Guardians of the Dark

Shadow Play

BIANCA D'ARC

This book is a work of fiction. The names, characters, places, and incidents are products of the writer's imagination or have been used fictitiously and are not to be construed as real. Any resemblance to persons, living or dead, actual events, locale or organizations is entirely coincidental.

No part of this book may be used or reproduced in any manner whatsoever without written permission, except in the case of brief quotations embodied in critical articles and reviews.

1st Edition
Copyright © 2011 Bianca D'Arc
Published by Kensington Publishing, Inc.

2nd Edition
Copyright © 2019 Bianca D'Arc
Published by Hawk Publishing, LLC

Copyright © 2019 Bianca D'Arc

All rights reserved.

ISBN-13: 978-1-950196-08-1

When Sam's sexy female co-pilot is marked for death, he'll stop at nothing to protect her while fighting the madmen who would unleash hell on the world.

She knows her life is in danger...

Emily asked one too many questions at the last board meeting and ended up having her car sabotaged. She's become more wary of voicing her suspicions, but she still has them. Someone is using the small charter airline her mother co-founded to smuggle drugs – or maybe something even worse. When a new pilot is hired, she is sure to check him out before trusting that he's just another fly boy.

He's on a mission...

Going on undercover investigations isn't exactly within Sam's bailiwick, but he's a highly qualified pilot and the best choice to embed in the small, charter airline on short notice. When he meets Emily, he's not sure if she's as genuine as she seems or if she's hiding some dark secret. Either way, he needs to find out. Working by her side, he soon finds himself intensely attracted to her quick wit and easy manner, but she's wary of him and he isn't sure of her despite the attraction that just won't quit.

Only by working together will they succeed...

When the time comes to trust each other, they will learn whether or not teaming up is the best way to end the deadly threat. Passion flares between them as the entire situation becomes incendiary. Will they be able to overcome their enemies and live to fight another day? Or will they go down in flames...hopefully taking the bad guys with them?

AUTHOR'S NOTE & DEDICATION

Note: This is the second edition of this book, which first appeared under the title ***Dead Alert***. I never liked the title and now is my chance to fix that—along with some continuity errors that made their way through the editing process and into the first edition of this book. I apologize for any confusion the title change may cause, but I feel very strongly about it and have wanted to change it almost from the very beginning, when the previously publisher demanded that all the titles of novels in this series had to have the word "dead" in them. I never liked that requirement and I've altered the two other titles in this set accordingly.

I'd like to thank my friend, Peggy McChesney for her help in finding, and hopefully eliminating, the problem points in the last two books of this series, especially. Thank you, Peggy! Any mistakes that remain are my fault entirely.

Dedication from the first edition…
This book is dedicated, as is all my work, with loving thanks to my mother, who I lost much too soon. She was my inspiration and my guide and I have been very lost without her these past months. And to Dad, who's been my rock through all of this adjustment and readjustment to the new normal. I love you, Dad.

I'd also like to remember Sherry Palmer Walter and her mother, Anna Palmer, who by all accounts had a lovely smile. Anna left us while this book was being written. While some might say it is inevitable that daughters lose their mothers, knowing that doesn't make it any easier. I'd like to think that our loved ones are always with us, guiding us, if only we are open enough to listen. Many thanks for your kindness during my grief, Sherry. I hope by the time this book comes out, you will have found some measure of consolation.

Thanks also to Suzanne, Shanda, Susan, and all my fb friends. I don't know what I'd have done these past months without you. Special thanks to Joy Roach, who came through for me—again—at the last minute. You are a lifesaver and a wonderful human being.

And last but definitely not least, many heartfelt thanks to my editor, Megan, for challenging me to try something a little out of my comfort zone. Thanks also for making allowances for my grief. I will never forget your kindness and forbearance during this time. Without you, my version of the zombie legend would never have seen the light of day—or perhaps I should say, the dark of night.

PROLOGUE

Fort Bragg, North Carolina

"I've got a special project for you, Sam." The commander, a former Navy SEAL named Matt Sykes, began talking before Sam was through the door to Matt's private office. "Sit down and shut the door."

Sam sat in a wooden chair across the cluttered desk from his commanding officer. Lt. Sam Archer, US Army Green Beret, was currently assigned to a top secret, mixed team of Special Forces soldiers and elite scientists. There were also a few others from different organizations, including one former cop and a CIA black ops guy. It was an extremely specialized group, recruited to work on a classified project of the highest order.

"I understand you're a pilot." Matt flipped through a file as he spoke.

"Yes, sir." Sam could have said more but he didn't doubt Matt had access to every last bit of Sam's file, even the top secret parts. He had probably known before even sending for him that Sam could fly anything with wings. Another member of his old unit was a blade pilot who flew all kinds of choppers, but fixed wing aircraft were Sam's specialty.

"How do you like the idea of going undercover as a charter pilot?"

"Sir?" Sam sat forward in the chair, intrigued.

"The name of a certain charter airline keeps popping up." Matt put down the file and faced Sam as his gaze hardened. "Too often for my comfort. Ever heard of a company called Praxis Air?"

"Can't say that I have."

"It's a small outfit, based out of Wichita—at least that's where they repair and maintain their aircraft in a company-owned hangar. They have branch offices at most of the major airports and cater mostly to an elite business clientele. They do the odd private cargo flight and who knows what else. They keep their business very hush-hush, 'providing the ultimate in privacy for their corporate clients,' or so their brochure advertises." Matt pushed a glossy tri-fold across the desk toward Sam.

"Looks pretty slick."

"That they are," Matt agreed. "So slick that even John Petit, with his multitude of CIA connections, can't get a bead on exactly what they've been up to of late. I've been piecing together bits here and there. Admiral Chester, the traitor, accepted more than a few free flights from them in the past few months, as did Ensign Bartles, who it turns out, was killed in a Praxis Air jet that crashed the night we took down Dr. Rodriguez and his friends. She wasn't listed on the manifest and only the pilot was claimed by the company, but on a hunch I asked a friend on the National Transportation Safety Board to allow us to do some DNA testing. Sure enough, we found remnants of Beverly Bartles's DNA at the crash site, though her body had to have been moved sometime prior to the NTSB getting there. The locals were either paid off or preempted. Either option is troubling, to say the least."

"You think they're mixed up with our undead friends?" They were still seeking members of the science team that had created the formula that killed and then turned its victims into the walking dead. Nobody had figured out exactly how they were traveling so freely around the country when they were on every watch list possible.

"It's a very real possibility. Which is why I want to send you in undercover. I don't need to remind you, time is of the essence. We have a narrow window to stuff this genie back into its bottle. The longer this goes on, the more likely it is the technology will be sold to the highest bidder and then, God help us."

Sam shivered. The idea of the zombie technology in the hands of a hostile government or psycho terrorists—especially after seeing what he'd seen of these past months—was unthinkable.

"If my going undercover will help end this, I'm your man." He'd do anything to stop the contagion from killing any more people.

Sam opened the flyer and noted the different kinds of jets the company offered. The majority of the planes looked like Lear 35's in different configurations. Some were equipped for cargo. Some had all the bells and whistles any corporate executive could wish for and a few were basically miniature luxury liners set up for spoiled celebrities and their friends.

"I hoped you'd say that. I've arranged a little extra training for you at Flight Safety in Houston. They've got Level D flight simulators that have full motion and full visual. They can give you the Type Rating you'll need on your license to work for Praxis Air legitimately."

"I've been to Flight Safety before. It's a good outfit." Sam put the brochure back on Matt's desk.

"We'll give you a suitable job history and cover, which you will commit to memory. You'll also have regular check-ins while in the field, but for the most part you'll be on your own. I want you to discover who, if any, of their personnel are involved and to what extent." Matt paused briefly before continuing. "Just to be clear, this isn't a regular job I'm asking you to do, Sam. It's not even close to what you signed on for when we were assigned as zombie hunters. I won't order you to do this. It's a total immersion mission. Chances are, there will be no immediate backup if you get into trouble. You'll be completely on your own most of the time."

"Understood, sir. I'm still up for it. I like a challenge."

Matt cracked a smile. "I hear that. And I appreciate the enthusiasm. Here's the preliminary packet to get you started." He handed a bulging envelope across the desk. "We'll get the rest set up while you're in flight training. It'll be ready by the time you are. You leave tomorrow for Houston."

"Yes, sir." Sam stood, hearing the tone of dismissal in the commander's voice.

"You can call this whole thing off up until the end of your flight training. After that, wheels will have been set in motion and can't be easily stopped. If you change your mind, let me know as soon as possible."

"Thank you, sir." Unspoken was the certainty that Sam wouldn't be changing his mind any time soon.

CHAPTER 1

"Got that new pilot coming in today, Em. My friend at Hobby Airport says he's sharp." As the head mechanic for Praxis Air and an old family friend, Buddy Hollister treated Emily Parkington more like a daughter than one of the senior pilots and part-owners of the charter airline.

Buddy was a pilot turned mechanic who was gifted when it came to keeping jets in good working order. He was a key member of the Praxis Air team and Emily thought of him as part of the family.

"I'm glad to hear it. That last guy was awful. I hate firing people." She shivered in memory, making Buddy laugh, as she'd intended.

Opening the refrigerator in the small break room off the main repair hangar in Wichita, she grabbed a cold soda and popped the top, drinking deeply. It was hot in the huge building today.

The outer door opened and a man walked in. She could see him through the large window that separated the break room from the main area of the hangar. Her temperature spiked a little higher as she got her first good look at the new pilot. The guy was smoking hot. Muscles filled out his tall frame to perfection and he had that confident pilot swagger down pat.

A grin revealed pearly whites as he strode across the room toward the office that was directly next door to the break room.

"I bet that's him," Buddy observed. "You better go rescue him from Sissy." The old mechanic cackled as he left the break room and headed for his kingdom—the repair bays where he was in charge of maintaining the Praxis Air fleet.

Sissy was the receptionist. She was divorcing husband number four at the moment and had been chasing all the single pilots and a few of the not-so-single ones too. No doubt she'd have her polished red hooks in the new guy the moment she laid eyes on him. It was only charitable to go save him.

Emily shook her head in disgust as she pushed through the adjoining door into the small office. There it was. Sissy had her hand on the new guy's arm as he filled out some forms. A counter separated them but that didn't stop Sissy the Merciless. Eyelashes batted and giggles abounded as she flirted for all she was worth. It was a little sad, actually.

God help her if Emily ever got so desperate to catch a man's attention. Of course, Emily's love life was nothing to crow about. A never-married workaholic was almost as pathetic to Emily's way of thinking, so who was she to cast stones?

Shrugging off her depressing thoughts, she decided to save the new guy before Sissy either scared him off or led him into the broom closet. Emily moved into the room and cleared her throat.

"Hi. I'm Emily Parkington. You're Sam Archer, right?" She walked up to the counter and held out her hand.

The new guy turned and that bright white smile dazed her for a brief moment. *Whew*. The man was even more potent at close range. Blond, blue eyed, and rugged, he was definitely easy on the eyes. He clasped her hand in his and the warmth of his callused grip made her weak in the knees.

"Pleased to meet you, Captain Parkington."

Oh, she liked the respect in his tone. She didn't often get that kind of response from the men she worked with. At least not until they knew who she was and that she owned a not-inconsiderable stake in the company. They treated her with more respect once they realized she could hire and fire them.

"Please, call me Emily." She remembered to smile as she regained possession of her tingling hand.

Damn. She was going to have to share a tiny cockpit with this mountain of a man. She'd have to get her inconvenient attraction to him under control.

"I'm Sam. Good to meet you."

"Sissy squared away most of your paperwork yesterday and Buddy said you did great on your check ride." She looked for a way to get him into the cockpit without making him feel like she was testing him. She was, but she didn't want him to know it.

Emily liked to do all the check rides for new pilots personally but every once in a while last minute charters interfered. When that happened, Buddy or one of the other long-time pilot employees filled in, but she still took the new pilots up on their first day to be certain they had the chops.

"The jet you passed on the way in was released from repair this morning. How about we take her up for a shakedown ride before we tackle the remainder of the paperwork?"

His charming smile only deepened. "Love to." He motioned for her to precede him out the door and into the hangar. The man had good manners, she'd give him that.

"You've had some military experience, haven't you?" A short stint in the Army was listed on his employment application and he definitely gave off the soldier vibe. Most of the guys she flew with who'd been in the service were Air Force or even former naval aviators. She didn't have much experience with Army guys.

"I was in for a couple of years," he agreed. Like many of the ex-military men she worked with, Sam Archer appeared to be a man of few words.

"I respect that. Thank you for serving." And she meant it too. She'd always admired those who chose to serve in the military and probably would've joined herself, if not for extenuating family circumstances. The death of her mother, for one. Her pesky brother and his Air Force aspirations, for another.

"My pleasure, ma'am."

She could tell he meant it. There was something in his voice that said more than his simple words.

"You miss it? The Army, I mean." She looked at him as they walked across the hangar. He was a tall man with long legs and normally she would've had to take two steps for every one of his but he was measuring his gait to accommodate her, which was extremely thoughtful.

One of his eyebrows quirked upward as he returned her gaze. "I loved everything about the service. The adventure. The travel."

"The waking up at oh-dark-thirty to exercise in the rain," she joked. "My brother is in the Air Force. He's told me a lot about that kind of thing. Or should I say, he's complained to me about it over and over again."

She chuckled at the memory and Sam grinned back at her. Time seemed to stand still as she gazed into his eyes.

A dropped hammer clattered loudly somewhere on the concrete floor of the hangar, breaking the spell. Wow. She really had to get control of herself around this guy if they were going to be flying together.

"I never mind physical training. PT is something I'd do anyway—drill sergeant pushing me harder or not."

She'd just bet he would. And probably did. The man had to be the most physically fit specimen she'd ever encountered in the flesh. Up close she could see the bulges of his muscles against the cotton of his shirt. When he raised his arms and those giant biceps flexed, she feared for his seams.

"So *be all that you can be* isn't just an ad slogan to you, eh?"

He joined in her laughter as they approached the jet she was aiming for.

"I've always liked a challenge. The Army gave me that. I think this job will too." His answer was only the slightest bit cagey.

She turned to look up at him suspiciously. She was getting mixed feelings about him. Usually a good judge of character, she trusted her instincts on new hires and people she met in her work, but she couldn't read him well at all. Something about him set her radar off. It could be the all too feminine discomfort of being so close to a devastatingly attractive male. Or it could be something far more sinister. Too many odd things had been going on at Praxis Air of late.

She didn't know this man. She hadn't hired him. That decision had been made by someone higher up the food chain. There weren't many people who had more pull in the company her mother had co-founded than she did, so her suspect list was short. All she knew was that something funny was going on at her beloved airline and she was going to figure out what it was come hell or high water.

This new guy could be innocent or he could have been brought in to further the conspiracy—whatever it was. She feared it had something to do with drug running, which would destroy the company if they got caught by the authorities. She couldn't let that happen. She'd been discreetly trying to find out what was going on for the past few weeks and was planning to handle it quietly, once she knew who was involved and exactly what they were doing. She'd hold her judgment about this handsome new pilot until she got to know him better.

"Well, the Lear 35 is challenging enough for me, but I've read your file. I noticed that you recently got the Type Rating for this jet. What were you flying before?" She knew, of course, but she wanted to hear it from him.

A pilot's log book recorded everything about their time spent in the air. It was sacred to each pilot. Something they kept with them at all times when on the job and reread to bring back memories of their early days. She reminisced over her logs from when she was a teen every once in a while.

Those times spent with her mother, learning how to fly, were some of the happiest moments in her life.

"Cargo planes mostly. Big lumbering whales. I wanted something a little sleeker in my next job. I'd heard the Lear 35 was a fun ride."

"That she is," Emily readily agreed. "Sturdy and dependable but small and fast. We fly a couple different configurations but they're all basically the same plane. This one is outfitted to carry rock stars." She gestured for him to board the little jet through the passenger hatch.

"Ladies first, ma'am." He motioned for her to precede him, those military manners coming to the fore.

She didn't want to argue when he was trying to be polite, so she went ahead, uncomfortably aware of him checking out her ass as she entered the passenger compartment. She stood to one side of the door so he could get the full effect when he cleared the doorway.

He whistled, clearly impressed. "Rock stars. You weren't kidding."

She looked around the luxury compartment with a feeling of pride. She owned a part of this gorgeous aircraft. This one, and all the others that were currently either parked outside or off on assignments somewhere. A fleet of fifty-odd jets built up from one lonely Cessna her mother had piloted back in the early days of the company.

"Rock stars, Arab sheiks, European royalty, the odd politician with lavish tastes. We've transported a lot of strange characters in this jet. I started calling it the rock star ride and the name stuck. You should see the back compartment."

They walked past the luxurious couch and table arrangement on their way to the rear of the aircraft. The table was essentially a bar, with slots for high-end liquor bottles and crystal stemware. It was all secured as it would be on a boat, against the natural motion of the aircraft while in flight. Everything was sparkling and shiny, cleaned and polished within an inch of its life. Even she was impressed, and she'd seen it many times. She opened the door to the back compartment and entered.

"You've got to be kidding me." Sam's voice came to her as she watched his reaction to the room.

It was essentially a bedroom. A huge bed took up most of the space, made up with the finest silk sheets in a deep burgundy color.

"We have different color sheets depending on the tastes—or sometimes the coat of arms—of the charter. Color choice is one of the riders in the contract. Goofy, huh?" She moved into the room and fixed a wrinkle on one corner of the soft bedspread. "You'd be amazed how picky some rich folks are. They want everything to their exact specifications."

She half expected some off-color comment about being in a bedroom so soon after meeting. Most pilots who looked as good as this one—and many of those who were a whole lot less good looking—fancied themselves as ladies men, and were usually always looking for their next conquest. Which was why she'd made it a policy to never get involved with a pilot.

"Being rich has its perks."

When he made no further comment, Emily smiled and led the way out of the cabin. He'd passed a test of sorts, though he didn't know it. For that matter, she hadn't realized she'd been testing him. Well. Wonders never ceased. It seemed like maybe she was flirting with the idea of breaking her own rule.

That wouldn't do. They had to work together. Spend hours and hours in a small cockpit. And there were bad things going on at her beloved airline.

So why now? Why did the hottest man she'd set eyes on in years have to show up on her doorstep at this particular moment?

Something was fishy here. Had to be. Emily had never been lucky in love. Hell, she'd never been lucky in *like*. She had a dismal track record with men. For Mr. Perfect to show up as a new employee at the same time she started to suspect something was very wrong in the company couldn't be a coincidence.

"Let's do the pre-flight inspection together," she suggested as she headed for the hatch.

"One walk around, coming up."

She frowned when he used the slang term. Normally the first officer would be doing the preflight inspection, commonly referred to as a walk around, to check for any obvious signs of trouble with the aircraft. This first time they flew together, Emily would do it with him.

The official testing had begun.

Sam liked the way his new lady boss handled herself as she subtly watched him during the usual preflight rituals. She'd let him take the lead on the walk around, asking questions and pointing out a few things peculiar to this particular jet. She definitely knew her aircraft. Sam was impressed with her knowledge and obvious intelligence, even as he chafed at the bit to get down to the business of his assignment. There were bad guys to catch and a possible conspiracy to uncover, not to mention a potential zombie horde to stop in its tracks.

Emily Parkington was not only a means to that end, but until he could clear her for certain, she was also a suspect. A very charming suspect, but a suspect nonetheless. She wasn't hard on the eyes either. Pretty in a girl next door way, her bouncy brunette hair and soft hazel green eyes were gorgeous. She was short, compared to him, but he guessed she was about average for women. Somewhere around five foot five or thereabouts. She had a trim figure with curves in all the right places. Sam had noticed how pretty she was right off the bat but he couldn't let that influence his investigation. She was still under suspicion. Just like everybody else at Praxis Air.

She'd let him take the stick on takeoff and he'd enjoyed the roar of the little jet under his command. She'd also watched him like a hawk as he went through each of the checklists necessary to complete before they could begin taxiing down the runway.

Sam was used to scrutiny. He hadn't become a Special

Forces officer without lots and lots of training and testing throughout his career. But being evaluated by a female superior officer was somewhat rare in his experience and this particular woman had the unnerving ability to get under his skin.

Her insistence on using exact terms for everything made him want to joke around with her, just to see if he could bust through her slightly officious exterior. The little crease between her eyebrows and slight pucker of her lips made him want to kiss her annoyance away.

Damn. That was a disturbingly strong thought. Sure, she was pretty, but Sam had a job to do here. He couldn't afford to have his head turned by a pretty face, no matter how appealing. Focus. That's what he had to do. Focus on the mission. The team was depending on him to follow this lead. It was the best one they had at the moment and it needed to be investigated as deeply and as quickly as possible.

Before another outbreak happened. Each time the creatures appeared, it meant a loss of innocent life. Each instance had been worse than the last and the biggest danger of all was if the creators of the deadly contagion managed to sell it. Hostile governments or terrorists, those unethical scientists and profiteers didn't care who they sold the technology to. It would go to the highest bidder if Sam and the rest of the team didn't stop them in time. The longer they remained free, the more dangerous it was. Given enough time, the transaction would be completed and the genie forever let out of its bottle. Sam had to work fast to prevent that and his first step was already underway.

Emily Parkington was a means to an end. She was either part of the conspiracy that was most likely brewing in the company or innocent of it. He needed to uncover which side she was on, but until he figured that out, she remained suspect. As did everyone in this place. He couldn't afford to get too close to any of them.

"Takeoff checklist complete. Moving on to the cruise checklist." Sam clipped his words efficiently as he mentally refocused on his mission.

"Roger," she replied crisply, flipping to the next checklist in the book.

She read through the items as he complied with each instruction. Some were as simple as checking a gauge, others required action such as setting a dial or flipping a switch. Old hat for someone who'd been flying as long as he had.

Emily Parkington put him through his paces in the air over the next hour and a half. She went through various scenarios to test his reflexes and skill with the jet. He enjoyed the challenges she set him and aced the test. He could tell how well he'd done by her silence as he worked through the various checklists prior to landing.

A few minutes later they were on the ground, taxiing back toward the hangar. Emily didn't say much until they rolled to a stop outside the massive door to the hangar in the space she indicated. He powered down and completed the paperwork before turning to her.

"How'd I do?" He couldn't help the grin he knew had to be on his face. He loved flying.

"You passed," she said after a moment. A hint of a smile lifted one corner of her mouth. Damn, she was pretty. Sam suppressed the thought as the silly grin faded from his face. He had a job to do. He had to get to it.

"So when do I fly for real?" The sooner he got on the schedule, the sooner he could begin checking out the cargo, clients, and routes. He was serving two masters in this endeavor and by far, the more important one was his commanding officer back on base.

"That wasn't real enough for you?" She climbed from her seat and headed out of the cockpit.

"It was plenty real," he clarified as he followed her out. "I meant, when do I get on the roster to fly charters?"

She opened the cabin door and headed down the stairs, turning to wait for him at the bottom. He clambered down the stairs and met her on the tarmac while another jet powered up nearby, making conversation difficult over the engine noise.

Emily pointed toward the hangar and he followed her inside and right into the office area. She reached behind the main reception desk and grabbed a clipboard, flipping through pages while he watched. She didn't babble. He liked that about her. Too many women seemed to think they had to fill every moment of silence with ceaseless chatter. Not Emily Parkington. She talked, but not incessantly.

She put pen to paper and flipped the clipboard to him. He caught it with one hand.

"You're on the schedule for a flight to Boise tomorrow at 9 A.M. That work for you?"

"Yes, ma'am." Sam felt that smile curve his lips again as he looked at his name marked in next to hers. They'd be flying together tomorrow. He liked the sound of that.

"You're first officer until you get a little more seniority with the company. Any problem with that?"

The slight lift of one eyebrow told him she was waiting to see how he'd react. The test wasn't quite over yet. She was feeling him out to see how he'd fit with her team.

"Fine with me, captain. As long as I get some stick time, I'm happy."

And as long as he was working for the company, he'd have a chance to poke around and try to learn exactly how they were involved in the forbidden zombie technology. He hoped, for Emily's sake, that she wasn't mixed up in it.

Being low man on the totem pole suited his purpose. He was there to gather intel on the company and its shipments and charters. If they were shipping top secret technology or ferrying rogue scientists and potential buyers, he would uncover it—with or without Emily's help. The clock was ticking.

*

"I'm setting something up and we'll need your jets."

The voice on the other end of the phone annoyed the snot

out of Scott, the new head honcho at Praxis Air. His father's untimely death had paved the way for Scott to take over and he wasn't asking too many questions about how that had all come about. He was in charge now and he was going to enjoy it. RHIP, the old man had always said: Rank Has Its Privileges.

The old man had been an Air Force officer and had run the small airline like it was his own personal air wing. Scott had never served, but he knew how to run a business. Cash was his goal—fast and lots of it.

The deal he'd worked with the professor guaranteed both and he was going to take the geek for all he was worth and then some. Too bad a few pilots had to die along the way, but it couldn't be avoided. Now, losing the jets—that had hurt. As had the National Transportation Safety Board investigations. Both problems adversely affected the bottom line but things were leveling out now. He didn't want any more *accidents*.

"What kind and how far?" Scott asked, wanting the facts before he committed to anything.

"Cargo at first. I need some equipment transported to the Pacific Northwest. If all goes as planned, I'll also need some luxury service for potential buyers from major hubs to a small airport along the Oregon-Idaho border. I'll tell you exactly where when the time comes. Think you can handle that?"

Scott thought about the logistics and personnel. Emily Parkington had asked one too many questions at the last shareholder meeting. He'd scared her off but she was as annoying as her mother had been—always watching him with disapproval in her judgmental eyes. He'd have to keep tabs on her. She had been flying most of the Pacific Northwest routes but that could be changed. He'd have to be subtle about it, but he thought he could do it.

"No problem. When do you want to start?"

"I've already started. The first of the new cargo shipments should be arriving in Wichita in a couple of hours. More will follow. Be sure they encounter no difficulties getting to their destination."

"Will do." Scott didn't like the man's superior tone of voice but for a cut of the deal he was willing to put up with it.

"Good." There was a slight hesitation. "And Scott, my boy…" The smug bastard made Scott feel about two inches tall. "See that your pilots keep their noses out of my cargo boxes this time. Do it personally. I'd hate to have to arrange another explosive decompression."

A bomb. That's what he meant. He'd already blown up two of Scott's toys. Those Lear jets didn't come cheap.

"Sure thing, Dr. Sugden." Scott used the man's surname purely to annoy him.

"Idiot! I've told you never to use my name over a phone line even if it is supposed to be secure. They have eyes and ears everywhere!"

Bingo. Scott had hit the bastard's paranoia button right on the nose.

"My apologies, sir." That little, subservient *sir* had always helped defuse his father's anger and it apparently worked on this science geek too. After a moment of silence, he seemed to calm down.

"Don't let it happen again." He cleared his throat and his voice calmed further. "I'll be in touch in a day or two, after the first shipment is completed, to schedule more."

The phone disconnected with an abrupt click. No goodbye. Just a click.

Sugden was a nutcase, that was for sure, but he was a rich one with what seemed like unlimited resources. And if the deal he was working on came through, Scott could finally buy that island in the South Pacific he'd had his eye on for a while. Owning his own island was something Scott had always wanted. The old man had left him rich, but not rich enough to do that. It was his goal and he'd do anything—anything—to get it. Including selling his soul to the devil.

In this case, the devil was a nutty professor who wanted to remake the world in his own image. Whatever. All Scott wanted was enough money to buy his island and transplant all the people and supplies he'd need to live out his life with a harem of beauties at his beck and call.

Was that too much to ask? A different girl for every day of the week. Hell, why not every day of the month? With enough money he was sure to find thirty or forty women willing to live on his oasis in the sea with him.

It was his fondest daydream. And if the rest of the world went to hell because of Sugden's little plague, so be it. Scott didn't really care.

CHAPTER 2

Someone was in the hangar with her, of that Emily was certain. Nobody should be here. It was way too early for the day shift of mechanics to arrive and there were no outstanding charters from this airport at this ungodly hour of the morning.

She'd come in at 2 A.M. to take delivery of a cargo job. The client was in an unaccountable rush to get the cargo loaded and ready for takeoff at 9 A.M. Emily couldn't figure out why. If they wanted it gone that badly, why hadn't they requested a night flight?

Under normal circumstances, she probably wouldn't have given it a second thought. Lately though, she'd been noticing more and more odd occurrences, particularly with cargo flights. They'd been getting an increased number of them too, when previously, Praxis Air had catered mostly to passengers. In fact, the Board of Directors had decided to outfit more jets for cargo hauling in the past year.

Emily hadn't agreed with the move at the time but she had been overruled. Since they'd dedicated more jets to cargo duty the number of cargo flights had gone up considerably, even though Praxis Air wasn't the cheapest or easiest way to deliver cargo.

Heck, if they'd wanted to make the airline into a cargo service, they could easily have done it by adding bigger jets that could haul more. They'd been approached numerous times by everyone from the popular overnight carriers to the US Postal Service about ongoing cargo contracts, but Praxis Air had always been about catering to elite clientele. Sometimes those elite had cargo, so they'd outfitted a few planes to carry it. Every once in a while, Praxis flew small, high priority items like emergency medical supplies as charity runs, but nothing on the scale of what they'd been doing in the past few months.

Something moved in the darkness of the deserted hangar. It was approaching four in the morning. The first workers shouldn't be here for another hour at least.

Emily grabbed a wrench from a nearby workbench. It wasn't much of a weapon but at least it was something.

There. Another sound. Something scraping along the concrete floor, barely perceptible. Emily edged cautiously closer, peering around crates and past machinery.

Something moved over by the cargo she'd just accepted from the late night delivery and her heart leapt into her throat. She hefted the wrench higher.

"You expecting trouble from an unhappy robot or something?"

Emily spun to face the source of the deep, male voice, ready to clobber him.

It was the new guy. Sam.

"What the *hell* are you doing here?" Emily lowered the wrench, her heart pounding in relief.

Then she realized how vulnerable she was all alone in the hangar with a pilot she'd only met the day before. And he was a lot bigger than her. Massive was a good word to describe his size in comparison to her petite frame. She tightened her hold on the wrench, keeping it at her side.

"I'm sorry." His tone was placating as he straightened from his crouch over one of the cargo containers. "I know I shouldn't have come in so early but I couldn't sleep. Kind of excited about my first day on the schedule."

He looked sheepish enough that she almost believed him. She'd give him the benefit of the doubt...for now.

"First day jitters? I thought only school kids admitted to that."

"You'll keep my secret, won't you?"

His grin was disarming and charming at the same time. She found it hard to resist the impulse to return it.

"Remember...I now have blackmail material to use against you and we should get along fine." She thought about the situation for a moment and decided to extend a bit of trust his way. "Come on, I'll buy you a cup of coffee since it looks like neither of us is going to get any more sleep before it's time to fly."

He kept a comfortable distance as they walked out of the cargo area toward the office. It was as if he knew how intimidating his presence and sheer bulk could be and was trying to minimize the effect. That was either incredibly considerate or potentially creepy, if he was trying to keep her calm before he struck.

It was a ridiculous thought, but one she couldn't help having. Women had to be careful—especially when they worked in a male dominated field like aviation. Winding up alone in the hangar wasn't the smartest move she'd ever made and she'd make a point not to repeat it. She had planned to leave right after the cargo handlers but she'd forgotten something in the office and needed to go back for it. Then she'd heard Sam...and now here they were. Together. Talk about unintended consequences.

"So are you going to tell me why you're so nervous about your first day on the job here?"

She pushed the door open to the small office lounge. There was a snack machine and most importantly, a coffeemaker. Emily started a pot brewing, always keeping one eye on her companion. He seemed safe, but she wasn't going to let her guard down yet. Thankfully, he stayed where she could see him, across the width of the room from her.

Sam shrugged. "I guess I wanted to impress my new boss. The grapevine says she's a stickler for protocol."

She liked that he would tease her yet keep his conversation on a professional level. If he kept it there, they'd get along just fine.

"Yeah, she definitely likes all her i's dotted and all her t's crossed. I'd watch myself around her if I were you." Laughing at herself helped ease her tension.

"I'll remember that. Thanks for the tip."

Too impatient to wait for the entire pot to brew, Emily placed one cup at a time directly under the stream of fresh coffee coming out of the filter compartment. When she had two reasonably full cups, she replaced the pot to collect the rest and headed toward the round table in one corner. She placed one of the cups in front of Sam, who had seated himself across from her.

She was still suspicious of him and his reasons for being in the hangar at this early hour, but since being discovered, he'd been nothing but polite and considerate. She wouldn't confront him about his presence here this morning any more than she already had—at least not until the hangar was full of people. She felt safe enough with him for now. She wasn't going to push it, but she would keep her eyes open and her suspicions carefully to herself.

She'd already asked one too many questions of the front office. Scott, the new CEO and majority shareholder wasn't her biggest fan. Emily still had some clout as a minority shareholder but the questions she'd been asking had been noticed by the wrong person. As she'd left the last shareholders meeting at corporate headquarters, her car had been sabotaged. The brakes failed and she'd managed to crash the vehicle without killing herself in the process. It had been a warning. A potentially deadly warning.

Since then, she'd been more careful. Something was definitely up with her beloved airline and she'd be damned if she'd let that weasel Scott ruin the company their parents had built. She just had to be more cautious in her queries.

And she wouldn't put it above Scott to insert a spy into the ranks to keep tabs on her. Sam could very well be a plant. Someone to watch her and report back to Scott if she put a toe out of line again.

Or maybe Sam was exactly what he seemed—another good time fly boy pilot flirting with every woman he met. Well, maybe he wasn't quite that bad, but he was certainly pouring on the charm with her. Of course, she was his new boss. Maybe he was trying to ingratiate himself with her for that reason.

She couldn't deny he was handsome, and his offbeat sense of humor definitely meshed well with hers. But could he be trusted? Was he part of the drug ring or whatever it was that had her driving planes full of high tech lab equipment around the country?

Yeah, she'd taken a few peeks inside the crates when she thought nobody was looking. She had a right to know what she was transporting, and the vague words on a few manifests had made her want to investigate. That hadn't gone over well with Scott the Louse when she had brought it up at the shareholders meeting, but after that one rather obvious attempt to silence her permanently, she'd stopped questioning things. At least in public.

Privately, she still kept her eyes open for an opportunity to learn exactly what was going on in the company and how to stop it. She wouldn't waste a second going to the authorities as soon as she had some proof of wrongdoing. Until she had evidence though, she had to pretend like she was being a good little girl and minding her own business.

"What did you mean about me expecting trouble from an unhappy robot?" His words came back to her now that adrenaline had ceased its pounding through her bloodstream.

"Well you looked pretty fierce with that wrench. If I were a robot, I'd have been really afraid."

Nonsensical, but funny. She found herself warming to his offbeat sense of humor.

"Good thing for you, you're not a robot then." They

shared a laugh and sipped coffee. "So what are you, some kind of secret science fiction fan?"

"Not so secret, I'm afraid. I love most all sci-fi movies. I don't get to watch a lot of television, but when I do, it's usually the science fiction channel."

"Star Wars, Star Trek or Star Gate? Which do you like best?"

"Do I have to choose?" he joked, getting into the spirit of her teasing.

"Fair enough. How about Captain Kirk or Captain Picard?"

"Tough call, but I think I'd have to go with Jean Luc Picard. I had a commanding officer like him in the service once, and I'd follow that man to hell and back. Kirk, not so much. Too many of the guys in red shirts wound up dead on his watch for my taste."

Oh yes, he was the sci-fi fan he claimed to be. About that, at least, she was sure he was telling the truth. She continued her subtle questioning as they talked, trying to gauge just who and what Sam Archer really was. One thing was for sure, he was a puzzle and she'd always enjoyed solving puzzles.

Sam and Emily spent the next twenty minutes discussing their flight plan and schedule for the upcoming charter. Emily only became aware of the passage of time when Buddy clomped into the break room in his heavy work boots, heading straight for the coffeepot.

"You're here early, Em," Buddy observed in his gravelly voice. Emily knew from long association that he wasn't the sunniest of personalities until he'd had his morning coffee.

"The cargo for today's charter was dropped off in the middle of the night. I came in to meet it."

"You've been here since then?" Buddy was clearly surprised.

"Well, I'd planned to go home but then I remembered I left my monthly reports on my desk and went back for them. By the time I was ready to head out, Sam was here and we got to talking." She didn't elaborate on how long they'd been talking. It had been a couple of hours, at least. Better to let Buddy think she'd gotten stuck working on her reports.

Buddy was like a father, or maybe a much older brother. He would've given her grief if he knew what had really happened. She'd let him know if necessary, but for now things had worked out well enough with Sam that she thought it was okay to keep her secrets to herself for a bit. After all, she'd have to spend a great deal of time alone with Sam in a small cockpit. She'd have to trust him with her life and vice versa. They'd made a start here. She hoped it boded well for their future working together.

She hoped Sam would turn out to be someone she could count on. She hoped like hell he wasn't involved in whatever it was that Scott and his cronies were doing. Whether her hopes were based purely on professional reasons, she wasn't entirely sure. Sam Archer was, after all, a total hottie.

After the rough start, the flight to Boise was smooth sailing. Sam hadn't been able to get a good look inside those high priority crates but he'd bet there was something fishy going on there. He'd gotten a peek at the manifest and the vagueness of what was written there was alarming. The contents of the crates were listed merely as *equipment* with no further information. Not what kind of equipment, the value of it, the locations of where it had come from or where it was going, merely that five boxes of equipment were being moved from one airport to another.

Sam knew that was far from standard. Cargo manifests at Praxis Air were supposed to record way more information than that. Part of the speech he'd gotten on his first day had been about how to fill out their paperwork and the importance of getting the most information possible. The office manager had shown him several examples of paperwork she considered filled out correctly and numerous versions of the wrong way to do it.

Even the worst of the bad examples were better than what he'd seen on the manifest for this shipment. The information provided by the sender was less than nothing. That nobody at Praxis Air had demanded more seemed impossible. Then he'd caught a glimpse of the signature on the woefully incomplete paperwork. It was signed by Scott Southerland, the new CEO of the airline and majority shareholder since the sudden death of his father a few weeks ago.

About the time Sam had been tapped to train for this undercover mission, Scott's father had met with an untimely end in a suspicious auto accident, clearing the way for Scott to take over. Apparently his signature on an essentially blank manifest was enough to get cargo rushed through to wherever he wanted it to go. Sam figured nobody wanted to question the new head honcho. Convenient.

"So what's the new boss like?" Sam asked conversationally once they were at cruising altitude.

It wouldn't take but a couple of hours to get to Boise but it was enough time to get bored with the scenery far below. Pilots usually spent flight time chatting about various things in between radio contacts with air traffic control, so it was normal for him to ask questions any new employee might ask.

"You mean Scott?" Emily seemed surprised by the question.

"I read about the senior Mr. Southerland's accident and wondered how his son was doing in his place."

"Scott's doing okay." Her answer was noncommittal at best and she didn't seem to want to pursue the topic. Odd. In Sam's experience, most long-time employees liked spilling the dirt to the new guy.

Emily's response took reticence to a whole new level. Sam decided to shelve the topic for later. He didn't want to spook her. Maybe she just didn't want to talk about Scott Southerland for some reason. Maybe he'd do better with a more general topic. He asked about the technical specifications of the jet and soon had Emily talking shop with relative ease. Once she was comfortable with him and their conversation he tried again to redirect it toward things he wanted to learn. After all, he had a job to do. He had a limited amount of time to get his investigation rolling.

"Do you do a lot of cargo jobs on this route?"

"Not in particular." Emily shrugged as she made notes in her log. "We fly stuff all over. And not just stuff, though we've been doing a lot more cargo lately for some reason. It's rather cyclical. Sometimes it's more business flights, sometimes more pleasure, sometimes more cargo."

While there wasn't anything wrong with her words, the tension in her shoulders seemed to increase on this particular subject. Where a moment ago she'd been talking easily about technical specifications of various jets, all of a sudden she was much more wary. Sam watched her carefully, his every sense on alert.

He really hated the thought that Emily could be involved in this mess. He admitted to himself the moment he'd met her, his objectivity where she was concerned had gone out the window. There was something about her. Something that made him want her to be innocent.

The landing at Boise Airport was uneventful. Sam completed all necessary paperwork under Emily's watchful eye. She definitely was a stickler for details. Sam noted the slight frown that wrinkled her brow when she went aft to check the cargo. Sam followed on her heels in time to catch her paging through the clipboard that contained the cargo manifests for this shipment.

She either didn't hear him or was too absorbed in what she was reading—or in this case, not reading—on the cargo list.

"Something wrong?" Sam tried to sound nonchalant. Emily started and looked up almost guiltily from the papers.

"No, nothing's wrong," she was quick to answer.

Something didn't sit right. In the short time they'd been acquainted Sam had already established Emily's penchant for filling out paperwork completely. He'd glimpsed those manifests and even from a cursory look he knew they were half-assed at best. Yet she wouldn't admit it to him. Not even to make a comment about how poorly others filled out forms, which would have been what he expected from her. Instead, she closed him out and denied everything.

He thought he could sense a bit of fear in her as well, and that concerned him. What was she afraid of? Was she worried he'd find out she was involved in covering things up? Or was she afraid of something else?

Either way, he'd find out why she was so jumpy on certain topics.

There was no time to pursue it any further. Sam could see cargo handlers approaching the jet out the window.

"Looks like they're eager to get us unloaded." Sam nodded toward the window. Inwardly, he wished he had more time.

Emily slammed the clipboard back in place and headed for the hatch. Sam barely heard the curse she let out under her breath. She was definitely upset about something and Sam was going to figure out what it was.

She opened the oversized cargo doors and Sam assisted when she directed him to perform small tasks. The cargo guys did the rest. Sam noted that these cargo handlers didn't wear the same uniform as the rest of the airport workers in the vicinity. They were some kind of special group with matching coveralls that held no insignia whatsoever. They had to have passed muster with the TSA in order to work at the airport but they weren't part of the regular airport staff. Maybe they were a private firm that worked for individual clients or something. Sam made a note to have the team look into it.

He could do little more than stand there and observe while the cargo was offloaded and whisked away, crate by crate. It chafed. A man more used to taking action, sitting and watching wasn't really his thing. He really wanted to find out where they were taking the cargo, but didn't see a way to do so without raising suspicion.

"We're refueling and flying on to Portland for a quick drop off. Grab a cup of coffee in the hangar, if you want one. We'll only be on the ground for a little while longer." Emily had come up beside him as he walked onto the tarmac, taking in as much of his surroundings as possible.

Sam flipped a casual salute in her direction on the noisy airfield and headed toward the small hangar a short distance away. They'd parked outside, on the section of airfield dedicated to charter airlines. A number of independent air services shared the hangar.

He greeted the office folks, keeping his eyes open as he learned as much as he could about this stop. The folk inside were friendly enough and pointed him toward the coffeemaker in the break room. Sam snagged two cups and prepared Emily's with cream and sugar the way he'd seen her take it back in Wichita.

Task done, he arrived back at the plane to find Emily nowhere in sight as the last of the cargo left the hold. A fuel tanker had come up alongside the jet and was doing its duty.

Sam knew he would have more opportunities to question Emily tonight when they had a layover in Portland before heading back to Wichita. It wasn't the greatest work schedule in the world, but such was the life of a charter pilot. In a way, it was useful to have the extra time with Emily. He wanted to know what made her tick.

Meanwhile, the best evidence he'd seen so far was being taken away on a beat up cargo loader. Sam watched the cargo roll down the tarmac with building frustration.

"Archer. You ready?" Emily shouted from a dozen yards away.

Turning away when the truck holding their cargo drove out of sight around a corner, Sam went to meet her. The mysterious cargo and any chance to find out what it had been, was gone.

"We're all gassed up." She was folding a piece of paper that was probably a receipt for the jet fuel as she spoke. "We need to be in Portland in two hours to drop off our last little bundle of joy for the day."

"Should be enough time," he commented. "Let's saddle up."

In addition to the five mysterious crates, there was one small box that had all its paperwork in order. It was heading to a business conference in Portland. Apparently, the client had been willing to pay top dollar to get it there as fast as possible. It was a prototype of a device that was being introduced at the conference that had been left behind by mistake, or so Sissy had volunteered when Sam had run into her this morning in Wichita before takeoff.

The flight to Portland and the big airport designated as PDX was quick and quiet. Sam's mind was working overtime on the problem posed by the cargo they'd dropped off. His instincts told him something was definitely fishy there, but he didn't have enough to go on in order to call for reinforcements. He didn't want to blow this undercover operation before it got started. And Emily's behavior was off. She wasn't a very good liar, which counted in her favor to Sam's way of thinking.

A little more time in her presence and he figured he'd be able to read her like a book—as much as any man was ever able to read a woman's mind. Which was to say, not much, Sam had to admit. But her tells were there. The way she tensed her shoulders and that little frown that wrinkled her brow. He'd noticed those and a few other things about her in the time they'd already spent together. He figured this layover was as good a time as any to begin deepening the relationship and trying to get a read on whether or not she could be trusted.

Sam had done a great deal of research on the charter industry, in general, before arriving for his first day at Praxis Air. John Petit had also given him pointers about undercover work. As a former Marine and current CIA operative, John had way more experience in this kind of operation than Sam, but he wasn't a pilot. Only a pilot could infiltrate into a position that could potentially give the team access to the information they needed, so it was up to Sam.

They'd made arrangements for Sam to check in by phone during layovers when possible and during his off duty hours. He had a secure phone that looked like a regular phone only the signal was scrambled. The other team members' phones had the codes to unscramble it.

Sam filled in his log while Emily parked them near one of the charter hangars at PDX. The charter area was on the opposite end of the airfield from the commercial hub that was Portland International Airport.

A very relieved and harassed looking secretary met them at the door to the small passenger concourse. Sam had carried the precious box marked with the company's logo from the jet to the terminal. This particular contract had included hand delivery to an agent of the client's company. The woman signed for the box and was off like a shot, headed for her conference. It would have been comical if the poor woman hadn't been so relieved to see the package delivered safely.

"Another happy customer," Emily observed as she finished the paperwork. "And we don't get our new cargo until tomorrow afternoon so we've got some time to kill and hotel reservations downtown. Wait until you see this hotel. I did a favor for the CEO of the chain once and he gives me a cut rate when I'm in town so you lucked out this time. No El Cheapo hotel for you." The humor in her expression was contagious.

"Can't wait."

CHAPTER 3

"You weren't kidding about this hotel." Sam looked distinctly out of place in the delicate interior of the lobby. "Is the whole place like this?"

"Not entirely. Wait 'til you see your room."

Emily went with him to his room to see his reaction. He didn't disappoint. She watched from the doorway as he took in the swaths of curtains and boldly striped wallpaper.

"Did you pick this special just for me or is the whole hotel like this?"

"Don't flatter yourself. This is standard issue for this place. You should see the more expensive suites."

"It's like a toned down Arabian Nights fantasy decorating scheme. What's with all the curtains?" He turned in a circle, dropping his overnight bag on the floor while she enjoyed his bemusement.

"It's their theme. They have a couple of hotels—this one is tame compared to the one in Seattle. Same decorating scheme, but much bolder colors. Dark red and bright lemon yellow."

"I guess I'm lucky. The pale yellow and cream are kind of nice once you get used to the big vertical stripes on the walls."

"Their restaurant is top notch," Emily informed him as she rolled her pilot case away from the door to his room. "Shall we meet there in an hour?"

She looked up from wrestling with her luggage to find Sam standing in front of her. He'd moved so quickly and silently, she hadn't known he was there. A little gasp of surprise escaped her mouth. One of his muscular arms rose to lean against the doorframe, crowding her space in an intimate way.

"Why the hurry? You could always stay here and we could get room service."

The huskiness of his deep voice almost had her purring—until she realized who and what he was. Just another pilot who thought he was Casanova, chasing anything in a skirt.

Dammit. He'd really had her going there for a minute. Too bad he was just like all the rest. She rolled her case down the hall as she shook her head with a smile glued to her face.

"Better luck next time, fly boy."

"Hey, you can't blame a guy for trying."

"Try me."

She hated the edge of steel that crept into her tone. She hated being bitter and fought against showing how her past experiences had turned her against certain types of men. She hated showing weakness of any kind in front of those who could very well exploit it. Working day in and day out in a man's world, she had to be tough. She couldn't afford to let many people see the woman she was underneath the professional pilot's exterior.

When she glanced back he was leaning against the doorframe, his muscular arms folded over his chest as he watched her walk away. The speculation in his eyes belied his easy grin. No doubt about it, the man was hot with a capital H, but he wasn't for her. Too bad. He really was a looker. Smart too.

But Emily wasn't ready to be one in a long line of women trailing out of his bedroom. She'd done that once and she'd vowed never to let it happen again. No more pilots. No more players. If she ever got involved with another man, he'd be a stable, secure type who wouldn't cheat on her. He'd be an accountant or a lawyer…anything other than a pilot.

The peace and quiet of her hotel room was a relief to Emily's frayed nerves when she finally reached it. Sam had been asking questions all day and she wasn't sure if that was just normal new guy behavior or something more sinister. Then that badly framed proposition. She still didn't know what to make of that. She was concerned she might be overreacting, but she couldn't be sure who to trust. She was beginning to see spies and assassins around every corner and she was afraid she was going nuts.

Scott and his veiled threats might very well have driven her around the bend.

Or maybe her suspicions were correct. Maybe something terrible was going on at Praxis Air and she seemed to be the only person who saw it. Maybe it was up to her to stand up to Scott and expose him.

The thought terrified her but there was nobody else. She had to do it. She owed it to her mother and to all the people who depended on Praxis Air to put food on their tables and money in their wallets. They had a loyal staff, many of whom had been with the company since the beginning. She wouldn't let Scott and his double dealings put them all out of work.

Secret flights and no-questions-asked charters were somewhat common in the industry, but the recent onset of fatal crashes that had plagued the company made her hackles rise. That, along with the odd cargo flights to and from backwater locations had her questioning the company and its new management. If Scott was running drugs there was every possibility Praxis Air could go under, its assets seized if and when the authorities caught them. That's why she had to do what she could to stop him.

Quietly, of course. The brake failure in her car made her wonder if maybe Mr. Southerland's *accident* had been entirely accidental. Just like those last two plane crashes. The NTSB final reports still weren't in yet, but a few questions had been raised about why those jets had gone down and operations had been halted for a while until every Praxis Air jet had been inspected and approved.

They were flying. For now. Another shut down could ruin their business completely. As it was, they'd lost customers over the recent problems. That was one of the excuses Scott had used to convert more of their jets to cargo haulers. He'd convinced the board but she wasn't sold.

Don Juan was waiting for her in the hotel restaurant when she went down an hour later. She'd taken the time to reinforce her defenses against Sam's charm. She had to work with the guy but that didn't mean she had to like him.

The problem was, aside from the overinflated innuendo of those last few minutes, he'd been the perfect gentleman. In fact, that last bit about sharing room service had seemed out of character with what she'd learned about him in the short time they'd been together.

She couldn't quite figure him out. Was he the player his smarmy invitation had implied, or something altogether different? A man like him probably didn't have to work too hard to get women. So why the abrupt and rather paltry attempt to get her?

Something didn't ring true. She'd be wise to stay on her toes with him. For all she knew, he could've been sent by Scott to spy on her…or worse. She didn't think he was a killer, but then, what did she really know about the guy?

Emily shoved those thoughts aside as she joined him at the table he'd already claimed. The restaurant wasn't too busy at this hour and the seating was designed in such a way as to provide the maximum of privacy for each diner. The atmosphere was intimate.

"Glad to see you're punctual," she said as she slid into the luxuriously upholstered booth he'd secured for them.

"I'm hungry. That sort of motivation will get me moving every time."

She laughed at his small joke as a server placed full glasses of water with elegantly thin wedges of lemon in front of them. Another man handed them each menus and began listing the specials for that evening.

When the waiter left, an uncomfortable silence fell between them.

"I should apologize for earlier. I didn't mean it the way it sounded—"

"Think nothing of it," she interrupted his rather painful apology. "Just don't try it again and we'll get along fine." Dammit, had she jumped to conclusions? She went back over his words in her mind and realized that it was a possibility. Embarrassment flooded her.

She didn't look at him as silence fell again. This was even more awkward than she feared. Most of the men she worked with wouldn't have batted an eye about propositioning her. But the enigma that was Sam surprised her yet again.

"I can't promise that."

"What?" She looked up from her study of the menu.

"I can't promise not to find you attractive, Emily, though I will try to curb my baser instincts and potentially indecent proposals in future."

His eyes sparkled in an inviting way. She should have felt discomfited by his words. Instead, she found herself amused. Amused and…intrigued?

No. That would never do.

"No problem. I get propositioned every once in a while. Jet jocks just can't help themselves. Forget it. I have."

"I guess you've dealt with your share of asshole pilots in your time. A girl as pretty as you must have had your share of problems."

She didn't know how to take the compliment. Had she been right the first time, thinking he was looking for a little nookie along with the room service? Or had it been an innocent proposal that she'd taken the wrong way? Sam confused the heck out of her.

Thankfully, the waiter returned at that moment to take their orders. After a short conversation with the talkative waiter about how the salmon special was prepared, they were alone once again.

Emily decided to take control of the conversation, to keep it from straying into dangerous or uncomfortable areas. She launched into a discussion of the ongoing airport construction at PDX and the different sights to see in the city. Before she realized it, Sam had maneuvered her into going with him to Saturday Market the next morning.

"We don't have to be back at the airport until mid-afternoon. If we meet for breakfast around nine, we can spend a couple of hours at the market before we have to head out."

"Sounds like a plan," Sam agreed. "I've heard about the market but I've never been to it before."

"It's worth seeing. There are lots of different kinds of things for sale and it's nice to walk around in the downtown area near the river. We can take the light rail to the market and hop on it again to get to the airport when we're ready to leave. It's very convenient."

They'd finished their main courses and were nibbling on desert by this time. More than an hour had passed while they talked about different things. Sam was a man of few words but oddly, he was a good conversationalist. Or maybe he was just good at letting her talk. He asked questions that made it seem like he was truly interested in what she had to say, which was refreshing but also somewhat worrisome. Only after an hour of talking did she realize she'd probably talked the poor man's ear off. Yet he didn't seem bored or annoyed with her. Curiouser and curiouser.

The attentive waiter cruised by one more time and Sam ordered a carafe of coffee. It seemed he wanted to stay longer, prolonging the conversation. She was amazed he wasn't making haste to get away.

They spent another half hour chatting over coffee. They formed a tentative bond of friendship over the meal, the earlier confusion over his maybe-proposition almost forgotten in light of their new camaraderie.

Sam let her get the bill on the corporate card though he made sure she wasn't going to pay out of her own pocket before allowing it. She liked that concern, even as she assured him they were traveling on an expense account.

"Pilots normally have a limit on meal expenses but you get a little more leeway when you travel with me," she explained. "I've been with the company since before I could fly, so I get a few extra perks." She wasn't about to go into the details of her minority shareholder status. If Sam lasted long enough with the company, she was sure he'd hear all the scuttlebutt from the other employees.

Not a one of them knew the whole story except maybe Buddy. He'd been with the company from the beginning and was a truly silent partner. Only the really old timers knew that Buddy was one of the co-founders of the airline and he'd asked them not to advertise that fact. He liked to keep a low profile and just be one of the boys. Emily respected that, even though she herself was often the topic of gossip surrounding her stakeholder status in the company.

They finished the carafe of coffee between them and lingered over desert. The crème brûlée had been as spectacular as she remembered it, but gone all too fast. Still, they sat companionably, talking over all kinds of topics until finally Emily began to notice the impatient looks some of the wait staff threw in their direction. It was near closing time and the staff probably wanted to clear up and go home.

"I think we'd better go." Emily nodded toward the bus boy heading in their direction.

Sam nodded and before she could rise, he was around the table, politely pulling out her chair. He had great manners. Most ex-military men did, in her experience. Still, it was nice to be treated like a lady for a change, instead of one of the guys.

The conversation didn't lag all the way up the elevator until they arrived outside the door to her room. She hadn't realized their destination until she was faced with the door that had her number on it.

"I guess this is my stop."

Darnit, she sounded nervous. Why did she have to sound wimpy all of a sudden? She thought they'd done a good job of repairing the damage caused by their earlier misunderstanding—though she was still unclear as to whether she'd misinterpreted his words or he really had been making a lame attempt at seduction. Either way, she wanted it put behind her as quickly as possible. She couldn't work with the guy with that kind of uneasiness between them. The cockpit was too close a space to bear that burden.

"Guess so." Sam didn't appear in any hurry to leave.

"Shall I call you in the morning before I head down for breakfast or do you want to meet in the lobby?"

"Call me." His voice dropped to a lower, more intimate tone.

Or maybe that was just her senses going into overdrive. Sam's presence had her on a knife's edge between simple attraction and outright arousal. She feared she was tipping dangerously toward arousal the longer she stayed in his presence.

Being all alone with him didn't help matters. The subtle lighting only made the mood more intimate.

"Roger that." She tried for a lighter tone and swiped her key card through the electronic lock.

Sam's hand rose to cover hers before she could push open the door. Her gaze flashed up to meet his and a little gasp issued from her throat. He'd taken her by surprise.

"I am sorry for my earlier poorly thought-out words." His voice surrounded her in warmth and mystery. "I truly didn't mean anything by what I said."

"Apology accepted. Let's just let it go." She hated that he kept bringing it up. She wanted it put behind them as quickly as possible.

"I'm glad you're a forgiving lady. Maybe you'll forgive this…"

He moved in on her, crowding her against the door. His big, hard body invaded her personal space but she couldn't find the strength of will to object. Everything female in her stood up and cheered when he pressed against her, her softness conforming to the ridges of his muscles. The man had a body to die for and her arousal kicked into overdrive as his head dipped lower.

He gave her ample time to evade his kiss if she so desired but the only thing she desired at the moment was him. She rose on tiptoe to meet his descent, their lips touching tentatively at first, then locking into an unbreakable ring of desire.

His hands went around her waist, dragging her closer as his tongue delved inside her mouth. Breathing ragged, she answered his thrusts with delicate parries that grew bolder as the kiss progressed.

Oh, yes. This is what she'd wanted since the moment she'd first laid eyes on him. Their easy conversation over dinner had only served to heighten her instant attraction to him. Sam was an intriguing man who grew more interesting the longer she knew him, not less. She couldn't say the same for most of the men she worked with—or even those few she'd dated in recent years.

So far, Sam was flipping all her switches and gearing her up for one hell of a flight.

Then he drew away.

Following his lips a short distance, she tried to prolong the kiss. But Sam was made of stronger stuff. He moved away, using his superior height to deny her his kiss, though he kept hold of her trembling body, tucking her head under his chin while his hands roamed over her back in a soothing motion.

"Forgive me," he whispered.

"There's nothing to forgive," she replied almost on autopilot. That seemed to be her standard response where he was concerned. It amazed her that they'd only known each other a couple of days. She already felt so comfortable with him.

"You're one hell of a woman, Emily." His voice grew stronger as his breathing grew steadier. It felt good to know he'd been as affected as she'd been from their kiss. She could feel the impressive ridge of evidence against her hip that he'd definitely been excited by their joined lips.

"So why did you stop?" Damn. Had she really said that out loud? She had a bad habit of saying whatever popped into her mind in moments of stress. This definitely qualified.

A low, sexy chuckle rumbled through his chest under her ear. Oh, she liked the feeling of that.

"I want you to respect me in the morning, Captain," he joked, setting her mostly at ease. "I swear I didn't mean to let it go so far but you tempt me like no other woman I've ever met, Em. I only meant to give you a friendly kiss goodnight but it morphed before I could control it and all I seem to do around you is apologize."

She placed a finger over his sexy lips as she drew away from his strong body. For the first time, she felt like she had the upper hand with a man. Somehow, for some strange reason, this big man was on the defensive. She didn't know what to think about that, but if it helped her muddle through the next few minutes, it was a good thing.

"And all I seem to do around you is tell you not to worry. Let's just let it be for now. You kissed me. I liked it. But it doesn't have to go any further than that."

"For now." He moved close again, intent in his eyes though he himself stopped before he kissed her again.

"Okay. For now," she agreed. "But know this. I'm not easy and I don't sleep around with every new pilot who joins my fleet."

He looked as if she'd slapped him as he let her go.

"Don't you think I know that already?"

"Just so we're clear." She backed off as well, glad to have some space between them so she could think more clearly. "I generally have a rule about getting involved with pilots. I don't."

"I'd heard that about you." A slow, wicked grin spread across his talented mouth. "But I have a rule of my own. I bend the rules."

She had to chuckle at that. His self confidence was truly something to behold. It was probably a big part of what made him a good pilot. Thinking on your feet and being certain of your decisions was a good quality in someone driving a high velocity aircraft where things could turn on a dime from good to bad to worse…to deadly.

"I'll remember that."

"See that you do." His smile warmed her and she found herself grinning back at him.

He dipped his head and for one shocking moment she hoped he was going to give her another of those amazing kisses. She held her breath in anticipation but he only bussed her on the forehead as he took the key card from her hand. He swiped it through the lock again and tucked it back into her hand. He turned the door handle and pushed the door inward, sticking his foot in the space he'd created, but didn't go any farther.

"Sleep well, pretty girl," he whispered near her ear then leaned back, letting her go. "Call me when you're ready for breakfast. And be sure to turn the deadbolt. These hotel locks aren't that great."

He gestured for her to go inside and wouldn't budge until she'd done so. She was definitely not used to this kind of treatment. It was as if he really cared about her safety. She looked at him quizzically as she stepped inside the open door.

"Close it and lock it, Em. I'm not leaving until you do."

She shook her head and smiled bemusedly as she shut the door. She went up on tiptoe to watch him before turning the deadbolt. Sure enough, he waited until the lock made the telltale snick. He gave her a tiny wave as if he knew she was watching, then turned and sauntered away silently down the hall.

Emily turned in the privacy of her hotel room and leaned her back against the cold door. It had been an interesting night. A lovely dinner filled with good conversation and then the most amazing kiss that had come out of nowhere. They'd gotten off to a rocky start with that strange invitation in his room, but he'd made up for it in spades.

If he flew as good as he kissed—and she'd already seen enough of his work in the air to know he was a competent pilot—then they were in for a wild ride.

If she chose to let this continue.

She still wasn't sure where his loyalties lay.

And that thought brought reality crashing back. What if all this had been some kind of ploy? What if he really was working for Scott? What if he was in on whatever Scott was doing to Praxis Air? What if he'd been sent to spy on her in some way, or keep her in line?

And what if her imagination was running away with her? She could be overthinking the best thing that ever happened to her.

Or the worst.

Darnit. Why was everything so confusing where men were concerned? Emily didn't know what to think anymore. She decided to give up for now and get some sleep. Hopefully everything would be clearer in the morning.

Sam found it hard to leave Emily and that was something he hadn't anticipated. Not only did she intrigue him on an intellectual level, but she fit in his arms way better than he ever would have expected. She was gorgeous. That went without saying. But she was attractive in other ways as well.

Sam had never been much of a skirt chaser though he'd had his share of playing around in his younger days. Nowadays, he wanted more than a roll in the hay from the women he chose to get involved with. He wasn't looking for a wife necessarily, but he wanted something more than a one night stand.

He wanted a friend. Someone he could talk to out of bed and enjoy in it as well. While his lifestyle and job didn't mesh well with the idea of a relationship in the traditional sense, after seeing the happiness of some of the couples on his new team, he wanted more.

He'd probably never find that, but it was something to

dream about. In fact, he had a pretty good idea that the woman he'd find starring in his fantasies of a future was the one he'd left only moments ago. Emily was funny, smart, and fit all his ideas of beauty both inside and out. While he still couldn't be certain of her loyalties, the picture he had developed of her so far was all too attractive for his comfort.

And he didn't have time. Sam couldn't afford to get emotionally entangled with anyone on this op. He had to keep a distance and stay as objective as possible. His mission depended on it. But after only a day or two spent with her, he knew it would hurt to discover that Emily was involved in the potentially treasonous activities Praxis Air was suspected of.

Time was wasting and he had to find out what was going on before another outbreak occurred someplace. The longer he took to complete his mission and uncover what exactly was going on at Praxis Air, the higher the odds of another zombie infestation. Each time the creatures had shown up, it got worse. More innocent lives wasted. More horror. More killing. Sam had to make that stop. To do that, he had to stop thinking about his attraction to a certain female pilot and start concentrating on his job.

He had to play the part of jet jockey lothario, but he hated it. He'd regretted propositioning her the moment he'd spoken the words, but part of his cover persona was to be a bit of a jerk. He found it hard to do with Emily, though. He didn't want her to think he was a jerk. Far from it.

Still, he had to present the rather shallow exterior of a man who had a girl in every port. A lot of pilots lived a free and easy sort of lifestyle. Sam knew plenty of guys like that and he'd come up with his undercover personality by choosing something that made sense in the world of aviation. He regretted it only when it came to Emily. Otherwise, the easygoing skirt chaser was the perfect cover for this particular job. And he was very much afraid he'd have to play the jerk again, no matter how much the real Sam didn't want to treat her that way.

Sam called in on his secure phone while he had the

chance. Commander Sykes picked up on the second ring.

"Sorry, sir. I know it's late but I couldn't get free before now to check in with you."

"No problem, Sam. I'm on the late shift for the next few weeks anyway, but you can call me anytime. Your mission is important. Don't hesitate to call."

"Yes, sir."

"Now, give me a sitrep. Have you learned anything yet?"

Sam launched into the requested situation report, detailing his activities since showing up for duty earlier that day and his plans for the next day. He gave his impressions of the various personnel he'd met so far and his plans to scout out the cargo manifests in more detail when he returned to the airline's home base in Wichita.

"The CEO signed the blank manifest personally. That, in itself, seems odd to me. It's like he wrote a blank check and nobody would dare question the missing paperwork because his name was on it. Emily didn't say a word, even though she's proven to be a stickler for protocol."

"Do you think she's in on it?"

"Too soon to say, sir. She seemed annoyed when she saw the manifest, but she went along with it."

"And there was no way to get a look inside the crates?"

"I tried early this morning but Emily intercepted me. She had accepted the shipment in the middle of the night. I'd thought she'd left, but she must've either come back or stayed in the office long after I thought she'd be gone. She caught me snooping, but I believe I was able to salvage the situation."

"She doesn't suspect you?"

"I don't think so. But she may have suspected something was fishy with the cargo, which is why she stayed. It's only a guess at this point. I haven't cleared her yet. For now, everyone is still on the suspect list. I'll let you know my findings as the situation develops."

"I'll try to have someone track the cargo after you dropped it off but I'm not holding out much hope. John Petit may be in touch with you in the next week or two. I have him working research for this op and he may also be able to provide some logistical support, if needed. In the meantime, if you need anything, call me."

"Yes, sir. Thank you, sir."

"And Sam," Matt paused. "Be careful."

"Roger that, sir. Give my love to the doc." Sam couldn't resist teasing his new commander about his girlfriend. Dr. Eileen McCormick had snared the commander's heart after healing Sam's.

She'd worked her medical magic on Sam back on Long Island before she'd even met Matt Sykes. Back then, they weren't altogether sure which team she was on, but her special serum—when injected directly into the heart moments after exposure to the zombie contagion—could save lives. It had saved Sam's life and he'd be forever grateful to her for it. As far as Sam was concerned, she'd more than made up for her initial involvement in creating the zombie contagion as part of the original research team.

Once she'd realized what they'd done, she'd put all her efforts into finding a cure. It still wasn't a perfect cure. It only worked on a small percentage of people. But it had worked for Sam and that's all that mattered.

"Stop flirting with my girl, lieutenant," came Matt's disgruntled reply. It had become a somewhat standard joke between them since Matt and Eileen had become a couple. Sam didn't have any romantic interest in Eileen, but he liked and respected her as much as he did the commander. It was harmless teasing between friends.

"Sir, yes, sir," Sam replied crisply to Matt's disgusted grunt.

"Call me when you have news. And Eileen says to take care of yourself. She doesn't want to have to patch up your bleeding ass again."

Sam heard a commotion in the background and realized he'd probably either woken the couple with his phone call or interrupted something a little more intimate.

The commander hung up before Sam could make a smartass reply but it was just as well. Matt was still his commander, for all their easy camaraderie. It was important to keep that boundary, even as their friendship deepened. Someday, when this was all over, they would probably hang out together, but for now there had to be a slight demarcation line between commander and those he commanded.

Meanwhile, Sam had work to do and time was not on his side. There was little he could do about it tonight. He decided to rest up. He'd have another chance for action again tomorrow and he wanted to be at his sharpest. Emily wasn't a fool and he had to be on his toes around her—whether she was on the good side, or heaven forbid, the bad.

CHAPTER 4

Sam dreamed of Emily. Hot dreams. Bothersome dreams. Dreams that had him taking a cold shower the moment he got out of bed and working to suppress memory of them when he met her in the lobby.

It did no good. The sight of her fresh face and creamy skin brought back the heated, sweaty imaginings of his overactive mind from the night before. That single kiss they'd shared outside her door had fueled his fantasies in a way no woman ever had before. To Sam, Emily was the stuff dreams were made of.

Erotic dreams, mostly. Although in other dreams they simply were together, laughing and enjoying their time together. Those dreams were almost as sweet as those that featured a heavy, sexual beat of them making love. At least in his mind.

Sam found himself grateful that she wasn't able to read his mind as he greeted her in the lobby of the hotel. She'd called briefly to say she was heading downstairs and he'd barely been able to grunt in response. He was doing better now but she still turned him on. He'd have to deal with it. They both had jobs to do and walking around with a woody wasn't going to help his cause—either with the woman or with the task he'd come here to perform.

"Are you feeling adventurous this morning?" Emily greeted him with a mischievous smile.

Oh, yeah. His dreams had definitely been adventurous, but somehow he got the feeling that wasn't what she was referring to. Still, best to be cautious. He leaned back on his heels and regarded her.

"Depends what you have in mind."

"Breakfast," she replied quickly. "But not here. This place has the standard eggs, bacon, and heart attack on a plate menu. I was thinking of something a little different. Question is, are you up for it?"

That daring edge in her voice was a siren's call to him. The more he got to know of her, the more he both dreaded and delighted in the fact that they seemed to be kindred spirits.

"I'm up for anything you can dish out, captain." Hell, he'd eat bamboo shoots and alfalfa sprouts if it made her happy. Lord knew he'd eaten worse in his time.

"I got us both set up for late checkout so as long as we're back here by noon, our stuff can stay in the rooms. What do you say we head out to parts unknown, get breakfast at a little bistro I'm thinking about, then head straight to Saturday Market from there?"

"Sounds like a plan." He nodded and followed her out of the lobby and down the street.

She was downright bubbly this morning and he wondered what had brought about the subtle change in her energy. Yesterday she'd been a cautious, calm professional. The day before she'd been slightly harassed and wary. Today she was open and free. Had he done that? Had their kiss brought out her lighter side as it had brought out the sexual perv in him?

Well, maybe not perv. But some of the things he'd dreamed about last night were definitely pushing the envelope. He wondered if she'd be interested in testing the kinkier side of life with him as he watched her sashay down the sidewalk slightly in front of him.

She turned suddenly and caught him staring.

"Do my eyes deceive me or was my first officer just ogling my butt? I could have you keel hauled for that, mister." The twinkle in her eye told him she was definitely kidding.

"Good thing we're not in the Navy, then." He caught up to her and took her hand in his.

He didn't know why he'd done it. He hadn't held hands with a girl since high school. Somehow, though, this felt right. Sort of old fashioned and good. Pure.

Unlike the steamy sexual thoughts he'd been having about Emily since last night. Better to tamp those down so he could function today. At least a little.

Being with Emily was proving harder on his self-restraint than he would have believed just two short days ago. She was a dynamo in a size petite captain's uniform and more competent in the cockpit than he'd have credited. Boy, had he been wrong about her. From the get-go, he'd had the wrong impression, gleaned from the thin personnel file and lousy photo he'd been given as background information before he went undercover.

She was nothing like the serious, harassed looking woman in the photo. There was something almost vulnerable about her at times that appealed to his protective instincts. At other times, she was fierce. A good partner to have at your back in battle. He'd never thought of any other woman in those terms. Not even the women warriors on his new team. Sure, he respected them all, but he didn't know them half as well as he thought he knew Emily after only a short acquaintance.

Of course, he'd never kissed any of them. Or had naughty dreams about them. No, that was just Emily. A woman who was working her way under his skin without even trying.

They walked toward the downtown area where the market was located. Emily stopped short of the busy market area and ducked into a small bistro.

Emily surprised him with her choice of restaurants. It had a fun ambience and eclectic menu. Lots of health food dressed up in appetizing ways. If she thought he'd be put off by the choices, she was sadly mistaken. He ordered fresh cinnamon wheat toast and a big portion of something called rice and raisins.

It was served hot and was basically a bowl full of seven or eight different kinds of rice that were mostly of the brown and long grain varieties, dotted with plump raisins. The waitress brought a bunch of fussy little dishes along with it, including a small carafe of milk and his choice of brown sugar, molasses, honey, or maple syrup and with a few different choices of chopped nuts and other things he could use to dress up the rice. He went to town, much to Emily's amusement, decking out his bowl of steaming rice and raisins with a little bit of everything.

"Nothing fazes you, does it?" She shook her head as he dug into his bowl of unconventional breakfast.

"Not much. I've eaten worse in the service, Em. If you want to stump me you'll have to try harder than this." He winked at her and they shared a grin as she buttered her whole wheat toast.

"Duly noted."

She nibbled daintily on the toast while he chowed down on the unexpectedly good concoction in his bowl. He'd have to remember this and try it sometime when he got back to base. He liked experimenting with different foods though he wasn't much of a chef.

"So what was your rank in the Army?" she asked out of the blue.

"Lieutenant. Wasn't that in my file?" He wondered if she'd read his file. Was she testing him or fishing for information?

"I only glanced at your file before they put it in the drawer. Officially, Buddy hired you. He's the one who read through all the statistics and reports. We do background checks on all our flight crew. You can't be too careful these days with all the smuggling and illegal goings on."

"Have you had problems with that kind of thing before?"

"No. Nothing like that. But I like to think our careful hiring practices are the reason we've been problem-free to this point."

"You did have a couple of fatal crashes in recent months, though. See, I researched you guys too, before I accepted the position." He tipped his imaginary hat to her belying the seriousness of his words. Hopefully if he kept everything in a friendly tone she'd continue to be open with him.

A frown wrinkled her brow. "Yeah, we had some bad things happen recently."

"A friend of mine said weather was most likely to blame for one of the crashes, and scuttlebutt had pilot error down for the other one. I asked around before I signed on the dotted line. I have a vested interest in my own safety, after all."

She chuckled but he could see she was still troubled by the reminder of the personnel they'd lost. Her tone was somber when she continued.

"The final reports aren't in yet but the NTSB cleared us of responsibility on a preliminary basis. The toxicology report on Ernie Young's body—he was the pilot involved in last October's incident—said he was drunk as a skunk. I knew Ernie liked to party in his off duty hours but I never would've thought he'd be stupid enough to fly in that condition."

"What about the other one?"

"There wasn't enough left of the plane or the pilot to do an autopsy. At least that's my understanding. There hasn't been a lot of information forthcoming on that investigation. I guess if we were implicated we would've heard about it by now."

"I suppose so." Sam chomped on his rice, allowing space if she wanted to continue. Sometimes silence was a useful tool to get others to talk. Sure enough, it worked with Emily.

"Still, it's strange we haven't heard much. I got the other information through a leak. One of the investigators knew my mother and was willing to give me a hint as to their findings. That's normal in this kind of situation where the airline isn't really to blame, or they're fairly certain that's the way the final report will turn out. If they think the airline is on the hook, you usually get a cease and desist order to stop flying or a bunch of inspectors show up to rifle through the books and interrogate personnel. None of that has happened. Either way, it's strange. I think we should've heard something by now."

"When is the final report from the NTSB due?"

"Who knows?" She rolled her eyes in frustration. "I don't think they've given themselves a cutoff date, which is also strange. The whole thing makes me wonder what's going on. Usually, they're more efficient."

"Could it have something to do with politics? I've heard sometimes the shift in political parties in Washington can affect how certain government agencies are run." He put that out there as a red herring. He wanted to see where she'd lead the conversation.

"No, I don't think so. The NTSB is usually safe from the worst of the political machinations. At least the investigative arm is. Most of those guys have been in the business for years. There's very little turnover in their ranks. They're all top notch in the field and they have connections all over the industry."

Once again, Sam waited to see if she'd continue, chewing his surprisingly delicious breakfast and trying to project his interest in her words. Once again, she didn't disappoint.

"I think it's more a case of someone being paid off or warned not to leak any information. I don't know who and I had no clue that anyone could really have that sort of power or why they'd use it in our case, but I'm leaning more and more toward that belief."

"That sounds serious."

"It is." Her expression was grim for a moment before she deliberately changed the subject. "But it's only a suspicion. How's your breakfast? I love this place. They have an inventive menu."

He let the conversation drift as they both finished eating and headed for the door.

"Do you feel like walking to the market? It's not too far and it's not raining, which can be rare in Portland."

"I'm up for a walk. Lead on, MacDuff." He opened the door of the restaurant for her and she preceded him out.

After days of comparative inactivity, Sam needed more than a little stroll, but it would have to do. He wasn't used to going days without a heavy workout or two, but he was in the civilian world now and most regular folks didn't keep themselves at the peak of readiness at all times. He'd had to lay off the more public workouts, like taking long runs with heavy weights, in order to fit in a little better. Plus, he just didn't have the time. The mission was on.

It might be a long-term assignment so he had to figure out ways to keep himself in shape while he did his job. He had a set of weights in his condo and was able to spend a few minutes here and there lifting iron to keep his muscles from turning to flab. That would have to do.

He began to notice more activity as they approached the market area. Looked like a good number of Portlanders and tourists were out in force, enjoying the uncharacteristically sunny weather.

Emily stopped abruptly as they were walking past a small dress shop. Sam was surprised. She seemed completely entranced by the Bohemian styles on display.

"I wouldn't have pegged you for a gypsy."

"You'd be surprised." A flush stole over her face before she turned away.

Sam caught her arm and coaxed her back around to face him. "Wait a minute. I think we should go in and take a closer look. I might be able to pick up something for my sisters. I'm a lousy shopper but those scarves look like stuff they'd like. I need your input, Em, or I'm sure I'll pick the wrong thing. You'd really be helping me out. What do you say?"

"You have sisters?" She looked like she was debating the idea.

"Two of them."

"Older or younger?" Yeah, she was definitely leaning toward giving in.

"One of each."

One delicate eyebrow arched as she looked up at him then relented with a sigh.

"Okay. So what's the occasion?"

"Vel's birthday is coming up and Ty's having a kid. I've been meaning to pick up some presents."

"Your sisters' names are Vel and Ty?" She walked with him into the shop as he broke out in laughter.

"Sorry, no. Those are nicknames that sort of stuck. Vel is Amy and Ty is Cathy."

"So how did those nicknames come about? Are they short for something?"

"Yeah," he admitted sheepishly. "Remnants of my Jurassic period. Vel is short for Veloci-sister. She's small and cute like a velociraptor, until she tries to bite your head off. Ty is short for Tyranno-sister Rex. She's the older, more frightening one."

Emily laughed out loud, as he'd hoped she would.

"You don't really call them that, do you?" He was enchanted by the laughter in her expression and if they hadn't been in the middle of a dress shop, he'd have taken her in his arms and kissed the life out of her right then and there.

"Believe me, that's better than some of the other things I called them when we were growing up. It's gotten to the point they kind of expect nicknames from me and get suspicious when I call them by name."

"So…a birthday and a birth." Emily moved farther into the store, tapping her chin with a slender finger while she examined all the colorful items on display. "Can you tell me more about your sisters? Besides which dinosaurs they resemble, I mean. Do you know either one's favorite color?"

"Amy likes pink. Cath's more into oranges, reds, and burgundies."

"Tall or short?"

"They're both about your height. Maybe an inch or two taller in Cathy's case. Both thin, though Cathy's supposed to be ballooning in a couple of months."

Emily shot him a dirty look that said she didn't appreciate

his comment. He liked that she'd stick up for his sister—a woman she'd never met. It said something good about Emily's sense of fairness.

"How far along is she?"

"Four months. She only told the family last week. She and her husband were keeping it quiet until they were sure everything was going to be okay." His voice grew more serious. "She's had two miscarriages."

Emily's eyes filled with compassion. "How about this?"

She swept a hanger off the rack and swirled the swath of brightly colored fabric over her arm. It was a dress that didn't have much of a waist. It would work really well for a pregnant woman. The fabric floated downward from an ornate neckline and was light as a feather. Some sort of gauzy cotton fabric that was dyed with bold orange and red flower patterns.

"I think we have a winner." He picked up the dress and folded it over his arm.

He hadn't intended to mix personal shopping with business but he figured he was killing two birds with one stone. He really did need presents for his sisters and if helping him shop drew him closer to Emily, it would help his mission considerably.

Plus the smile on Emily's face made his gut clench in a mix of pleasure and dread. He was falling fast for the pretty pilot. That hadn't been part of the program but he would have to deal with things as they came at him. He'd always been quick on his feet. He'd just have to figure a way to handle the attraction that sparked between them whenever they were together.

"How about this for Amy?" Emily lifted a delicate pink shawl from one of the tables and held it out in front of him, displaying the fabric. It was thicker than the dress and even softer.

"What's it made of?"

"Raw silk."

"Fancy." He took the shawl out of her hands and added it

to the growing pile on his arm. "She'll like that. Now, what do you want as a reward for helping me? How about that blue number over there? You'd look killer in it." His gaze moved to a form fitting Chinese brocade dress displayed on a mannequin, then back to her. He'd noted the way she eyed the silk dress when they'd walked in.

"No, I don't want anything for helping you."

"At least let me buy you lunch."

"We're on an expense account. The company is paying for our lunch." She rolled her eyes at him.

"Can't blame a guy for trying. Come on, I saw the way you were looking at that blue dress."

"It wasn't the blue dress," she caved in, moving toward the rack of dresses like a bear to honey. "Though the blue one is pretty." She looked through the hangers checking sizes until she found the one she wanted. "This is the one I was looking at." She pulled it from the rack and held it in front of her as she looked into the mirror a few feet away. She was totally entranced by the floaty black dress.

It was the typical little black dress most women wore but with a Bohemian twist. The skirt was short and flirty, made of whisper thin fabric and the top part would hug Emily's curves like a lover.

Damn. Sam wanted to see her in that dress. He wanted it bad.

And then he wanted to see her out of it. Doing the things he'd done with her in his dreams last night. All of them. All night long.

Sam cleared his throat around the lump that had formed there, moving the bundle of fabric over his arm so that it hid his rather blatant reaction to those provocative thoughts. Luckily Emily was still totally absorbed by the dress, looking at it with longing in the mirror.

Then she glanced at the price tag and her expression fell.

"Well, there goes that. Too rich for my pocketbook." She put it back on the rack, but not before Sam peeked at the size. She seemed to lose interest in the store then, a sad little crinkle at the corners of her eyes.

He didn't quite understand. If she was the sole heir to her mother's stock in the airline, why didn't she have enough money to buy a dress? Furthermore, she was a fully employed pilot with years of seniority in an airline her mother had founded. Where was her cash? Was she just thrifty or was there some other reason?

Suddenly, he wanted to shower her in gifts. He wanted to spend some of the money he had socked away for a rainy day on her. It didn't make sense, but there it was.

"Why don't you go on ahead while I pay for these," he suggested. "Snag me a couple of those shepherd's pies you were telling me about. Extra onions."

She seemed grateful for the excuse to leave the store. Sam was glad too. He gave in to impulse and added two more items to his purchases before he brought them to the counter to pay. When the saleslady asked if he wanted them gift wrapped, he decided to go for it. He'd never have time or the supplies to wrap his sisters' gifts otherwise and the festively colored paper might keep a certain lady pilot from looking too closely.

Whether or not she'd ever get a chance to open that particular box was still up in the air but Sam was a man who liked to be prepared for all contingencies. An impulse had driven him to buy those things but that didn't mean he had to give in all the way. He'd hold the package in reserve and see where events led him.

For now, he had lunch to eat and a plane to catch, in that order.

The flight from Portland to Denver was uneventful. Another high-powered corporate client wanted some files hand delivered to their representative who met the jet at the airport in Denver. From there it was a quick hop back to Wichita.

The sky was cloudless and dark outside the cockpit, lit only by pinpoints of stars and a sliver of reflective moon as the jet cut through the air speeding toward its destination. This kind of quiet peace, above the clouds and close to the stars, always made Emily introspective.

"I once heard about a ceremony overseen every year by the Dali Lama where a group of Buddhist monks spend days and days creating an intricate design out of sand. They lay the pattern grain by grain in painstaking detail. It's a gorgeous artwork in a circular design they call a mandala."

"I've seen it," Sam replied mysteriously.

She didn't want to question his wording but it made her wonder about him. Did he mean he'd seen it *in person*? It sure sounded that way. But maybe he meant he'd seen it on television, the way she had. She was a fan of documentaries and had watched an hour-long program about Tibet that had included footage of the ceremony. She chalked his response up to that and let it pass. The moment was too solemn and the mood too intimate to break by questioning his choice of words.

"At the end of the ceremony, when the mandala is finished, they sweep it away. Destroy it deliberately." She paused, letting the silence be filled with that thought for a moment. "I never understood how they could spend so much time creating a thing of such beauty and then demolish it." Dismay filled her voice.

"It's all about the impermanence of life," Sam said quietly.

She looked at him, surprised by his quick grasp of the concept it had taken tragedy for her to understand. Perhaps he'd learned it the same way. Perhaps he'd lost someone dear to him. She couldn't tell much from the firm set of his jaw as he stared out the cockpit window, but the tense set of his broad shoulders made her think maybe she was right.

"Yeah, I get that now."

"You lost someone." It wasn't a question. He turned his head to meet her gaze as he spoke, pinning her in place with compassion etched into his handsomely weathered face. He knew. He understood.

"My mother." It was her turn to look away. To hide her

pain as she stared at the infinite sky in front of them. "She was my best friend. My role model. The only person in my life I could truly trust."

She paused, gathering herself. She hadn't been this close to tears in a long time and it shocked her that she was able to open up to this man—this new person in her life—so readily. She wasn't normally so willing to expose her secrets to anyone, much less someone she'd really only just met. But something about Sam seemed innately trustworthy and it felt good in a bittersweet way to remember and talk about her mother.

"She was a pilot. A trailblazer in this profession dominated by men." Yeah, her mom had been one in a million. It was freeing to remember and to be able to share the memory with another pilot who might understand. "She taught me how to fly when I was in high school."

"Cessnas?" he asked, naming a common brand of prop planes that many people learned to fly in.

"Piper J-3 cub," she corrected his assumption.

"A tail dragger." He used the nickname applied to planes with landing gear near the tail that required a special technique to land. "Those cubbies are too small for me. I flew one for a while when I was a kid, but I shudder to think about squeezing into that tiny cockpit now."

She laughed with him. The man was big with a capital B and the cockpit on the two-seater cub was small. He seemed to take up more space in the jet too. He wasn't fat—not by any stretch of the imagination. He was all muscle from what she could see. The seams of his uniform shirt strained against his biceps and deltoids as he flipped overhead switches and moved around the cramped quarters of the jet. She couldn't help but notice. A girl would have to be dead not to notice Sam Archer.

Of course, she knew too much about pilots to get involved with one. Most of them had a girl in every city and weren't good prospects for a woman who demanded fidelity. They lived on the edge, and while she could understand that, she also expected faithfulness in any relationship she engaged in, whether it was a simple business deal or a more personal relationship.

Maybe that's why she had so few friends lately. People had let her down more than she cared to admit and she'd grown a tough exterior, unwilling to let anyone near enough to hurt her again.

There was something about Sam that made her want to break her own unwritten rules. He'd already made her lower her guard enough to talk about her beloved mom. She didn't do that easily or readily and was a little surprised she'd brought up the topic at all. His quiet acceptance and calm understanding made her want to share her deepest thoughts with him and she found herself almost unable to resist.

Realizing that made her cautious but something inside her felt relief at finally being able to talk to someone. That part of her overruled the skeptic—at least for now. In the background, her saner, more logical side would be on guard in case he proved unworthy of her trust.

"How about your dad?" Sam broke the short silence that had fallen. "Was he a pilot too?"

"Good Lord, no." She laughed at the thought. "He's a math professor at Princeton."

"No kidding." Sam's reaction was a lower key version of the usual response she got from that revelation.

"Dad's too smart for his own good. He's great with the abstract world of advanced mathematics but not so good with everyday life. Still, he means well." She shrugged. "Mom was the nurturer and the adventurer. Poor dad was just along for the ride most of the time, but he loved her with all his heart. They had what I consider the perfect marriage. A true partnership. When mom died, it broke his heart and he's never fully recovered, though he's found solace in his work—and taken on the task of keeping me and my brothers in line. I think we drive him a little crazy. Except for Leo, he doesn't understand any of us at all."

"Leo?"

"Sorry. Leopold is what they named my baby brother. He's working on his Ph.D. in mechanical engineering. Dad *gets* him. He doesn't really understand why I'd want to be a charter pilot or why Shotgun opted for the Air Force Academy out of all the choices he had. Shotgun is my twin brother's nickname. His real name is Henry but we were always fighting over the shotgun seat in our high school driver's ed class, so I started calling him that and it stuck."

"You're a twin?"

Sam knew how to parse words, she thought with inward humor. He didn't say more than he had to but he certainly knew how to get his point across. He was the proverbial *man of few words*, but somehow it didn't make him seem antisocial, just reserved.

"Yup. And my crummy brother gets to fly sexy Air Force jets while I opted for the civilian route. He never lets me forget it either." She grinned, remembering their last conversation. "But to be honest, I'd had enough of always stealing his spotlight. Everyone made such a big fuss over me when I got my pilot's license. They almost forgot Henry got his the same day. I would never admit it to him and I'll kill you if you ever repeat this, but he's a better pilot than I am. He has the killer instinct I lack. I dither while he makes lightning fast decisions. I think he's a natural born fighter pilot and I'm content to let him shine. We were always together as kids and I do miss him, but I know this is the best route for both of us."

"You must love him a lot."

"That I do," she agreed. "We're twins. We shared everything when we were little. We grew apart as we aged though mom taught us both how to fly. It'll never be the same as it was when we were small, but we'll always have a special bond that nothing can break. To this day, I always know when something's gone wrong with him. I woke up in the middle of the night when he had an accident in ejection seat training and broke his collarbone. I knew immediately that he'd been injured. It was hell trying to get through to his commander but when I finally got the man on the phone his first words to me were that Henry warned him I'd be calling."

"Does it go both ways? Does he know when you're in trouble?"

"I think so but we haven't had a chance to test that as much. See, I'm less accident prone than he is. Or maybe it's just that I take fewer chances than he does. Shotgun lives life on the edge. I prefer the safer route to most destinations."

"But where's the fun in that?" Sam teased.

She looked over at him, sitting so close in the small cockpit and was snared by the twinkling light in his eyes. Yeah, he had a little bit of the daredevil in him—the same daredevil that had led her twin to the Air Force. She saw a kinship between them that she hadn't really acknowledged in her conscious mind before. Now she knew what it was.

They were both warriors. Sam may not be in the service anymore but he definitely had that soldier vibe going strong around him.

CHAPTER 5

When Sam reported in, Commander Sykes surprised him by making it a conference call. John Petit, the CIA operative who was working on their team, was pulled into the call to fill Sam in on some research he'd been doing.

"I figured out why your girl is pinching pennies," John said with no preliminaries.

"Do tell." Sam was more interested in the information about Emily than he really should be but it couldn't be helped. If she was in trouble, he wanted to help her if at all possible.

"Seems her little brother got cleaned out by a femme fatale who is now doing twenty to life for doing the same thing to a few other witless young men. She got convicted on a manslaughter wrap when one of the men came after her. Seemed he'd finally figured out what she was doing, raiding her boyfriends' bank accounts for all they were worth. He brought a knife to a gunfight and she killed him. That's what finally brought her down."

"So Emily's supporting her brother because he got swindled? What about the rest of the family?"

"Nobody else seems to know about it. From what I pieced together, baby brother didn't want to face his dad or the rest of the family but he did confide in Emily. She's been paying his tuition—he doesn't qualify for financial aid and the banks won't loan to him based on the way his girlfriend ruined his credit. Emily's been supporting him for a little under a year now. To his credit, he's got two part-time jobs in addition to being a full-time grad student, but his sister is still paying for the big ticket items."

It was noble, if stupid. Emily was sacrificing to help her brother save face. No doubt he'd feel like a fool if his stupidity became known. So she'd come to his rescue and bailed him out. Little brother probably had no idea how much strain he'd put on his sister financially and Sam would bet she'd never tell him. He'd needed help and she was there to give it. It was a nice thing for her to do and it only made him like her more.

"She's a regular Girl Scout. Nothing else on her public records and no other files that I could access. She's not on the radar of any government agencies as far as I can tell. I don't think she's involved in anything illegal—or if she is, she's either new to it or damn good at hiding her tracks."

Sam liked the sound of that. It echoed what he'd been thinking. Where Emily was concerned, it was good to have a conscience check from an objective source. He'd gotten too close to her and wasn't sure he could look at her coldly, without seeing the beautiful woman that had so captivated him from almost their first moments together.

"What about her other brother, the Air Force jet jock?"

"He flies all kinds of black ops, Sam. A real Special Operator. He's done work for the Agency, which is the only reason I was able to find out that much. I called in a favor from a friend who'd worked with him. They call him Shotgun. No idea why. He came in with the handle and managed to keep it through flight training."

Sam smiled on the other end of the phone line. He knew Emily was responsible for that nickname and it said something for her twin that he'd kept it. Often, pilots didn't really have a say in what people dubbed them. Henry

Parkington had to have tried really hard to keep the name his sister had given him and reject all the others his crewmates tried to stick him with.

"I'm putting his name on my reserve list," Matt chimed in. "I spoke to his commanding officer and if his sister stays clean and we need another pilot, I believe he'd be a good choice."

Now that was saying something. Sam knew what it took to get on Matt Sykes' short list. He wasn't one of the most respected Special Forces commanders in the services for nothing. Before he'd gone totally underground with this mission, operators had vied for spots on his team. Sam was proud to serve with the man and take his direction. He'd bet good money Shotgun Parkington would feel the same.

Sam only hoped they managed to resolve this mission before it became necessary to add more personnel to the team. The sooner this problem was eradicated, the better as far as he was concerned.

"I'm sending John out to see you. He'll bring new gear for you. The techs have come up with some improvements that will enable you to carry in plain sight."

"That'll be most welcome, sir."

Sam had been carrying a regular sidearm, as a lot of charter pilots—many of whom were ex-military—routinely did. But the ammunition it held was strictly conventional. If he met up with a zombie, he'd have one hell of a time trying to destroy it without the special toxin they'd been using to dissolve the creatures on a cellular level.

"He's arranged some private shooting range time so you can get familiar with the new weaponry. Expect him tomorrow."

Sam wasn't on the schedule to fly again until the day after, so it worked out perfectly. He looked forward to seeing his teammate. He'd been in the field alone for a while now and it was a new and sometimes awkward feeling for a man who was used to functioning as part of a team.

"I look forward to it."

"Frankly, I'm getting nervous," Sykes admitted, surprising Sam with his candor. "We haven't seen any of the creatures in a while now and I'm not fool enough to think the rogue scientists have packed up their toys and gone home. Something's brewing out there and you're in the best position to find out where and when. Keep your eyes open, Sam."

"Yes, sir."

They ended the call and Sam went over the mission in his mind one more time before falling asleep with a renewed sense of urgency and thoughts of Emily Parkington in his head.

John Petit showed up on Sam's doorstep around noon the next day, holding a case of beer and a package of steaks. The rented condo he was living in came with a small patio and basic charcoal grill. To any observer, it looked like two old friends getting together for a day of sports, beer and steaks.

John informed him they'd get to all that—after they took a little trip to the private shooting range John had lined up. Sam got into John's rental car and welcomed the small talk about various team members as they made their way to the secure location. John did the driving and Sam noted the careful way he watched his mirrors to be certain they weren't being tailed.

When they reached a dirt road that led to a large steel building set back in the distance, John didn't hesitate.

"We keep places like this in various parts of the country and abroad," he said as they approached the plain structure.

A man walking a big German shepherd met them as they neared the gated steel fence that surrounded the property. The man wore no uniform but he had a military stance that was unmistakable.

John flashed his credentials and the guard let them through the gate with little fanfare. There was no one else in sight, and after the guard had closed and locked the gate behind them, even he and his dog had disappeared.

"We've got the place to ourselves for the next couple of

hours," John said as they pulled up to the building.

John stashed the rental car inside a small lean-to on one side of the structure, where it wouldn't be easily visible. They got out of the car and John stopped to grab a large duffel bag out of the trunk before he preceded Sam inside the building.

To say Sam was amazed by the interior of the building would be an understatement. After a rather plain lobby-type area, the hall John led him down opened into what looked like an apartment, complete with a state of the art communications suite. John bypassed it all, leading Sam down two flights of stairs to a shooting range that must've taken up the entire length of the building and then some.

Sam began to get the idea that the building above ground was only the tip of the iceberg. What lay beneath was much more extensive. John was only showing him the area they needed—the fully equipped shooting range. Sam was impressed despite the abbreviated tour. He could only guess what other surprises this building housed, but he'd bet they were substantial.

John took it all in stride, dropping his duffel bag on a table located conveniently at the shooting end of the range. He unzipped it and began sorting through the equipment stashed inside.

"I've got a present for you." John grinned as he pulled a black holster from the duffel and tossed it toward Sam.

He caught it, noting the weapon it contained.

"I already have a handgun."

"Not like this. And especially not with the ammo I brought. This new stuff will take down a zombie. No need for dart guns anymore."

Now that was good news. Sam could carry a normal looking gun. The dart gun, on the other hand, was too hard to explain should someone see it.

Many pilots were ex-military and liked to be armed, though it was difficult for commercial pilots going through TSA in big airports to carry. Charter pilots though, that was a different story. On the routes he was flying and the airports they visited, Sam could easily carry the Ruger SR-9 John had just given him.

"Why the Ruger? The Glock is standard issue." Sam examined the unloaded weapon closely.

"The Ruger has metal magazines and a new style safety."

That made a lot of sense. The metal magazines had to be safer for carrying toxin than the plastic mags of the Glock. And Sam had heard the stories of guys who stuffed a Glock in their pants and accidently shot themselves in the leg because they screwed up the safety. Looking at the safety on this weapon, he could see it was a bit more secure.

"Nice." Sam sighted down the barrel experimentally.

"The four inch barrel on this makes it about the same size as the Glock 19, which is considered a compact. There's a three and a half inch version of this weapon that takes a ten round magazine. The seventeen round mags fit, but they hang out the bottom a bit so we thought we'd go for the full size."

"Good decision. I'd rather have more rounds in the clip than a half inch off the barrel length. The weight feels good." He tossed the unloaded weapon from hand to hand, checking the grip on either side. He'd trained himself to shoot both right and left handed with accuracy.

"That was the consensus of the team. Even the girls liked the slightly larger version. It had less kick for them."

"What about the bullets?"

"Frangibles with a special payload." John took a large metal ammo box out of his duffel bag and placed it gently on the table. "The science team refined the toxin. This new stuff—they call it T2—is a gel and it only takes a small amount to dissolve one of the creatures. Each bullet contains enough to do the job."

"T2? No kidding."

"Yeah." John smiled. "Seems the lab ladies have a sense of humor. They said it stands for Toxin Number Two, but a few posters of Arnold Schwarzenegger have recently started showing up on the walls of their lab."

Sam laughed at that. He liked both of the medical doctors

on the team and had been under their care when he'd been infected. Both ladies were serious, dedicated medical professionals but he knew first hand they had good senses of humor.

"Has T2 been field tested?"

"Not in a real world scenario but all the lab tests indicate it should be five times as potent as the liquid T1. This ammo is one shot, one kill, and you can use it in an airplane, if you have to."

Frangible rounds didn't punch holes in the fuselage of a pressurized airplane. Instead, they broke up on impact. The tech guys back on base must have taken that technology one step further to develop a bullet that could hold a small quantity of the more potent T2 toxin.

"These frangible bullets deliver the payload into the target, breaking apart and spreading the toxin on impact," John went on. "From there, the toxin will spread rapidly through the target. It used to take four T1 darts to dissolve a target, each loaded with a couple of milliliters of liquid. This new stuff has a higher viscosity and fits nicely inside the frangible bullet housing."

"Ingenious." Sam examined one of the bullets, handling it carefully. The toxin was deadly to all human tissue. It would kill an uninfected person as easily as it killed a zombie. "How safe are these to carry?"

"Safe enough. Just keep them in the metal mags and store the mags in two or three layers of heavy plastic. You're the field tester on this unless we have another outbreak somewhere."

"Hopefully I won't have to use them."

"Yeah, there's that," John agreed. "But we know the remaining scientists are actively trying to sell the technology. Sooner or later the creatures will show up again. You're the best bet we have of finding them before they become a real problem."

They spent the next hour in target practice with dummy frangible rounds. No sense contaminating the range with deadly T2. All Sam really needed was some practice with the new firearm. He wanted to get the feel of it before he might possibly have to use it in the field.

Once Sam was satisfied he'd become competent with the new weapon, they headed back to his rented condo. John didn't have to leave for a few hours yet so they would put the steaks on the grill and kick back for a while. Even operatives had to eat sometimes.

It was the first time Sam had gotten to use the outdoor grill and he enjoyed getting it going. John had brought a couple of cold cans of beer out onto the patio along with a few dishes and utensils for the steaks. They were almost ready when the doorbell rang. Instantly, both men went on alert.

Sam shot John a quick look and he knew John would circle around front through the shrubbery while Sam went back inside to answer the bell. They'd both be ready if trouble had come to Sam's door.

Sam took a look through the peephole and his alert level dropped while his concern grew. He opened the door. It was Emily. She looked nervous and a bit embarrassed.

"What can I do for you, captain?" He liked calling her that as both a reminder of her position of authority over him and therefore his mission, and because he thought it was cute that she outranked him.

"I'm sorry to bother you on your day off but I think maybe you might have dropped this in the cockpit and I thought I'd return it to you in case you needed it. The cleaning crew found it this morning." She held out her palm, on which was laying a small black cell phone.

What to do? The phone wasn't his but it might contain information that could help his mission. It was clearly a burn phone—one that had been bought pre-paid, likely for cash, and was therefore pretty much untraceable. He recognized the logo of one of the many pre-paid cellular companies that specialized in that market.

He wanted to know what calls that phone had made before it had been either discarded or lost. Or maybe it had been placed in that cockpit as a way for someone else to communicate with one of the pilots. Whatever the case, he really wanted to know what might be on the memory chip of that little black box.

But in order to do so, he'd have to claim it. Worst case scenario, it belonged to one of the other pilots and had been innocently lost. Questions would be raised if the other pilot was looking for it and Sam claimed it now. Or worse, this could be a test, and claiming the phone would condemn Sam in Emily's eyes. He didn't want that. He needed to buy some time.

A quick, nearly imperceptible hand signal had John moving out of cover, a set of keys in his hand as if he'd come from his car. He walked right up to the door, distracting Emily as intended.

"It wasn't in the car," he said. Sam easily picked up the story.

"You should check your bag again, dude. Sorry, Emily, this is an old friend of mine. John, this is Emily. He's in town for a few hours. We were grilling some steaks out on the patio. Why don't you join us? There's enough for three."

"Oh, no, I couldn't impose."

"No imposition, ma'am," John said smoothly, turning on the charm. "In fact, a pretty lady like you will brighten the place up. Don't leave us by ourselves." The exaggerated puppy dog face made her laugh and Sam could see she was going to relent.

Good. He had a few minutes to sort out his response to the phone question. With John's help, he might be able to get a look at the phone without claiming it.

"If you're sure," Emily said softly. This was the first time Sam had seen her hesitate. In the air and in the hangar, she was a take-charge kind of woman. Here, in his temporary home, she seemed shy and reluctant to intrude.

"Come on in," he insisted, opening the door wide so she could squeeze in under his arm. He could've moved back to let her enter but he wanted the moment of closeness. He wanted to breathe in her delicate scent and feel the warmth of her body as she passed close to his.

Once she'd gone in, he moved behind her, letting John secure the door after himself.

"Come out to the patio. I left the grill unattended."

He passed her and led the way out to the small backyard. She seemed interested in his home in a purely domestic way. He'd had women check out his bachelor pad before but where most of his previous encounters left him with a feeling of being stalked like prey, this time he wished he could show Emily his real home, not this impersonal rental.

"Nice yard," she commented as he picked up the tongs and saw to the meat.

"Thanks." Sam eyed the cell phone. He really wanted to know what secrets it might hold, but he had to play it cool.

John saved him from having to make more small talk by reentering with another place setting and a cold beer.

"Sam has some soft drinks in the fridge if you'd rather have that," John said, holding the beer can up questioningly.

Emily took it from him with a friendly grin. "No, this'll taste good on a warm day like today. Thanks."

"How do you like your steak?" Sam asked. "These are already heading toward medium. If you want rare, speak up quick."

"Medium well sounds good. Is there anything I can do to help?"

"No, ma'am. Sit back and relax. We'll do the work," John was quick to volunteer as he set the plates next to Sam by the grill. That done, he took a seat at the patio table across from Emily. "So let's see that cell phone you found. It's not yours, is it Sammy?"

Finally, some action. Sam took his cue from the CIA operative. No doubt John had a plan.

"Not mine," Sam readily agreed as Emily put it on the table.

John picked it up and started pushing buttons. "I'm a tech guy. Maybe I can figure out who owns this little fellow."

"I tried, but I didn't recognize any of the numbers and there aren't any names saved in the memory." Emily watched what John was doing but she probably couldn't see much from her vantage point.

"I see that," John agreed, a frown wrinkling his brow as he continued to push buttons. "Maybe I could look up some of these numbers on the laptop." His words trailed off and John stood as if preoccupied and went into the house, taking the phone with him. He was smooth. He didn't give Emily a chance to object.

John was inside for a few minutes longer than was strictly necessary but Sam distracted Emily by serving up the steaks. By the time he had everything laid out on the table, John was back, his absent minded professor act firmly in place. Sam had to give him credit. He was very convincing.

John brought Sam's laptop outside with him and proceeded to type up a storm while Emily and Sam began to eat. Sam suspected a lot of what John was doing was just for show but he could just as easily have been sending the numbers from the memory of the phone to the team at the same time.

"Do you know anybody named Jose Vargos?" John finally asked.

Emily's eyes widened as she swallowed a sip of her beer. "He's one of the new mechanics. He joined the company about three months ago."

"Well there you go. It's probably his phone. His home number was the last one called." John handed the black rectangle back to her with a funny little grin on his face.

"That's amazing. How did you find that information? I tried looking up the last number but it came up unlisted."

John's grin widened as he sat back in his seat. "I have my ways."

Sam threw a scrunched up napkin at John's head, getting into the spirit of their cover story. They were supposed to be old friends. In reality, they'd only been working together a short time. Still, Sam thought he knew enough about the other man to call him a friend.

"Johnny's a tech geek."

"I'd say he's a tech wizard." Emily looked both impressed and curious.

"It's how I make my living, ma'am," John supplied smoothly. "I'm an IT consultant."

"IT?" she asked.

"Information technology. Computer stuff," John clarified as he dug into his steak.

"Funny. I would've pegged you for a soldier." Emily was looking down at her plate so she didn't catch the significant look that passed between John and Sam.

"Well, I was a soldier. Once upon a time. Uncle Sam trained me to use computers and a rifle at about the same time. I guess you never lose that military bearing, eh?" He kept his tone carefully light.

"Something like that," she agreed. "So is that where you two met? In the service?"

Sam was content to let John handle the cover story. He was better at lying than Sam was. He'd had way more practice as a CIA operative.

"No ma'am. I'm a Marine. I didn't mix with Army dogs."

Emily looked puzzled. "Don't you mean you *were* a Marine? You're not still in the service now, are you?"

"No, ma'am. I retired some time ago but once a Marine, always a Marine. I'll consider myself a jarhead until the day I die."

"*Semper fi.* Isn't that the expression?" She smiled at him over her half-empty beer.

"Yes, ma'am." He raised his beer can in salute and they had a toast. "*Semper fidelis.* Always faithful."

They drank to the Marine motto and Sam was relieved to see that any suspicion that had been in Emily's expression was gone. At least for now. The CIA boy was a grand master at selling a cover story, that was for certain.

"If you don't get a move on, you're going to be *always late*," Sam teased. It was about time John took his leave.

Sam was looking forward to a little private time with Emily, here in his temporary home where they'd be on equal footing. On the job, she was definitely in charge. Here, it was different.

Maybe it wasn't the smartest thing he'd ever hoped for, but he wanted whatever time he could get with Emily. He wasn't thinking with his head, but something a little farther down, inside his chest…something that beat harder at the mere mention of her name.

Other things got harder too, but he tried his best to ignore those baser instincts for now. He had to keep his priorities clear. The investigation came first, Emily second. He'd done what he could for the mission today already. Now there was time to see how far Emily would take him and how far she'd let him go.

John left without much more ado, promising to call in a couple of days. To anyone, they sounded like old buddies who liked to keep in touch. To be honest, it felt that way, too. In the short time Sam had known John Petit, he'd come to respect him and felt the bonds of friendship forming between them. Given half a chance, they could be lifelong friends.

Of course, neither one of them might live very long. Not on this mission. That stark reminder hit Sam square between the eyes as he closed the door behind John. Emily hadn't tried too hard to leave, though she'd made the token protest about letting Sam get on with his evening. It hadn't taken much to convince Emily to stay for a nightcap and a short discussion of their upcoming flight plans.

Both of them knew they didn't have all that much to discuss as far as the job went. The routes they'd take were well established and the only changes that would occur would happen right before takeoff and depended on the whims of the customer or possible bad weather patterns.

Emily had finished her beer with dinner and opened another one that she was sipping slowly. There was no doubt in Sam's mind that the small amount of alcohol had worked to lower a few of her inhibitions and brought out a bit of a wild streak, if he wasn't mistaken. Emily was looking at him with an intensity he found hard to ignore as he rejoined her on the patio.

It was early evening, just starting to get dark. He turned on the bug zapper and lit a string of patio lights that lent the place a festive yet intimate atmosphere. He couldn't have planned it better himself if he'd decorated the condo.

He took a seat next to her on the extra wide lounger meant for two people. They'd abandoned the patio table around which they'd eaten dinner after clearing the plates away and moved over to the lounge area. There was a small fire pit in the center that he didn't bother lighting. It was too warm and the twinkling patio lights were enough ambience for now.

Emily didn't move away when he sat next to her. In fact, she snuggled into him when he raised his arm to wrap it around her. She fit next to him as if she'd been made to go there. That stray thought was both unsettling and kind of nice.

"You know, Em, I really enjoy working with you."

"I like working with you too," she said softly, her head resting against his shoulder.

"But I like you like this even more."

"Like what?" She tried to look up at him but he preempted her by moving downward, capturing her lips with his for a smoldering kiss that hinted at the passion that lay beneath the banked flames.

When he pulled away, her eyes were half closed in pleasure and her expression was dreamy. It only made him hotter.

"Like you want me to kiss you again," he belatedly answered her question.

"I do want you to kiss me again." Her voice was a drug to his already heightened senses.

"Are you absolutely certain? It's not the alcohol talking? I don't want you to regret this in the morning." He drew closer, his lips nearing hers as their voices dropped to breathy whispers.

"I haven't had that much and the only thing I'll really regret is if you stop now. Ride on, Sir Galahad."

He chuckled even as his lips moved a breath away from hers. "I'm nobody's knight in shining armor."

"Oh, I think you'd surprise yourself."

She didn't get to say more because his mouth claimed hers in a much hotter, more adventurous kiss. He rolled with her on the wide cushion of the chaise so that she was beneath him, open and receptive to his kiss, his heat, his body.

One hand claimed her waist and the other rose to gently cup her breast, shaping her softness through the thin layers of cloth that separated them. She moaned and pushed upward, into his touch, telling him without words of her desire.

They were both fully clothed, like teenagers exploring the forbidden. But the heat they generated was hotter than anything Sam had ever felt. He'd never experienced a woman more made for him than this one. And he feared he never would again.

That stray thought jolted him out of the drugged reverie of her kiss. He drew away, staring down at her. A woman who quite possibly could be his downfall. Suddenly, he didn't care. If being with her, tasting her, taking her would bring later doom, he would live for today.

He swooped downward to retake her lips but one slim hand rose to press lightly against his chest. The slight pressure of her hand stopped him.

"What is it?" His voice coaxed, his gaze zeroed in on her swollen lips, wanting badly what she kept just out of reach.

"Are you sure about this?" The doubt in her voice made him meet her gaze.

"You're not?" he countered.

"Technically, I'm your boss. I shouldn't have let this happen."

He grinned. "Don't worry. I won't sue for sexual harassment."

She laughed at that and the mood turned intimate once more. "Okay. But will you respect me in the cockpit?"

"Oh, Em. I'll respect you no matter where we are." He moved off of her, wanting this to be clear between them before taking their relationship any further. It was important to him and he sensed it was equally—if not more—important to her as well.

Sam moved back into his original position, sitting at her side on the wide chaise, his arm around her shoulders. She didn't object.

"You're the boss, Em. In the air. In the cockpit. Even here. If you say no, I stop. But if you say yes…" He turned to face her, daring her with his smile to follow where their passion for each other led.

"If I say yes…" She placed her hand over his heart, stopping him once more. "It won't be tonight. I'm not easy."

Sam laughed outright, his tense muscles easing. He understood where she was coming from. No woman wanted to be thought of as cheap.

"I never thought you were, Emily. In fact, I believe you're worth waiting for, no matter how long you make us wait." He kissed her forehead and settled comfortably back against the cushions of the chaise, his arm still around her, keeping her close.

She sighed heavily but remained next to him. In time, the tension in her shoulders eased.

"This is nice," he commented. "Watching the stars with you could become a habit."

"They're clearer at forty thousand feet." Her mumbled comment made him laugh.

"That they are. But I can't hold you like this in the cockpit." He kept his voice low and as seductive as possible. He wanted to keep her in this pliable mood for as long as she'd let him keep her there.

"Yeah, the FAA might object."

"Or the passengers. I wonder what they'd think if someone saw us canoodling in the cockpit?"

"Canoodling?" She turned her head to look up at him, the sparkle of laughter in her pretty eyes. "What kind of word is that?"

"Sue me for being old fashioned." He shrugged, enjoying her teasing. "You bring out the long buried gentleman in me, Emily."

She sat back, snuggling into his half embrace. "I'm glad."

CHAPTER 6

They watched the stars roll by for about an hour before Emily finally stretched and stood up. She had enjoyed her time with Sam tonight. It had been altogether unexpected and completely captivating. She had to be careful, lest she fall completely under his spell.

That meant she had better leave before she forgot all her sensibilities and jumped the man. No, that would never do. Not if she wanted him to respect her in the morning. No, she had to leave. Now.

The first part was getting her legs to cooperate. Finally, after a few minutes of sternly lecturing herself, she had managed to rise from the comfortable chaise. Now came the hard part—actually leaving.

"I really should be going." Darnit. Even to her own ears, she sounded reluctant to leave.

Sam stood up and she realized how tall he was all over again. The man was a giant compared to her more petite stature. She should be used to it, having been towered over by her brothers all her life, but Sam was imposing in a new, very male, very sexy way. She liked the feeling of it, even as it scared her a little. He was raw power. A caged tiger that could come out to bite her at any time. Dangerous yet alluring.

And there went her temperature, skyrocketing toward the stars. She had all too vivid an imagination around Sam Archer. Pilot or not, she was about to break all her rules when it came to getting involved and she didn't care a bit. Sam was worth the risk. She had a feeling being with him might very well ruin her for any other man but the little daredevil voice inside her was cheering her on, saying *ruin away*!

"I understand."

Wait. What did he understand? For a minute there, confusion reigned. Had she somehow said something out loud?

He began escorting her toward the patio door, back inside the house. When he didn't touch her or head toward the nearest bedroom, she began to relax. She hadn't given herself away. Not yet, at least. She'd better make good her getaway before she succumbed to temptation.

"Thanks for dinner and the stargazing," she said as they neared the door. She'd picked up her purse from the couch and tucked the strap over her arm. "I really enjoyed meeting your friend."

A frown marred his brow. "Forget him." He took her by the hand and drew her closer, his head dipping so that his lips were a breath away from hers.

His kiss this time was designed to imprint him on her senses. At least, that's what it accomplished and the possessive way his arms came around her made her feel claimed in a very basic way. Protected too, come to think of it. Sam had a way of making her feel safe. It wasn't something she'd thought out. It was intuitive.

His big hands roamed over her back and down to cup her rear, drawing her into his hard body. Yeah, that felt really good. Dangerous, but really good. She wanted to stay like this, pressed against his hardness, yet she craved more. And feared it.

That thought was the only thing that gave her strength to pull away.

Sam let her go by slow degrees, releasing her lips last of all. Then his hands dropped away from her body and they stood facing each other for a timeless moment, both breathing hard. "What were we talking about again?" she only half joked. Sam gave her the grin that she was coming to recognize as the one that made her stomach flip. One of his hands squeezed her hip as if in approval.

"That's my girl."

"We're flying to Omaha and back tomorrow," she reminded him for lack of anything more coherent to say.

"I remember." He released her but didn't step out of her personal space. He simply leaned against the doorjamb and looked at her. That look spoke volumes and invited her to throw away common sense and jump his bones.

But that would never do.

"Can you be at the hangar a little early?" she asked, clearing her throat and trying to hold on to her sanity. The man was too handsome for his own good—or hers.

"Sure. Why?"

"I'd like to go over the schedule and give you some charts to study."

"Sounds good."

"Yeah, it does." Man, that sounded inane. She had to get out of there before she managed to embarrass herself even more. "So I'll see you tomorrow."

"Count on it."

Emily's request allowed Sam the perfect excuse—and the perfect time—to do a little sneak and peek around the Praxis Air hangar and office. If asked, he could truthfully say she'd asked him to come in early and his curiosity could be passed off as boredom, as long as he didn't get caught doing anything too suspicious.

He had to take the risk, though. His mission, and his nature, demanded action. He'd spent a lot of time cooling his jets so far and not enough time working on the issue of killer zombies and the fact that this airline could be unknowingly—

or worse yet, with full knowledge—transporting the deadly technology. Either way, if it was passing through Praxis Air, Sam had to find out, and soon. It had been too long between outbreaks. The situation was ripe for another and Sam didn't want to be caught short with nothing to show for his efforts if, and when, the shit hit the fan again and the creatures started killing people.

Sam started his recon in the office, paging through cargo manifests and flight plans. He began to see a pattern and headed out into the hangar to see if he could confirm his suspicions by taking a look at some of the cargo that was stored for flights later that day. Of course, the moment he opened one of the heavy duty packing cases tagged to be shipped to a small airport on the Oregon-Idaho border, Emily caught him.

"Um…what are you doing, Sam?"

Caught red handed Sam couldn't do anything other than cop to being caught with his hand in the cookie jar. He held up his hands and turned around to face her. She'd snuck up behind him without even trying, her rubber soled shoes making little sound on the concrete floor. He decided to try to brazen it out.

"I'm sorry. I got here a little earlier than I expected and got bored, so I thought I'd take a look around."

Her eyes narrowed. "Taking a look around includes opening up cargo crates?"

"I was always too curious for my own good." He gave her a smile and a sheepish shrug. He wasn't sure if she was buying it.

"Look, Sam. Curiosity isn't a good thing to have around here lately. If you know what's good for you, you'll keep your nose out of the cargo boxes and not ask too many questions."

Oh, he didn't like the sound of that. Was she warning him off? Was she involved in the illegal activity? Covering for someone else? Part of the conspiracy? He hoped to hell she wasn't. It would destroy him to have to kill her.

"Why? Is it against the rules?" He did his best to keep his

tone light.

She folded her arms over her chest. She'd probably meant it as an aggressive pose, but it looked more protective to him. Not much to go on, but it gave him hope that she wasn't as deep in this as he feared.

"Let's just say that asking too many questions could get you fired. Or worse." Those last two words were mumbled almost under her breath, but Sam heard them. He was paying close attention to every move she made, every word she spoke. This was too important to let anything go unobserved.

"Consider me warned then." He deliberately brightened his smile and tried to be as charming as possible. "I'll do my best not to let curiosity get the best of me again. Of course, once I have the commute time figured out so that I can get here with more accuracy, I probably won't have time to spin my wheels waiting. Idle hands always got the better of me, even when I was a kid."

She tilted her head as if still unsure how to take his words and incriminating actions. He'd messed up. Whatever trust they'd been building was in doubt now. He'd just set himself back a bit both personally and with his investigation. He'd have to figure a way to get them back to where they were as quickly as possible. This mission—and this woman—were too important.

And that thought stopped him dead in his tracks. When had Emily begun to rank right up there in his priorities with his mission? Saving the world from the zombie contagion *had* to come first. Nothing was more important than that.

Then there was Emily, who suddenly had become just as important to him. If not more so. And he wasn't sure that she was on the right side yet.

Man, he was so screwed.

"Let's go to the office. There's some paperwork we need to finish before we can get going."

Her expression said she was reserving judgment about his presence here and his lame excuse for snooping around. That would have to do for now. It would take time and some maneuvering to repair the damage he'd just inflicted to his own cause.

Sam followed her into the office and did as she requested. He'd done his homework in here already and his pocket held a tiny digital camera with which he'd photographed the flight plans and manifests he'd found questionable. He'd upload them to the team later, when he was back at his condo, or sooner if he could find a secure connection and a couple of moments free from observation.

He'd noticed what he thought was a pattern in the flights to the Pacific Northwest. He'd ask the team to confirm his initial suspicions with further research, but he had a hunch that's where the rogue scientists were holed up—or perhaps that's where they planned to be in the near future. Someone who went to pains to remain anonymous had certainly had a lot of boxes of mysterious equipment delivered to that area in the past few weeks.

Only a small portion of the contents were listed on the cargo manifests. That raised questions in his mind. The airline hadn't transported that much scientific equipment in the past. At least not to such remote locations and for such mysterious clients. Every other cargo list from prior years that contained anything remotely scientific was usually destined for a reasonably big city airport being shipped either to or from a legitimate scientific business, laboratory, or hospital.

The more recent manifests that had caught his eye had obscure senders and receivers in backwater locations. One or two like that could be put up to random coincidence, but the quantity he'd been able to locate in a quick, covert search made him think there was a fire somewhere beneath all that proverbial smoke. Something was up in the Pacific Northwest.

They used different airports, but all the questionable invoices went to that region. He hoped the team could help him discern a pattern in the shipments that might help narrow down the target area a little more. That region was vast and sparsely populated except for a few big cities here and there. The rest of the area was mountainous and held many ranches and farms as well as miles and miles of forest. It was a good place to hide.

Also a good place to carry on with highly dangerous research. In fact, it was a near perfect hiding place. No wonder the team had lost track of their quarry.

Not for long, if Sam had anything to say about it. This was the information Sam had been sent to find and the reason they'd needed someone on the inside to begin with. He'd gathered enough to start the more analytical-minded folks back at base on the hunt. All in all, it had been a good morning.

Sam still had a full day of work ahead, during which he could further his relationship with Emily. While not strictly an essential part of the mission, getting in Emily's good graces could be quite useful to the successful completion of his goal. It was also something he wanted on a personal level. He wanted to get to know her. He wanted to be able to vindicate her if she wasn't involved. And he wanted to be near enough to be able to protect her in case the shit hit the fan and she was in the line of fire.

Emily wasn't immune to the zombie contagion. Hell, she probably didn't even know such horrors existed. Sam hoped like he'd never hoped before that she had no idea what dark things existed out there in the night.

If it turned out that she knew and was helping spread the research by transporting it around the country, he'd have to take her down. The thought turned his expression grim. He knew his duty and would perform it to the best of his ability, but he wouldn't enjoy it. In fact, he began to wonder if he would ever recover from such an eventuality where Emily was concerned.

But he'd cross that bridge when they got to it—if they got to it. Today was for flying and getting to know her better. It was a good day.

There was an uneasiness between them at first as they

headed toward Omaha. They went through the various checklists quietly and efficiently. Finally Sam had had enough.

"Bad weather ahead. We're on IFR into Omaha," she stated almost mechanically, not looking at him.

"Sure thing, boss. I Follow River."

There. That got a rise out of her. Emily looked up from her clipboard and shot him a suspicious look.

"You do know what IFR means, right Sam?"

"What? We're back to testing again? I thought I'd already proven to you that I am fully qualified to fly this jet." The clipped tone in his voice couldn't be helped. He was disappointed both in himself for getting caught snooping and in her for being so suspicious of him all the time. "Give me a little credit there, captain."

Okay, now disgust was creeping into his tone. He tried to throttle back on the emo, as his twelve-year-old niece would say, but found it difficult. Emily had a way of getting on his last nerve and making him vulnerable in a way he hadn't expected.

"Humor me."

Sam liked the challenge in her voice. Finally, he was getting an honest response from her. Too bad he'd had to piss her off to get it.

"Let's see. I've also heard it as I Follow Road. But I don't see any roads around here to follow."

"Cute." Her expression said it was anything but. "If you're trying to get on my nerves, it's working."

"Never let it be said I annoyed the queen of precision."

"Do you *want* to lose your job?"

"Not necessarily," he countered, glad to finally have some spark in their conversation even if it did skate very close to the edge of ruining his mission. "What I *want*..." His voice pitched lower, seeking a more intimate tone. "I want us to go back to where we were yesterday, when I was kissing the breath out of you at my front door. I *want* the Emily who fisted my shirt in her hands so hard your nails left little indentations in the cotton long after you were gone."

That gave her pause. He could tell by the way her breath caught and her eyes sparkled.

"She's not here. You're stuck with me. Get over it."

He laughed at her flippant comeback.

"*Touché*, captain. You have wounded me to the core." He sighed dramatically and let the silence stretch in the tiny cockpit as the jet hurtled through the cloudy skies toward their destination.

"It's a shame really." He finally spoke when she started fidgeting. He'd let her stew long enough. "I liked that Emily. I think I could have fallen for her, given half a chance. And I do know that IFR stands for Instrument Flight Rules. I just like teasing you. You rise to the bait every single time."

He sent her a smug grin that took the edge off the serious words he'd spoken prior to his last teasing remarks. Let her think about that for a while. Let her come to terms with the issue he too was struggling with—their undeniable attraction.

"If you were one of my brothers, I'd be trying to strangle you right now."

She seemed to recover quickly now that he'd established a lighter tone. He'd managed to say a few things he thought had needed saying between them and still end it on a teasing note. Not bad, if he did say so himself.

"I'm not your brother, Em." He made sure to catch her eye and hold her gaze a few, significant moments before turning back to the controls. When she swallowed nervously, he knew he'd gotten his point across. He didn't want her thinking of him as one of her brothers. No, sir. That wouldn't do at all.

"I bet they gave you a hell of a time growing up though. I would've thought you had grown a thicker skin having a twin brother and all."

"Are you kidding? He was the worst offender. Shotgun teased me all the time. And I mean *all* the time." She rolled her eyes in memory.

"No wonder, if you're so easily engaged." He chuckled at the way her lips pursed.

"It's not nearly as bad as it once was, but he still manages to yank my chain every once in a while." She grew somewhat contemplative. "I don't know why you manage to bring out the shrew in me too, Sam. Sorry I snapped at you."

"And I apologize for baiting you. It wasn't very professional of me and I'm sorry."

"Truce?" She looked at him sideways as if both relieved and still a bit suspicious.

"Truce," he agreed readily. Anything to get them back on better footing. He thought he'd jumped a hurdle and was glad to see her smile again. He hadn't liked the hurt suspicion in her eyes.

"Red alert," he teased lightly as the radio crackled to life. It was air traffic control.

Any further deep conversation ceased as they came closer to their destination and had to begin landing clearances and checklists. Sam communicated with air traffic control and then the tower as Emily brought the jet in for a landing.

They were transporting passengers today and Emily was glad to see the back of them as they piled into a waiting limo headed for a business meeting. Emily and Sam had to hang by the airport. They were on call for the next few hours, until the businessmen were done with their meeting and ready to leave.

"How about some lunch?" she asked Sam as he joined her inside the terminal.

"What did you have in mind?"

"There's a couple of choices. Pizza, deli, fast food, fried chicken."

"Let's check out the deli, if that's okay with you."

"Fine with me." She led the way to the deli. They had a decent selection and she'd eaten there a couple of times.

Sam ordered a giant meat filled sandwich, as she expected, while Emily got a salad.

"That's all you're eating?" Sam didn't look impressed with her plate as they sat down to eat. Come to think of it, she wasn't too impressed with it either. Sam's sandwich looked a whole lot more appetizing but those last few pounds she was trying to shed were stubborn.

"I'm on a diet." She tried to end it there. It was embarrassing talking about her weight with a man she was attracted to. She hoped he'd leave it alone as she dug into her tasteless lettuce, keeping her eyes lowered to her plate.

A big hand came into her field of view and half of Sam's sandwich landed on top of her plate of wilted lettuce. She looked up at him in shock.

"You don't need a diet, Emily. You're perfect just the way you are. Now eat up. We have a long day ahead of us and you need your nourishment."

He seemed genuinely upset by the idea that she'd deprive herself to lose a few pounds. Emily didn't know what to make of it. Not only had he given her a compliment but he'd given up half of his monster sandwich for her. She was oddly touched. Especially when he opened his bag of chips and shook out a portion of them on her plate. He kept the rest for himself, but he was definitely splitting his lunch with her. Providing for her. Nobody had ever done that before.

It was the act of a caveman. A thoughtful caveman, but a caveman nonetheless. Somehow, instead of being offended, Emily was deeply moved by his actions.

She'd sat in stunned silence while he filled her plate. She knew she had to say something, but she wasn't sure how to react.

"Thank you," she said finally. It didn't seem to fit the situation, but it would have to do. Emily took hold of the sandwich half and bit into it. It was absolutely delicious. She thought maybe she'd made a sound and looked up to catch the amused gleam in Sam's eyes. Yeah, she'd made a noise. How could she help it? The sandwich was *that* good. "Sorry."

"Don't apologize. That little moan was sexy, Em." He winked at her and she felt her cheeks heat with a blush as she returned her attention strictly to the sandwich.

Damn the man. He really knew how to get to her.

"You shouldn't have given up half your lunch to me," she protested, even as she took another bite of sandwich heaven.

"Don't worry so much. If it makes you feel better, I'll let you buy dessert."

"Dessert?" She gulped. "If I hadn't planned a big lunch, what makes you think I intended to have dessert?" She took a sip of her diet soda, meeting his amused gaze.

"You were operating under the erroneous conclusion that you need to lose weight. I disagree and, after all, I'd be in position to know whether or not you need to shed a few pounds. I had my hands all over your curvy hips and tight tush last night. Believe me, they're perfect."

Her mouth went dry as his voice dropped to that intimate, rumbly purr. How could he get her all hot and bothered sitting in an airport deli, for goodness sake? The guy ought to come with a warning label.

"Well…" She had to clear her throat and take another sip of soda. "Thank you for that endorsement but the scale says otherwise. I don't plan on dessert today but you're more than welcome to get something for yourself. I shouldn't be eating this sandwich." She shook her head as she took another bite. "But it's so good," she said in between mouthfuls.

"I like it when you give into temptation, Em." There was that sexy tone again. It made her want to squirm in her seat. "You should do it more often."

With him around? Emily was afraid she'd be doing it more than was good for her.

She was saved from answering when her cell phone rang. She looked at the number and answered. It was one of their charter passengers.

"Eat up. We have to be back at the hangar in half an hour. Our passengers concluded their business sooner than they expected."

Sam didn't have to be told twice. He practically inhaled the rest of his lunch and was finished well before Emily. He cleaned up while she ate the last bite and they headed back to the hangar together moments later.

"Guess our FOWs got lucky today," she said as they went through the terminal to the pilot's entrance. "They'll probably be in a good mood on the way home."

"FOWs?" Sam asked, as she'd expected.

"Friends of Warren. This is Omaha. Who did you think they were going to visit? Their meeting was at Berkshire Hathaway."

Sam looked amused at her little joke. Omaha was the headquarters of one of the most famous investors and businessmen in the country, if not the world. Emily had flown more than one charter of folks eager to meet with the man himself.

"No kidding." He seemed impressed.

"Try not to listen if any of them give you stock tips. Praxis Air officially frowns on insider trading."

She felt surprisingly lighthearted after their meal. Enough to joke around with him, though she still wanted to know why he had been peeking in the cargo crates this morning. She wasn't one hundred percent sure he was telling the truth about that, but she also found it hard to distrust him. Everything she learned about him made her like him more. She hoped she wasn't that bad a judge of character.

CHAPTER 7

As predicted, their passengers were in a boisterous mood on the way home. Champagne flowed in the cabin as they celebrated some business deal or other. Emily didn't know exactly what they were celebrating and she didn't really care. It wasn't her job to care about that sort of thing. All she was supposed to do was fly the plane and get her passengers where they wanted to go on time. As long as she did that, it was all good.

Normally, the *hands off* attitude was one she cultivated in her pilots and herself when it came to their clients. Of course, this was a routine job for a reputable business client. The flights she'd become most interested in lately were anything but routine.

As she drove the jet through the clouds on the quick hop back to Wichita, she thought about the problems that waited for her back at base. This trip was a break from her worries but it would be over all too soon.

Those cargo crates Sam had been nosing around were of interest to her as well. She wanted to know what he'd seen inside, if anything, but didn't know how to ask without potentially causing herself more trouble.

She hoped Sam wasn't working for Scott Southerland but

she didn't have definitive proof one way or the other. She'd been going on her gut instinct with Sam so far. Unfortunately, Sam had a way of confusing her senses until she wasn't sure what was up and what was down. She wasn't sure whether to trust her instincts with him or not.

"Penny for your thoughts." Sam's voice broke into her reverie.

She sighed heavily and brought her attention back to the cockpit and the approach they were about to make back to their home air strip. Sam was landing the jet this time while she worked through the checklists and handled the radio calls.

"They're not worth that much."

"You sure? You looked worried. If anything's troubling you, I can be a pretty good listener when necessary."

"There's nothing wrong. Really. I suppose I didn't get enough sleep last night and it's catching up with me."

"Couldn't sleep? Funny, there was a lot of that going around last night." She met his gaze and saw the fire leap within. An answering arousal shot through her veins as he smiled invitingly. "Next time, you should come over to my place. I'd be happy to rock you to sleep anytime, Em."

As long as that rocking included the joining of bodies she could see so clearly in her mind's eye, she doubted she'd get much sleep. He would tire her out though. Of that she had little doubt.

"Kind of you to offer," she tried to bring the conversation back to safer ground. His innuendo had just about melted her socks off. "But I'm sure I'll catch up on my nap time tonight."

A radio call interrupted their conversation and it was all business until Sam set the jet down, light as a feather on the rainy runway in Wichita. The passengers stopped to thank them and the leader of the group handed out hundred dollar bills as if they were mere pocket change. Tips for services well rendered.

Emily saw Sam's bemused expression as he pocketed the

hefty tip. It didn't look like he was used to big spenders and being in a service industry where every once in a while, good service was rewarded with an awkward awarding of cash.

"Can I keep this or is there some policy against accepting tips?" Sam whispered as the charter passengers walked away.

"You earned it. It's yours." She smiled at him. "If a client wants to tip, that's their prerogative. We don't encourage or discourage it. It's purely up to the client and there's no rule against accepting. A lot of our guys supplement their income with passenger trips. You make more tips when there are actual people on board than cargo. That's why the new emphasis on cargo flights has been somewhat unpopular among the pilots."

Sam's attention was caught by something over her shoulder. The little frown between his eyes made her turn to see what, or who, was coming toward them. She shaded her eyes to see better and then let out a little *squee* as she ran to meet her twin.

Henry swept her into a big hug and swung her around, manhandling her. He gave her a smacking kiss on the cheek as he lowered her back to the ground.

"When did you get in? How long can you stay?"

"I landed about an hour ago and I have to leave tomorrow morning."

"That soon?"

"I already checked your schedule, squirt. I know you've got a flight tomorrow afternoon so even if I could stay longer, you wouldn't be here."

"Okay, okay. I just missed you. Really, really missed you." Much to her surprise, tears gathered in her eyes.

"Hey now, little sis. What's wrong?"

She hadn't been able to confide in her twin about her suspicions. He hadn't been home since well before the board meeting and the near miss right after it that had scared her so badly.

She blinked back the tears and pasted on a bright smile. This wasn't the time or place to tell him. They needed privacy.

"Not here. I'll tell you later."

"You sure?"

"Yeah. Later. Don't worry. And don't let on that there's anything wrong."

"I don't like the sound of this, sis." His frown deepened and she could've kicked herself—or him—for being seen like this. If Scott had her under surveillance, she didn't want her watchers to see anything out of the ordinary.

"For goodness sake, try not to look so grim." The annoyance in her voice must've gotten through to him. He wiped the frown from his face and casually looked around. She knew the moment his attention was snagged.

"Speaking of grim, who's the giant staring me down like he wants to rip me apart limb from limb?"

She looked over her shoulder and sure enough, Sam was watching them with a speculative look in his eye. She tried her best to suppress the little thrill that went through her at his marked attention. Was he jealous?

"That's the new guy. Sam Archer. He's flying with me for the next few weeks."

"Really?" Now her brother's somewhat hostile gaze settled back on her.

"Don't look at me like that. He's strictly a coworker. Stop imagining things."

"I'm not imagining the way he's looking at you. Or at me." Henry seemed intent on watching Sam, and Emily rolled her eyes. "Don't look now, but your new guy is coming this way."

"Not *my* new guy. *The* new guy," she tried to clarify but there was no time. A second later, she could feel Sam behind her. Henry held out his hand and Emily turned sideways so she could see them both.

"I hear you're Emily's new copilot. I'm Henry Parkington."

Did she discern a hint of relief in Sam's expression when Henry identified himself as her brother? Maybe she was imagining things.

"Good to meet you. I'm Sam Archer."

"So my sister said." They ended the handshake and began the time honored male tradition of sizing each other up. Emily had seen this before. It was the modern day equivalent of beating on their chests and swinging from trees, or so she'd always believed.

"You're the twin," Sam observed.

"Yup." Henry put one hand on her shoulder in a clear message of ownership.

She allowed it for a moment, then stepped deliberately away in her own show of independence. She knew how to play this game. Being the only girl in a family of overprotective men, she'd picked up a thing or two over the years. She decided to break the tension and leave the boys to their testosterone party.

"I have to finish up a little paperwork and then we can go," she told her twin.

"Sounds good, squirt." He touched her arm as she turned to go. "I don't have wheels, so I'm dependent on you for transport."

"I'll meet you by the parking lot door in about ten minutes. Okay?"

"Roger that." He tipped his hat at her as she walked away.

She looked back to see the two men talking. They seemed to be conversing the whole time she walked toward the hangar. What could they be talking about? She had the sinking feeling they were talking about her. Oh, not out in the open, but skirting the issue the way men did when they wanted to make a point. The idiots.

"Are you interested in my sister?"

Straightforward. Sam liked that.

"I think that's between me and your sister," Sam hedged.

Henry Parkington cursed under his breath. "So you are interested in her."

Sam folded his arms over his chest. He wasn't going to confirm or deny until he had no choice. Here was an opportunity to learn more about Henry and his twin. He'd take it and run with it while he could.

"Just watch your step, Archer. I watch out for my sister."

Sam nodded. "I have no doubt on that score. But you should realize she's a grown woman. Whether she and I get together or not, that's our business. Not yours."

He thought he might've overplayed his hand but he couldn't help but speak his mind. This situation was suddenly too important to him on a personal level. If the gods were smiling and Emily turned out to be an innocent bystander in this dangerous drama—and if she was as interested in Sam as he was in her—then he wanted to be up front and honest with her family from the outset. He knew damn well that was a lot of ifs. Still, something inside him told him he had to be himself with this man, her twin, if there was to be any hope of a future.

Of course, he was just dreaming when it came to the future. He doubted a woman like Emily would want him. Not with all the baggage currently accompanying him wherever he went. There was the dangerous nature of his job along with the unknown and potentially life threatening side effects of the serum he'd taken to save his life when exposed to the zombie contagion.

Then there was the whole zombie thing. Until that was resolved, he shouldn't even begin to entertain the idea of getting involved with anyone. Especially Emily. He didn't want her exposed to that. If his gut was right and she was innocent, he wanted to keep her safely away from any possible action on the zombie front.

Henry was watching him, holding his tongue while he took Sam's measure.

"What's your story? You're military."

"Army," Sam confirmed.

"You must not have been out long." Henry was clearly fishing for information. Sam would have to tread lightly.

"Long enough," Sam hedged.

"What unit were you in?"

"82nd Airborne. Why? You going to check me out? I thought Em said you were Air Force." Sam let the challenge come out in his voice. Let Emily's twin know he wasn't a pushover.

"I have friends in the Airborne," Henry countered. "But somehow I get the feeling you were more than just regular soldier."

"You have good instincts." Sam figured it wouldn't hurt to hint at the truth.

His heavily doctored personnel file for Praxis Air contained some of this information. It wouldn't hurt his cover. The real danger could come from lying outright to Emily's brother. That could cause big problems for his cover story.

"Rangers?" Henry asked. Sam nodded in reply. Henry's mouth thinned to a frowning, unhappy line. "Green Beret?"

"Need to know," Sam said, both confirming and stating the need for quiet on this topic.

"Shit." Henry said a few more curses under his breath before turning back to Sam. "So what the hell are you doing here?"

"I'm a pilot. I needed a job. Here I am." Sam shrugged.

"And that's all there is to it?"

"If it weren't, I still couldn't tell you."

Another round of cursing followed before Henry turned back to him.

"Who, exactly, could tell me?"

"Nobody you know." Sam could see Henry was working up a good head of steam so he decided to cut him some slack. "However, if there turns out to be more to it, I think you'll be finding out soon enough."

That stopped Henry in his tracks. Steely blue eyes turned on Sam. "You wouldn't be shitting me, would you?"

"No, sir." Sam had said more than enough. Anything more and he might as well draw the other pilot a diagram. "You'll have to be satisfied with that for now."

"I'm not satisfied," Henry said quietly, his frustration

clear. "Not with any of it. But I'll live with it for now. But know this—if you set one toe wrong, I'll have your ass in a sling, Spec Ops or not. Is that clear?"

"Clear," Sam acknowledged. The man had a right to try to protect his sister. It said a lot for him that he cared enough to try.

The tension lasted for a few more seconds before Henry began to relax.

"So I outrank you?"

"I believe you do, Major Parkington."

"What's your rank, Archer?" Henry seemed more curious now than hostile. They were on more familiar ground now with this discussion.

"I'm a first lieutenant."

"Present tense?" Henry nodded to himself and Sam realized his potential mistake. It wasn't that big a deal but after what had come earlier in their conversation, it was significant.

Sam shrugged. "Once an officer, always an officer."

"True," Henry allowed. "What did you go to school for?"

"Aeronautical Science, believe it or not. I went to Embry-Riddle." That was the truth and had been included in Sam's cover story. His lifelong love of flying had led him to study it in college. He'd perfected his skills over the years to the point where he could fly pretty much anything with wings.

"Why didn't you go Air Force?"

It was a common question. Anyone with his aviation background could have had his choice of spots in most of the armed services, yet he'd chosen for deeply personal reasons.

"My dad served in Nam. He was a Green Beret. When I joined up, there was no question but that I'd go Army like him."

Sam hadn't taken the easy route. If he'd joined the Air Force, no doubt he'd be equal or higher ranked than Emily's brother. But Sam's skills as a pilot were secondary to the plethora of combat talents he'd had to develop as a special operator. He wouldn't change his choices, even if he could.

He loved being a Green Beret like his father before him. Tradition was important to him and he had a strong belief that his choices had led him to this place—to being in the right place at the right time with the right skills to get this most important of jobs done.

"Family loyalty is something I understand." Henry's gaze turned hard again. They had an uneasy truce but the protective brother wasn't far away.

A piercing whistle got their attention and Sam turned toward the hangar to see Emily waving at them.

"Was that her?" Sam asked. That whistle had been one of the loudest and most piercing he'd ever heard.

"The girl's got talent," her brother replied as they began to walk toward where she waited in the shade of the hangar door. "She perfected that ear shattering whistle when we were kids. Drove our father crazy when he was trying to work."

"I bet it's hard to grade papers with sounds like that breaking your concentration."

"She told you about our dad?"

Sam tried hard not to sound smug but it felt good to surprise the other man. He nodded as they walked together toward Emily.

"And how you got your nickname, Shotgun."

"No way."

"Way," Sam replied.

Henry let out an appreciative, if disbelieving, whistle. Seemed the talent for expressing themselves via sharp noises ran in the family.

"You move fast, lieutenant. You've been with the company how long? A month or two?"

"Actually, just a couple of days."

"Damn."

Sam looked over to see Henry's jaw clench. He was prevented from saying anything else because they'd arrived at the door. Emily was clearly getting impatient, and a little suspicious.

"You two talking about me?"

She'd chosen the direct approach. Sam could respect that.

"As a matter of fact, we were talking about me," he replied, giving her a playful wink.

Her whole demeanor changed. She went from defensive annoyance to outrage in the blink of an eye. Sam was glad the outrage wasn't directed at him. He wasn't sure he could have survived the full frontal assault she was about to rain down on her brother.

Henry Parkington was made of sterner stuff than Sam had believed. He gave his sister a grin that only seemed to inflame her anger more. She gave him the dirtiest look Sam had ever seen before turning on her heel and stomping off toward her car.

"Wish me luck," Henry said as he turned to follow his sister.

"You're a braver man than I, Shotgun," Sam complimented the pilot heading into the tornado of his sister's temper.

Henry only laughed. "Her bark is worse than her bite." His gaze left his sister's retreating form and settled on Sam once more. All amusement faded. "But I'm the opposite. You mess with my sister, you should remember that."

"I have no intention of hurting her in any way." Sam knew that was parsing words at best. Sure, he didn't *intend* to hurt her, but if she was involved with the conspiracy, he might have to kill her.

The emotional aspect was even more of a minefield. Sam didn't know what he wanted where Emily was concerned except that he needed to protect her and wanted to make love to her. All night. Every night. For a long, long time.

She was quickly becoming an obsession. A fire in his blood he didn't know how to quench.

In all likelihood, he'd hurt her when this ended, even if she wasn't on the wrong side. If they got involved romantically, he couldn't foresee much of a future for them. He couldn't foresee much of a future for him and any woman. Not with the job he did and his new medical condition that made him immune to the zombie contagion and able to heal faster than any normal person. Who knew what other side effects the serum he'd been given could have long term? He didn't want to expose anyone, much less Emily, to that uncertainty.

"See that you don't," Henry ordered him, a wary look in his eye. "Emily is the most important person in the world to me. I'd do anything—kill anyone—for her."

Once again the earsplitting whistle rent the air, spoiling Henry's badass vibe. Sam had to hand it to him, he may not be a special operator, but he had the attitude down. They both looked over to see Emily at her car, peering over the roof, glaring in their general direction.

"You coming, or what?" she shouted to her brother in an exasperated tone.

Henry held up one hand to her, indicating he was on his way, but he turned to face Sam.

"Just watch your step, lieutenant. I protect my own."

"Understood. I do the same. And as long as Emily is my copilot, I'll watch out for her in the air and on the ground."

A new respect entered Henry's eyes for a fleeting moment. They'd reached detente. For now. How long it would last was anyone's guess. Best case scenario, this could be the start of a lifelong friendship. And if Commander Sykes tapped Henry to join their team, it could be the beginning of a good working relationship as well.

Or it could be the beginning of the end for both twins if they were aiding the terrorists trying to sell the zombie contagion to the highest bidder.

"I can't believe you gave Sam the third degree." Emily slammed her refrigerator door and popped the top on a soda can before placing it in front of her twin.

Henry sat at the breakfast bar in her small kitchen, his expression alternating between annoyance and worry as they discussed his encounter with her new copilot. And why was he annoyed? Emily was the one who had to work with Sam every day. She was the one Henry had embarrassed with his questions.

"He's more than he seems, Em. That dude has Special Forces written all over him. You need to be careful."

"Oh, come on. There's nothing in his file except a stint in the Army after college."

"There wouldn't be if he was Delta Force or some other kind of black ops guy. I'm serious, sis. This is one guy you don't want to get tangled up with. He's bad news."

"He's a talented pilot and is becoming a friend. I'll make my own decisions where he's concerned."

"Sis, come on. If he's here, something is up. I don't buy that he's not in service anymore. He's too rough, too lean. He's still on edge and ready for action. He's not retired. He's here on an op."

"You've got to be kidding…" Emily trailed off as she lost steam. All her suspicions about the airline came rushing back to her.

"What? What is it?"

"I've…" She didn't know where to begin. She'd been keeping it all to herself for a long time, not wanting her brother to get involved. She didn't want to endanger his career—which is exactly what she'd be doing if he decided to go AWOL to protect his twin sister.

"Come clean, Em. What have you been keeping from me?"

She was well and truly caught now. She had no choice.

"I think Scott's using Praxis Air to smuggle drugs. Or something." She shook her head in annoyance. "I don't know exactly what he's doing but there have been a number of weird cargo shipments. High tech stuff sent to obscure places. Never the same airport twice. And I think the two recent crashes had something to do with it. Whatever *it* is."

Henry grew utterly still. She knew that look. He was taking in data and trying to come up with a logical answer. Henry had inherited at least that analytical skill from their dad.

"Tell me more. What have you seen that makes you suspicious?"

"Scott has plans to change more than a third of the fleet to cargo carriers. It's already begun in a big way. I've flown a few of the cargo runs. Mostly they keep me away from them since the board meeting."

"What happened at the board meeting?"

"I made the mistake of confronting Scott about it. The manifests for those flights weren't filled out properly and every one of them I've seen has had his original signature on it. It's like he signed a bunch of blanks and gave them to someone carte blanche. But the origins and destinations are never the same, nor are the sending and receiving parties. The only common factor is Scott's signature on those forms. It's like the clients are going out of their way to be as anonymous as possible."

"Which isn't what I'd do if I wanted to really be anonymous. They aroused suspicion by being too cautious." Henry was thinking aloud, puzzling through the facts she presented him with. She could work with him in this mood. She only feared what would happen when she told him what came next.

"After the meeting, I nearly drove off a cliff. I found out later, my car had been tampered with. I think Scott did it, or ordered it done."

"God, Em!" Henry jumped to his feet but the danger had long since passed. "What makes you think Scott was behind it? And how do you know for sure it was tampering?"

"He delayed me with some cock-and-bull story about having coffee with him after the meeting, though he had assistants coming and going while we chatted about stuff he already knew. He was asking me about hangar business we'd already gone over in the meeting. It was like he was delaying me, though I only realized it later, when the mechanic showed me the cut lines and asked me if I wanted to file a police report. He was upset when I declined but I told him I'd handle it."

"Who was the mechanic?" Henry's brows lowered into an ominous frown. She'd bet he already knew the answer.

"Buddy. I called him on my cell phone after the paramedics took a look at my scratches. I was okay and I didn't want to go to the hospital. Buddy understood and came to get me. He also took a moment to check under my car while the wrecker hoisted it up onto a flatbed. There wasn't much left of it that wasn't damaged, but you know Buddy."

"Best mechanic in the entire United States," Henry confirmed Buddy's oft-repeated boast.

"He saw right away that my car had been sabotaged. He wanted me to involve the police but I figured that would only make things worse. If Scott was involving Praxis Air in something illegal, I wanted a chance to shut him down without ruining the company in the process. I had to try. For mom."

"While I understand the sentiment, I can't agree with your decision." Henry gave a long suffering sigh and sat back down. "The police should handle this. If there is something illegal going on, they're the ones to uncover it. Not you. Not Buddy. I can't believe he let you talk him into this." Henry was heading toward anger and she didn't want to go there with him. She was too tired. Too drained from the emotions of the last few minutes. She had to get him back on track.

"Regardless, I've been keeping an eye out. The cargo seems to be mostly high tech scientific equipment. The little I've been able to sneak a peek at is way beyond anything I've seen before but there were a few things I recognize. Centrifuges, all kinds of lab glassware, something called a mass spectrometer according to the tag on its side and a few Geiger counters and radiation monitoring badges. I also saw a little crate that had a gamma counter and a giant crate that had a beta counter in it. I did a quick internet search and both of those are used in medical labs to do quantitative analysis of radioactive compounds."

"Doesn't sound like drugs. This could be so much worse than drugs, Em."

"Don't you think I know that? But then, what about all

the regular lab equipment—distillation equipment, Bunsen burners, flasks, beakers, and all that stuff? That could be a drug lab. Or maybe it's both. Maybe Scott has his fingers in more than one cookie jar and is smuggling stuff for anyone who'll pay."

"That's exactly what I'm afraid of, sis. Damn," Henry cursed. "Have you told anyone else about this?"

"No. Only Buddy. And he warned me not to talk about it to anyone. Even him. We've been pretending everything is normal and neither one of us has said anything since the wreck. We're just both keeping our eyes open."

Suddenly Henry was on the move. He opened his knapsack and began rummaging through it. All kinds of electronic doodads came out to be strewn across her living room couch. He'd always been a techno geek and it looked like nothing had changed much in the years they'd been pursuing vastly different careers.

At length he came up with a small box that looked a little like an old fashioned transistor radio. It had an antenna on one end and Henry moved around her house, pointing the antenna at various objects and heights after switching it on.

"What are you doing?"

"Not a word, Em." His tone was as stern as she'd ever heard it. "I mean it."

He passed by her and moved into the kitchen, checking it thoroughly. When the box began to beep, Emily jumped.

"Hell." Henry looked disgusted as he reached inside one of the flower pots that lined her kitchen window and pulled out a little black pebble.

On closer inspection, she saw it wasn't a pebble. On her brother's palm lay what looked like the tiniest microphone she'd ever seen.

"Someone's been in here." The proof was in her brother's hand. Emily felt sick. Someone had violated the sanctity of her home and planted a listening device in her kitchen.

"Pack your things. It's not safe for you here, Em."

"Stand down, Parkington. I'll take it from here." A tinny

voice issued the order from the bug in her brother's hand. It was a two-way device then. Whoever it was could both hear and speak to them.

"Who the fuck is this?" Henry was definitely pissed now. He also seemed a little less tense. Like maybe this wasn't the disaster they had at first believed.

"Go to the back door," the voice replied.

Henry pulled a pistol from the holster he'd had hidden under his pant leg and flipped off the safety. He motioned for her to take cover behind the kitchen island. Then he went to the back door that led right into the kitchen and peered out the small window inset in the wood.

"Son of a bitch," he swore, flipping the lock open and swinging the door wide. He didn't lower his weapon but the set of his shoulders seemed to relax a fraction from what she could see. "You bugged my sister's home?"

Emily couldn't see who was at the door from her angle and she was too frightened to move without Henry's all clear. She didn't want to do anything that could get her twin shot.

"Just doing my duty, sir."

Dammit. That was Sam's voice. Emily stood from her hiding place.

"Would you mind telling me exactly what the *hell* is going on here?" Oh, she was mad now. Mad and scared. It wasn't a good combination.

CHAPTER 8

"I bugged your house, Emily. I'm sorry but I had to know which side you were on in this." Sam didn't look one bit sorry for what he'd done and she still had no idea why he'd done it.

"What exactly are we dealing with here, lieutenant?" Henry had that crisp note of military authority in his voice. He'd really perfected that over the years. It impressed even Emily and she'd been his shadow all their lives.

"Need to know, sir, and you're not in my chain of command."

"Chain of… So then you're still in the military?" Emily asked, putting things together in her mind.

Sam grimaced. "You're putting me in a tough spot, Em. Everything about my presence here is need to know. I can't tell you anything. I shouldn't have revealed this much but when you found the bug, I couldn't let you run for the hills. It could blow the operation and this is too important."

"More important than my sister's life?" Henry got right up in Sam's face, but Emily was glad to see that Sam didn't take the bait.

Instead, he seemed to deflate. His reaction puzzled her.

"Believe me, I'd love to get her out of here right now but this is a matter of national security. Hell, it's bigger than that.

You have my word that I'll do everything in my power to keep her safe from harm."

Henry stilled. Emily knew he was thinking, weighing the possibilities and deciding on his response. But this was her life they were discussing. Her safety.

Her decision.

"I'll stay, Sam. If it'll help end whatever is going on at Praxis Air. I want to help in whatever way I can."

"Em—" Henry began, but she silenced him.

"My life, my decision, big brother." She knew that hurt him. They were almost the exact words he'd spoken to her when he'd signed on for the Air Force instead of joining the family business. That decision had broken her heart but in the intervening years, she'd come to see the wisdom of his choice.

"So what are we dealing with here? Is it drugs?" Henry persisted in asking questions Sam refused to answer. "Something worse than drugs? Organs? Body parts? Radioactive materials for terrorist purposes?"

"You know I can't answer. Suffice to say we're actively seeking intel from Praxis Air and leave it there."

"You were sent here undercover?" Emily felt betrayed. It was silly, but that's the feeling that engulfed her.

Sam moved toward her then checked his motion as if unsure of his reception. That small movement made him more human to her and eased the pain in a funny sort of way.

"So what is a Green Beret doing on an undercover assignment inside the borders of the United States? Whatever your mission, I guess it's big enough that *posse comitatus* has gone out the window." Henry rolled his eyes, clearly growing more upset by the moment.

Emily knew her brother was referring to the law that limited the power of the federal government to utilize the armed forces of the United States for law enforcement purposes. It was one of the basic tenets of law that had come into being after the Civil War. If Special Forces soldiers were being used undercover in a law enforcement action, they had to have express authorization from Congress.

This was bigger than she'd imagined. And much more dangerous, if this was the man they'd tapped for the job. She'd heard about Green Berets. They didn't mess around. They were reputed to be the best of the best in the Army and she didn't doubt Sam fit that bill to a T.

"This is insane," she whispered.

"You won't get an argument from me on that." Sam let out a giant sigh that somehow helped her relax a fraction.

His reaction was real. His frustration with the situation was subdued but evident to her in the way he spoke and moved. She'd gotten to know him well in the short time they'd been together. They'd clicked. And that hadn't been an undercover operative doing his job. All she had to do was take one look at the pained expression on his face to know at least part of it had been as real to him as it was to her.

"Why did you bug my kitchen? Did you think I was in on it?" She walked right up to him, wanting the truth, no matter how hurtful it might be.

"I bugged your place to clear you, Em. Please believe me. I didn't want you to be involved in this and I'm trusting my instincts to believe this isn't all some big ruse to get me out in the open. I'm trusting that you're as innocent as I want you to be." He walked right up to her and looked her in the eye. "I'm trusting you, Emily."

The moment felt significant. She didn't want to ruin it with doubts and fear. This was a pivotal moment. She had to make a choice.

"And I trust you, Sam." She saw the satisfaction in his gaze as she spoke the words that might forever alter her fate.

"Are you sure, Em?" her brother interjected.

"I'm sure." There was no hesitation. She was following her instincts. Right now, her instincts were telling her that Sam—and no other—could protect her in this suddenly much more dangerous situation and perhaps salvage something of her mother's airline. "What can I do to help?"

"Emily!" her brother shouted in disapproval.

"Nothing," Sam replied. "Just keep doing your job and let me handle the investigation."

"No way." She refused to sit on the sidelines while he risked his neck. Not when she could help.

"Be reasonable, Em," her brother appealed.

"I know the airline like the back of my hand. I grew up in it. I know where most of the skeletons are buried."

"Yet you couldn't figure out what was going on before someone tried to kill you," her brother countered. "It sounds like Lieutenant Archer knows more. He's already way ahead of you. Let him handle it."

"Like hell I will." She glared at her brother.

"Let's ratchet this down a notch," Sam suggested in a reasonable tone. "Major Parkington. You'll probably want to verify my claim. I'll try to have one of my superiors contact someone in your chain of command but we have to keep this quiet. Who do you trust?"

"Lieutenant Colonel Frank Trautman, currently stationed at the Air Force Academy," he answered without hesitation.

"I'll make a call." Sam turned on his heel and walked out the kitchen door into her tiny backyard.

Emily saw him unclip a cell phone from his belt. He didn't go far, just far enough away that she couldn't hear his side of the conversation. She watched him from the open doorway while her brother seethed quietly a few feet away.

"If you stay, I want you to have every last contingency planned out ahead of time. The jets are your best way to escape if you need to get out of town in a hurry. Just make sure Buddy keeps an eye on the planes. I trust him, but there are rats in the kitchen and anyone could easily sabotage a jet sitting on the sidelines. Otherwise use public transportation. Cars are too easy to track down and it's harder to murder someone in public and get away with it."

"Jeez, Henry, I never knew how totally paranoid you'd become. Will you lighten up? I know how to take care of myself. I've been doing it just fine without you these past few years."

"Dammit, Em. You've never been in danger like this before. Nobody's ever sabotaged your car before. I still can't believe you didn't tell me." He began to pace, his anger returning.

"And have you do what exactly? Run to my rescue? I learned to stop asking you to fight my battles when we were in second grade, Henry."

Sam disconnected his call and walked back toward the door. "He's coming back."

"Do you really trust him, sis?" Henry asked in a low, terse voice.

She didn't have to think about it. "Yeah, I do."

"I hope you know what you're getting yourself into," was all Henry could say before Sam reentered the kitchen, closing the door behind him.

"You should be getting a call shortly," Sam told Henry as he pulled out a chair and sat, looking like he had all the time in the world. "It's up to you if you want to wait or we can get started now. I already heard the bit about your car being sabotaged." Both men gave her identical disapproving frowns at the mention of her car. "Have you received any direct threats or other attempts on your life?"

"Scott's remarks at the board meeting are a matter of public record. He told me to stop questioning his authority or he'd make my life difficult. I took it as empty words…until I almost went off the road."

"And to be clear, the Scott you're referring to is Scott Southerland, CEO of Praxis Air?" Sam asked.

"One and the same," she confirmed.

Henry's cell phone rang. He unclipped it from his belt and took a look at the number.

"That was fast," he mused as he answered the call. Emily listened unabashedly to his end of the conversation though he didn't talk much. Mostly he listened and grunted now and again, looking worried. After a few more terse words, he ended the call and nodded at Sam. "Identity confirmed. Em, he's a special operative on a covert team assigned to discover what's going on with all the mysterious shipments you've been noticing at the airline. That's all I got. Damn." He paused. "That, and suddenly I'm being recalled from leave and sent to meet with someone named Commander Sykes." Henry's gaze zeroed in on Sam, who nodded.

"He already had his eye on you because of your familial connection to the airline," Sam confirmed. "Looks like you're going to be joining our merry band. Welcome aboard."

"So this is a good thing. You'll be on the inside of this covert team. Able to help. Right, Henry?" Emily tried not to worry about her brother getting any more involved in this mess. She'd learned firsthand that whatever was going on, it could be potentially fatal.

"From afar, it sounds. I'm not too happy about that. I'd rather stay here with you."

"I think that would be a little too obvious at the moment," Sam countered. "If we tip our hand too soon, we won't catch them. They'll go to ground and we'll have a hell of a time picking up the trail again. These guys are good. And we're on the clock. The longer they're out there, the bigger this problem becomes."

"What problem are we talking about, exactly?" Emily challenged him. They were talking circles around the real issue and she'd had enough. She wanted to know what was going on. "If it's not drugs, what is it? Henry's going to be let in on the big secret and I'm in the thick of it. I think I deserve to know."

Sam looked troubled but remained silent.

"She needs to know, lieutenant, so she can recognize the danger and defend herself."

"You'll be read in by the proper authorities, major," Sam told Henry before turning his gaze on Emily. His eyes softened when he looked at her and she could see the indecision, the warring thoughts racing through his mind. Finally, he seemed to come to a decision.

"I can tell you it's not drug smuggling, but it is smuggling. They're moving technology. Very dangerous technology. And people with interest in buying this technology. And possibly the incredibly dangerous results of this technology." He seemed to take special care not to reveal exactly what the technology was they were skirting around discussing, but it was more information than she'd had before. At least now she knew the general idea of what they would have to be on guard against.

"I'm assuming it's a weapon of some sort," Henry began to analyze the information in his typical way. "And the buyers of this kind of thing would be terrorists, criminals, or perhaps foreign agents."

"Good guess," Sam nodded, his eyes narrowing on Henry.

"So we should be on the lookout for out-of-the-ordinary passenger charters as well as the weird cargo flights," Emily said.

Sam stood, clearly angered by her words. "*We* shouldn't be on the lookout for anything, Emily. This is my mission. You're going to keep your nose out of it as much as possible. I nearly choked when I heard you tell your brother that there had already been an attempt on your life. Southerland—or whoever is pulling his strings—already suspects you. You're to stay out of this. I mean it."

"And how do you propose to do that when we'll be flying together?" She marched over and stood toe to toe with him.

"Pass me off to another pilot then. I won't endanger you any more than I already have."

"But I can get us assigned to any flight you want. I have my pick of the charters. I can choose the ones that we want to target. If you fly with someone else, you'll get the luck of the draw. I can't interfere to the extent of rearranging the flight schedule for you. That would be too out of the ordinary and would definitely raise suspicion."

"And how do you propose to keep her safe if you're flying different routes?" Henry added. For a moment there, as she stood looking into Sam's eyes from only a few inches away, she'd almost forgotten her brother was there. "I hate to say it, but I think she's safer with you than off on her own. If I know my twin, she won't stop snooping because you tell her it's dangerous. Even wrecking her car didn't slow her down much." Henry sounded disgusted and Emily only shook her head. He knew her better than anybody. He shouldn't be surprised she'd pursue the bastard who had tried to kill her.

"While I appreciate the sentiment, I can take care of myself, you know."

"Yeah, arousing suspicion to the point they tried to kill you was really a smart move." Henry's sarcasm was not helping her hold on to her temper.

"How was I supposed to know? I still don't really know what we're dealing with here," she turned an impatient glare on Sam, but he seemed as immovable as stone, standing there, watching the siblings hash it out. "But I agree with Henry. I'm safer with you than on my own, Sam. And I can help your investigation without drawing undue attention. I always get to pick and choose my flights because I'm one of the owners. None of the other pilots have that luxury. You're better off working with me than trying to keep me out of it."

Sam looked resigned and a bit angry, but he finally relented. "All right. But you have to promise to follow my lead, Emily. I'm the only one who can handle it if we encounter anything…dangerous." She didn't understand the slight hesitation in his words, but let it pass. He was relenting, seeing reason. She wasn't about to question it now. No, that would come later.

"I promise I'll behave."

She made a joke out of it, but this was a breakthrough moment for her. She wasn't going to be sidelined. She'd have a chance to help stop whatever was going on at Praxis and maybe save the airline. It was important to her. The airline had been important to her mother and it was the last piece she had left of that life. She didn't want to see it go down in flames. Her mother wouldn't have liked that at all.

"I want your word of honor that you'll look after Emily, lieutenant." Henry sounded as serious as she'd ever heard him. It was touching, actually.

"You have my word," Sam answered solemnly. "I'll protect her to the best of my ability and put her life before my own."

Whoa. That was some heavy stuff he'd just said and Sam looked like he meant every single word. Things had gotten very serious, very fast in her small kitchen.

"My leave is officially over," Henry grimaced. "I'm to fly out and meet my new commander. It's all very irregular, but they told me to hop in my jet and fly it directly to Fort Bragg. Emily, I'll check in with you when I can, though I won't be able to talk to you about any of this over the phone, I expect." He took her hand and led her a few feet away from Sam. He was going to say goodbye. She hated this part. She hated being separated from her twin, but it had become necessary as they grew older. They each had their own lives to lead.

"You take care, Shotgun," she whispered, hugging him and kissing his stubbly cheek.

"Same goes, kiddo." He kissed her cheek and squeezed her tight. "I don't know Sam well, but I know his type. His word means something. He'll take care of you but you have to do your part." He was whispering near her ear so Sam couldn't hear. "Don't make his job hard, squirt. Follow his lead and keep your head down. I'd die if I lost you."

Tears gathered behind her eyes at his heartfelt words. "Same goes on your end. You be careful too."

"I will if you will." He drew away to give her one of those patented Henry smiles. He could charm almost anyone into anything with one of those smiles.

"Agreed." They shook on it as they had when they were little kids, both grinning at the familiar routine that had begun any number of misadventures when they were small.

They broke apart and Henry turned to Sam. "I'm trusting you." He held out his hand and Sam reached to take it, giving it a solid shake.

"I won't let you down, sir. Give Matt Sykes my regards. He'll give you my number." Sam patted his cell phone. "The lines they issue us are scrambled secure satellite. When you're on the team, we'll be able to talk if I'm in a safe location. I've already asked the commander to issue one for Emily so you can talk to her more freely. She'll have to be careful where she uses it though. I'll show her how to choose and secure her locations sufficiently."

"I'd be grateful to you," Henry replied. "Being a twin is a funny thing." It was hard to have to describe the connection to someone who hadn't experienced it. Emily had tried before and knew what Henry was getting at. "I've felt something was wrong here for a while now but I hoped Em would come to me before anything big hit the fan." He turned to look at her, his gaze going between her and Sam, including them both in his words. "That's why I finally finagled leave to come see her. I'm glad now that I did and regret I didn't do it sooner."

"I only got here a few days ago," Sam said quietly. "The timing on your leave was perfect as far as I'm concerned. Until I heard you two talking, I had to keep Emily on the suspect list. Now, thanks to those few moments, the good guys have gained two new allies." He shrugged one shoulder. "Things have a way of working out."

"That's a good way of looking at it," Emily said. "But I'm still mad that you bugged my house. How could you, Sam? Honestly." She exaggerated her words in order to break the solemn mood and it worked.

"Just doing my job, ma'am." Sam tipped his nonexistent hat at her and grinned.

Henry looked at his watch and grimaced. "I've got to go. I'm going to take the family plane back to the civilian airport near the base, drop it off at the Praxis hangar, then hop a cab to base so I can get my jet. Can I take your car? I'll leave it at the airport. I'm sure Sam would be happy to drive you over to pick it up."

Sam nodded agreement as she got her keys from her purse and gave them to Henry.

"Walk me out, sis." Henry put his arm around her

shoulders as they walked to her front door. Sam stayed behind, giving them a moment of privacy. "Call me as soon as you get the secure phone. Be careful where you call from. Sam will help you figure out what's safe and what's not. Listen to him. Learn from him. He's been doing this covert stuff longer than you—or me, for that matter. Follow his lead."

"Roger wilco." She tried to joke with him but sometimes there was no getting around Henry's serious side.

At the front door he hugged her one last time and kissed her cheek. Then he was gone. Out the door, in her car and down the driveway to the street beyond. She watched until her car turned and went out of sight.

"Your brother seems like a straight shooter."

Sam had come in from the kitchen soundlessly. Emily jumped when he spoke from right beside her.

"You scared the life out of me. Make a sound once in a while, would you?" She shook her head as she caught her breath. Sam only laughed at her.

"Sorry. It's my job to be stealthy. It's become a way of life."

"It's not normal, Sam. Human beings make noise when they walk into a room. The brush of a shoe on carpet. The sound of rustling fabric as they move." She was frustrated and frightened by the recent turn of events and it came out in her conversation. She didn't mean to take it out on him but he was a handy target. Luckily, he seemed to understand. His eyes were kind when she met his gaze.

"Your brother will be okay, Emily. They won't let him in on the truly dangerous stuff my team is involved in. I know that for a fact. He doesn't have the right…training." There was that awkward hesitation again when he went searching for words. There was something strange going on for certain. She just hoped they could put a stop to it so she and her brother could get on with their lives.

"This is truly dangerous, isn't it? I mean, more than your garden variety criminals are involved."

He nodded, holding her gaze. "There's a great deal I can't tell you but believe me on this—Henry won't be in much more danger than he would be on his regular job. He'll be used for his flying skills. That will be the extent of his contribution to the team. That, and you. You and Praxis Air are the links that brought him into the fold. If the airline hadn't been involved, you and he wouldn't have come to anyone's attention. As it is, you *are* involved and we all have to make the best of the situation that we can."

"I can understand that."

"What's the family plane Henry mentioned? Do they keep one specific jet set aside for you at Praxis?"

"It's a relic of the old days. The first plane our mother flew for Praxis when they were setting up the airline. An old cargo job. A mid-sized Cessna. Buddy keeps it in good condition and we take it out every now and again for fun. Lately she's been put back into service a time or two when we had last minute cargo charters, but she sits idle for the most part."

She wished suddenly for the old days, when her mother was still alive and Scott was in school and nowhere near the management of the airline. Scott's dad would never have gotten involved in anything so illegal and underhanded. He'd been a trustworthy man. Otherwise, her mother would never have gone into business with him and their other partners.

Emily yearned for those carefree times, almost wishing she had never noticed anything wrong. For a mad moment she wished she could go back to the way things had been before Scott had started systematically changing the airline. Back when things were normal and reasonably happy. Secure.

She shook her head, closing the door and locking it. When she turned around, she pinned Sam with her gaze. They had work to do.

"The first thing I want you to know is that I don't like having my privacy invaded. I'll forgive you this time but if you ever bug my home again, there will be hell to pay." She knew as she spoke the words he would smile and she was glad when he did. "Now, the first thing I want you to *do*, is remove those listening devices. I suppose you hid them all over the place."

"Yeah." He had the grace to look sheepish. "I'll take them out." He leaned over to the big potted plant by the door and lifted a black pebble from the dirt.

"Show me where they are. I want to at least learn something from this if I have to go through the indignity of having my home bugged. Show me how to spot them."

To his credit, Sam went through her home and showed her not only where he'd hidden the bugs, but other locations where they could be hidden without being seen. Some of them were pretty ingenious, like under the rim of her porcelain umbrella stand. She never would have thought of that in a million years.

He led her around the living room and kitchen then proceeded down the hall as if he were very familiar with the layout of her home. Which, in fact, he was. He'd snuck in here to plant the listening devices, after all, which still freaked her out if she let herself think about it. If Sam could do it with such ease, so could other people with his skills. Bottom line—her home wasn't the safe place she'd thought it was.

Her thoughts were troubled as he led the way to another doorway. She stopped short when she saw where he was headed.

"In the bathroom?" She was outraged. Was nothing sacred?

"Just doing my job, Emily. They trained me to be thorough."

"A little too thorough if you ask me." It didn't bear thinking about what kinds of sounds he could have been privy to.

"Exactly how long ago did you break in and place the devices?"

Sam grinned at her over his shoulder as if he knew exactly what she was thinking. She felt her face heat with a blush.

"The day before I started working at Praxis Air."

God. That was longer than she'd have thought. It also meant something else.

"So I've been a suspect from the very beginning?"

"Everyone who works at Praxis is a suspect," Sam replied. "Right now, you're the only one I've been able to clear. Everyone else might still be on the take, so be careful who you talk to and what you say to them."

"Even Buddy?"

"Especially Buddy," he came back, stronger than she would have expected. "I don't like that he didn't insist on reporting the tampering on your car. That he let it go could mean he's in on it."

"Or it could mean he respects my judgment," she countered.

Sam's mouth thinned to an annoyed line but he didn't rise to the bait. Instead, he reached for the listening device hidden above her medicine cabinet.

"Don't worry. The fact that you sing in the shower is safe with me."

"I do not sing in the shower." She was appalled to think he'd heard her.

"Yeah, I guess I shouldn't really call it singing."

She punched him in the arm. "I'll get you for that someday, Archer. Payback's a bitch."

"I'll look forward to it." He turned to face her, pocketing the bug as he'd done with all the others. "And I'll dream about sharing this shower with you sometime." He advanced into her personal space until she could feel the warmth of his body though he didn't quite touch her. "I bet I could give you a real reason to sing."

His voice had dropped to that sexy tone that made her melt. His head lowered so his words sounded right next to her ear, his hot breath drifting over her skin, raising goose bumps of awareness all over her body.

"Are you making a pass at me?" Her voice was breathy and weak. Weak like her knees became as Sam's head dropped lower and his lips brushed over the sensitive skin of her neck.

"If you have to ask, I must not be doing it right." He closed the small gap between their bodies, his hands going around her waist as he drew her against his hard frame. "Damn. I've been wanting to do this for hours." His lips covered hers, his tongue running along the seam of her mouth, unzipping her lips and delving inside. She gave in with a whimper of need.

She hadn't known how badly she'd been craving him until he kissed her. Then it all came back in a rush. The heat of him. The passion in his touch. The need that only he seemed able to inspire in her.

Her senses swam as he lifted her in his arms. She felt motion as he began to walk but she was too caught up in his kiss to realize where he was going until he lowered her gently to her bed.

The softness of the cotton comforter under her was as welcome as his hard body over her. Sam was moving fast but Emily didn't care. She'd dreamed of him since that first kiss they'd shared. She'd dreamed of this. And more.

He broke away and sought her gaze. He was breathing as hard as she was, both of them caught up in the moment.

"Tell me you want this, Em. Tell me now if you want me to stop."

She thought about her answer for all of a second. Her heart knew the answer right away.

"Come here, Sam." She wound her arms around his neck and drew him back down for a sizzling kiss as her fingers played in the short ends of his hair.

One of his hands went to her waist, burrowing under her soft cotton shirt to touch the skin of her abdomen. The warmth of him was incredible. His touch was skilled and exciting. She wanted more.

Would he move upward or downward? She wanted both equally.

When his hand stroked upward on her ribcage as his tongue danced with hers, she moaned. He apparently took that as his cue, sliding his hand right up under her shirt. He covered one of her breasts for a moment only before grasping the edge of the cup and pulling it downward with some force.

With a simple touch, Sam made her feel wanton. She craved his touch like her next breath and her desire only spiked higher as his hand shaped her bare breast. His fingers plucked at the nipple with care, pinching lightly as if learning her shape and her response.

Soon that wasn't enough. She wanted her shirt off. She wanted his off too.

Emily moved her fingers to the buttons on his shirt, fumbling at first. Eventually she found the coordination to release those small buttons from their holes and pull the shirt out of his waistband. Within moments, she was touching hot, hard, male flesh.

She wanted more.

Apparently so did Sam. He released her, sitting up for a moment while he stripped off first her shirt and then his own. Her bra followed in a slow movement while he held her gaze and spoke not a word. He was watching her carefully, seeming to gauge her reactions, but she had no ability to hide how turned on she was by his every movement. So far, Sam was her dream lover. He had anticipated her needs and delivered what she wanted. She only hoped she was experienced enough to do the same for him.

Somehow she doubted her meager experience with the opposite sex would match up to Sam's. Anybody who looked like him and lived the fast-paced life he must lead probably had more women than he knew what to do with. She didn't like the idea that she was one of many, but she wouldn't pass up this chance. She wanted to be with him regardless of what had come before or what would happen next.

"Do you have a condom?" She had to ask. She'd assumed he'd be prepared but she needed to be sure before this went any farther. She was being impulsive here tonight, but she wasn't a fool.

Sam reached into his back pocket and retrieved his wallet. From it he pulled two or three foil packets, throwing them onto the nightstand.

"I've had these in here for a while, but they're still good. I've also recently had a full medical workup, Emily. I'm clean of disease. Disgustingly healthy, as a matter of fact."

He made a face she couldn't quite interpret but she saw the truth in his eyes. He wouldn't lie to her about something this important. Sam was at heart an honest man regardless of the subterfuge he was sometimes forced to employ in his work.

"I'm clean too, but I'm not on birth control, so we need to use something."

"I'm okay with that, Em. The last thing I want to do is make trouble for you with a disease or otherwise." He cupped her cheek, then ran his fingers through her hair, his voice dropping low as he drew closer. "This is supposed to be about passion and desire. A gift from each of us to the other. A thing of beauty and mutual pleasure."

When he talked like that, he gave her a glimpse into his inner soul. The soul of a poet. An artist. A sensitive man hidden beneath a tough exterior. He only made her like him more.

Daring greatly, she ran her hands downward, over his chest and muscular torso, then cupped his length through the fabric of his pants. Sam shivered but let her explore for a moment. But she didn't want to wait. Her body was already screaming for satisfaction. It had been far too long for her and her desire for Sam was greater than any she'd ever felt.

Her hands went to his belt, working the leather and brass of the buckle free. Then she attacked the button and zipper, wanting the barrier between her and her goal gone as quickly as possible.

"Help me," she pleaded softly as her fingers fumbled, unable to work fast enough to suit her.

Sam complied, rising slightly to help ease open the zipper. Emily didn't wait. As soon as she had an opening, her hand slipped inside, battling through the layers of fabric to finally touch flesh.

He was rigid and warm, the velvety texture of his skin contrasting with its hardness. He was also big. Bigger than she'd ever had. It would take work to accept this into her body, but she imagined it would be well worth the effort.

She wrapped her fist around him and squeezed. Sam moved away after only a moment of this treatment and she was disappointed to have her prize taken out of reach too soon.

"Much more of that and this'll be over before it starts." His smile charmed her and the movement of his fingers to her waistband made her forget her disappointment.

He made short work of her pants and panties, caressing her skin in long sweeps of his large hands, up and down her legs. He held her gaze as he spread her legs, making room for himself between. She was centered on the queen sized bed, totally naked on her soft comforter. Sam still wore his pants though they were unzipped and in danger of sliding off his narrow hips. Silently she rooted for them to slide off. She wanted to see what she'd only felt up 'til now.

But he was in charge of this show for the moment and she was content to let him lead. Sam knelt between her knees, arranging her to his satisfaction. She was nervous but willing to see what he wanted. It had been a long time since she'd had a lover. A long time since she'd tried anything truly adventurous. Being with Sam and letting him do what he liked was an adventure. So far, it was an amazingly good one.

Sam's hands stroked higher up her inner thighs, converging on the point that ached for his touch. When he got there, one hand rested on her pubic bone, the other delving into her folds, touching and probing, teasing and stroking.

She was slippery, ready for more but he teased her a bit longer, rubbing light circles around the distended nub that craved his touch. Her stomach flipped and her limbs began to shiver with pent up desire. Only then did he stroke lower once more, one large finger sliding within as if testing her fit.

She squirmed. She couldn't help it. The feeling was incredible. His thick finger stretched the place that hadn't seen much use in too long to mention. She creamed around him, easing his way, wanting more.

"How does that feel, sweetheart?" he whispered, his gaze rising to capture hers.

"Good," she replied on a breathy moan as he added another finger to the first.

Yeah, that was a tight fit, but it felt really intensely wonderful. She wondered how good his cock would feel and she didn't want to wait much longer to find out. Foreplay be damned. Just being around Sam was foreplay enough for her, let alone being naked and spread wide on her bed for him. She was already primed and ready to go.

"Just good?" he prompted with a teasing tilt to his head and a grin lurking at the corners of his mouth.

"Better than good," she admitted. "Sam, don't make me wait. I want you now."

"Are you sure, Em? Be sure."

"I'm sure. Finesse can wait until next time. This first time I just want you. Hard and fast and now. Don't wait."

He made a humming sound, deep in the back of his throat. She thought maybe her headlong response had gotten a rise out of him in more ways than the obvious one. Emily knew a large portion of sex was mental. Her eagerness for him seemed to be an additional turn on for Sam. She'd remember that for next time. It took a while to get to know what your lover liked. She'd learned something she could use to bring him more pleasure in the future—however long or short that future relationship might be.

Sam shucked his pants and boxers, letting them fall to the floor at the side of her bed. When she got her first look at him, she realized her estimation of his size had been a little off. He was longer than she'd thought and a nice size around. Yeah, that would make a tight, hot, incredibly arousing fit.

And she most definitely wanted it. Now.

Sam prowled up over her on hands and knees like a jungle cat. His body heat was tremendous. Warm and comforting. Strong and powerful, like almost everything else about him. He smelled so good. His natural musk wasn't overpowering and made her senses come alive in appreciative response.

She licked his shoulder, wanting to taste him. Salty and clean. He tasted like more.

Sam growled in the back of his throat as her teeth nipped at his skin.

"Let's put that mouth to better use, shall we?" he growled, settling over her. Then his mouth claimed hers in a tempestuous kiss that went on and on.

She lost track of time and space as he took possession of her passion. A moment later—or maybe it was an hour—he slowly took possession of her body. Sliding within, inch by inch, moment by moment, he was careful not to hurt her. He pressed steadily, using a rocking motion when necessary to use her body's lubricant to aid his path. Eventually his strategy worked and he sat fully within her tight sheath, ready for more.

"Is it okay, Em?" he gasped, breaking the kiss so he could meet her gaze.

She nodded. "Yeah."

"Want more?" He smiled down at her. He was by far the sexiest man she had ever been with.

"Oh, yeah." She returned his smile with interest.

He began to move in earnest, sliding slowly at first, but with some force as he pulled almost all the way out, then stroked home in one long thrust. Sam repeated the motion, watching her face. He was probably trying to gauge her reaction. She was quickly learning that Sam Archer was an incredibly considerate lover. She liked that and so much more about him. She had to be careful or she'd lose her heart to the man.

When she wrapped her legs around him to urge him to move faster, Sam took the invitation and ran with it. His thrusts became shorter and more powerful, eventually turning into hard digs of his hips, stroking into her heat. It felt glorious.

Emily began to make little keening noise as her passion rose higher. She was close to something momentous. Like flying too close to the sun. And she wanted to go higher. She wanted to touch the sun and explode, then float back down to Earth secure in Sam's arms. She knew instinctively that he would keep her safe.

"Are you ready, Em?" His hot breath panted over her damp skin like a caress. She was straining toward completion.

"Almost," she cried out. "Sam!"

She shouted his name as the first waves of pleasure broke over her body, making it clamp down around his, jerking and convulsing in wave after wave of orgasmic spasms.

She felt Sam join her in bliss as his muscles tensed on a final hard thrust. He strained above her, his eyes clamped shut as his body seized the pleasure they had created together.

His warmth engulfed her, sweeping her into another round of pleasurable contractions that drove her higher. She'd never done that before. It felt so good to let go so completely with Sam. He was a talented and considerate lover. And as he began to move again within her—slow, sweeping strokes that milked the last of their pleasure from both of their bodies—she flew to the sun one last time, shocking her into a scream.

She screamed his name as she came.

Sam woke Emily twice more in the night to make love. He didn't think he'd ever get enough of her sweet body and honest responses. Guilt flooded him as he realized what he'd done. He should never have touched her. He should have been strong enough to resist the temptation of her. He was on a mission. Perhaps the most important one of his life. He shouldn't have given in to the very personal need he had for this woman, but he hadn't been strong enough to resist her allure.

Even after a full night of loving her, he found it hard to

resist claiming her again. He had to be stronger than this. He had to be better. If he failed, the entire world might suffer the consequences. Steeling himself, he let her go and got out of bed as quietly as he could.

He watched her sleep for a long moment, teetering on the edge of climbing back in and having her again. In the end, he found the strength to get up and begin his day. There was work to be done and nobody here but himself to do it.

CHAPTER 9

Emily awoke to the smell of coffee. That was different. Usually, she stumbled her way into the kitchen half asleep to make the first pot of the day. But today was different.

Today was the day after the night before. The night before where she'd slept with Sam.

She stretched, feeling sore in all the right places, bringing back memories of their night together. After a moment of luxuriating in those wicked memories, her brain switched into full gear.

The smell of coffee meant that Sam was still here. That was a good sign. Wasn't it? Would things be awkward between them now or easier? Had last night been as earth-shattering for him as it had been for her?

Somehow she doubted it. Not a guy with a body like a Greek god come down from Mount Olympus, and skills in bed she hadn't even realized were possible. No. Sam Archer was in a different class entirely from the kind of men she usually got involved with—the kind of men who were interested in her.

Sam was here because of his job. Maybe yesterday's seduction had been all about keeping her close and lulling her into blindly trusting him. Maybe it had been about making her fall in love with him.

She sat up in bed, clutching the rumpled sheet to her chest as realization hit.

If that had been his plan, he'd succeeded beyond his wildest dreams. Finding out he was on the right side of the law had broken through the final barrier, allowing her heart the freedom to attach itself to him. She was very much afraid she was starting to love him.

What a mess.

"I made breakfast if you're interested." Sam's voice came to her from her open bedroom door.

Their eyes met and she was touched by the soft, almost relaxed expression on his face. This was the first time she'd seen him this way and it gave her a little thrill to realize she was probably a large part of the reason why he was so relaxed this morning.

"What? No breakfast in bed?" She decided to keep their interaction light hearted. The heavy stuff could come later—if there was a *later* for them as a couple.

"You know, I considered it, but then I looked at the clock and realized that if I climbed back in that bed with you, neither one of us would ever make it to work today. We're running a tight schedule as it is."

"What time is it?" Her eyes widened when she caught sight of her bedside clock. He was right. They really did need to get going if they were going to make their charter.

He laughed as she scrambled out of bed. "I already grabbed a shower. Breakfast will be waiting when you get out."

She noticed then that he was freshly shaven and wearing his pilot's uniform. He'd come prepared. She'd ask him about that over breakfast. For now, she had to hustle if she was going to shower and dress and still have time to eat. They had a big day ahead of them.

When Emily arrived in the kitchen a few minutes later, she looked good enough to eat. Sam had enjoyed nibbling on her the night before but it had only seeded a hunger that grew the more he was around her. She could easily become addictive.

"You happened to have a spare uniform with you?" she asked as she sat at the table. He liked her straightforward style. There was no messing around. No beating around the bush with Emily, unlike the other women he'd been involved with over the years. She was a refreshing change.

"I always keep a change of clothes in my trunk. Several, in fact. I've got camo gear, black fatigues for night work, gym clothes, and since coming here, a spare uniform. I like to be prepared."

"What are you, a Boy Scout?" she joked, seeming to relax at his answer.

"Weren't you listening? I'm something even better—a Green Beret officer. We wrote the book on being prepared."

She chuckled, digging into the eggs and toast he'd made. It wasn't fancy, but it was hearty and decently cooked. He was good with breakfast foods and grilling but anything fancier and he was lost.

"Look, Em, I didn't plan last night. I'm not saying I didn't think about it. A lot. But I didn't plan for it to happen the way it did, where it did, or when it did. But I'm sure glad it did."

She burst into laughter. Here he was, trying to be serious and reassuring and she was laughing.

"Sorry." She must've seen by his expression that he hadn't been joking. "You just sounded—" She stopped herself midsentence. "Never mind. I'm glad to learn you aren't that calculating when it comes to seduction. I admit, I was wondering if you'd been playing me. I wouldn't like that, Sam. I know we've been thrown together by circumstance and it's true I've been drawn to you from the moment I first saw you." A becoming flush of rose entered her cheeks at the admission. "I know this situation is one in a million. I just don't want to be played."

"I respect that. And I wouldn't do that, Em. Please believe that."

Her expression changed and a small smile lifted the corner of her mouth as she looked at him with her head tilted to one side.

"I believe I do." She stood from the table and took the plates to the sink, leaving them there for later. "Thanks for making breakfast. We've got to get moving if we want to make it to work on time."

"I thought being the owner, you had more leeway than other pilots?" He wasn't arguing, merely teasing her as they gathered what they'd need and headed for the door.

"I do. But clients are clients and when they want a flight at a certain hour, it has to go at that time."

"Poor boss lady. Slave to the clock." He laughed with her as she locked the door behind them and they headed for his car. Her car was already at the airport from when Henry had driven himself there the day before.

He unlocked the door to the big SUV for her and waited while she got in, closing the door behind her. Then he got in on the driver's side. He started the vehicle and headed for the airport, watching his mirrors closely for the first few blocks.

When he had to stop for a red light, he turned to Emily, gently reaching to cup the nape of her neck in one hand and pulled her close for a deep kiss. He only surfaced when the car behind them honked, indicating the light had turned green and he'd been too lost in kissing Emily to notice.

Damn. He had it bad.

He got the vehicle going again and cleared his throat, trying to rein in his raging hormones.

"I was wondering when you'd get around to a good morning kiss," Emily quipped as the silence lengthened.

"To be honest, I knew if I kissed you back at your place, we'd never leave. As it was, I lost track of the passage of time. You make me forget everything when I kiss you, Em."

And now he was getting sappy. He'd never spoken such things to a woman before. Of course, he'd never felt such things. Emily confused him. Or rather, his emotional turmoil where she was concerned confused him. But one thing was perfectly clear after their night together—making love to her could make him forget everything. Mission, duty, and danger be damned. When they were together, nothing else could penetrate the state of bliss she created.

He knew without having to think too hard about it that only Emily had this effect on him. She was special. Special, and very dangerous to him on a personal level. She was the kind of woman a man gave up everything to be with. Sam wasn't so sure he was ready for the commitment. He wasn't sure if he was capable of it.

There was the added uncertainty of his medical state. The serum he'd been given to save his life had changed him on a fundamental level. He had more in common with a comic book superhero now than he did a regular human being. He healed super fast. He doubted anything short of decapitation would kill him now, though he didn't want to test it. He wasn't completely invulnerable, but it was a close thing, or so he'd been told by the docs who had worked on him.

He should have been dead from the zombie contagion long ago but he'd been saved. And changed. He wasn't sure what the future held for him medically. The stuff they'd used to save his life was highly experimental and long term effects were totally unknown. So he didn't know if he really *had* a future anymore.

He'd have to be satisfied with whatever Emily would give him here and now. He couldn't think of the impossibility of a future with her…or worse, without her. Wanting to be with her after this mission was over had quickly become a strong desire. But he wasn't fool enough to actually believe it could happen.

For one thing, Emily was a lady through and through. A smart woman with resources of her own. She didn't need a rundown soldier like him. She could have any man. He hoped she'd choose to be with him for a while at least but he wasn't fool enough to think she'd want him for anything long term. She'd marry a doctor or a lawyer and settle down in the 'burbs. The life of a soldier's wife was too rough for her.

"You have hidden depths, Sam Archer. I didn't know you were such a smooth talker." The light in her eyes warmed him as he met her gaze.

"You bring out the long buried gentleman in me, Emily. I'm not usually known for my language skills." He had to laugh at himself because that statement was nothing but the truth.

"I find that hard to believe."

"Believe it. I once went a week without speaking a single word to anyone. Not on purpose. It just happened. I only realized it when I started to say something and felt my throat didn't really want to cooperate. I was hoarse from not talking for so long."

"Were you on vacation?"

"That's the amazing part. I was working. Back then I was only a green second lieutenant, fresh out of school. I did a lot more following of orders than giving them and all that was required of me was a salute and the completion of the assigned task."

They arrived at the airport and parked near the Praxis Air hangar. In fact, Sam was able to park in the space right next to Emily's car.

Sam spotted Buddy standing in the doorway, wiping his hands on a dirty rag. There was no doubt the old man saw them arriving together in Sam's SUV. From the pointed look Buddy gave him, Sam knew there would be words between himself and Emily's self-appointed protector later.

"Crap."

The unladylike word from Emily's lips made Sam grin. She'd noticed Buddy watching them.

"I guess I should have asked this before, but do you mind if people at work know we're together?" Sam kept his voice pitched low so only she could hear as they headed across the parking lot toward the door.

"To be honest, I hadn't thought that far ahead yet, but it looks like the cat is already out of the bag. At least with Buddy. He won't talk but I bet he's not the only one who noticed my car parked here last night. No doubt there will be talk. Even if nothing had happened, there would have been talk when they saw you give me a lift today."

"So the question is, do you want to give them something to really talk about?" He offered his hand, letting it be her decision whether or not she took it.

She seemed to think it over for a second as they walked, then she apparently came to a decision. She took his hand and moved closer to his side. Something about her actions made him feel about ten feet tall.

"Is Buddy going to give you hell for getting involved with me?"

"Probably." She paused. "Either that or tell me how relieved he is that I finally found a guy I like. He seems to have appointed himself as my surrogate parent since my mom died. I'm thinking the chances are fifty-fifty. He'll either be glad or think I've lost my mind."

"I'd bet on the latter if his scowl is anything to go by."

"Yeah, you may be right about that," she murmured as they neared the door. "Good morning, Buddy," she said, trying to ease past the old man without pausing for conversation.

Buddy wasn't about to let that happen. He blocked the door subtly, with his rounded body, pocketing the rag he'd been using to clean his hands. His gaze swept from Emily to Sam and back again before zeroing in on Sam.

"I noticed your car was parked here overnight, Emily. I assume Henry left it here on his way out of town. What surprised me was that you didn't come get it last night."

"I had other plans." Emily squared her shoulders and faced the older man down. She had courage when it came to standing her ground, Sam was learning.

"With him?" Buddy's gaze narrowed unflatteringly on Sam.

"As a matter of fact, yes. Sam gave me a ride in this morning so I wouldn't have to take a cab."

Sam liked the way she didn't lie, but she also didn't give in to the older man's bully tactics. What he learned about what they'd been doing the night before was up to Emily. Sam would respect her wishes whatever she decided.

Buddy eyed him suspiciously but it didn't bother Sam. He stood fast and said nothing, letting Emily take the lead. This was her world, after all. She'd have to live with these people when he was gone.

Thinking of that even in an abstract way annoyed him. Sam didn't want to think of a future without Emily in it but that, in all likelihood, would be his reality.

"We've got an early charter, Buddy. If you'll excuse us, we need to get moving." Emily moved daintily past the big man and went through the door. Buddy grudgingly stepped aside to let Sam follow.

They really did have an early charter and no time to waste. Emily settled the paperwork while Sam went through the preflight checks on the jet. It was another one of those strange cargo runs, which fit perfectly with Sam's plans. With Emily on board, he'd probably be able to get a much better look at the contents of the crates that had already been loaded into the belly of the plane.

They were headed to West Virginia today. Coal country. Land of lots of caves and nooks and crannies. Sam thought it a perfect place to hide if you wanted to go to ground.

The charter was an overnighter. They'd be bringing cargo in and taking another load out the following day. The layover might give Sam time to do some serious recon. He had every intention of covertly following these boxes to their destination.

They got off the ground with little fuss. Sam had taken the opportunity to search the cockpit and hold during his preflight to make sure there were no listening or recording devices that shouldn't be there. They would be able to speak freely on board.

Once they hit cruising altitude, Sam unbuckled himself from his seat.

"Where are you going?" Emily asked as he wormed his way out of the tiny cockpit.

"I'm going to take a look at the cargo."

Her lips thinned in worry but she said nothing as he worked his way aft. The crates were sealed tight but Sam had a knack for breaking into the boxes in such a way that nobody would ever know he'd been there. He popped the cover on the first one and found lab equipment. He didn't know exactly what the apparatus was off hand, but he knew he'd seen something like it in the team's labs back on base. He snapped photos of the contents of that box, and each of the others, with his secure phone, sending them via satellite to the tech crew before he'd even finished putting all the covers back on.

He rejoined Emily in the cockpit a moment later.

"Everything okay?" he asked as he slid into the copilot's chair and refastened his safety harness.

"Smooth sailing. What was in the crates?"

"Laboratory equipment. I didn't recognize most of it but the techs back on base will be able to identify what it all is, I'm sure."

"How?"

He patted the phone on his hip. "I sent them photos. They're probably already working on it as we speak."

"Pretty nifty."

"Not as nifty as you." Oh, man. He had it bad. Sam had never said anything cornier in his life, but her smile was worth it. She didn't seem to find him awkward at all, which was a minor miracle.

He reached out and took her hand in his, rubbing her knuckles with his thumb. He needed to feel her skin. That small touch brought back memories of the incredible night they'd spent together. Emily was a special woman. Of that he had no doubt.

The radio broke into his thoughts, air traffic control issuing guidance for their flight. They were beginning their approach to the small airstrip in the hill country of West

Virginia. There were larger airports in the general area with lots of commercial traffic, so they had to pay close attention to the instructions from the ground to navigate the busy airspace.

Before long, they were on the ground and the cargo was being unloaded. Sam watched, pretending to do paperwork while the cargo handlers did their thing. He was ready to move as soon as the cargo left his sight. The airfield was small and he should be able to follow it, providing Emily arrived with the rental car in time.

He'd sent her off as soon as they landed to pick it up. They were staying overnight and one of the perks of her position was that she could spend the money on a car rental that most other flight crews weren't allowed. As a result, they had a nondescript sedan waiting for them. All they had to do was get it and get going. With any luck, she'd be in the lot waiting for him when the cargo van they were loading the crate on took off.

As it was, Sam couldn't have planned it any better. As he walked out to the parking area, which was adjacent to the airstrip, he found Emily waiting there for him, keys in hand. She'd even thought to let him drive.

"I figured you had more experience tailing someone than I did," she joked in a quiet tone as she tossed him the keys.

"You figured right, ma'am. Hop in and let me show you how it's done." Sam threw his overnight bag into the backseat and climbed behind the wheel.

He could still see the old white cargo van trundling toward the airport exit. There was an advantage to being in such a small airport. There were few buildings, lots of wide open spaces, and a great deal of visibility.

"Did you do the check?" he asked tersely as he started the car.

"Yes, sir." She flipped him a mock salute and took the small black electronic box from her jacket pocket. "I do believe it's all clear." He'd given her the box, which was designed to check for listening devices, before leaving the jet and asked her to give the rental car a discreet once-over.

"Just to be safe…"

He took the box and flipped a switch that would create electronic interference with any signal that might be transmitting from the vehicle.

"We'll leave this on so nobody can track the car," he told her, placing the box out of sight, in the center console. "We won't be able to listen to the radio or use the GPS, but nobody can track our movements via the GPS unit in the car either."

"Nifty." She turned her attention to the road. They'd left the airport exit and were on a four lane highway. "Is that what we're following?" She pointed to the truck.

"Yes, indeed. The big white whale. We got lucky. That thing shouldn't be too hard to track, so I can hold back a bit and still keep an eye on it."

He did just that for the next forty-five minutes as the delivery truck led them on a circuitous route through small towns and wooded areas. The terrain was hilly with steep grades in some places. They went through some obvious coal mining area where piles of the black rock lay around roadside buildings and dump trucks trundled past stacked high with it.

Eventually, the white truck slowed and turned into a narrow driveway.

"What do we do now?" Emily asked as he passed the driveway and kept going on the small mountain road.

"We look for a place to stop or turn around so I can go check out what's up that driveway." Just up the road he found what he needed. "This is perfect."

He pulled into a small parking lot. There was a convenience store of sorts with a set of broken down gas pumps that were probably installed in the 1940s.

He threw the car into park and opened the door, looking around. The sun was beginning its descent over the hills, causing dark shadows to creep across the land. The place looked deserted but he couldn't see around the corner of the building from his vantage point and it was heavily wooded. It didn't really matter though, because all he wanted to do was switch drivers so Emily could drop him off along the side of the road on the way back down the mountain.

"Sam?" The tone of Emily's voice caught his attention. She'd stopped in her tracks, halfway around the front fender. Her face was turned toward the side of the building he still couldn't see.

Without hesitation, Sam joined her. He saw immediately what had stopped her cold. There were two men on the ground. One prone and one kneeling over him. Both wore dirty, tattered clothing, but the kneeling one was covered in blood. It dripped downward from his mouth and the ends of his sharply taloned fingers.

"Oh, crap." Sam reached for the gun strapped to his ankle.

"What is he doing?" Emily asked, stepping forward as if to help. Sam stopped her by grasping her upper arm. She turned to meet his gaze, clearly confused.

"Get in the car and lock all the doors. There might be more of them. If anyone comes toward you—even if they look harmless—drive away. Get to safety. Do you understand?" He issued the instructions as quickly and quietly as he could, trying to instill a sense of urgency. He didn't want to draw the creature's attention just yet.

"I won't leave you here by yourself. I can help." It touched him that she thought of his safety, but her concern was completely misplaced.

"No. You can't. I'll be all right. I've dealt with this before, Em. Trust me. If one of them scratches you, you're dead. And I mean dead. No turning back. You die and then come back as one of them to spread the contagion."

"What about you? They could kill you too." Her voice rose along with her fears, it seemed.

"Shit." The creature looked up, spotting them. "Get in the car now, Em. No arguments. I have to deal with this."

The creature rose and started toward them.

"Sam?" Emily froze as she got her first real look at a zombie.

"In the car!" He put some force behind his words and she finally got moving. Emily finished her half circle around to the driver's side, seated herself behind the wheel and locked the doors.

Sam had never used the frangible bullets before. Now was his chance. He only hoped they worked as advertised.

He took aim and fired while the creature was still about ten yards away. He hit it in the chest. The impact of the bullet made the creature stagger slightly, but it kept coming. It lurched in that steady, rhythmic way he'd come to associate with the creatures.

As it drew closer, he saw the bloodstains around its mouth. They were all a fresh, bright red. They hadn't had time to dry. With any luck, the poor soul on the ground was the only victim. Otherwise there would be dried blood on the creature's clothes and older, brownish stains of dried blood around its mouth and on its hands.

He counted the seconds in his mind, hoping the zombie would disintegrate sooner rather than later, but he really had no idea what this new version of the toxin could do. He'd have to report in to the rest of the combat team as soon as he had some hard data on how the new weaponry worked—if it worked.

The zombie was only five feet away and the toxin still hadn't taken effect. Sam began to back away, bumping into the side of the car. Emily had the car idling, waiting, ready for action.

"Move the car, Em. Take it about ten yards toward the road." He spoke in a clear, loud voice so she could hear him through the closed windows over the soft purr of the engine.

She did as he asked. Sam never took his eyes off the zombie or stopped the count in his head. Twenty seconds now and no sign of stopping.

Sam backed off. The zombie followed. Twenty-five seconds.

The zombie's face slid, its jaw dropping off its hinges as the rest of him followed close behind. When Sam mentally reached a count of thirty seconds, the creature was a pile of steaming goo and dirty clothes on the ground at his feet.

"Stay put," he shouted to Emily.

He saw her wide-eyed nod as he took his satellite phone from its holster at his hip. Speed dial connected him with Commander Sykes.

"Sir, we've got a situation." Sam spoke as he walked cautiously toward the victim, lying still on the ground.

"Where are you?"

"West Virginia. Coal country."

"I'll have the techs triangulate your signal while you give me a sitrep."

"I just eliminated a single creature. Single frangible round. Thirty seconds from impact to dissolution. The creature killed one victim at a small, backwoods gas station convenience store. From the looks of him, he was the clerk. Sending photo now." Sam used the camera feature on the sophisticated phone to send an image of the dead man.

"Are you secure?"

"Emily's in the car, but sir, she saw the creature. I'll have to tell her." Sam searched the rest of the area, keeping an eye on both Emily in the idling car and the victim. Sam would have to deal with that poor soul as well, but he had some time yet.

"Understood."

"I think I know where this creature came from. We followed a cargo van from the airport to a location down the road from here. We stopped to turn around so I could do recon of the area but encountered this situation before I could scope out the driveway the van turned into."

"I've mobilized the combat team. They're on their way. They should be there in about an hour. Do recon and report back before taking action, if possible. It would be better to let the team handle this to preserve your cover should this not be the main infestation. The intel you've gathered to date leads me to believe there could be multiple locations we'll need to mop up."

"Understood. I'll take care of the victim then continue recon."

"I sent cleanup specialists with the combat team. Do what you can to secure the area but recon is the priority for the next sixty minutes."

"Yes, sir." Sam saw the victim stir, coming back to life—if you could call it that. He was dead, but his corpse was reanimated by the contagion.

"Gotta go, sir. The victim is getting hungry."

Nobody had ever explained to Sam why the creatures seemed so eager to eat people. The contagion acted on dead cells to elongate hair, teeth, and nails, the latter two becoming pointy and sharp. The fingernails in particular, turned into hard, yellow claws and made good weapons, which the creatures used to disfigure their victims in gruesome ways.

The attendant rose. Half his face was missing and his intestines were hanging out of a giant hole in his abdomen. The first creature had been playing with his kill and it wasn't pretty.

Sam took aim and fired. Once again he counted. Twenty-nine seconds later, the attendant was another pile of dirty fabric and organic goo, roughly four feet from the other one. At least the cleanup team wouldn't have far to travel between kill sites. Sam marked each of the piles of debris with small electronic wafers that would lead the cleanup teams directly to the hotspots. Not one particle of the contagion could be left behind. The entire area would get a thorough cleansing but the remains would be packed up and shipped to the laboratories back on base where the science team would study them.

Sam took a look inside the store and did a perimeter check around the building. No signs of any more creatures. That was good.

Now for the place the delivery van had disappeared.

Sam went back to the car. Emily opened the doors for him. Before getting in on the passenger side, he took his bag from the backseat and pulled out a camouflage shirt. If he was going to do recon in the woods, he wasn't going to wear his white uniform shirt.

"Is it safe?" Emily leaned over the center console to peer up at him.

Sam shrugged. "Safe enough for now. Be ready for anything and keep your eyes open."

He stripped off his white shirt and quickly dressed in the green and brown one. Then he looked at his pants and grimaced. He didn't want to take the time to change completely but his chances were better for not getting caught if he was outfitted correctly.

"What *was* that?" Her voice trembled with remembered fear.

"What did it look like?" He didn't want to be difficult but the situation had just gone to hell and he didn't want her to be in the line of fire. He shucked his pilot's dress shoes and took off his pants right there in the parking lot, in full view of anyone who might be passing on the road. Luckily, this road was sparsely traveled. In fact, nobody had passed in the whole time they'd been there. That was good. The cleanup team might have time to get here and contain the site before anybody else happened along.

"It looked like..." she trailed off, her tone uncertain.

"Go ahead. Say it."

CHAPTER 10

"It looked like a zombie." Her gaze flew to his, the ghost of a self-conscious smile hiding at the corner of her mouth.

Sam nodded. "That's what we've been calling them." He buttoned his camo pants and pulled out a pair of combat boots from the bottom of his bag. "What they are is a science experiment gone wrong. A team of scientists, selected and hired by the military, were working on ways to make soldiers heal faster. What they ended up creating was a contagion that kills people and reanimates them into what you just saw."

"Dear Lord," she breathed.

Sam propped one foot on the lower edge of the car door and bent down to lace up his boot. All the while, he kept a careful watch on their surroundings.

"Keep a sharp eye out, Emily. There could be more of them. For some reason, the creatures seem intent on spreading the contagion and making more of themselves by scratching or biting people. After death, the contagion does something to their nails. The formerly dead cells regenerate into longer, sharper versions that are ten times as strong. They can scratch you bad and infect you with the contagion at the same time. That happens, you die and rise again to become one of them."

"It's like something out of a horror movie," she exclaimed, clearly appalled by the situation.

"Welcome to my world. I've been fighting these things the past few months. That's why I went undercover at Praxis Air. A couple of the scientists who developed this technology want to sell it to the highest bidder."

"Are you kidding me?" Oh, she looked angry now. "Spread this like a weapon and have us all kill each other? Unchecked, this could wipe out everyone, couldn't it?" Emily grasped the implications quickly, he'd give her that.

"That's the fear." He couldn't tell her about the special few who were immune to the contagion. That information was more top secret than the rest. Immunity was something that would make the technology even more expensive to the right buyer. If the user could pick and choose who would be immune and who would not, the contagion could be used as a weapon without fear of the consequences.

Sam finished tying his other boot and took one last look around before climbing into the car. He shut the door and turned to Emily. She still looked shaken but she hadn't become a pilot without learning how to handle unpredictable situations. She was holding up well.

"I've still got to find out where that van went," he said softly.

"What's the plan?" She visibly held her fear in check, which he appreciated. She was turning out to be a good partner in this totally screwed up situation.

"I want you to drive me back down the road to the curve just beyond the driveway where the van disappeared. I'm going to bail out of the car—"

"Bail out?" she interrupted him, looking appalled.

"It's easy. You slow down to about thirty miles per hour and I'll jump out. I've done it before and it's the best way to avoid being seen. Stopping on a curve isn't safe."

"Neither is what you're planning," she interjected.

Sam had to grin. He liked the way she argued with him, but he didn't really have time for it now.

"Do you trust me? Seems like you have so far, Em." When she grudgingly nodded, he continued. "So trust me now. This is the easiest and safest way for both of us. I know what I'm doing and I won't get hurt if you do as I ask."

"Okay. So I slow to thirty and you bail out. Then what?"

"I'm going to do a sneak and peek to see if I can find out what happened to our cargo while you continue down the road, then turn around at that coal company lot we saw down the hill and come back this way. I'll meet you back here at the gas station in about forty-five minutes. By that time, you might see some of my teammates here, cleaning up the area. If so, pull in. If they try to run you off, tell them Commander Sykes knows. Only that. Commander Sykes knows. You'll be challenged with two questions. They'll ask you what the color of the day is. You say orange. Then they'll ask what the animal of the day is. You'll say the penguin."

"Are you kidding me?"

"I know it sounds ridiculous but it's the pass code. They set it up before I left for this undercover assignment. Just go with it." She nodded and he looked at his watch. "Okay, we need to get going."

"Are you really sure about this?"

"Absolutely. Don't worry. It's my job and I'm good at what I do. Now drive on, captain. Time's a-wastin'."

She gave him a worried look but managed to get the car on the road. It didn't take long to get to the driveway where the van had disappeared.

"All right, just past this next curve, slow down to about thirty." Sam readied himself, his hand on the door handle.

"For the record, I don't like this."

"Don't worry so much." He winked at her but she didn't respond. Nothing would prove to her that he wouldn't be hurt doing this until he did it.

Sam watched the road and the upcoming curve. Almost there.

"I'm going," he said as he opened the door and rolled out of the moving car.

He sprang to his feet out of the diving roll and stood to see her brake lights still on as she slowed, but didn't stop the car. He waved at her before melting into the trees. He watched for a moment to see her safely around the next bend. He wasn't thrilled about leaving her alone and unarmed knowing there were zombies in the area, but she was in a moving vehicle. As long as she kept moving, she should be relatively safe. As long as there wasn't an army of zombies out there.

The thought made him pause.

"Oh, hell." He couldn't worry about it now. He had work to do.

Sam spent the next fifteen minutes moving through the woods as quickly and silently as possible. He followed along parallel to the driveway until it ended at what could best be described as a shack.

He could see the crates standing alongside the small structure. There was one man walking from the shack into a darker, wooded area behind it. The terrain rose steeply and there was a mountainside not too far from the back of the shack.

Sam stalked the man through the woods, keeping off to one side, hoping to discover where he was going. Sam's suspicions were raised when he saw the pitiful surface structure. Those suspicions were confirmed when Sam caught sight of the gaping maw in the earth, almost hidden by the dense forest ahead of his quarry. Sure enough, the man disappeared into the mouth of the huge cave.

Sam's further reconnaissance only confirmed that the shack was simply a delivery station. The real action was going on inside that cave. Sam sat back in the forest and watched for a few moments. His patience was rewarded a few minutes later when an older man in a blue lab coat followed the first man out of the cave and headed back toward the shack.

Sam had counted only two small vehicles parked near the shack. There was the possibility that the two men he'd seen were the only two here. There was also the possibility that more bad guys were hanging out inside that cave. Sam had to find out which was the truth. The team would need that recon when they got here.

He decided to take a quick look to see what the men were up to. He slid back through the woods in time to see the first man open several of the crates. It looked like the guy in the lab coat was inspecting the equipment and giving instructions to the other man. In Sam's mind, lab coat was the brains. The other guy was the muscle.

When it looked like they were going to unpack the crates, which would take some time, Sam decided to head back to the cave to see if he could get a closer look. He approached with stealth, using the senses he'd developed over years of field work to note things about his environment. For example, there weren't any obvious booby traps or sensors in the area. The whole setup didn't have a lived in look. He'd bet the scientist and his friend hadn't been here long.

Of course, they'd been around long enough to lose at least one zombie. Sam approached the cave entrances from the side. The mouth of the cave was wide and squat. The men had emerged from an area about five yards to the left of Sam's position.

He examined the entrance of the cave minutely before he moved forward. As he'd thought, the place was empty except for a few boxes and tables. There was a caged area with a raised table in it. That looked new. There was still construction debris around the base of the bars. Sam would bet they'd installed it after they lost the guy he'd dealt with at the convenience store.

Sam didn't go far inside the cave. Just a few feet. Enough to get a general idea of what was inside, but not far enough to get caught inside should the men from the shack come back. Sam glanced at his watch. The team would be there soon. He had to get clear to meet up with them.

He made his way out of the cave and faded back into the woods. The convenience store wasn't far as the crow flies. Sam decided to trek back through the woods and scout the trail for the team.

He found nothing that would slow down the team. The approach was clear. Whoever had set up that little hole in the ground hadn't secured it very well. Perhaps they'd thought being in a cave would be defense enough. Boy, were they going to be proven wrong in a big way. Sam couldn't wait to see it happen.

When he got to the convenience store lot, he approached from behind—probably the same way the zombie had. Only there was no unsuspecting clerk for him to surprise. Instead, he was challenged at the perimeter of the woods by one of his teammates.

"About time you joined us." Xavier Beauvoir, Green Beret captain and all around Cajun badass, greeted him.

"Doing my sneak and peek, as ordered, captain."

Sam went into detail about what he'd seen as they walked toward the front lot of the store. He wasn't surprised to find the place had been cordoned off and taken over by his teammates. The evidence of the two men he'd had to shoot was already gone. He could see techs in hazmat gear following the blood trail around the grounds. They wouldn't leave anything to be discovered later by unsuspecting and unprepared locals.

Sam also saw the rental car. Relief flooded him so hard he almost missed a step. Emily was safe. She'd gotten past the low-key guards and was talking with Simon Blackwell, former Navy SEAL and the original zombie hunter.

Simon had been the first man to prove immune to the contagion and he'd led the way for the precious few who'd followed. Emily smiled at something Simon said then glanced in Sam's direction and the smile turned into a huge grin of relief. He could read her now. She was as pleased and relieved to see him as he'd been to see her. But they didn't have time for a sloppy reunion just yet. Sam had to pass along his intel and help his team.

As soon as the other guys saw him, they gathered around. Simon left Emily at the car with one of the support staff.

John Petit and his sister, former police officer Sarah Petit, who was also Xavier's fiancée, walked toward him from the other side of the lot. Donna, newly engaged to John was walking on his other side. It was strange to have women on his combat team, but Sam had gotten used to these two over the past months. Both were tough, though Sarah was a much better shot than Donna. Ultimately though, the thing that made them most suitable to the team was that they were both immune to the zombie contagion.

The only personnel sent to confront the zombies—or into any situation where zombies were expected—were the fortunate few who had already been proven immune. Sam had been made immune by the serum Dr. McCormick had developed, as had their team leader, Matt. Another scientific intervention had made John immune. The rest of the combat team had been attacked and survived because they were naturally immune. Simon, Xavier, Sarah and Donna. They gathered around, exchanging short greetings before the informal debrief began.

Sam told them everything he'd seen at the cave and they quickly devised a plan.

"You look like you're a little light on equipment, Sam," Xavier observed. "Go get whatever you need out of the truck. We'll head out as soon as you're geared up."

Sam gave Xavier a quick salute and headed for the truck parked close to Emily's rental car. She saw him and pushed past the man who'd been talking to her to intercept Sam. He waved the other man off and motioned her to join him as he picked up a combat vest from the truck.

"Did you find where that thing came from?" Emily's voice was breathless with what sounded like worry she was trying to hide.

Sweet of her, but not necessary. Still, it was nice to have someone worry about him again. It had been a long time since anyone had given a damn about whether Sam lived or died, except maybe his teammates.

"Yes, ma'am. They're in a cave not far from here. We're

going there now to solve the problem."

"You're going with them?"

"I scouted the place. I'm going to lead them to it." He grabbed a spare rifle and slung it over his arm. The vest was already loaded with clips of the specially marked ammo. He'd done a quick check before slinging it on.

"You'll be careful?" Emily's tone made him stop to take a look at her. She was more than worried. She was terrified. Hiding it well, but he could see it in the depths of her gaze.

Sam took a moment, sweeping her into a quick hug. He kissed her cheek, not caring that the rest of the team was probably watching his public display of affection. Emily had just been rudely introduced into the realities of zombies roaming the woods and eating people's faces. The least he could do was take a quick moment to offer comfort and reassurance.

"I'll be fine, Em. I've done this before. Don't worry. Besides, I only saw two people at the site. Should be easy work." He let her go, knowing he had little time. "The sooner I go, the sooner I'll be back. Wait here. Let them debrief you. Tell them what you saw. Every detail is important. I'll be back before you know it."

"I'll hold you to that, Sam." She gave him a tentative smile and he admired her grit. Few women he'd known would have handled this situation with so little fuss.

Sam gave her another quick kiss, onlookers be damned.

He left her by the truck and headed back toward the team, who were waiting for him with a variety of expressions on their faces.

"Getting chummy with your new boss?" Sarah asked with a knowing grin as he rejoined the group.

"Give me a break, Sarah. Emily's had a rough day."

Sam took point, leading the way back through the woods. The first few yards were within the larger perimeter the support team had set up so there was still an opportunity for low-key conversation.

Xavier and Sarah walked beside him. "How did the

frangibles work out for you?" Xavier asked.

"Twenty-nine to thirty seconds to take effect," Sam reported. "One shot, one kill."

"Ooo-rah." Xavier made the soldier's sound of approval in a quiet tone. "I was hoping they worked as advertised but we haven't had a chance to try them in the field yet."

At that point they passed the perimeter guard and Sam moved into the lead. They'd travel in silence, using hand signals only from here on.

When they reached the edge of the woods beyond the shack, Xavier took the lead. He signaled for Donna and John to remain on watch there while the rest of the team went on to the cave entrance. Donna was the least skilled of the combat-qualified members of the team but John was one of the best. Together, they'd already proven to be an effective team. They could take care of any potential problems from the shack while the rest of them dealt with whatever they found in the cave.

Sam didn't think they'd find much besides the two men he'd already spotted, but it was always best to be on guard. A battalion of creatures could come at them from the depths of the cave. Sam really hadn't had that much time for recon so it would pay them to tread lightly.

The two men he'd originally seen were captured with little fuss by John back at the shack moments after Xavier gave the order to strike. Sam rushed the cave with the rest of them, surprised to find two more people inside. They were in the caged area, chained to tables. No doubt, they were to be the next test subjects...the next zombies.

"Looks like we got here just in time," Sarah commented, shouldering her rifle.

The two prisoners were both female. Both young and dressed for a night on the town, not a night spent doing evil science experiments. They were gagged but when they saw the team, they began to struggle against their bonds and try to scream. Sarah opened the cage and tried to reassure the girls.

When they were sure the cave didn't go any deeper and

there was nobody else inside anywhere, Xavier and Sam made their way back to the shack to back up John and Donna. As it turned out, there was no need. John already had both of the men wearing handcuffs, well and truly caught.

"Looks like we've got this under control. You should probably go back to your lady friend and get on your way." Xavier sidled next to Sam and spoke in low tones. "The commander wants you to stay undercover as long as you can. Judging by what I see here…" He looked around with disdain. "I don't think this is more than a small offshoot. There are more of them out there and we need to track them all."

"Roger that, captain," Sam agreed.

He headed back through the woods to the convenience store with a light heart. This wasn't the big haul they'd hoped for, but it was something. One less scientist, perhaps, capable of unleashing that madness on the world. One less criminal trying to exploit the terrible technology. That definitely was something.

And the fact that they hadn't caught the big fish he was angling for only meant he got to stay on the case a little longer. On the case and in the cockpit…with Emily. While he wanted to wrap up the mission as soon as possible and catch the bad guys, he also wanted to be with Emily.

Opposing forces there, but so it goes. Sam was challenged by the sentries in the woods as he neared the convenience store lot, as it should be. They let him through and he immediately sought Emily. He came up behind her as she stood leaning over the open door of the rental car.

"Are you ready to go?"

She spun to face him. "Dammit, Sam. I told you to stop sneaking up on me."

He moved in closer and leaned in for a deep kiss. He made it last, letting them both enjoy the sensations of life and hunger for a few moments before he raised his head.

"How are you, Em? Dealing with what you saw?"

Her eyes went from dreamy to troubled in a few seconds

flat.

"I'm not sure. Nobody around here will talk to me since I finished answering their questions. They just keep telling me to wait by the car."

"You have to understand, everything about this mission is top secret, Em." Sam backed off, putting about a foot of space between their bodies. She was too distracting up close and personal. "But after what you've seen, there's no way to keep you out of it anymore. I still need to figure out where the remaining scientists might be hiding or conducting further experiments."

"And you think they're using Praxis Air to get around?"

"It makes sense. Private flights. Nobody needs to know who you're transporting or where you're taking them. Same for the cargo."

"It does make sense." She shook her head in a frustrated gesture. "Dammit," she cursed. "It makes too much sense. All that laboratory equipment. All those small airports. All the blank cargo manifests with Scott's signature at the bottom so nobody dared question them."

"And let's not forget the attempt to silence you," Sam added.

She rolled her eyes. "How could I forget that?" She slammed her hand down on the hood of the car. "I can't believe Scott would be so foolish as to risk everything for something like this." She shook her head again. "Scratch that. I *can* believe it. Scott is a complete moron. Has been all his life. A self-centered, egotistical, mini-megalomaniac. I didn't want to believe he'd risk the airline running drugs, but this is so much worse. I mean, drugs are bad enough, but this…"

Sam covered her hand on the roof of the car, offering comfort. "I know. This is a nightmare. I've been dealing with this reality for a while now and it doesn't get any easier. The only thing we can do is work hard to shut them down and stop this madness before it goes any further."

"Amen to that." She took a deep breath, seeming to gather her courage before his eyes. "So what now?"

"Now we get back on the road and go to the hotel. Maybe stop for dinner beforehand somewhere. We act normal. Like nothing's gone on here and we've had no part in it."

"I don't know how good an actress I am," she looked worried. "But I'll do my best."

"You'll do fine, Em. You've done really well up 'til this point. Nothing's really changed except now you know what's going on and what to look for. Actually, things have gotten easier, not harder. Before, you didn't know what was going on. You could only guess."

She sighed, looking around at the activity on the site. "Now I understand why they say ignorance is bliss."

He chuckled and she joined him. She had grit and he liked the fact that she was bouncing back from her first—and hopefully only—zombie encounter relatively quickly.

Xavier popped out of the woods and headed for them.

"Here comes trouble," Sam said to Emily, only half joking as they turned to face the approaching man.

"Ma'am," Xavier nodded to Emily. "I'm Captain Beauvoir. How are you holding up?"

The Cajun smiled at her, oozing charm. Sam didn't like that at all. He leaned back against the car and slid one arm along the roof behind Emily, clearly staking a claim the other man could read. It wasn't necessary. Sam knew Xavier was already attached and very much in love with Sarah, but Sam couldn't help the caveman impulse. Xavier saw it and smirked. The smug bastard.

Sam liked the guy enough to take the teasing with good grace. He supposed he deserved it. He'd been as quick as the rest of the team to tease Xavier when he'd come back from the mission on Long Island engaged to the woman he'd been sent to question.

"I'm okay, captain," Emily answered simply. Good. She wasn't inclined to get chatty with Xavier, which suited Sam just fine.

"Good. Sam, are you ready to resume the mission?" Xavier turned his attention to Sam with a nearly audible snap.

Something was up. Sam went instantly on alert.

"Yes, sir. We're ready to go whenever you like."

"Best if you leave now. We've got locals coming. Can't keep them out of it much longer and I don't want you two seen."

That spurred Sam to action. He moved to the truck, which was now parked only a few feet away, and relinquished the rifle and ammo clips.

"Better take a few extra rounds for your handgun," Xavier advised. "Replace what you used and add an extra clip or two."

Sam was more than happy to follow that order. He did it quickly and was ready to go in under a minute.

"What about your outfit?" Emily asked as he walked toward the passenger side of the rental car.

"You drive. I can change in the car." Sam caught Xavier's eye over the roof of the car before he got in. "Tell Sykes I'll be in touch at my regular check-in."

"Roger that. Stay safe, Sam. Good work today."

"Thank you, sir. Give my regards to the rest of the team." Sam saluted his superior officer and climbed in the car.

Emily had already started the engine and got the car moving toward the two-lane road within seconds. They passed a convoy of county police cruisers and trucks as they made their way down the side of the mountain. Luckily, Sam had already ditched his camo shirt in favor of the T-shirt he'd worn beneath, though in these parts many hunters probably wore camouflage. Still, it wouldn't do to draw unnecessary attention of the local police. He didn't want to end up in some police report somewhere that the team couldn't control.

He'd gotten away clean today, keeping his undercover persona intact. He wanted to keep it that way as long as possible, both for the good of the mission and for his own reasons. Most of those reasons had all too much to do with the woman sitting next to him in the driver's seat.

"Where to?" Emily asked as they arrived at a crossroad.

"Let's head back toward the airport. There ought to be a

restaurant in that area. We can stop in and grab some dinner."

"Would you mind if we get it to go? I mean, do you think it would look suspicious? I don't know if I'm up to a crowd after..." She let her words trail off but he knew what she meant. She'd been through the wringer emotionally, if not physically. She had a lot of new and utterly crazy information to assimilate. He'd been through it too. He knew she needed time and quiet space to think through all she'd learned.

He took a close look at her. She was a little pale but otherwise seemed okay. Still, perhaps it was better not to test her reactions in public this soon after learning the reality of his mission and seeing the gruesome effects first hand.

"Yeah, we can get something to go. Bring it to the hotel and eat in our rooms. Or better yet, how about room service?"

"Oh, that sounds even better." She looked relieved and Sam was glad he could ease a little of her burden.

"I recall you once said you weren't my knight in shining armor," she mused quietly as she drove toward the airport at a sedate pace.

He remembered the conversation. "I'm still not, Em. I'm just a soldier. Doing my job."

"You might like to think so, but there *is* something special about you, Sam. And nothing you say will convince me otherwise. You saved us today. When I panicked, you knew exactly what to do—what to say to get me moving and how to deal with a situation I couldn't have imagined in my wildest dreams. What I'm trying to say is..." She paused, looking at him for a moment, taking her eyes off the road on the straightaway. "Thank you." She turned back to the road but the emotionally charged moment lingered.

"You're welcome." His voice was quiet but she felt the import of the moment. The sun was quickly setting and the atmosphere inside the cabin of the car grew even more intimate. "Thank you too," he said awkwardly.

"For what?" She was surprised by his words.

"For being a good partner. You're rock solid, Em, even though you've never trained to deal with something like this. I knew right away that you were a competent pilot—and we both know that means something—but you're good on the ground too. I wasn't sure if your courage in the air would translate. For a lot of pilots, it doesn't. But you did good today. Thanks for trusting me."

"I do trust you, Sam."

The moment was broken by the turn of the steering wheel. They'd arrived at the hotel.

CHAPTER 11

It was a slightly better hotel than he'd expected. One of a chain of moderate luxury hotels he'd been to once or twice before. Sam hefted his bag and made sure Emily was okay with her little rolling case. He'd offered to carry it for her but she was independent enough to want to do it herself. It wasn't heavy, so he acquiesced.

When they got to the front desk, he found they'd reserved two bronze level rooms. This chain labeled their rooms bronze for the base level room, which was the least expensive, silver for mid-level, gold for what he would equate to business class, and it also had a few platinum level suites for the highest level of luxury they offered. Sam didn't blink when Emily asked if they could have adjoining rooms, but a jolt went through him. She didn't want him to be far away. He liked that.

Of course, it could be that she was still scared from her zombie encounter. Sam wasn't above capitalizing on that. He'd keep her safe. And he wanted to keep her close too—as close as possible. So deciding, he stepped up to the desk, planting himself next to her.

"Can we nix the two bronze rooms and upgrade to platinum?" he asked the clerk. The young lady behind the counter smiled, looking from Emily to Sam and back again.

"Is that what you want, ma'am?" the helpful girl asked Emily.

Emily looked up at him and he felt his heart melting. Damn. Just that hopeful, cautious look in her eyes made him want to give her the moon, if he could.

"Is it possible?" Emily turned back to the clerk. "Do you have a gold suite available?"

"Platinum," Sam corrected as he fished his credit card out of his wallet and passed it across the marble counter toward the clerk. The girl smiled and tapped the keys on her computer terminal.

"Yes, we have one platinum suite left."

"Excellent." Sam grinned and put one arm loosely around Emily's shoulders.

She was tired. She had to be wiped out from the heinous events of the day. The sooner he could get her to the suite and in bed, the better. She deserved to be pampered and he was just the man to do it.

They got the key and rode the elevator up in silence. There was a lot to say, but most of it wasn't suitable for public consumption. Discretion was the better part of valor in this case, even if the hotel seemed relatively quiet.

Sam kept his arm around her shoulders. He could feel the slight tremble. He figured she was due for a little breakdown considering what she'd seen that day. He'd pushed for the suite not only because he wanted to make love to her again. He definitely wanted that. He didn't think she was up to it right now, though.

He'd wait. He'd wait for her as long as he had to. She was worth it.

That thought should have startled him. Instead, it felt comfortable. Lived in. Like part of him he wasn't ever going to give up willingly.

Just like Emily.

Only he knew that was impossible. She didn't belong to him and with all the crap that was going on in his screwed up wreck of a life lately, it would be cruel to ask her to be a part of it. All he could have was now. The mission. The moment. That's all anyone ever had, after all.

But if he were going to fantasize about the perfect future, he'd have Emily in it. At his side. Sharing his life. Partners in the air and on the ground. For as long as they both shall live.

And didn't that sound domestic. Sam nearly laughed at himself, but checked the impulse as the elevator whisked them to the platinum level. There were only a few suites up here at the apex of the building. Each of them had a rooftop patio, or so he believed.

They got off the elevator in silence and Sam guided Emily to their door. He swiped the key card and ushered her inside.

"Wait here." He positioned her just inside the door and dropped his duffel next to the wall before he went to check out the suite.

He didn't think anyone or anything was waiting in the suite for them, but it was best to be sure. Being careful saved lives.

"The room is safe," he reported as he strode back to Emily a few minutes later. She'd stayed exactly where he'd left her and the look on her face was tragic.

"Is it safe to talk?" she asked in a whisper.

"Yes, Em." He'd already checked with the small device he'd had in his pants pocket. She looked about ready to crumble, so he stepped up to her and took her in his arms. "Come here, sweetheart," he whispered, pressing her head to his chest.

They stood like that for long, long minutes. Her trembling amplified as she let go. Her breathing became ragged though she seemed to be fighting the urge to cry. When she began to quiet down, he reached behind her and flipped the locks on the hotel door, never letting go of her small body.

"It's okay, Emily," he whispered against her hair, drawing her closer in his arms when he'd secured the door. He'd keep her safe. It was his duty and his honor.

"I'm sorry, Sam." Her voice sounded choked, as if she was

fighting strong emotion in addition to the tears.

"You have nothing to be sorry for, sweetheart. I'm the one who dragged you into this. It's me who should apologize. I know what you saw today had to be jarring."

She laughed brokenly. "You can say that again."

"You're safe now."

He patted her back and stroked her hair, offering what comfort he could. Little by little, he felt her trembling decrease until she was resting comfortably against him.

Then everything changed.

Emily made the first move this time. She raised her head, seeking his lips for the kiss she wanted deep in her soul. She needed his touch, his warmth, his reassuring presence, but more than that, she needed him. His lovemaking. His love.

She didn't dare hope for that particular miracle. She'd gotten her hopes up before, but no man had ever declared his love for her—not seriously. She'd always been so focused on her career and following in her mother's footsteps. There hadn't been a lot of time for boyfriends, though she'd had her share. Just nothing serious.

She didn't think she'd get that from Sam either, though the more she was around him, the more she wanted it. She wanted him to be the one. The man who would go down on one knee and ask her to be his bride. She may be a modern career woman, but she was an old fashioned girl at heart.

But tonight wasn't about love. It wasn't even about sex. It was about caring and reassurance. About his strength and protection making her feel safe and secure. She'd learned there were awful things in the world today. Things she never would have believed if she hadn't seen it with her own eyes.

All that had stood between her and horrific death today had been Sam. He'd proven equal to the task and given her the gift of his protection and skill. Tonight she'd give him her thanks in the most basic, earthy way. It was his reward—her reward too. She needed to feel alive tonight after learning so much about the most awful death she could imagine. She needed to feel Sam. His strong, protective presence over her, on her…in her. She needed him like she needed her next breath.

So she kissed him and he didn't disappoint. No hesitation. No questions. He took her invitation and kissed her back with all his might. Just what she needed.

She wanted it fast and hard. She wanted it raw and elemental. What she'd been through had thrown her world off its foundations and she needed something to nudge her back toward sanity.

She knew, without a doubt, Sam could do that for her. He'd rocked her world the last time they'd been together. Emily wanted that same earthy energy now. Needed it. Needed him.

"Now, Sam. I don't want to wait," she panted when he released her lips.

His hot mouth slid down her neck, his fingers doing away with the fastening of her pants, letting them drop to the floor even as he pushed her back against the wall near the door. His fingers went to the buttons on her blouse next, releasing them in a frenzy as her need climbed higher. His impatience matched hers.

She pushed at his T-shirt, rubbing it up and over his rippling abdomen and rock hard pecs. He eased away for just a moment to rid himself of the stretchy fabric, flinging it over his head while she worked on the closure of his pants. A moment later, he was hot and hard in her hand.

Emily met his gaze as she squeezed him, daring him with her eyes to take what he wanted. What she wanted to give. What she wanted to take in return from him. There was no waiting. No need for further preliminaries.

"I need you now, Sam."

"Are you sure?" He seemed surprised but willing. She could feel just how willing in the palm of her hand.

"Get a condom." Sanity prevailed in one tiny part of her mind, thank goodness. Sam reached for his wallet.

She shucked her panties and kicked her shoes off and the fabric away while he covered himself. What should have been an awkward moment was nothing of the kind. It was a moment filled with unbridled need and desperate yearning, waiting for him to claim her.

He came back to her in seconds. His muscled arms lifted her up, against the wall, holding her in place while his covered cock slid along her cleft. He pinned her against the wall with his body weight, coaxing her thighs around his hips while he used one hand to test her readiness.

"Eager little thing, aren't you?" he teased as his hand came away wet, trailing up her torso to the lacy white bra she still wore. He pulled one cup downward, baring her nipple, then circled it with that wet finger, watching it peak for him.

She shivered in his arms, making a sound in the back of her throat that surprised her. It was needy and demanding. Almost desperate. The way she felt about him was all those things in that moment. All that, and so much more.

She began to slip down the wall a little, prompting him to plant both of his big palms on her butt, hoisting her higher. His head bent to her other breast and he used his teeth to pull the cup down. Then his mouth was on her, his moist breath bathing the peak of her breast with heat that started a lightning fire that raced from that point, straight to her core. Her stomach contracted, even as he lowered her fractionally, impaling her on his rigid member.

Finally. She moaned as he slid deeper, biting her lower lip to keep from screaming when he pushed all the way inside.

His mouth covered hers, making her open for him. When he drew back, he stilled, catching and holding her gaze.

"Don't hide from me, Em. Don't hold in those sexy sounds you make when I'm inside you. I want to hear it all."

"I can't," she breathed, scandalized by the idea that someone might hear through the thin walls of the hotel. Scandalized, she realized, but also titillated a tiny bit at the naughty idea.

"Yes you can, sweetheart." He gave her an audacious wink. "Do it for me."

His muscles tightened as he held himself in check. She saw

a muscle ticking on the side of his firm jaw. She stretched upward and kissed him there, working her way downward over his sexily stubbly cheek until she reached his lips. Hovering, she rubbed her lips over his.

"I love this, Sam, but if you don't start moving your ass right now, I'll scream all right and you won't like it at all."

He laughed outright at her threat, breaking the tension. The sparkle of something that looked like joy in his eyes moved her. She closed the short distance between their mouths and kissed him deeply as he began a sure, steady rhythm with his hips.

"As you wish, my lady." His tone was playful and powerful at the same time. Perfect. Everything about his possession was perfect.

Powerful thrusts pushed her against the wall. The width of his cock rubbed her most sensitive spots, compelling her toward a peak higher than any she'd ever known.

He started out strong and soon spiraled higher. The steady rhythm turned into something more erratic as they raced together toward a precipice. His loving was hard and fast. Within moments she was moaning, unable to hold back, just as he'd wanted. She'd give him her cries of passion. She'd give him her sounds of pleasure. She'd give him anything he wanted in that moment, if only he'd keep doing what he was doing to her pleasure starved body.

"Sam!" she screamed his name as her peak neared.

Her short fingernails dug into the hard muscles of his back, holding on for dear life as her body rode up the wall and slid back down again with each sweaty thrust.

"Come for me now, Em," he ordered harshly, his breathing as jagged as hers.

He rode her hard and fast right up into the sky, hurtling them both toward the distant stars, each one a new and exciting pop of pleasure that took Emily by surprise. She almost forgot to breathe for a minute as the most amazing orgasm broke over her, making her numb to any discomfort and blind to anything but the intense pleasure that flooded through her.

"Sam," she whispered against the side of his neck. He clutched her close, supporting her through the storm that quaked her entire body.

"I've got you, Em," he whispered back after a moment.

He lifted her away from the wall after another few minutes to catch their breath and walked them farther into the room. Sam lowered her onto the king size bed in the center of the main room, following her down and settling at her side.

"Wow."

The single word from Sam made her chuckle. She was pretty speechless too. Never in her life had sex been so tempestuous, so urgent. Never had she responded to a lover the way she responded to Sam. Of course, she'd never had a man like Sam as her lover. He was strong in more than just the obvious ways. Mentally, physically, and emotionally, she thought he might be the strongest man she had ever known. Nothing seemed to phase him. Not even running into a zombie eating someone's face in the shade of a convenience store parking lot.

That thought brought it all back. She rolled on her side to look at him.

"That thing in the parking lot…that was real, wasn't it?"

He rolled toward her and propped his head on one elbow. He caught her gaze and she could read the concern in his eyes.

"Real as it gets, I'm sorry to say."

She sighed. "I was hoping maybe I'd been hallucinating or something." One side of her mouth lifted in a self-mocking grin.

He lowered his head and kissed the corner of her mouth, taking her smile and replacing it with a renewal of the passion that had so recently gripped them. It wasn't the runaway freight train of before. This was something much less desperate but also much more powerful. At length he drew back, holding her gaze.

"I'm sorry I dragged you into this."

His statement took her by surprise. She'd been gearing up for round two while apparently he'd been thinking of something completely different. She switched gears, following where he led. It was important he understand that none of this was his fault.

"I would have stuck my nose into what was going on at Praxis anyway. All in all, I think I'm safer working with you than on my own."

"I'll do my best to keep you safe, but if we ever run into one of those creatures again, promise me you'll get as far away as fast as you can. Don't hesitate. Don't worry about me. Just run. I can take care of myself. I've been fighting these guys for a while and I know how to handle them without getting myself killed. I wasn't kidding when I said that one scratch from them and you're dead. You'd end up joining their little zombie army."

"They're that contagious?"

"It's not a disease, but yes. A single touch and you're infected. Death is pretty quick. Then your body is reanimated and you go off to make more."

"That's awful." She shivered, remembering what she'd seen. The man had looked absolutely ghastly to her.

"Yes, ma'am." He put his hand on her hip. "It's also a real mood killer. So why are we talking about this when I have you naked—" he looked her up and down, grinning, "—make that half-naked, in a bed?" He chuckled, moving his fingers up to the bra strap hanging off her shoulder. "Sorry I was in such a rush before. I didn't even take time to completely undress you."

"I was kind of in a hurry too, in case you didn't notice." She grinned back at him, moving closer as his hand went around to her back and the closure of the lacy bra. A quick flick and a pull and he had the hooks undone. "I can't believe you just did that with one hand. Makes me think I'm not the first woman you've charmed out of her bra."

He stilled. "No, you're not the first," he answered in a low, intense voice, holding her gaze. "But you're the most important to me."

"You mean that?" she whispered, the mood growing serious.

"Yeah, I do." He sighed. "Emily, I didn't mean for this to happen. I never expected—" He trailed off and regrouped. "I read your file when I agreed to take this mission and you intrigued me from the start but I never intended to seduce you. It's not part of the mission. It's not something I planned. It happened because frankly, I can't keep my hands off you." He looked chagrinned. "In the middle of a mission is not the best place for romance, but I…care…for you, Em. More than any other woman I've ever known. I wanted you to know that so there will never be any doubt in your mind. Making love to you was never part of my plan. I consider it a gift. Just as I consider you a gift. Someone I never thought to meet who has made a big impression on my life."

Wow. He was really serious. Emily was touched deeply by his admission. She'd bet a year's salary that he'd never said anything like that before to any of the women he'd undressed. The words seemed too rusty, too unrehearsed. They were from the heart—or the nearby region.

He hadn't said he loved her, but that was too much to expect. He'd gone farther than she thought he would and that meant a lot to her. She reached up and cupped his bristly jaw.

"I care about you too, Sam. And you've made a big impression on my life too, in the short amount of time I've known you. You're like a tornado," she joked, trying for a lighter mood. "You turned me upside down and inside out but I like where I landed." She patted the big bed and stretched one of her bare legs over his thigh, rubbing along the length.

His pants were only partially off. She realized abruptly that he still had his boots on. She began to laugh as her foot made contact with the leather.

"Do you always wear your boots to bed?"

"Only when I'm in a hot zone or some smoking hot lady makes me too crazy to remember my own name. Though I will admit, it hasn't happened often. Never, in fact. You're a first for me in many ways, Emily."

He levered himself upward until he was sitting on the side of the bed. She admired the rippling muscles of his six-pack abs and massive arms as he bent over to unlace the boots. His back was muscled too and his shoulders were wide, tapering to a luscious V above a butt that would cause wars if women made up the Army. Speaking of smoking hot, he was definitely making her burn in very eager places that wanted him again.

Who needed downtime? With Sam, she was roaring to go again almost immediately. Now *that* was something new too. She'd never been quite so eager as she was with him.

"Bet I'm your first lady pilot," she teased, knowing her odds were good. Flying was still, by far, a man's occupation.

"Are we talking as a friend or as a proverbial notch on my belt?" He threw her a look over his shoulder. "By the way, I don't keep count. There haven't been so many in recent years that I don't remember them."

She didn't know if that was a comfort or somehow disturbing. Was he letting her know that he'd remember her after he left? Or was he saying that he wasn't an inconsiderate cad who kept score on how many women he'd conquered? She didn't know what to think but she wasn't going to let it throw her. She had him now, and other women be damned.

"First commercial pilot you've slept with, then." That narrowed the field. Most female pilots weren't employed in commercial aviation. She rolled to her back, unwilling to meet his gaze should the answer be no. She shouldn't have started this avenue of conversation. She should have let sleeping dogs lie.

Sam disposed of his boots. She could hear them make two soft thuds on the carpeted floor as he set them down. Then his pants whooshed down his legs to be left where they dropped. She felt his knee make a depression on the side of the bed, tilting her slightly toward him but she kept her eyes closed, refusing to meet his gaze.

Then a kiss landed on her belly and her eyes flashed open. She watched as he worked his way up her abdomen, pausing at her breasts, laving and sucking alternately hard and soft in a rhythm that had her gasping in moments. He was thorough this time, drawing out her pleasure. His mouth and one hand worked her breasts while his other hand delved between her thighs, rubbing, swirling, testing, fingers plunging deep in a teasing prelude of things to come.

It didn't take much to make her fully aroused and ready. She moaned in the back of her throat as a small climax overtook her. He whispered words of praise and encouragement as he brought her higher still. When she couldn't take any more, he lifted his head and met her gaze, coming closer as if to kiss her. But he stopped a few inches away.

"For the record," he said in a gravelly voice. "You are the first and last pilot of any kind that will ever grace my bed. I can't imagine ever meeting another lady flyer who got under my skin the way you do."

He didn't give her time to respond. He lowered his lips to hers and took her mouth in a hard, slow, tempestuous kiss. A moment later, his fingers were replaced by something thicker and longer, and way more satisfying.

The loving was slow and deep this time, sending her into spiraling waves of pleasure so intense that she didn't know where one left off and the next began. Never one to experience multiple orgasms before, Emily was fast learning the kind of man it took to bring out her long hidden wild side. One man in particular. This man.

He rode her hard and drew out every stroke to give her the utmost in sensation. He mastered her body as he'd mastered his own, not letting the pace drop or speed, keeping it steady until he seemed satisfied that she'd given him all she could for the time being.

Only then did he let go, allowing his pace to rocket out of control. She struggled toward the stars with him as he plunged into her, sending them both into orbit with sensation and an agony of pleasure so intense, she thought maybe she blacked out for a few seconds.

All she knew was that when she opened her eyes again, Sam lay at her side, breathing hard, his honed body more relaxed than she'd ever seen it. She'd done that to him. Wrung him out as he'd wrung every last ebb of tension from her. He'd given her a gift of relaxation and pleasure and caring.

Yes, she felt truly cared for as he lay beside her. His big hand reached for hers and he absently interlaced their fingers, his eyes closed as he caught his breath. It felt good to just….be. To be still. To be with him. To be cared for by someone she also cared about.

Of course, her heart was fully involved. The caring had morphed into full-blown love somewhere along the line, but that was entirely her fault. If she spoke that word around him at this point, he'd take off running and she wouldn't blame him. It would take time—if ever—to be able to admit the true depth of her feelings for him.

For now, it was enough to have their mutual caring out in the open. It felt good and was more than she had expected. Sam, for that matter, was more than she'd ever expected in her life. More intense. More commanding. More masterful. Just more of everything she found desirable in a man.

And for the time being, at least, he was hers.

That pleasant thought in mind, she drifted into a gentle, replete sleep.

Sam woke her a little while later with gentle kisses as he lifted her into his arms and carried her toward a door that led to the most luxurious hotel bathroom she'd ever seen. A giant Jacuzzi tub was set on a platform among a waterfall of flowers and green, growing plants. The hotel staff must take a lot of time caring for the hothouse flowers.

Emily looked upward to discover part of the secret behind why the indoor garden was so lush. Stars twinkled at her through a huge skylight centered over the tub. It had a shade that could be pulled over it for privacy, but aside from a few airplanes and maybe a satellite or two, there was nobody up there who could possibly see them. Still, it made her feel like she was outside almost, being able to see the moon and stars beaming down on them.

"You drew a bath?" Emily finally looked downward to notice the steaming water and the fine sheen of bubbles that floated on its surface. He'd left the jets off for now, but they were clearly visible between the bubbles. That and…lights? The tub lit up from beneath.

"Wow. This place is fancy." Sam lowered her feet to the floor, setting her down next to the tub.

"Nothing but the best for my lady." He winked at her again in a way she was coming to think of as charming.

Nobody ever winked at her. Not like that. Not in a way she didn't find either grandfatherly or lascivious. Sam put a whole new spin on the simple gesture that made it intimate and sort of special. Just between them.

"Do you need a moment or do you want to soak now? I'd planned on sharing the tub with you. It's big enough for a platoon." He looked pointedly behind her, at the massive tiled oasis of hot water.

She felt the blood rush to her cheeks as she realized why he asked. At least he was considerate enough to anticipate her possible needs. She'd noticed another door that led to a private toilet area. Whoever had designed this place had thought of everything.

"I'll only be a minute. Hop in. I'll join you in a few." She tried to skirt around him to beat a hasty retreat toward the private toilet but he snagged her waist and hauled her in for a quick kiss.

"To tide me over," he explained when he let her go. "Hurry back. You might have to call the Coast Guard to fish me out if I get lost in there."

She laughed, put more at ease by his teasing as he let her go. She took a few moments to answer nature's call and clean up a bit before rejoining him. He looked so relaxed, head back on the small inflatable plastic cushion that was strapped to the rim of the tub. His eyes were closed and his arms were stretched along the oval rim. He looked at peace.

She stood at his side for a moment, just looking at him. He really was the most handsome, fit man she'd ever seen in the flesh, so to speak. His body was as perfect as Michelangelo's David. He didn't have any scars, which she thought odd, now that she realized what he did for a living.

His eyes opened. She was caught staring.

"Like what you see?" One corner of his mouth tilted sexily upward.

"Oh, yeah." She moved closer, stepping into the tub. He took her hand, guiding her to face him, coaxing one foot over his hips so she straddled him.

Suddenly her mouth went dry as she met his smoldering gaze. Her position made her vulnerable and was all too blatant. Her thighs were open, her pussy bared to his gaze as he sat up—on the perfect level for…

"Oh my Lord…" she exclaimed as he kissed her there, his tongue snaking out to wind around the little nub that made her knees go weak.

His big hands landed on her ass, supporting her as she began to tremble. Just that easily, he had her all hot and bothered again. Sam Archer was probably the naughtiest lover she'd ever been with and she had a sneaking suspicion she hadn't seen even a fraction of his tricks yet. The thought should have scandalized her but it only made her hotter. There was something about being with a bad boy who knew how to touch a woman and push her to her limits.

Sam licked her, showing his skill and she burst into flames. A short climax followed by intense afterglow made her limbs weak.

"You'd better let me sit down before I fall down," she only half joked.

"I've got you," he whispered against her tummy. His hands supported her on the way down, never letting her go. At least not far.

She ended up facing him, perched over his thighs, straddling him. Her knees splayed to the sides in the wide tub, her heels somewhere around his knees. He was rock solid beneath her. Warm, slippery from the soapy water, and the look in his eyes made her heart stutter.

"Thank you."

"Any time." He almost purred with satisfaction. "I really like watching you come."

She felt the heat rise to her cheeks but her belly jumped in reaction. He said the naughtiest things sometimes that really turned her on.

"Maybe I can return the favor." She reached between them and grasped his semi-erect cock in her hand. It was his turn to jump.

But he covered her hand with his, stopping her when she would have continued.

"Time for that later. Right now, we're going to relax and enjoy this tub. I've never seen anything like it. Have you?"

He eased back against the headrest and cuddled her close so she rested on top of him, her head in the crook of his neck, her breasts flattened against his chest. Their bodies slid sinuously together in the soapy water.

"Only in magazines. I didn't think people actually did garden tubs for real. Only for photo shoots."

She felt languorous after the lovely climax he'd given her. The hot water was the perfect temperature and the company wasn't bad either. Sam felt good under her. His arms stroked over her back, soothing away any remaining tension and making her feel cherished.

"If I ever buy a house, I'd like to have something like this in it."

"Me too," she agreed lazily.

That was the last thing she remembered until he roused her with a kiss sometime later. The water had grown tepid and her skin was wrinkling up in places. It was time to get out.

"Sorry I fell asleep," she murmured, embarrassed.

"Don't be. I take it as a compliment that you feel safe enough around me to let your guard down. I like it." His smile warmed her.

Slipping only a bit, she climbed off him and out of the tub, all too aware of her pruny fingers and toes. She reached for the giant bath towel and wrapped it around herself, suddenly self-conscious. Sam grabbed her from behind, towel and all and pulled her backward into a big bear hug.

He seemed to be in a playful mood, which suited her fine. She liked seeing the carefree side of him, knowing she was seeing the real Sam, not the super duper secret agent.

"I believe I promised you room service."

Her stomach rumbled as she remembered how hungry she was.

"I hope they have a good restaurant. I could really go for a cheeseburger right about now."

"A cheeseburger?" He let her go as he snagged a smaller towel and dried off before casually wrapping it around his hips. "I didn't picture you for the cheeseburger type." He flipped the drain so the water would flow out of the tub.

"What type am I?" she challenged playfully.

"I had you pegged more as a health food girl. Salads and sprouts. That sort of thing."

"*Au contraire.* I eat salads when I'm being good but for comfort food, give me a good all American cheeseburger any day."

"A girl after my own heart," he joked as they headed together toward the bedroom.

Dinner consisted of cheeseburgers with imported gourmet cheddar cheese and the fanciest French fries Sam had ever seen. It was delicious. More so because of the company than because of any special treatment the chef had given the burgers.

They were too caught up in each other to really pay much attention to the food. After finishing the food, they went back to bed for what remained of the night. Neither of them got much sleep, but when they did sleep, it was in each other's arms. Sam discovered he liked the feel of her against him, though he'd never been much for cuddling with anyone else.

Emily was teaching him new things about himself all the time. He'd never really met anyone like her before. Oh, he'd enjoyed friendships with many professional women. He'd even dated a few. He liked and respected the women who'd been drafted onto the team but Emily was something else altogether.

He realized suddenly the most likely reason. He was in love with her. Had to be. The feelings she inspired in him couldn't be anything else. Sam wasn't one of those guys who fell in and out of love every day. He thought he'd probably loved his high school girlfriend, but that was only a pale glimmer compared to what he felt now for Emily.

There was nothing he could do about it now, he realized. Love had caught up with him at last—at the worst possible time. Sam didn't know how it was all going to shake out for him and Emily. He'd do his best to protect her. From the zombies and their makers. From the snakes in her own company. And from himself, if it came to that.

For now, all that mattered was that she was in his arms. In his bed. He fell asleep feeling smugly satisfied with that particular thought and didn't rouse 'til morning.

CHAPTER 12

When they got to the airport the next morning, Sam was hyper aware of their surroundings and the possibility for trouble. If someone had seen them or suspected them of being involved in the raid the day before, there could be trouble. With that in mind, he did an extra thorough examination of the jet with Emily's help. They'd discussed it over breakfast and agreed to get to the airport early in order to check things over as best they could.

Emily helped. She knew this model of jet better than he did and was invaluable in checking for small things that could turn their flight into a crash real fast. Sam kept watch while she checked the engines and steering mechanisms. She did the same for him as he checked other parts of the plane. Then she climbed in and he watched the outside of the jet as she activated various switches, making bits move about.

Everything looked okay and they were done in plenty of time to pick up their charter and head off into the sky. Before long, they were headed back to their home base in Wichita. They'd shared a lovely morning, talking about all kinds of things and sharing a new closeness that hadn't been as easy between them before their shared adventure—and the aftermath marathon session of lovemaking last night.

"So, how do you want to play this when we get back to work?"

"What do you mean?"

They were cruising safely and Sam figured it was a good time to strategize for tomorrow and the continuation of his mission.

"I mean this. Us. Do we go back as a couple or do you want to try to keep this under wraps? Buddy knows and others may have seen your car parked in the lot all night, but do you want it out in the open or do we keep them guessing?"

She seemed to think about it for a moment.

"What's better for your mission?"

"We'll make a soldier out of you yet." He couldn't help but compliment her reasoning. She'd impressed him, putting the good of the mission ahead of her personal comfort. Then again, he shouldn't have been too surprised. Emily was an altogether different sort of woman from those he'd been involved with before. "It would be better to have our relationship out in the open," he answered honestly. "It would give us a reason for always being together and it might act as a distraction in case anybody wonders what we're up to."

"Okay then. Out in the open it is. But no necking in the hangar. I do have certain standards to maintain."

He liked her sense of humor. Reaching over, he ruffled her hair, then smoothed it and pulled her in for a quick kiss.

"If we didn't have a passenger back there, I might seriously consider initiating you into the mile high club right about now," he whispered when he pulled back. They had one passenger hitching a ride back to Wichita, but he was safely ensconced in the rear cabin with the soundproof door closed between them so they could talk freely.

"Mile high club?" She pretended innocence, though he could tell she damn well knew what he meant. Every pilot had heard the stories about the informal fraternity of people who'd had sex in flight.

"Oh, yeah." He nipped her earlobe, then sat back in his own seat. "You tempt me beyond all reason, Em. But one of us needs to fly the plane."

She gave a heavy, dramatic sigh. "If you say so."

"Emily..." he growled. "Don't tempt me."

She laughed outright then, the sound charming an answering smile out of him. He never would have believed the stickler of a boss he'd met only a few days ago would turn out to be such a tease. Emily definitely had hidden depths he was only beginning to plumb. He looked forward to learning more with eager anticipation. But that would have to wait until they were safely on the ground.

"I was thinking, since we have a free afternoon, it would be pretty normal for me to spend the ground time doing paperwork," Emily volunteered, changing the subject. "If you want to get a close up look at the manifests and flight plans, I have a private office at the hangar. I don't use it much, but it is there. No windows and the door locks."

"I like the way you think." He sent her a lascivious grin that made her laugh. He liked to hear her sound so carefree and happy. And he liked being the one to make her feel that way.

"We can get to the hanky panky later," she said in a mock stern voice. "But I don't mind if people think that's what we're doing. It's all in a good cause. Meanwhile, you'll be able to get a much closer look at what I've been able to pull together of the suspicious manifests and corresponding flight plans. I made electronic copies of everything and hid the USB drive in my office."

Sam was impressed at her forethought. "That'll save me a lot of time."

She grinned at him. "Yeah, I thought so. All I've been able to make of the information so far is that there's a predominance of flights to destinations in or near the Pacific Northwest. I only started gathering the records a few weeks ago and haven't had time to really look into it yet, but that much was pretty obvious. I had to be cautious in the way I dug up the documents. I didn't want Scott or anyone who might work for him to know I was making inquiries."

"Smart move. Do you think anyone knows you've collected all those documents in electronic form?"

"It's doubtful. I got them all off different computers and didn't put them into a single file. I saved them to the USB drive one at a time. I also have some of the hard copy from flights I actually made. I keep copies of all my flight information going back a year or two. I didn't pull the individual flight data hard copies, but it's all in there, waiting. I marked the folders with a little tear on either the tab or the edge so I'd be able to find them again when needed."

"Good thinking. We can pull those files and take the USB drive back to your place. I have a laptop in my duffel bag that nobody at Praxis Air can trace. It's on an independent network and we can use it to send the data back to the analysts at my home base and see what they've already made of what I sent them on my own—which wasn't much."

"Well, we can change that now that we're working together." She sent him a bright smile. "We're on approach. Let's land this puppy and get to work."

A short while later, they were on the ground. Their passenger had disembarked and they had gotten only a few odd looks as Emily led Sam into her private office and closed the door.

"They're definitely grouped right in this area," Sam said to Emily a couple of hours later. They'd poured over her hard copy records together and a pattern emerged as he put the odd flights she'd earmarked together into some kind of order.

He drew circles on a topographical pilot's map Emily had pulled out of one of her other filing cabinets. It was a map of the Pacific Northwest. In particular, he was looking at a large section in the less populated areas of Eastern Oregon, Washington state, and upper and mid-Idaho. It was a big area, but at least they'd gotten that far with the information at hand.

"That's a lot of ground to cover," Emily commented as

she stood beside him. They had cleared her desk and were standing around it. The office was a mess with papers everywhere, but they were definitely onto something.

"Hopefully the team on base will be able to narrow it down with the information on the drive."

One of the first actions Emily had taken after locking her office door was to go to a secret compartment in her antique desk and retrieve the USB drive. She'd given it to Sam for safekeeping before showing him the way she'd marked the file folders for the flights she'd actually made herself.

"I don't know about you, but I'm starting to get hungry. We skipped lunch and it's close to dinnertime." She rubbed her midsection as she spoke and Sam became aware of his hunger—both for food and for her. Since they'd first made love, he just couldn't get his fill of Emily's sweet body.

He began to put the files back in order. "Yeah, let's put this place to rights and get out of here. I think we've given our coworkers enough to talk about for one day, don't you?"

Emily walked over to him and put her hands on his waist, tugging slightly at his neatly tucked shirt, deliberately disarranging it. Then she ran her fingers through his short hair, dislodging a few of the longer stands on top a bit, making it messy. He got the idea when she reached up on tiptoe and kissed him hard, grinding her lips against his.

Two could play this game.

Sam took great pleasure in messing up her pretty hair and tugging at her clothing so she'd look adorably rumpled and sexy as hell. Any red blooded male seeing her like that was going to think all kinds of lascivious thoughts, but he figured it was okay. She was going home with him. Not anybody else. He was the lucky bastard who'd have her in his bed tonight. The gods were smiling on him in a big way.

Before he could forget himself and drag her clothes off right then and there, he pulled back, taking stock of her pink lips, the sexily tousled hair, and wanton disarray of her clothes. Yes, there was no doubt about it. She looked hot.

"Damn, baby." Sam couldn't keep from expressing his

appreciation.

"Back at'cha."

He liked the breathless quality of her response.

"Let's hurry and get these files back where they belong so we can finish what we started."

"And get dinner," she reminded him. She worked with him to refile all the folders and put everything back to rights quickly.

"Dinner's on the list. As is reporting back to base. But then you're all mine, Em, so be warned."

"I can get behind that," she agreed with a sexy grin that made him want to push her up on the desk and have his way with her right there. But it would have to wait. At least until they got back to his place.

They finished refiling the folders at record speed and Sam ran a critical eye over the office to see if he could discern any obvious differences from when they'd first entered. Everything had been put back from where they'd gotten it and the place looked good.

"We're good to go," he nodded at the condition of the room. They worked well together as a team no matter what they were doing, it seemed.

"All right." She patted her messy hair and looked like she was trying to compose herself before opening her office door. Just as she would probably do if they really had been in there making love all this time. "Let's do it."

She nodded to him and opened the door. There wasn't exactly an audience waiting outside watching the door with bags of popcorn in their laps, but there definitely were more people in the outside office area than there had been before. Most of them looked over when they stepped out of her office.

Sam quickly slid his arm around her shoulders and put his body between the onlookers and Emily, shielding her. It was something he'd normally do in this situation, so it wasn't out of character. And it established them as a couple without any room for doubt. The way she snuggled into his side spoke loud and clear of shared intimacy.

They walked the gauntlet of the back office together and out into the hangar and then the parking lot without speaking to anyone. It was pretty clear that everyone present saw them and the possessive arm Sam had around Emily's shoulders.

"A little blatant, don't you think?" Emily challenged when they'd gotten out into the parking lot.

She might be complaining, but she wasn't moving away. In fact, she seemed more than comfortable with his display, snuggling closer and putting her arm around his waist. It might be for the benefit of the gawkers clustered in the open hangar door. Or it might be because it felt so darn good. At least it felt darn good to him to have her close.

He bent and placed a quick kiss on her temple.

"Just staking my claim. You don't mind, do you?"

She craned her neck to meet his gaze as they walked toward their cars.

"I don't mind. I kind of like giving them something to gossip about. It might keep some of them from wondering what I've been up to snooping around lately."

"The old bait and switch," he agreed. "It'll fool the casual observers, but if there's anyone really serious—anyone who was sent to deliberately watch you—it might only arouse further speculation. Still, either way, we can use it to our advantage. And I get a little primitive thrill out of staking my claim." He shook his head, amused by his own reaction. "Can't say that I've ever felt that particular caveman instinct before."

"It's okay, Tarzan. I don't mind playing Jane for a little while." They'd arrived at their cars and she turned to face him. Her smile teased him and gave him an oddly light sensation in the vicinity of his heart. "So long as it's understood that we're partners, not master and servant in private, I can play the little woman in public. For now. Though you understand, it goes against my independent nature."

He laughed outright at her over the top delivery, as she'd

probably intended. She laughed with him and they had a moment of shared amusement before she stepped away from him. She fished out her keys from her purse and turned toward her car, which was parked right next to his.

They'd decided to take both cars back to her place where she would pack a fresh overnight bag and water her plants. Then they'd head to his place, which was safer. He'd chosen it for its reasonably secure location and he'd made some improvements since moving in that included some early warning sensors in case anyone tried anything.

Everything went off without a hitch and they were at his place inside an hour. They'd picked up Chinese take-out on the way and ate dinner at his small table. He'd taken a moment to start up the laptop and send the documents from Emily's USB drive to the techs on base. That done, he sat back to enjoy dinner with her before he checked in with the commander.

After that…well, he had big plans for Emily after everything else had been handled. He only hoped they both still had the energy. Neither of them had gotten much sleep the night before and while Sam was used to pulling all-nighters and functioning well on little sleep, it was clear Emily wasn't. She was yawning around every bite of her lo mein and her eyelids had taken on a decidedly sleepy cast as the food hit her system.

No doubt within twenty minutes, she'd be out like a light. Sam felt his plans being pushed back through no fault of his, but it was okay. He wouldn't push Emily beyond her limits. She'd already had to deal with a lot and had risen to every challenge. She deserved his respect and his care. He would put her needs first and it was looking increasingly like her most pressing need after dinner would be sleep.

Recalculating his plans, he decided he could handle that. He was disappointed, but he consoled himself with the knowledge that he could hold her warm little body next to him in his bed until she was rested enough to join in some of the more adventurous ideas he'd been entertaining for the evening.

"You finished?" Sam nodded toward the half-eaten plate in front of her. She had been picking at her food for the past few minutes.

"Yeah. I'm afraid my eyes were bigger than my stomach. We can save this for tomorrow maybe." She stood and repacked the take-out containers, stowing them in his fridge with Sam's assistance.

When she'd yawned for the third time in the space of a couple of minutes, Sam simply picked her up in his arms and headed toward the bedroom. She squeaked a bit when he lifted her but her arms went around his neck and her head settled into the crook of his shoulder.

"Where are we going?" she asked sleepily.

"You're going to bed. Then I'm going to check in with the base before I join you in dreamland. Then maybe a little later on, we'll wake up and have some fun."

"Sounds good." She slurred her words slightly, exhaustion kicking in now that she'd eaten.

He placed her on his bed, pulling back the covers from under her and taking a moment to undress her. He made short work of it. Otherwise, he'd be overly tempted, and he'd yet to take advantage of a nearly unconscious woman. He wouldn't start tonight. And especially not with Emily. She meant too much to him to abuse that way.

No, when they made love, he wanted her with him, awake, aroused, and wanting him as much as he wanted her. He could wait a few hours until she'd had a chance to rest up a bit.

That didn't mean he didn't enjoy every moment of taking her clothes off. It was still a new enough experience that he lusted over each inch of skin he revealed. He paused once or twice to place gentle kisses on her belly button and then up to her breasts. She moved into his touch, seeking more, but her eyes were mostly closed and she was half asleep already.

Much more of this and he'd lose all willpower. Having her naked in his bed was a sight he enjoyed all too much. Steeling his resolve, Sam pulled the covers over her and made himself leave the room. He still had work to do and a check-in to make with his team commander.

He left the bedroom and headed for the kitchen. It was the best soundproofed area in the condo and he had equipment stowed there that looked like regular kitchen appliances that contained sophisticated jamming devices. He'd checked the house when they'd first arrived, but it was standard operating procedure to use extra precautions whenever possible in a situation like this.

Commander Sykes picked up on the first ring.

"Good work on collecting all that data, lieutenant."

"Emily gets the credit for that work, commander. She's been gathering that information over the past few weeks. All I did was pass it along." Sam was a strong believer in giving credit where it was due.

"Please give her my thanks then, Sam. And keep an eye out for the phone we're sending her. It should arrive at your place by courier any time now."

They spent a few minutes going over particulars about the preliminary data and Sam's suspicions. Matt Sykes was a good CO. He encouraged independent thought, especially when he sent men into the field on their own.

"Emily's going to try to put us on the Pacific Northwest flights starting tomorrow. We'll concentrate in that area unless the team comes up with something else out of the documents I sent you."

"Good plan. Report in when you can. We're on twilight shift here now that the night activity has settled down. There's always someone to answer the phone and you have my direct number if there's an emergency."

"Yes, sir." Sam liked Matt's friendly approach to command. He had a way of inspiring loyalty by giving it in return.

Although Matt was a Navy SEAL who'd been sidelined into the command track by injury, Sam was glad to have been assigned to his command across services. It had been jarring at first for an Army guy to take orders from a swabbie but only a few days into the new assignment, Sam had come to realize Matt Sykes was one of the most talented commanding officers he'd ever have the good fortune to serve under.

"Oh, and you can tell Ms. Parkington that her brother is now part of the team. We're going to keep him and his shiny new F-35 Lightning ready in case we need air support."

Sam was impressed. Those jets were the newest and best that had come out of the Joint Strike Fighter program designed to come up with a brand new, more versatile aircraft that could replace the aging air fleets of the United States and its allies. Sam had read that the F-35 was being developed by the United States and the United Kingdom and a few other friendly governments. Emily's brother must be one hot flyer if he'd gotten assigned to the elite group that was putting the new fighter jet through its paces.

"From everything I've heard about it, that jet will be an asset to the team, sir."

"I've been reading up on it. Supposed to be quite a versatile piece of equipment." Matt's conversational tone invited further comment.

"I believe it was designed to serve multiple purposes. It's a single-seat, single-engine stealth aircraft. They say it can be used for close air support, tactical bombing, and direct dogfights. It's supposed to be ultra-versatile and very high tech."

"It looked pretty slick when it landed. Got a lot of people talking. Most of the pilots on base have been trying to talk to Parkington about the jet but he can't say much, which suits me fine. Though I could've wished he flew something a little less conspicuous, it's good to have the best the Air Force has to offer at our disposal, should we need it."

"What about servicing the jet?" Sam knew that a new jet like that couldn't be serviced by just anyone.

"He'll go to his home base for that. In fact, after this initial debrief, he'll probably go back and stay there until we need him. It's better for the jet and he's centrally located. Being in flyover country is probably the best place for him to offer support should we need him almost anywhere in the country."

"Roger that, sir." Sam liked the plan. Though they didn't know Henry Parkington well, Sam knew without a doubt the man would never endanger his sister's life.

They ended the call after a few more minutes and Sam straightened up the house a bit. He didn't want Emily to think he was a total slob. He'd left a few things lying around that took only a few minutes to put away. By then the courier was at the door.

He was dressed as a pizza delivery guy, complete with pizza box that he made Sam pay for before turning it over—in case anyone was watching. Sam suspected he was one of John Petit's CIA friends, but the man was gone before Sam could blink.

Sam took the box inside, opening it to find a smaller box taped inside. There were some interestingly tiny electronic gizmos along with a new cell phone for Emily. She'd be happy to be able to talk to her brother, he knew. He'd give her the phone tomorrow morning. He had plans for the rest of the night.

Taking the phone with him into the bedroom, he plugged it into the charger on the nightstand before undressing. He took a quick shower before joining Emily in bed. Pulling her close in his arms without waking her, he enjoyed the feel of her warm body against him for a while before drifting off himself.

Emily woke to find herself snuggly warm. Sam spooned her from behind and one of his arms rested around her waist, the hand reaching upward to toy with one tight nipple. She felt his warm skin touching hers and realized they were both naked.

Correction, she was naked. He already had a condom on. Oh, she liked that even better.

Going from zero to sixty at light speed, she tried to turn in his arms but he wouldn't let her. His strong arms clamped around her, holding her just where he wanted her.

"Where do you think you're going?"

"Well, I was going to jump your bones, but you aren't cooperating."

She enjoyed the rumble of his chuckle against her spine.

"I had something else in mind."

She loved the low rumble of his voice when he was in this mood. She could easily get used to it—given half a chance.

"Really? Will I like it?"

"I can pretty much guarantee you will." He tweaked her nipple, making her squeak. It didn't hurt exactly, but nobody had ever touched her with quite that much force. Shock followed a frisson of pure pleasure that radiated down her spine. "If you don't like anything I do, say the word and we'll try something else. There are lots of things I want to try with you, Emily."

"Mmm. Now that sounds promising."

His hand moved downward, sliding between her legs and lifting her top leg backward, draping it over his. The position left her very exposed and conscious of her own vulnerability. Did she trust him? The answer came back without hesitation. Yes.

His hand slid around, cupping her butt cheek and squeezing.

"How's that? Comfortable?" His tongue licked at the sensitive skin of her neck as he spoke near her ear.

"I'm okay."

"Okay?" He sounded disappointed. "By the time we're through, you'll be more than okay, sweetheart. I promise."

That was one promise she couldn't wait for him to keep.

His hand dipped lower, into the dark crevice and lower still until his fingers slid in the slippery wetness of her body preparing itself for him. He played for a minute, rubbing her clit with an expert touch, driving her passions higher. Then he slid inside, testing her readiness.

One finger was joined by another and then another until

three wide fingers stretched her. She knew from experience his cock wouldn't disappoint and she wanted him. Now.

But he held her on the precipice, not allowing her to move.

"Sam?"

"You like that, Em?" He slid his fingers in a pulsing rhythm that made her moan. "Want more?"

"I want you, Sam," she nearly shouted. He knew how to touch her, to make her come. Or not. Depending on his whim. "Please!"

"Oh, I like that. Hearing you beg me to fuck you."

A little thrill went through her at his use of the crude word. She'd heard worse, of course, but she'd never had a lover speak that way to her. She liked it. At least when Sam was the one talking. She wasn't sure she'd have appreciated it from any of the few men she'd been with before.

"Please, Sam," she repeated. He was holding her back, keeping her teetering on the knife's edge of pleasure.

"Please what? Say it, Em," he dared her.

She gasped as he pushed inward with a touch more force. It felt heavenly, but it still wasn't what she wanted. What she craved. What she needed.

"Please fuck me, Sam," she whispered.

"Well, when you put it like that…" He growled, biting down on her earlobe as he removed his fingers and replaced them with what she really wanted.

He thrust inward from behind, his way made easy by the foreplay and her astoundingly immediate response to his merest touch. She was his to command and he'd already proved it. All he had to do was trail his fingers along her arm and she purred. It was that easy. That amazing.

His angle of attack made things…interesting. She'd never quite done it this way before. He held her by the hips, thrusting slowly into her. Each breath came on a gasp of air as he pumped her closer to an earth-shattering peak.

One hand reached around to stroke her clit and she cried out as pleasure overtook her. Sam was a steady, pulsing presence behind her, around her, within her as she reached that first climax. What promised to be the first of many, though she wasn't sure she'd survive.

There was the sensation of motion and she found herself on her hands and knees, Sam behind her, still inside her. He lifted her hips until her ass rose high in the air, at perfect hip level to receive his deep, deep thrusts.

"Okay, sweetheart?" he asked, stilling until she answered.

"I'm good," she gasped. "Just do it."

"Do what?" He ran the fingers of one hand up and down her spine in a soothing, scintillating caress. "What do you want me to do, Em? Or should I say, *who* do you want me to do?" He chuckled, the sound translating into soft pulses that she felt all through her body emanating from where they were joined.

She knew what he wanted her to say. He'd already gotten her to say something she'd never said to a lover before. She'd liked it and he knew it. He was pushing her boundaries, daring her, and she'd never been much good at resisting a challenge.

"Do me!" she shouted. "Dammit, Sam. Do me already. You know you want to." That last was whispered on a moan as he began to move.

His hips thrust forward as his hands pulled her back onto him. She moved with him, eager for whatever he would give her. The penetration from this angle was amazing. She only wished he'd move faster.

The pressure was building again and she knew the peak this time would be higher than the last. Higher and more satisfying when he finally let her have it.

"I like the way you beg, captain." His use of her title jarred her. It made this kinkier, and somehow more exciting. "I want to hear more of it."

She remained silent to see what he'd do. Would ignoring his request drive him over the edge? She wanted to drive him as crazy as he was making her.

A smack sounded through the room as his open palm

landed on her ass. Oh my Lord, he'd actually spanked her. That wasn't something she'd anticipated, but it had felt surprisingly good. It cut through the dizzying pleasure, bringing it into sharp focus. Honing it until she was ready to scream for more.

"Defiant, captain? I think I like that even better than hearing you beg." He leaned over her, making her very aware of her size in comparison to his. His presence engulfed her, his heat making her feel small, vulnerable, yet strangely powerful. "Because when you're defiant, I get to punish you. Do you like to be punished?"

She hesitated before answering. "I—I don't know."

"I think you do. I think you know damn well you liked being spanked. Shall we try it again?" He rose, resuming his position behind her. Sure enough, a moment later, his hand smacked down on the other cheek with an echoing sting.

She let out a little sound this time, not quite a squeak, not quite a moan. It was something in between.

"Yeah, baby." He rubbed the stinging spot gently, with circular motions. "I knew you liked it. Don't try to hide it. I like it as much as you do."

She'd think about what that meant later. For now, she couldn't think of anything beyond the intensely focused pleasure that was building inside her with every movement, every minute.

"Now beg," he reminded her. "Let me hear you beg, baby."

She bit her lip to keep from giving in.

"Oh, so you want more punishment?" He sounded inordinately pleased. "I can do that too, but in the end, you'll give in. I'll see to it."

Two quick smacks, one on either side, made her shriek. He laughed and it sounded triumphant. Then the real torture began.

Sam slid into her, his hands gripping her hips hard. He began a heavy, pounding rhythm that pushed her closer and closer to the stars she sought so desperately. Only to pull her back from the precipice before she could get there.

"Give it to me, Emily," he commanded.

She moaned, caught in the grip of a tidal wave beyond her ability to control. She surrendered to it. Surrendered to Sam.

"Please!" she cried. "Please, Sam."

The pleading seemed to do the trick. Sam sped up, pushing harder, the way she wanted. He knew exactly what she needed. A few moments later, she tipped over the edge into the abyss, but he was there to catch her. Sam followed her, his embrace keeping her safe, his body protecting hers as they flew through the stars together.

She screamed his name as she came. In the end, she thought she heard him shout something too, though she couldn't be sure. She was too far gone in her own pleasure.

The bliss overwhelmed her. The passion shook her to her soul. She flew without a plane, with only Sam's strong arms to support her.

"I've got you, Emily," he whispered as he lowered her to the bed and disengaged their bodies. She still pulsed with pleasure, her breathing harsh and irregular.

Sam was winded too as he positioned her on the bed next to him. They both gulped in air as their shared climax began to fade into a lovely afterglow. Sam put his arm around her, tucking her into his side. That felt good. The possessiveness of his grasp felt even better.

"I never knew you were so kinky," she whispered, amused now that the crisis of pleasure had passed.

"You ain't seen nothing yet, Em. Stick with me and you'll learn all sorts of naughty things."

"Is that a threat?" She craned her neck to look into his eyes. She was joking and he smiled back at her.

"It's a promise. One that I look forward to fulfilling—anytime, anywhere."

"I'll remember that." She snuggled into the pillows, needing to rest.

"See that you do." He kissed the crown of her head.

She fell asleep with a smile on her face.

CHAPTER 13

"This looks promising," Emily commented to Sam as they headed for their jet.

The trip was a quick cargo hop to Portland International Airport, known as PDX, and back. The cargo had come in from a small airstrip near Norfolk, Virginia, overnight and was being split into two shipments. One was going to PDX. The other to Boise, Idaho. The bulk of it was going to Boise in one of the newly outfitted, strictly cargo jets. They'd take a smaller set of boxes in a passenger jet to PDX.

They'd opted to take the PDX flight because the second leg of that trip would net them a few passengers who were on their way to a tiny airstrip in the wilds of Eastern Oregon. Emily agreed with Sam's conclusions that something was up in that region. They'd tried to hide it but when looked at as a whole, all those mysterious shipments seemed to center around that geographic area. It was also pretty wild up there. Farm country that was somewhat mountainous and desolate. There was lots of room up there to do all kinds of things without anyone being the wiser.

Sam had cautioned her against talking in the cockpit until he'd had a chance to check it for bugs. They'd also done a thorough but nonchalant check of the jet's systems, looking for any possible sign of tampering. She didn't think the bad guys would want to blow up their own cargo, but it couldn't hurt to be too careful. Sam would also discreetly check the cargo before they took off, to be sure that it wasn't a bomb.

They were in the thick of things now. Since their encounter with that creature in West Virginia, Emily understood exactly what was at stake here. She and Sam had to find out where the bastards who wanted to sell that heinous technology were hiding out.

Emily taxied to the runway while Sam checked the cargo. He rejoined her in the cockpit with a few seconds to spare, giving her the thumbs up that was her signal meaning the cargo was not potentially explosive. She shot them into the air and Sam took care of the communications with the tower and ground control until they were at cruising altitude.

When they began to level off, he started fiddling with some electronic gear he had in one of his pockets. At length he gave her the all clear signal and she relaxed a fraction, knowing they could talk without fear of being recorded. There was no real viable way to listen in on them live while they were in the air, but a bug could record for later playback and get them in trouble once they landed, he'd warned. It made sense and she was being ultracautious now that she knew what they were up against.

"This came last night, along with your phone," Sam said, pulling out a long, thin wire that had a little flat oval on one end.

"What is it?"

"A way to eavesdrop on our passengers after we pick them up at PDX." He leaned over in the small cockpit space and examined the bottom of the soundproof—and bulletproof—cockpit door. "There seems to be just enough space in the seal for me to wiggle this under. Or over," he added, looking at the roof. "Once they're aboard and they've settled a bit, I'll slide this baby into the crack of the door. It's the latest in spy gear. Supposedly undetectable. I guess we'll find out."

The devil may care grin he sent her made her want to

laugh. And worry. She did both, knowing it was futile to try to tell him not to do something potentially dangerous. Danger was his middle name, it seemed, cliché as it was. He'd come alive when they were in West Virginia, fighting for their lives. And he hadn't been the man she'd first met since.

This was the real Sam Archer. The warrior. The daredevil. She loved that about him, as much as it frightened her. Her only consolation was that he had to be damn good at what he did if he'd stayed alive this long. She had faith in his abilities and she knew he was getting top of the line equipment in this fight. The little gizmo in his hand proved it. As did the new cell phone clipped to her hip. The government wasn't sparing any expense to stop this horror in its tracks, and she was glad of it.

They should have never tampered with such things to begin with but now that the genie was out of the bottle, they had to do everything in their power to stuff him back in. More than the safety of the nation depended on it. Life itself depended on getting this technology under control and completely out of circulation.

"Yet another good reason to have taken the PDX flight," she commented.

"Yes, ma'am. Cargo is one thing, but passengers inevitably talk, even if it's only to complain about my flying." He winked at her and she laughed, knowing there was usually very little to complain about his competent hand at the stick.

"Are you going to give them something to complain about?" she challenged.

"If I must." He sighed dramatically, but she knew he'd do whatever it took to get the information they needed. If these passengers had it, he'd get it out of them and they'd likely never even know.

"So what's in the cargo this time?"

"Nothing much. Could be a red herring meant to throw any watchers off the trail. Bundle the shipment together as far as Wichita, then split it in two. One is the real shipment. The other is useless junk going to a dummy drop point. I'm betting that's what we've got. If not for the need to get the passengers, those crates might've ended up going to New Mexico or someplace else, unrelated at all to the action up here. It's like laying a false trail in the woods."

"Clever."

"Well, unfortunately the people we're dealing with aren't dopes. Most of the tech folks on the original projects were medical doctors or Ph.D.'s. Some had multiple doctorates. Not stupid people. The few that we've already stopped were either a little crazy, had delusions of grandeur, or visions of being super rich and all powerful."

"Nice bunch of folks," she said dryly.

He laughed and shook his head. "One of the female researchers went completely around the bend. She turned her ex-husband and his trophy girlfriend into zombies and took over their lake house. Since the creatures don't like direct sunlight, they need to go to ground during the day. She took great pleasure in telling them to go jump in a lake. The creatures took her literally and walked into the deepest part of the lake to hide from the sun."

"You're kidding." She was appalled.

"Afraid not. They're dead. They don't need to breathe. They could hide down there all day and walk out of the lake at night to do their nasty work."

"I'll never enjoy a day at the lakeshore again." She shivered, imagining seeing something like that creature from the convenience store walking out of a peaceful lake to ravage the countryside.

"Never fear. That's what we're going to stop. With any luck, you and I can shut them down completely. We've accounted for almost all the original scientists except one. A charming fellow named Dr. Sugden."

"You've met him?" Sam's voice had an edge when he said the man's name.

"No, ma'am. I've not had the dubious pleasure. But from the things we've been able to piece together after the fact, it looks like Dr. Sugden maneuvered his way onto the team by employing some pretty underhanded tactics. He had one of the leading scientists in his field discredited with false rumors. Everyone later realized the man was innocent but by then the choice had been made to put Sugden in charge. Then, when it began to look like the goal they'd been working toward had taken a horrible turn, it was Sugden who pushed to test the experimental substance on cadavers. I hold him responsible for that first outbreak that killed so many of my brothers in arms. Their blood is on his hands."

A cold look had entered Sam's eyes as he went on. "I believe that bastard knew damn well what would happen when he shot up those corpses with the contagion, yet he did it anyway. Then he ran away with the technology and put it up for auction to the highest bidder among several hostile foreign governments. If I ever meet the man, it will be my pleasure to put a bullet between his eyes. I only regret I can't make him suffer the way my teammates did."

Sam was staring out the cockpit window into the distance, and Emily knew the memories that tightened his muscles must be terrible. She reached out to him, putting one hand over his. He turned, taking her hand in his as he looked at her.

"I'm sorry, Emily. I'm a violent man. It's best you know that from the beginning. I've led a hard life but I've never reveled in killing. The part that scares me is that I would probably dance on Sugden's grave given half a chance, for what he did to my friends and me."

"You're only human, Sam," she whispered. The moment was tense. She wanted to comfort him and reassure him that wanting the man dead who had killed his friends wasn't a terrible thing. It was understandable, under the circumstances.

"See, that's the thing…" He let go of her hand and turned back to stare out at the sky. "What happened changed me. Forever. There's no going back to what I was."

He looked so torn. So sad. Again, her instinct was to comfort him.

"I suppose that's to be expected. Life changes us. The things that happen to us and how we react to them make us who we ultimately become. And from where I'm sitting, you've taken all that life has dished out to you and done good with it. You haven't let it beat you down. You haven't let it turn you bitter or stop you in your tracks. You're out here, actively doing something to make the world safer. That's a win in anybody's book, so give yourself a break, Sam. You're doing fine."

His expression lightened as he seemed to consider her words. At length he shook his head, his tension leaving him.

"I'm glad you have such faith in me, Em."

"Always." She smiled at him and neither said much more until they began their approach to PDX.

The cargo was whisked away as they refueled. They had to wait for one of the passengers. There were to be two men. A Caucasian fellow with a thick accent Emily thought was Russian or something like it was already waiting when they landed. Sam handled the refueling and paperwork with the jet while Emily dealt with the passengers. They'd agreed beforehand that it would be best for Sam not to have direct contact with them, in case he spooked them somehow. It was pretty hard to hide his stature and unmistakable military air.

A lot of pilots had that vibe but Sam was a little more intimidating than the others she'd dealt with. Her brother had pegged him for Special Forces right off. One soldier, it seemed, had a way of recognizing another. They'd take extra precautions in case Sam's demeanor spooked any of the passengers. He'd told her he didn't want to blow it when they'd already come this far and she agreed. Besides, it was more natural for her to deal with the passengers since she was the senior pilot on this team and had been with the company much longer.

What she hadn't realized was that Sam would be skulking around the jet, using his phone to take surreptitious photos of the two men they were to transport. She didn't think anybody else would realize it, but she now had the same phone he carried and had been introduced to its rather surprising features that morning. It could take photos from a camera secreted in its tip.

Which was exactly what Sam had pointing toward her as she walked across the tarmac with their two passengers. The second man had shown up a few minutes late. He was Asian, probably Chinese if she was any judge, but she couldn't be sure. Their names were not listed on the flight manifest and she knew enough not to ask. That's the way it had been since Scott had taken over, though many of the celebrities she'd flown before had avoided talking with the "little people" like her as well and didn't list their names on the manifests—only those of their managers and support personnel. Often they'd list fictitious names, if they listed any at all.

This new policy, though, was taking things to an extreme. Celebrities were one thing. Everybody knew who they were. But in the past, businesspeople had always been required to show I.D. and give their real names for the records in case there was an accident or some question later. Their insurance carrier demanded it.

Only Scott didn't seem to give a damn about legalities lately. He'd sent down the directive and suddenly it was law. They'd fly anybody, anywhere. No questions asked.

Emily was glad it was starting to unravel. With any luck, they'd catch the bad guys and end this soon. Then she could go back and rebuild what Scott had destroyed—if there was anything left to rebuild.

Of course, that would probably also mean the end of her time with Sam and she couldn't be happy about that. He'd given her so much in the short time they'd been together. He'd made her feel special and cherished. He'd made her feel loved.

That was something rare in her life. She had the love of her family, of course, but there had been precious few men she'd fallen for in her lifetime. And of those few, fewer still had fallen for her in return.

She didn't know if Sam loved her. He cared about her. She knew that with certainty. But love? She didn't dare jinx what they had by bringing it up. They both knew their relationship was doomed from the start. Their jobs and responsibilities would be hard to reconcile even if they did both want to pursue the relationship beyond the end of this mission.

Increasingly though, she wanted to keep him in her life. She was contemplating ways they could make that happen. A long distance love affair was better than nothing at all, she figured. But it would take two to make it work, and so far, Sam hadn't said anything about the future. She sure wasn't going to bring it up. Not yet. She didn't want to say anything that could ruin what they had. The time would come when she couldn't put it off any longer. That would be soon enough.

Emily saw Sam finish his walk around and slip up the stairs into the jet before she and the passengers got there. He was already doing the preflight in the cockpit when she ushered their guests to their seats and showed them the various amenities. There was a fully stocked bar and snacks on board should they desire to eat or drink. This wasn't the fanciest jet in their fleet, but it was often used for high powered businessmen who didn't want to deal with commercial flight schedules.

She shut the door between the cabin and the flight deck and locked it for good measure. They'd communicate with the cabin via intercom from here on in. All of their jets were carefully designed so that the intercom could not be tampered with. Their business clients demanded the utmost in privacy, which included that the pilots not be able to overhear any business that might be discussed in the cabin during flight.

No matter. Sam had his new gizmo to try out. Hopefully it would work and they wouldn't get caught. Emily felt her heart race as she slid into her seat and joined Sam in the procedures necessary before getting the little jet off the ground.

"Did you take pictures?" she asked as they rocketed into

the air.

"You saw that?" He seemed concerned.

"I don't think anyone else would have realized it, but I'm familiar with the phone and its abilities now."

He nodded, seeming to put his worries aside. "I sent the images back to base. Hopefully somebody back there will be able to I.D. our guests, though I have a sneaking suspicion I know who they are already."

"Really? Who?"

"Not yet. I want to be sure first."

"Tease," she accused playfully.

He waited until they were about fifteen minutes into the flight to deploy his little gizmo under the door, in the corner, where it wouldn't be easily seen. He put a small earpiece in one ear, taking off his headphones. The mic plugged into a small black box that looked like one of those miniature radios joggers wore on armbands. It had a dial he played with until he seemed satisfied that he could hear what was going on.

Emily flew the plane, trying to hold her curiosity in check, but it was a hard thing. She wanted to hear what he was hearing but there was only one earpiece. She'd have to wait until he chose to tell her what was going on back there.

Finally she couldn't wait. She tapped him on the shoulder, drawing his attention.

"Anything?" she mouthed.

He shook his head. "Negative. They're drinking but not saying much of anything useful."

At least it was working. The little gizmo was picking up the cabin conversation and hadn't been detected. So far, everything was stable.

It was only moments later when Sam suddenly tensed.

"Bingo," he said absently, listening intently to the conversation in the cabin.

It was a good thing. The flight wouldn't last much longer. It was only a quick hop from PDX to a small airstrip on the Oregon border with Idaho. Sam seemed to notice they were beginning their descent and he took the earpiece out to talk to her.

"Can we find a way to stay over? Maybe invent a malfunction with the jet?"

She thought about it for a moment. "Yeah, I can complain about a sticky rudder. That should ground us for a bit."

"Sounds good. Work it out so we can stay overnight. There's something going on here I need to check out. This thing records digitally," he pointed to the little black box. "I can download it to my sat phone and send the file back to base. I'll do that as soon as our guests deplane. This is hot intel. I'll need to act on it and have a plausible reason to stay in the area while I check it out."

"I'll deal with the jet and the mechanics. I'll throw a hissy fit if I have to, in order to get one of our mechanics up here from Wichita. They'll arrive tomorrow, so that'll give you tonight and part of tomorrow to do what you need to. Good enough?"

"Perfect," he replied, a predatory grin stretching his lips. He was on the hunt and enjoying every minute of it, judging by that dangerous expression.

Emily landed the jet while Sam split his attention between cockpit duties and continuing his eavesdropping. She had no idea what he was hearing from the passenger cabin, but judging by the set of his jaw, it was something juicy.

They landed and Sam had to pull in his surveillance gizmo before she could open the cockpit door and help the passengers out of the cabin. She let him stay in the cockpit while she dealt with the pleasantries. She waited until the passengers were gone before asking for hangar space for the allegedly faulty jet. She set the wheels in motion to have the jet housed here for the night while demanding one of the Praxis Air mechanics fly in first thing in the morning to look at it.

Once she had that all settled, she looked around for Sam. She found him leaning against the hangar wall. He looked smugly satisfied.

"So what now?"

He swooped down to kiss her cheek, pausing to whisper in her ear.

"Now we follow the transmitter I planted on their rental car."

"You didn't." She was truly impressed. She hadn't thought there'd been time to get ahead of them or that he'd be able to get close enough to place a tracking device.

"Oh, ye of little faith." He drew back and gave her a teasing grin.

They got a car from the rental guy. They were lucky. He only had one left in the lot. This airport was tiny compared to where they'd come from. A few minutes later, Emily was behind the wheel, taking directions from Sam. His phone may have looked like hers, but she quickly learned it had a few extra features. Somehow it was able to follow the tracker he'd planted on the bad guys' car. He was able to direct her to turn right or left from quite a distance away, which meant their targets wouldn't know they were being followed.

"I still don't know how you got close enough to put a tracker on their car," she mused.

"It was really a thing of beauty. I threw on a windbreaker over my uniform shirt as soon as I got out of sight and headed straight for the parking lot. There were only a few cars and only one with someone in it. I watched while the waiting man went to meet our two passengers. While he went to get them, I casually tagged his car with a tracker chip. They're a variation on the chips we use to mark kills, only a little stronger. They use satellite technology, like our phones do."

"This is a satellite phone?" she patted the new phone clipped to her belt. "It's not any bigger than a regular cell phone and it doesn't have that weird antenna I've seen on other sat phones."

"You've probably seen the commercially available sat phones. These aren't on the market. Hell, they're not even available to most military outfits. Our team already had the model you're carrying but when we added a CIA operative to the team, he upgraded a few of us to the one I've got. Real James Bond stuff."

He seemed like a kid with a new toy and it made her smile. She'd seen that look on her brothers' faces many times.

"So who are we following?"

"If I'm not very much mistaken, Aleksander Krychek and Bin Zhao. Two potential buyers of the zombie tech. Krychek is a freelance arms dealer who pretends he's a businessman. He's made billions off the death of others with the arms he's supplied—often to both sides of a conflict. Zhao's background is shadier, though I personally think he's working for one of the unfriendly governments on the other side of the Pacific. Could be North Korea, China, a few others. He's Chinese by birth but even our CIA friend had a hard time digging up any more than that."

The seriousness of the situation was driven home by his words. This was bigger than anything Emily had imagined in her naïveté. By comparison, she almost wished it had been a simple drug ring operating in her airline.

"Why only two buyers? Wouldn't the seller want to open this up to a broader group in order to get more bids and raise his profit?"

"Normally, yes, but this technology is too hot. We've been a half step behind them since the beginning, constantly gaining ground. We've taken care of many of the original threats. We believe only this one single corrupt member of the original team remains. He's got to be cautious. Inviting more people to bid means disclosing the nature of the weapon to them and increasing his risk. All he needs are two competitive bidders to get a good price and it looks like that's exactly what he's got."

"But why would they travel together if they're on opposite sides? They didn't seem very chummy, but they were cordial to each other from what I saw."

"Some ridiculous notion of honor among thieves, no doubt. Both men seem to live the high life and enjoy all the trappings of the elite rich. They make a show of being polite and businesslike in their outward dealings but they're both ruthless when there's blood in the water. Don't let the urbane act fool you." Sam kept his eyes glued to the small color screen on his phone that displayed a GPS map while he spoke. "But the more likely reason they came in together is simple logistics. They probably flew to PDX separately from wherever they were in the world and the seller—Sugden—provided transport to the meeting place. If they don't know where they're going, they can't set up a snatch and grab. It's a wise precaution on Sugden's part. These kinds of men would gladly kill him and each other if it meant they could grab the technology free of charge."

"Wow. I find it hard to believe."

"Believe it, Em. Your life depends on your taking this seriously."

"Oh, I do," she was quick to protest. "It's just that I find it hard to wrap my head around some of this stuff. It seems so unreal—like a movie playing out and I'm trapped inside."

"I know what you mean, but trust me, this is about as real as it gets."

"I understand, Sam. Truly I do. Don't mind me. I just…" she trailed off, not knowing how to express what she was feeling inside. It was such an alien world she'd stumbled into.

"Are you starting to feel a little bit like Alice when she fell down the rabbit hole?"

She was surprised by his understanding, though she guessed she shouldn't have been. He'd probably already dealt with this persistent feeling of disbelief back when he'd first learned there were actual zombies in the world.

"Did you feel the same way when you learned about it?"

"That would be a giant affirmative." He let out a big sigh. "Don't worry, you'll get used to it. Either that, or it will all be over by the time you come to grips with it. Pray for the latter and in the meantime, keep on truckin'. As long as you can continue to function and work toward the goal of eliminating this threat, the better off you'll be. Take my word for it. It's not good to feel useless."

The terrain was getting more desolate the farther away they got from the airport. For the past few miles, all they'd passed was wire fence meant to hold in cattle, though there were few in sight, and acres and acres of farmland.

"It's pretty empty up here," she commented.

"Lots of space to do things where nobody would know," Sam agreed. "And we're about to head into more mountainous areas if they keep going the way they're going now. Logging country that's still heavily forested in most places. Perfect for the creatures because of the dense tree cover."

"You said they don't like sunlight, right?" She didn't want to ask, but she probably needed to know more about the zombies if they were going into the lion's den.

"Most encounters have been at night or in shade, like heavy tree cover or inside a dark building. They don't usually come out in the open unless it's dark outside. They move deceptively fast. They never run, but the slow, steady pace eats ground. If you encounter one, run as fast as you can. The newer models are capable of basic strategy and they'll surround you like wolves—encircle you so you have no way out." He watched the scanner carefully. "They're slowing. Looks like they're heading down a private road. Probably a ranch driveway or something similar. Be ready to stop the car. I'll tell you when."

"You're not going to bail out on me again, are you?" she asked, only half joking.

"Maybe. But I think there's enough room on this road to pull over. If you recall, that road in West Virginia had no shoulder and the spot I needed to get out was on a blind curve."

"Are you trying to convince me that the reason you scared me half to death and risked life and limb jumping out of a moving car was for safety?" The convolutions of the male mind still managed to astound her sometimes, despite being Henry's shadow the majority of her life.

"Yes, ma'am." He shot her a quick glance and she could

see he was laughing. "I'm all about safety."

"You'd better be," she muttered, following a long, sweeping curve of the road as it rode up the side of a heavily wooded hill.

"We should be entering a small town in a few minutes. Keep your eyes peeled for a bed-and-breakfast. There are lots of them in this part of the country. If we can find one close to where our targets just stopped, we can use it as a base of operations."

"So do you want to tell me what Zhao and Krychek were talking about during the flight?"

He frowned and a muscle ticked on the side of his jaw. Whatever it was, it had to be something bad.

"A demonstration." His voice was grim.

"Wait. Do you mean they're going to kill someone and turn them into….one of those things?" She was horrified at the idea.

"Yeah. Apparently Sugden promised them they'd see proof the technology worked as advertised before the bidding began. Our buddies, Butt and Ugly, were saying how the demo had better be really good to justify the multimillion dollar price tag Sugden was asking for."

"How far do you think Sugden will go? With the demonstration, I mean." She was almost afraid to ask.

"For that much money?" Sam sighed heavily. "The man's already proven he has no conscience. I think he'll go as far as he can without getting caught, and he won't care who he kills in the process. Which is why I have to stop him."

They'd entered the sleepy little town perched on the side of the mountain. A few blocks into the village, Emily spotted a sign.

"Just what the doctor ordered," she said with some satisfaction, though thoughts of what Sugden had planned disturbed her on a deep level. She stopped the car in front of the bed-and-breakfast. It looked quaint and had a pseudo-Victorian façade. "Do you want me to go in and see if they have a vacancy?"

"We should go in together. It would look more natural."

"But you want to stay and keep an eye on your GPS, don't you?" She could see it in his expression.

"Yeah. But I can walk and chew gum." He opened the car door and got out, still watching his phone. "Get your sweater out of the back. Put it on over your uniform shirt. You do the talking. I'll be just another stressed out yuppie glued to his PDA." He still had his windbreaker on, which made them look a lot less like pilots and a lot more like a couple out for a casual ramble through the countryside.

Sam's plan worked like a charm. Within moments they were ensconced in an upstairs room with a private bath. The rental car was parked around back under cover of a big carport, not visible from the road or even from the air.

"This is good," Sam said, checking the view from the window. "We're not too far from the GPS hit as the crow flies and it looks like it's straight uphill through this woodland. I should be able to get there on foot from here."

"Are you sure?" She looked at the uncertain terrain at the back of the house. Their window faced the back of the house, looking out onto the steeply graded mountainside. "It looks a little rough."

"Piece of cake," Sam countered, keeping one eye on his phone while he reached for his big duffel bag. He pulled out items of clothing and a big pair of well worn boots.

"This Clark Kent changing into Superman routine is becoming familiar," she mused as he shucked his dark uniform slacks and pulled on a pair of camo cargo pants. An olive drab T-shirt replaced the white one he'd had on under his white pilot's shirt.

He laughed outright at her comparison as he laced up his boots. All the while, he kept one eye on the GPS screen, probably to be sure his target stayed where he expected it to stay.

"So what's the plan?" she asked as he finished his transformation from charter pilot to Green Beret.

"I'm going to hike up there and take a look around before

night falls, to see what we're up against and what the setup is. I'll be back in about ninety minutes. Then I'll call in to the base and make my report. Then we have dinner and coo at each other like we're in love." Her heart stuttered when he mentioned the "L" word, but he breezed past it. "Depending on what I find up there, I might go back out again. In fact, it's more likely than not."

"What do you want me to do while you're doing all that?" She didn't like the sound of him doing all the work and her sitting around counting the cabbage roses on the wallpaper.

"You're going to stay in the room and pretend we're having a good time all by ourselves. Keep up appearances while I sneak away. Call your brother, if you're bored. Tell him how annoyed you are that I've left you sitting here while I'm having all the fun." He dropped a kiss on her forehead as he teased her.

"I don't know that I'd call risking your life fun," she muttered as he chuckled and moved toward the window, opening it wide and peeking out. It looked like he was scoping the area in preparation for a jump. Was he serious? They were on the second floor.

She squeaked when he lifted his foot and stepped over the sill. He paused and turned a grin on her that at any other time would have made her tummy flip. He was just that sexy. But not when she was worried he'd break a leg or crack his skull on the way down.

"Don't worry, Em. This is what I do for a living and if you're around me for any length of time at all, you'll soon learn I'm really hard to kill."

"Is that supposed to comfort me?"

"Come here, Emily."

His voice was pitched low. He straddled the windowsill, one leg dangling outside the building, the rest of his body inside. She almost didn't want to obey the command in his voice, but in the end she was powerless to resist him. She went to him, moving closer when he clasped her waist and pulled her in for a deep, drugging kiss.

How he could dangle twelve feet off the ground and still kiss the sense out of her, she'd never know. He released her lips and his gaze met hers.

"Please try not to worry about me, Emily, although I have to admit I'm touched that you do." His grin charmed her. "Trust me, I'm really good at my job. They wouldn't have sent me if I weren't."

His reasoning did bring some comfort. He'd known exactly what to do at the convenience store in West Virginia and he was calm, cool, and collected in the cockpit. She'd seen his flying skills and some of his fighting skills already. He had to be the best of the best if they'd tapped him for this all-important job, she reasoned.

And she could see he needed her to pull herself together. She didn't want him worrying about her worrying. Anything that distracted him from keeping himself safe was bad. She shored up her reserves and tried to give him a smile.

"I do trust you, Sam. Now go before someone sees your leg dangling out the window. Just be careful."

"Always." He ducked his head out the window and moved to the side.

CHAPTER 14

She hadn't seen it before but there was a trellised metal pole running down the side of the building. Glancing upward, she saw it was attached to a lightning rod. Seemed odd to have a house equipped like that out here on the side of a mountain, but people did all kinds of strange things to protect their property from any possible threat. In this case, she was glad of the sturdy structure that allowed Sam to climb down safely. No doubt, he'd come back the same way, unseen by anyone inside the house. Handy.

Emily watched him climb silently down the pole and melt away into the woods. He was gone in less than a minute, completely out of sight. She tried to see him in the woods but it was impossible considering the dense foliage. She gave up and closed the window, leaving it unlocked for Sam's return.

Taking Sam's advice, she pulled out her handy new phone and called her brother, Henry. A short way into the conversation, she realized that Sam had probably known that by her calling Henry, she'd be alerting the team about what Sam was up to at that moment. He'd probably planned it that way. Having her tell her brother that Sam was doing reconnaissance was as good as making a report to their commander.

She had no doubt that Henry would report in minute detail what she told him. His questioning was too detailed. He wanted a rundown of their actions since waking up that morning. She gave it to him, hoping to help Sam's mission in some small way. It was clear that Sam was too busy to make the report himself, and she wanted someone to know where they were and what he was doing should Sam run into trouble.

Sam was right. The phone call to Henry did make her feel better. She learned that he was still at Fort Bragg for the time being, but he'd be returning to his home base later that day. They talked around the whole zombie issue, but it was clear he'd been briefed on the mission and what they were up against. Finally, she just had to tell him what she'd seen. She wanted Henry to comfort her as he had when they were children.

"It was awful, Hank." That particular nickname didn't come out until the situation was dire. It felt pretty dire now, as she remembered what she'd seen in West Virginia. "That poor man. It was like something out of a horror movie."

"It's okay, punkin." His soothing voice over the phone helped, as it always had when they were little. "I haven't seen it in person, but I've heard all about it. I still can't quite believe it's possible."

"Believe it." Her tone was wry. "It was the most terrible thing I've ever seen in my life. They have to stop this. They can't let this go any farther. And I can't believe Scott got Praxis messed up in this. What in the world was he thinking?"

"I think he was probably looking for a fat paycheck."

"He's already CEO. He makes a lot of money running Praxis Air. How much money can one person want?"

"For some people, there's no limit. They want everything. Too much is not enough."

They talked for a few more minutes before ending the call. Henry was supportive, as always, and worried for her safety. He made her promise multiple times to be careful and to do exactly as Sam instructed should they get into a dangerous situation. She began to understand how annoying her warnings must have been to Sam after Henry had made her promise for the third time. She made a resolution not to be so bothersome when and if Sam returned. She'd keep her fears and insecurities to herself and trust that he knew what he was doing. She'd try, at least.

She had begun to pace when she heard a soft swishing noise from the direction of the window. Sure enough, Sam was lifting the sash from the outside, then climbing nimbly inside. She rushed over to him.

"How did it go?"

His mouth was set in a grim line. "They're holed up on a big ranch just over the ridge from this town. It's rugged terrain but they found a clear spot for the ranch house and outbuildings. No easy cover for approach to any of the structures, which makes ground surveillance difficult, but they're definitely there. I may have seen Sugden pass one of the windows. I'm about fifty-five percent positive it was him." He looked annoyed. "I have to be sure he's up there before we call in the cavalry. The show won't start without him and if he's not there, we have no reason to storm the place and tip our hand. I'll tell you one thing, though, whoever is running the show up there, they've got their own small army. Lots of men with lots of firepower."

"That's not good." Her heart sank at the news of what Sam and his teammates might be going up against. At the same time, she was relieved they'd found their quarry. With any luck, this horrible situation might be coming to an end. "When do you think they'll begin their demonstration?"

"Good question." Sam moved into the room and drew the curtains on the big windows before turning on the lights. It was still light out but Emily figured he didn't want anyone looking in at them, just in case anybody could. "I don't know Sugden well enough to predict, but I know some folks who do." He pulled out his phone and hit speed dial. The call was connected almost instantly.

Sam reported his findings while Emily listened

unabashedly to his side of the conversation. She made a mental note of the coordinates he gave for the ranch he'd scouted. She also committed his description of the layout of the place to memory…just in case. He was pretty adamant about not letting her help, but if he got into trouble, she wouldn't just stand by. She'd do whatever she could to help, regardless of his wishes and admonitions.

When Sam had finished his report, he sat back to listen. Whoever he had on the other end of the line apparently had a lot of information to impart. When he finally ended the call, he didn't look happy. He flipped the phone closed slowly, then tapped it against the point of his chin, seeming to contemplate his next move.

"What did they say?" Emily couldn't take the silence. Funny, that, when it was Sam who was the man of action. Emily was supposed to be a bystander at this point, but she couldn't help feeling involved in this—whatever it was—up to her neck.

Instead of answering her question, he came back with a few of his own. "Do you think we can take a few days off? Sort of a lovers' getaway? Or would that bring mongo trouble down on us both from the airline?"

"I could do it. It won't be easy, but I can swing it. How many days do we need here?"

"At least two, maybe more."

"I'll get us taken off the flight schedule for the week."

She reached for her phone and made the necessary call while Sam got out their topographical maps from his pilot's case. She'd wondered why he hadn't left that stuff on the plane but it made sense to her now. He'd need those maps if he was going to be running around in the hills.

Sissy, the receptionist, teased her a bit but complied when Emily told her what she wanted her to do. She ended the call with a click, knowing she was going to catch hell from Buddy when they got back—if they got back. Emily began to worry that they were getting into something very dangerous up here in the hills and their odds of survival weren't very good at all.

"We're clear for the week," she reported.

Sam looked up from his charts. His expression was taut with tension, but he seemed otherwise relaxed.

"Come take a look at this."

She was surprised by his offer, but went to stand beside him. He'd covered the room's only table with maps.

"This is where we are now." He pointed to a spot on the map. The concentric rings indicated elevation on this map and she was well familiar with how to read it. His finger traced a path over the ridge and stopped. "This is where they are. The ranch seems to take up most of the top of this hill and down into this small valley. Between us and them, right here—" he pointed to a spot on the map where the elevation rose sharply, "—is a no man's land of rocky forest and steep slopes. That should provide some cover for the town should things at the ranch get out of hand."

"What did your commander say? Is he dispatching me to help?"

His mouth thinned to a grim line. "Not yet. Other reliable intel from the team puts Sugden in Virginia. They're going to check that out before moving the show up here."

"I thought you said you saw Sugden through the window."

"Not clearly. I can't be positive it was him and the intel is solid that he's elsewhere right now. He's the big fish. If they can catch him before he gets here to do his demonstration, it's over. I hope the team gets him in Virginia and we don't end up dealing with him here, but just in case, I'm going to do more recon tonight."

"Don't you need to sleep sometime?" she challenged, concerned for his welfare. Tired men made mistakes. It was as true for pilots as it probably was for soldiers.

"I'll catch a combat nap, then head out. With any luck I won't be gone all night."

"Just most of it, I'll bet," she muttered. He chuckled at her response and some of the heavy burden that had settled on his shoulders seemed to have lifted for a few minutes.

"Yeah, I'll be out most of the night but look at the bright

side." He put one arm around her waist and drew her close for a quick cuddle. "With any luck, we can spend all day tomorrow in bed." His head dipped and he kissed her long and slow, giving her a preview of what they might enjoy when she finally did get him in bed for any length of time.

He drew back all too soon. The moment stretched out between them as she looked deep into his eyes, mesmerized by the emotion she thought she read there, though he didn't speak it out loud. It was still too soon, perhaps. Or maybe she was fooling herself to dare to hope that he felt about her the same way she felt about him.

She stepped back, out of his arms, and the moment died.

"What do you want to do for dinner?" She had to think of practical things and get her head out of the clouds.

They'd been on the road since landing and hadn't taken time to eat. As a result, hunger was starting to make itself known.

"There's a restaurant two blocks away in the heart of town and a convenience store just beyond that. I say, dinner first, then we pick up some supplies at the store in case we get hungry later. We'll be keeping odd hours so it might be wise to make use of the mini fridge in here. If for nothing else, at least keep some cold drinks on hand in case you get thirsty."

She noticed the small fridge in one corner for the first time. It was well camouflaged, as was the small, white microwave that sat on top of it. A coffeemaker was on the tiny console table outside the bathroom along with complementary coffee and tea fixings. They'd definitely found a B&B with all the amenities in the middle of nowhere.

"Did you bring any casual clothes with you?" Sam asked, already rifling through his duffel bag.

"Don't worry. I'm a past master at packing for all occasions. I had to learn the hard way to be prepared for any contingency when I started flying. You never know what the client will want you to do or invite you to attend while you're in a strange town."

"Really?" Sam looked interested and less tense, so she

went on. Anything to help him be at ease.

"From rock concerts to art showings to business dinners. It doesn't happen often, but certain repeat clients will sometimes leave an invite for me as a perk if they know I'm at loose ends."

She went to her small bag and took out the small black ball that was the most useful item of clothing ever. It was made of jersey knit that didn't wrinkle and had a few variations on how to wear it. She opted for the rather conservative black sweater—rather than the black mini-dress configuration she thought Sam would've liked—and threw a big, colorful scarf around her shoulders.

Fluffing her hair with her fingers, she was done in under five minutes. She turned around to find Sam watching her.

"Impressive. I bet you could give lessons on urban camo. I'd never peg you for a pilot now. You look good enough to eat." He moved in but she evaded him.

"Real food first, then you get to eat me." She blushed at the way that sounded but he only laughed.

"I'll hold you to that, sweetheart." He held the door for her as they left their room and went out of the B&B the conventional way, waving to the nice lady who ran the place on their way out.

Sam had changed too. He'd opted for his black pilot's pants and dress shoes with the olive drab T-shirt and windbreaker. It was cool enough in the evening up here in the mountains to warrant the jacket, so nobody would remark on it. It also provided cover for the giant handgun she'd seen him tuck into his waistband. Her eyes had widened, but she hadn't said anything to him about it. It was enough to know he was armed and ready for anything.

They were seated in the restaurant with little fuss and made quick choices from the simple menu. The food was piping hot and very good. She filled the void in her stomach with the home cooking and was relaxing over a second glass of iced tea when Sam reminded her of why they were here.

"I want to get back and sleep this off before I go out

again," he said in a low voice. "Are you almost ready to go?"

He'd refrained from mentioning anything to do with his mission during what turned out to be a most pleasant dinner. Suddenly it was all back. All the tension. All the fear. She put down her glass of tea.

"Ready when you are."

He paid the bill and they stopped at the small convenience store to get supplies before heading back to the B&B. They were quiet on the way back. Not that they'd had much to talk about at dinner, or since leaving their room at the B&B. Emily was in a somber mood, scared to death of what the night might bring to Sam, all on his own, out there in the wilderness.

She knew he was highly trained and could take care of himself, but that didn't stop her from worrying. She knew also that he had to go out and do his duty. There was nobody else here who could stop Sugden and protect the people of this sleepy little mountain town should things get out of hand. It was up to Sam and she had to stand by him, support him, and help him in whatever way she could.

They walked arm in arm, like two lovers out for a relaxing evening stroll. They were lovers, but the stroll was anything but relaxing. The owner of the B&B was a little old lady named Mrs. McGillicuddy. She waylaid them on their way back into the house, stopping to chat and remind them about breakfast in the morning.

Emily had one moment of discomfort when Sam told their hostess that they wouldn't be needing room service during their stay. He politely implied that they'd be up in that room humping like bunnies, which made Emily blush as Mrs. McGillicuddy playfully swatted Sam on the forearm with the magazine she'd been reading when they walked in. Luckily, the old lady didn't appear to expect Emily to say much and before long they made their escape to the rented room, locking the door behind them.

"Wake me at eleven thirty," Sam said as he peeled off the windbreaker he'd been wearing. He placed his handgun on the bedside table after checking the safety and kicked off his shoes before collapsing on the bed. He was asleep moments later.

That was a neat trick. No tossing and turning, trying to go to sleep for him. Sam simply decided to conk out. The next thing you know, he's asleep.

Emily sat in the room's overstuffed chair and turned the television on low to catch up with the local news. She also took a good long look at the maps, committing the area to memory. You never know when the information might come in handy, she reasoned, and it gave her something to do besides worry about what was to come later that night for Sam.

Sam woke at Emily's gentle urging, at exactly eleven thirty. He felt rested and ready to take on whatever might come his way in the woods that night. Emily leaned over him to one side of the king size bed. That would never do. He wanted to feel her against him, if only for a few moments.

He wrapped his arms around her waist and tugged her off balance, controlling her descent, breaking her fall with his body. She was soft and warm against him. That was more like it. Without warning, he caught her mouth with his, loving the mellow taste of her, the sweetness of her lips and the soft sigh of her breath as she surrendered to him. He liked the sound of that best of all.

Sam would have loved to stay like that, with her as a warm, wiggling, living blanket all night, but duty called. Much as he didn't want to move, he had to leave soon to see if he could find out exactly what was going on up on the mountain.

Reluctantly, he ended the kiss, drawing away from her.

"Do you know how to handle a handgun?"

She looked at him quizzically for a moment. "Yeah. Shotgun and I used to go plinking out in the woods in the summer when we were teenagers. I got a Ruger 9mm a few years ago and have kept up with target practice whenever one of my brothers wants to go to the range with me, which is at least once a month. Why?"

"I'm going to leave one of my weapons with you. I picked up an extra in West Virginia." He was glad now that he had. He rolled her to a sitting position as he got up and went to his duffel. He took out the black holster and checked that the gun was safe before handing it to her. "This model isn't that much different from your Ruger in concept. Take a look."

She handled the handgun with confidence, showing him she knew what she was doing. She clicked the safety on and off a few times, checking the empty magazine and familiarizing herself with the operation of the weapon. She asked a few questions and he answered, showing her the features of this particular weapon. Once he was satisfied she had the basic operation down pat, he handed her two additional clips of ammunition.

"Don't mess with these bullets. They're frangibles, loaded with a toxin that will turn any organic matter to a pile of goo in about thirty seconds. You see one of those creatures, you shoot it one time and count to thirty. Don't waste the ammo making multiple shots. It won't dissolve any faster and chances are if you see one zombie, you'll see more. If any of the creatures gets this far, there will have been too many for me to deal with alone. Don't look for me. Don't wait for me. Do what you have to do to get to the car and get the hell out of here. Call the base. Get help, but whatever you do, don't stay here."

"You're scaring me."

"Good. This is serious. That said, I honestly don't think you need to worry about anything tonight. This is only a precaution. I want you to know what to do if there's trouble. Being prepared is half the battle."

She still looked frightened and he regretted having had to put that look on her face. "I got it. If I see one of those guys, I shoot it and run as fast and as far as I can. I get help. But what about you? If they get past you, does that mean you're dead?"

"No." He had to reassure her on that point at least. She looked so afraid for him it was touching, really. "I have a lot of experience with these guys and all kinds of tricks up my sleeve. Try not to worry. If you have to run, don't assume I'm gone. I'll be in touch with base if at all possible. Worst case scenario, you can get a sitrep from them."

"Sit rep?" she repeated, clearly not understanding the jargon.

"Situation report," he clarified. "We can keep in touch by phone. They can double as field radios in a pinch. I have an earpiece." He dug the little bugger out of his pants pocket and stuck it in his ear. "I can call you on Tac One. Give me your phone. I'll show you."

He spent a few minutes showing her the hidden features of her phone. There were several Tactical channels.

"It's like the walkie-talkie feature on some phones," she commented.

"Yeah, it's like that but it doesn't make noises that would give us away in the field."

"Can you stay on the radio with me for a bit while you go out tonight? If there were trouble I could phone it in for you while you dealt with it."

"That's sweet of you, but don't you want to get some sleep?" He was touched that she'd want to monitor him and help keep him safe.

"I doubt I'll be able to sleep much until I'm sure you're doing okay. Can we try it at least for a while?"

He drew her into a hug. "Yeah, we can." He kissed the crown of her head, deeply moved by her desire to help keep him safe. It had been far too long since anyone had really cared about what happened to him.

He left a few minutes later, after giving her the rest of the lowdown on the frangible rounds and how to handle them. He went over a few more safety points while he changed into his camo gear. Then he climbed out the window and down into the tree line before he could change his mind. He called her using the radio feature on their phones a short while later.

"Hey sweetheart, you got your ears on?" he whispered into the headset, keeping his voice low.

"Where are you?" she asked.

"Just reached the top of the ridge. Not much going on up here but it's a beautiful night for a little sneak and peek. The stars are out but there's only a sliver of moon. Brisk. Just enough chill in the air to make you feel alive."

"Thank you for the weather report." She couldn't keep the wry amusement from her tone and he had to suppress a chuckle.

Silence stretched while he navigated the last bit of heavy woods before the tree line. The ranch house and outbuildings sat in the middle of a large clearing. He couldn't get much closer without being seen. He sat back to wait and see what could be seen from this vantage point. He'd move around the perimeter over time to view all angles, but he might as well start here. He had a good view of the largest barn and the front of the two story farm house.

"I can see the house." He took out a small set of binoculars from one of his cargo pockets. "Looks like there's a party on the upstairs deck. Zhao and Krychek are both there along with a buffet table stacked with finger foods and drinks." He looked around, scoping out the barn.

Sam could only see the back side of the barn and the open space between the front of the barn and the house. A man walked rapidly over the ground toward the house, his back to Sam. He entered the house, shutting the door behind him, then reappeared several moments later on the balcony with Zhao and Krychek. He faced Sam. It was Sugden.

"Oh, crap." Sam drew his weapon.

"What is it?" came Emily's worried voice in his ear.

"Sugden is here and the viewing party is up on the second floor. I think the demonstration is about to start." Silence greeted his words and he knew Emily was worried. That couldn't be helped.

"Should we call for help?"

"Yeah. I'll do that but I want to get a little more intel for them first."

"What are you going to do?" Her voice was rock solid though he knew this news disturbed her. That pilot training certainly made for a cool head in times of crisis. He was glad of that now.

"I'm moving to a new position so I can get a better look. I'm going to sign off with you in a few seconds and call this in to the team."

"How long do you think it'll take for them to get here?"

"Several hours. I'll have to hold down the fort until the cavalry shows up." He was in position. He now had a better view of the opening of the barn, though he was still off to one side so he could keep an eye on the viewing party on the balcony. "Hold on, sweetheart. I've got to make that call. I'll be back on with you as soon as I can. Hang tight."

He switched from the radio function on the unit to the sat phone function and placed the call. Commander Sykes picked up on the second ring.

"Sir, I've got a visual on Dr. Sugden here in Idaho."

"Are you sure," Sykes barked.

"I've got eyes on him right now, sir. He's sitting on a balcony with Zhao and Krychek. Looks like they're about to view a show. They've got refreshments set up and are unreachable from the ground. Wait...I have activity. Confirmed. One zombie heading out of the barn on the ground level, toward the viewing party's location on the balcony."

Shots rang out. Sam scanned with his binoculars until he saw muzzle flashes in the lit area between the barn and the house.

"Shots fired," he reported. "There are three men on the ground, firing at the creature. It's moving toward the closest." As Sam watched, that first gunman went down with one long scrape of the creature's claws. Despite multiple direct hits from the gunmen, the creature kept going, taking its steady, menacing steps seeming unstoppable. "He's toast. One gunman down in the dirt. The zombie is closing in on the second."

Then the second man went down. The third tried to run, but the zombie caught him as he scrambled for cover behind one of the vehicles. No doubt he was trying to get into the car to get away but it had been locked against such a circumstance. The third man died in a spray of bright red blood as the zombie's claws severed his jugular. Then the creature began feasting and Sam's stomach turned at the sight.

He reported it all to Matt Sykes, even as he heard sounds of furious activity on the commander's end of the line.

"We're gearing up. We can be there in four hours. We'll chopper in on the other side of the ridge and jog it in to meet you. Can you hold position?"

"So far, the activity seems to be localized between the house and barn but I'm not sure what's going to happen when those three casualties rise to join their maker."

"Understood."

"Sir, I noted a good sized clearing when I was on my way in." He gave Sykes the coordinates so the team could use the spot to either land a chopper or rappel in from one, depending on what the team leader decided to do when they got here. The situation could have changed drastically by then, so it was best to leave all options open.

"Where is Captain Parkington?" Sykes asked.

"Back at the B&B. I've been in touch with her since I left there and she's aware of some of what's going on."

He wasn't sure if the commander would be on his ass about disclosing the events of the evening to a civilian before he'd reported in to his commanding officer, but no way was Sam going to leave Emily out of the loop. Her safety was of paramount importance to him and if he couldn't be there to see to it himself, he wanted her on guard for danger, armed with all the intel he could give her. If that got him in trouble with his CO, then so be it.

"That's all right." The approval in Sykes' voice took Sam by surprise. "You might as well give her the sitrep so she can be on guard. Is she armed?"

"Yes, sir. I gave her my spare with the special ammo." Sam knew that hadn't been authorized, but he'd live with his decisions and their consequences.

"Good." Apparently, there weren't going to be any consequences to that particular decision right now. "Keep her in the loop when practical and tell her to stay put as long as she's safe where she is."

Sam switched over to Tac One after ironing out a few more logistical points with the commander. Sam would call back to base with further updates as things on the ground developed. For now, he had a moment to warn Emily to be careful.

"Emily? Come in, Em." He kept his voice low though the woods here were dense and full of wildlife. Sam had climbed a tree to get a better vantage point and now rested against the trunk, most of his weight on a large, branching limb.

"I'm here." She sounded competent and eager, which translated in pilot terms to scared and anxious.

"Bad news. This is going down now. One zombie just made three more. They haven't risen yet, but it's only a matter of time. The team is on its way."

"Tell me what I can do."

"Sit tight and don't leave the building. Don't even leave the room. Hole up and wait for the all clear from me or one of the team. Their ETA is under four hours. There are at least four infected creatures now, maybe more. By the time the cavalry arrives, there could be a lot more. Keep the weapon I gave you loaded, and on you at all times. Don't go anywhere without it. Just be careful who you shoot. That toxin is as lethal to living people as it is to the creatures. One shot, and whatever you hit is dead. No going back."

"I get it," she replied. "But is there anything I can do to help you? As you said before, it's not good to feel useless."

"Right now, the best way to help me is to keep yourself safe."

"I'll do that. And you do the same, okay?"

"You may not be able to reach me on the radio. I'll probably be on the phone a lot of the time or otherwise unable to talk." He didn't want her to worry over much if she tried to reach him and couldn't. "If you run into trouble, remember what I told you. Get out of Dodge and head for the hills. Help is already on the way and they're better equipped to deal with this particular problem than you."

"I understand. Sam…" She hesitated, which was out of character for her. "I…" She was having a hard time spitting it out, but he thought he understood. The situation was dire enough that he wanted to get something off his chest. Maybe she did too. And maybe if he went first, it would make it easier.

"I didn't want to say it this way but…I think I…I love you, Emily." Silence met his soul-bearing, so he tried to give her an out. "Stay safe for me. We'll sort the rest out later, okay?"

He'd thought it might make it easier, but maybe he'd just made everything a lot more awkward. He waited, breath held for her to speak. Finally, she broke her silence and her voice was breathy with emotion.

"I think I love you too, Sam."

Damn, but he loved the gentle way she spoke the words that made his heart lift. He'd never wanted to hear those words from a woman as badly as he had in that moment. He felt about ten feet tall but this was the absolute wrong moment to be sharing such intimate thoughts.

"I want to kiss you so bad right now, Em."

"Me too."

"But it'll have to wait. I sure picked a bad time to bare my soul, huh?" He chuckled into the headset wishing he had her right there, in front of him, in his arms. "I've got to go now but remember what I said and sit tight. I'll be back before you know it. Love you, Em." He tried out the words, savoring the feel of them on his tongue. They felt right.

"Love you too, Sam. Stay safe and come back to me." The love word felt even more right when she said it to him. He could listen to her say that over and over. Maybe for the rest of their lives.

But he had things to do first before he could go back to that sleepy little town and claim his woman. First he had to make things safe for them to spend the next couple of weeks holed up in bed, solidifying the claims they'd just made on each other. He looked forward to that with every fiber of his being.

First things first. He had zombies to track and kill. And a mad scientist and his buyers to stop. Nothing would stop him now. Not with Emily and the promise of love that could last a lifetime waiting for him back in town.

CHAPTER 15

One by one, the three dead men began to rise. Sugden stood up and began to gesture as the creatures started walking toward the balcony, stopping just below as if wondering how to get up there to their quarry. Luckily for the men who watched from above, climbing seemed beyond the zombies' poor intellects.

The creatures stood and watched. All but the last one was mostly intact, though they were all stained red with their own blood. The last one had fared much worse, having been nibbled on by its maker. His nose was gone. Only a red, gaping hole marked where it had been. Gruesome was a good word to describe it, Sam thought from the safety of his makeshift tree stand on the perimeter of the woods. He could see the details through his binoculars, the area between the barn and house well lit by floodlights.

Sugden was holding forth, like a lecturer in a college class who liked to listen to himself talk but at length he finally turned to survey his creations. It looked like he was giving them simple orders to walk to the barn and back again. They did this a few times before Sam spied the rifle. Sugden had it leaning up against the balcony rail. He must've placed it there before Sam had gotten on scene. It wasn't visible until

Sugden picked it up and took aim at one of the zombies.

He shot five times and Sam heard right off that the retort wasn't that of a regular weapon. Sam was familiar with the sound. It was a dart gun. Apparently Sugden had come up with his own version of the toxin that destroyed the zombies.

Sam started counting, trying to gauge how effective Sugden's concoction was. It was a full two minutes before the creature staggered to a halt and fell to its knees. It didn't dissolve the way Sam was familiar with. Instead, it lay on the ground in a large, lumpy pile. It was immobilized. That was the important thing. But Sugden's toxin didn't seem half as potent as the stuff Sam had loaded in his handgun at the moment.

The other three zombies saw what happened to their friend and scattered. Sugden fired after them but only hit two of them and only with one dart each from what Sam could see. The man couldn't hit the side of a barn with a flamethrower and he'd just turned his gunmen into zombies. That wasn't great planning on his part.

It'd be up to Sam to track the creatures through the woods, then quietly take them out when he was far enough away that the sound of his gunfire wouldn't be noticed. Sam had had more difficult missions, but he wasn't sure when.

"Son of a bitch," he muttered under his breath as he dropped from the tree he'd used as his hiding place.

Now he'd have to hump it through the dark forest after a couple of zombies to make sure none got into town. He had three creatures on his hands. He didn't want to let them multiply the problem by creating more.

Emily had absolutely no warning when the door to her room at the B&B burst in. She was caught completely off guard with no way to defend herself.

Added to that was the shock. The intruder was none other than Scott Southerland and he had a huge gun in his hand, trained on her chest.

"Scott?" He was the dead last person she'd expected to

see. She'd thought she was relatively safe as long as she stayed inside the B&B.

"You're coming with me, bitch." His voice was a low, urgent snarl. "And if you make one sound on the way out of this mausoleum, it'll be your own grave."

Yeah, now that was pretty clear. The jig was up.

"Why?"

He actually laughed, though it sounded more like a disgusted snicker.

"You've interfered in my plans for the last time. I plan on making a clean getaway and my friends will know what to do with you to keep it that way. Now come on." He waved the gun again and she stood, glad she'd put the ankle holster on under her jeans when she'd changed a few minutes ago. The phone was in her pocket. She only hoped Scott didn't notice it. "Where's your boyfriend?"

"Who?" She tried to bluff but knew it was going to be an uphill battle as she preceded him out the bedroom door.

"The new pilot," he sneered. "Come on, I know he's been poking around in my business. Just like you. And for that, you're going to pay." He nudged her with the barrel of the gun as she hesitated at the top of the stairs.

She walked downstairs, trying to think of how she could get out of this. Nothing came to mind. Scott had the gun and he looked ready to use it.

"I don't know where he went."

"Maybe so," Scott allowed. "But I guess it doesn't matter. If he's out in the woods, he'll be dead by morning."

She gasped allowing some of her dismay to show. Let Scott think what he wanted. He'd always underestimated her as a pilot because she was female. Maybe she could use that to her advantage somehow in this situation.

He prodded her toward the front door, which was unlocked. It shouldn't have been at this time of night. That's when she looked over her shoulder into the living room and saw Mrs. McGillicuddy tied to a chair, her eyes wide and full of tears with a gag in her mouth.

At least Scott hadn't killed the nice little old lady. That was something, she supposed. There weren't a whole lot of other guests, but somebody would find Mrs. McGillicuddy at some point, so she should be okay. Emily's future was less certain.

She didn't see any alternative but to get in the red Porsche waiting at the curb. The roads in the town were empty this time of night. Most of the respectable citizens of the sleepy burgh were fast asleep in their beds. Although it went against her better judgment to get in the vehicle, she went along with Scott's demands for now. She'd get her chance…she hoped. She just had to wait for the right moment.

As it turned out, the two who'd been hit with one dart apiece were relatively easy to track. Sam followed them over the ridge line and dropped them within sight of the B&B, though they'd have had a hell of a time getting down the incline the way they moved.

The new ammo and increased range of the weapon made it a lot easier for one man to take out multiple targets from farther out in faster time. The two creatures were down to piles of organic goo in mere minutes.

He'd totally lost track of the third one though. Sam dropped markers on his two kills and took a quick look around. It was hard to tell in the dark woods without proper night vision gear, but he couldn't pick up sign of the third creature.

Deciding to circle back to the ranch, Sam took only a moment to check that the light was still on in their bedroom and their rental car was still in its parking spot behind the B&B. Emily was safe enough for now. She'd stay put while he dealt with the threat in the woods.

Strengthening his resolve, Sam turned back to the dark forest and wound his way back through the trees, keeping a sharp eye out for the last of the three amigos. It didn't sit well with him that there was definitely a creature out there, bent on killing, but Sugden was the real target. Sam had to keep eyes on the scientist and his buyers to be sure they cut off the head of the snake.

Prioritizing two awful choices, Sam moved back into sight of the barn and ranch house. Sugden and his two buyers were still on the balcony. They were seated around the table now, talking earnestly. Sam guessed the bidding was on.

He called in to base to give them a sitrep and have them warn the drop team that there was at least one zombie on the loose in the woods between their drop zone and the ranch. Maybe they'd get the bastard on their way in. In a perfect world, they'd get him before he managed to kill anybody else and spread the contagion.

Sykes answered before the first ring faded. "Sitrep," he barked.

Sam filled him in on events since their last call had ended.

Suddenly, a red Porsche sped up the drive, spitting gravel as it came to a stop in the pool of light between the barn and the house. Sugden stood, agitated as he yelled something down at the man who stepped from the driver's side.

It was Scott Southerland. Now that wasn't what Sam expected. He watched as the scene unfolded.

Scott was obviously shouting up at Sugden and Sugden was shouting back, his expression angry. Trouble in paradise, perhaps?

Scott stalked around to the passenger side and threw open the door.

"Son of a bitch!"

"What is it?" Sykes asked sharply but Sam didn't respond. He was too busy watching the scene unfold.

Emily stood from the passenger side of the car and for one heart stopping moment, doubt crept in. Was she there voluntarily? She wasn't tied up or anything. Not that he could see.

Then sanity prevailed. No way was Emily playing for the wrong team. She had to have been coerced to accompany Scott out to the ranch.

A moment later, Sam saw the handgun Scott held. Sam tried his best to see if he could tell the model and barrel size.

He couldn't tell if it was the gun Sam had given Emily being used against her—in which case the ammo was absolutely lethal and he couldn't afford to let Scott get off even a single shot. If it were a regular gun with regular ammo that was bad enough, but the toxic frangibles were a lot worse.

Scott prodded her with the gun barrel toward the house but Sam still couldn't tell from this distance whether it was her gun or not.

"Sam! Are you there?" Matt Sykes' voice came to him as if out of a fog and Sam had to refocus.

"I've got to go, sir." Sam had to do something. He didn't know what yet, but he'd better come up with something real fast.

"No way, Sam. Wait for backup." It was clear that was an order even though Sykes didn't say the words.

"I can't, sir. Scott Southerland just pulled up in a Porsche. He's got Emily. He's holding her at gunpoint in the hot zone." Sam dropped from the tree and prepared for action. "I hate to do this, but I'm going Elvis on you. Sorry, sir. You can court martial me later. If I make it."

"Dammit, Sam!" Sykes was clearly losing patience. "The team is almost there. Wait—"

Sam cut him off, closing the phone and tucking it into its holder at his waist. He'd never disobeyed a direct order before. Then again, he'd never seen the woman he loved held hostage by a couple of zombie-making madmen before either. Today was a day of firsts. Hopefully it wouldn't be his last.

Sam maneuvered around the perimeter to edge closer to the house. Closer to Emily. There was a point, still in the tree line, that was only about fifteen yards from the house. Sam hadn't used it before because it offered no view of the balcony, only of the barn door and part of the space between the house and barn, where the Porsche was currently parked.

He'd trade visibility for proximity and hope it didn't come back to bite him on the ass. Or that nothing else got close enough to bite him, come to think of it. There was still a zombie unaccounted for. Which only spurred him to greater speed in closing the distance between himself and Scott. He wanted to hear what the bastard was saying to Sugden. As Sam got closer, he began to be able to make out the words.

"—she's been nosing around this operation too long. I found her in that little town just over the ridge."

"How did you track her?" Sugden seemed to have calmed down from when Scott had first shown up, if his voice was anything to go by.

"She wasn't hiding her movements. She called in to the office this afternoon and had herself taken off the flight schedule. She's never done that before. I placed a few calls and found out where she'd last used the company credit card. Bingo. Back-of-beyond, Idaho. Too much of a coincidence not to check it out."

"Good thinking, Scott. You've done well."

Why did the scientist's tone suddenly set Sam's teeth on edge? The man was planning something. Sam went on even higher alert. Scott still held Emily in front of him like a prize—or a shield.

"You going to let us into the house or do I have to yell up to the balcony all night?" Scott finally asked, sounding suspicious.

Jeez, *now* the man finally realizes he's been stuck in the open? Sam didn't give the guy credit for much in the brains department.

"The house is locked up," Sugden replied. "But don't worry. You'll be all right down there. We're just concluding our business. Stay put until we've finished the meeting."

With that, Sugden stopped talking and Sam could only assume he'd returned to his meeting with the buyers. Scott shifted his weight uncomfortably. It was easy to see he didn't like being dismissed.

Sam spotted movement at the doorway to the barn. On the far side.

Oh, crap.

That last zombie was back and he was stained red with blood. He'd made at least one kill while he'd been out in the woods. And now he was stalking Scott Southerland from behind. When no warning came from the balcony, Sam knew Sugden had left both Scott and Emily to the wolves.

Sam couldn't let that happen.

He didn't give a rat's ass about Scott Southerland, but Emily's life was worth any sacrifice. He broke cover and ran toward them, firing on the run.

His first bullet went wide, embedding itself in the barn door behind the tableau of zombie, Scott, and Emily.

She saw him first and her eyes widened in fear. Scott reacted sluggishly, but still managed to bring his handgun around to take a wild shot at Sam, assuming he was the real source of threat. But he wasn't.

"Behind you!" Sam shouted. "Get down!"

Firing another of the frangible rounds, Sam nailed the zombie in the chest this time, but there was that thirty second window during which the toxin did its thing, and the creature was too close. Much too close.

One bloodstained, clawed hand reached out and slashed Scott's neck and back. Blood spurted as Scott finally realized the true danger came from behind. Scott shot wildly, most of the clip in his handgun going into the façade of the ranch house or up into the air. A lucky shot clipped Zhao, knocking him down, but Sam couldn't see much more than the fact that he was unconscious. He might even be dead.

Sam didn't really care. He wanted any possible threat to Emily eliminated and that zombie was much too close to her. Scott went down under its claws and his gun went flying. Emily dodged and wove away but she didn't get clear.

She came up, Scott's gun in her hand, aimed at the balcony. Sam quickly realized, she was keeping Sugden and Krychek at bay.

In his haste to get to her, he hadn't cared about them. If they shot him with a regular bullet, he'd heal. Even Emily had a better chance with conventional firearms injury than with the zombie.

Sam slowed, keeping in the shadow of the house, using it

for cover.

"Sugden!" he shouted to be heard above Scott's death screams as the zombie savaged him.

The zombie looked at Sam, but didn't stop gnawing on Scott, pinning his arms and legs in a savage display.

"Who are you?" Sugden shouted back.

"Someone you don't want to know. Thing is, I can let you walk away from this, as long as you don't harm the girl." He had to shout to be heard on the balcony above the noise of Scott's screams, which were beginning to die down as life left him.

"You're the lover," Sugden said as if piecing the information together. "Convenient."

"Em," Sam used a low, urgent whisper that only she could hear. "Get behind the car, then work your way into the barn. Close the door and bar it."

She shook her head slightly. Just once.

Dammit.

"Sweetheart, that thing can't hurt me. That's why they sent me. But it'll kill you and break my heart. Promise me you'll get clear."

Her eyes widened, just a bit, but she nodded almost imperceptibly as she held Scott's sparsely loaded gun trained on the balcony. She began to slowly edge away. Thank God.

That's when he saw the slight bulge in her right pant leg, down by her ankle. Good Lord, she had the frangible rounds on her. They might get out of this yet.

"You got my gun with you?" he asked urgently. Again she gave a slight nod. Damn, she was cool under pressure though he knew she had to be quaking in her shoes. He sure as hell was. "When you get to the barn, take it out and use it. I doubt Scott left much ammo in his pistol."

Knowing she at least had that small protection, he refocused his attention to keeping Sugden at bay. He could easily shoot her, just for fun. Sam was banking on the idea that Sugden wanted to see her eaten by his creation first. An added bonus to his demonstration.

"Do I have your word? Let the girl go and I'll get you out of this," he shouted up to the balcony.

"Out of what? I see only two people standing in my way and my little friend down there will take care of you both soon enough."

Oh yeah. It was official. Sam didn't like this guy at all.

"What are you going to do when half the town is eating the other half and coming after you too? How will you get your buyers to safety and complete the transaction?"

"That one down there is the last. When he's done with you two, I'll dart all three of you. End of problem."

"Then you didn't take a good look at the amount of blood on him," Sam yelled. "He's been out in the woods, making friends. I wonder what direction they'll go in and how long it'll take for them to spread the contagion enough to make a small army?"

Sugden seemed to hesitate. "I have plenty of darts."

"Yeah, and they don't work too good, do they?" Sam countered as the zombie finally finished with Scott and turned his attention to Sam, the source of all the noise. It was as good a time as any to show Sugden something he might need if he planned to sell this tech. He took aim and fired one round into the creature as it came toward him.

"Start counting," he yelled up to Sugden even as he started a silent countdown himself. He moved in the shadow of the building, leading the zombie around, waiting for it to disintegrate.

And then on the count of thirty, it slid into oblivion. A pile of goo on the flagstones leading up to the house.

Silence from above as Sam watched Emily edge closer to the big barn doors. She'd have to close those. Otherwise, it was an open invitation to every zombie in town to join her in there. They liked enclosed, dark places. Only the light at the front of the barn was on right now. The interior was still dark.

"You like my ammo?" Sam taunted, keeping Sugden's attention on him while Emily made her slow getaway. She was moving at a good pace, making no sudden movements. With any luck, she'd already be behind cover when Sugden realized what she was doing.

"Who are you? CIA?"

"Now, now, Dr. Sugden. You started this escapade with the military, what makes you think they'd just hand it over to the feds? Is Bin Zhao dead? My employers won't be happy to hear that."

"You're saying you're military? A Chinese agent?"

Sam liked how easily Sugden could be led. For a brilliant man in certain areas, he was proving stupid in most others. Sam could use that to his advantage.

"How is he? Don't lie to me now," Sam cajoled.

"Dead. Southerland got lucky with a headshot."

Sam weighed whether or not he could believe that along with what he'd seen out of the corner of his eye as he'd been running. It made sense. Zhao was probably dead. If Sugden really thought he was some kind of foreign agent, he had incentive to keep the man alive. On the other hand, if he lied and Zhao was dead, lying about it wouldn't help him.

"That's unfortunate. How about you, Mr. Krychek? You okay?"

"Who are you?" Krychek shouted back in lightly accented English.

"As I said," Sam kept stalling while Emily edged away from the line of fire. "I can get you out of this safely. I've got the ammo you'll want if you ever decide to use this technology. Sugden's darts suck from what I've seen. They take too long to work and you need far too many of them. There's also the problem of range and equipment. My ammo can be shot from regular firearms and achieve similar range to regular ammo."

"So now you're an arms dealer?" Sugden snapped angrily. He was losing his cool. He didn't like not being the smartest one in the room and the ammo thing clearly annoyed him.

Sam watched Emily clear the barn door. She was behind the wall, safe from darts. Maybe not higher caliber bullets, but the darts were the main thing he was worried about right now. That and zombies. So Emily was safe enough for now.

"I can get you out of this. For a price." Sam stalled for time, taking his phone off his belt and hitting speed dial.

He had to keep Sugden talking, to buy time for the team to arrive. Depending on how many people that zombie had killed before returning here, Sam would need their help to clean up this mess.

"What do you want?" Krychek asked. It sounded like he was getting impatient with letting Sugden run the show. "How much for the ammunition you're using?"

Sam held the phone to his ear. Sykes answered.

"Sir, Emily's inside the barn, taking cover. Scott Southerland is dead. Bin Zhao is dead. Sugden and Krychek think I'm a renegade out to sell them the T2 toxin. I'm parlaying with them now to stall for time."

"Ten million," Sam shouted upward in response to Krychek's question. He continued to haggle with him in between reporting back to Sykes.

"I took out all but one of the creatures. I finally got him a few minutes ago, but there's evidence he killed while he was out of my range. The woods probably contain one or more zombies rising from the dead right about now. Tell the team to be cautious when they get here."

"They're twenty minutes out but we have one other alternative if you and Ms. Parkington can get clear." Sykes spoke as rapidly as Sam did, in between haggling with the foreign buyer.

"Sir?"

"How many unfriendlies on site?" Sykes asked.

"Sugden killed all his men for his demonstration," Sam replied. "I'm convinced the only people left on site are him and Krychek."

"How fast can you clear the area?"

Scott Southerland's Porsche stood between Sam and the barn. From his new vantage point, he could see the keys dangling in the ignition. They could be gone at a hundred and twenty miles per hour if they could just get into the Porsche and drive away before it got shot up.

"Southerland's sports car is here. A red Porsche," he told Sykes, trying to figure a way to get them both in it and get out of there.

"Work it, Sam. Try to get in that car. I've got Parkington—the Air Force Parkington—in the air and armed to the teeth. He's got smart bombs that can take out the entire hilltop without anyone knowing he was even in the area. Or so he and his commander assure me. I've got clearance from the President. All we need is a clear shot. You've already given me the coordinates from the GPS in your phone."

"Stand by." Sam firmed his resolve and knew what he had to do.

"You want this ammo, right?" Sam yelled up to the men on the balcony. "I've got the formula for the toxin as well. Kill me and you'll spend months reverse engineering. That is, if anything survives the blast."

"What blast?" Sugden shouted.

Sam stepped into the light, one hand up, clutching his phone. "This is a trigger device. Dead man switch." Sam didn't think either of the men could tell what he was holding from that distance in the uncertain shadows cast by the floodlights. "I fall, I blow up. Considering the size and shape of the charge, you'll probably go with me."

Krychek began to applaud. "Well played, my friend," he said, walking toward the balcony railing. He actually wore a smile on his face. This cold bastard was in his element now, it was clear. Haggling over life and death with desperate men.

"I'm going in there—" he pointed over his shoulder toward the barn "—for a few minutes to let you talk this over. Give me a shout when you're ready to deal. You can call me Sam."

Krychek was going to speak, but Sugden's arm across his chest silenced him. Sugden wore a shit eating grin that made Sam nervous. He knew—or thought he knew—something

Sam didn't. *Shit*. The die was cast now, he had to play it through.

Sam headed for the barn, never taking his eyes off the men on the balcony.

When he cleared the door, he ducked to the side and spun around, looking for Emily. She was safe. Standing a few feet away, near what looked like a row of barred cells that contained stainless steel tables and a variety of high tech medical equipment. Sam had seen something like this before.

"Emily," he breathed her name as she rushed into his arms. He hugged her for a quick, timeless moment before setting her away from him. "When I give the signal, I want you to jump in the car. We need to clear out of here as fast as possible so your brother can do his stuff."

"My brother?" Understanding dawned in her eyes even as she asked the question. She knew what her brother's fighter-bomber could do. She understood the concept of air support better than most other civilians.

"You're using the frangibles. Good girl." He nodded to the gun she'd taken out of her ankle holster.

"Scott's gun only has three rounds left," she said quickly. He'd seen the other weapon tucked into her waistband at her back.

They were as ready as they'd ever be. It was time to make a move.

"Commander?" Sam reconnected with Sykes over the phone. "Did you hear all that?"

"I did," Sykes confirmed. "Parkington's on station, awaiting the order. As soon as you're clear, I'll give him the go."

"Roger that, sir. Stand by." Sam clipped the phone to his shirt so he had both hands free.

"I'm going out first," he told Emily. "I'll distract them while you climb into the Porsche. If anything happens, I want you to get out of here as fast as possible. Don't wait for me."

"But—"

He cut her off. "No arguments, sweetheart. Trust me." He

paused a moment to drop a hard, all too fast kiss on her lips. It wasn't enough—a lifetime in her arms would never be enough—but it would have to do for now. "Please do as I ask, Em."

She gave in, her expression conflicted, but she nodded. "Be careful, Sam." He could tell she wanted to say more. There just wasn't time.

"Sammy boy, come on out so we can discuss terms." Sugden shouted across the distance between house and barn.

"This is it," Sam told Emily. "Be ready to move."

She nodded, her teeth clenched and jaw tight. She was nervous, but she was a trooper. Cool under pressure, like any good pilot, she'd get the job done. God, how he loved her.

"I'm coming out," Sam called. "Don't try anything or I blow this place."

Sam unclipped the phone and said one last thing to Sykes. "I'm putting the phone on speaker so you can hear what's going on, sir. Keep it quiet on your end please."

Sykes agreed and Sam took a step out the door. He kept his phone in his hand as if it were the trigger mechanism he'd claimed it was, knowing Sykes could hear everything more clearly now that he'd switched it to speakerphone function.

"Oh, shit!"

Sam had walked into an ambush. A half dozen zombies gathered around the entrance to the barn, with more behind them. Sugden had been a busy boy. He'd made an army of the undead, hiding them somewhere inside the house, Sam guessed. There was a side door that had been closed before and was now open. The creatures were coming from there.

Sam started firing but he wasn't going to be able to take all of them out. Not before they reached him. And not before he ran out of ammo.

A piercing whistle broke through the night.

Dammit. Emily hadn't stayed put like he'd asked. Instead, she'd sidled out of the barn and had used her earsplitting whistle to draw the zombies' attention. They headed toward her *en masse*. But Sam wouldn't stand for that. He kept firing.

The report of his handgun split their attention between himself and the new target Emily presented.

Then Emily was next to him, firing at his side. Damn, she was beautiful. But he didn't want her here. The creatures were too close and she wasn't immune to their contagion.

"Get in the car and get out of here."

"Not without you." She kept firing, even as they held their low voiced conversation. A quick glance upward told him they didn't have much time.

"I love you, but you've got to get out of here now, Em."

CHAPTER 16

He loved her. No equivocation. No weasel words. He'd said it before, but she'd almost been afraid to believe.

"I don't want to leave you here."

"You have to. These things can kill you with a single scratch. Get in the car. Put as much distance between yourself and this place as possible. I'll catch up with you."

"I'll drive. You keep shooting from the passenger seat."

She thought she had him convinced when he moved around to the other side of the car, closer to the advancing army of zombies. Emily ducked into the driver's side and closed the door, praying Sam would get in on the other side. She couldn't be sure. Sam had a hero streak a mile wide and a foot deep.

The first of the zombies he'd shot were disintegrating but there were just too many of them. They were only a few yards away now and closing fast. She started the car.

"Come on, Sam!"

She thought she'd won when Sam turned toward the car but a gunshot stopped him cold. The bullet ricocheted off the passenger door, making a pinging sound.

Sam turned, firing even as he raised his arm toward the balcony. Krychek went down hard as Sam's bullet hit him in the chest.

Krychek had shot at Sam—or at the car. She couldn't be sure what his target was. Either way, he'd died for it.

Sugden took aim with his rifle at that point, both of his buyers dead, but he didn't get a chance to fire even one dart. Sam drilled a hole between his eyes and he dropped to one knee, then collapsed. Dead.

That left the zombies. They were getting close enough that Emily could see their faces—or what was left of their faces. Every one of them had dried bloodstains around their mouths and down the front of what was left of their clothing. Many were missing pieces. Noses, fingers, ears, lips. One was more gruesome than the next. All were a ghastly grayish color.

"Sam?" They really needed to get away from here. The creatures were cutting off their escape route. "Sam!"

She looked at him. He was talking to his commander by phone, shooting all the while. He hooked the phone to his shirt and reloaded his handgun with a new clip. He needed help. Emily leaned out the window and fired off as many shots as she could from the awkward angle, trying to make every one of them count. She fired until she was out of ammo but it still wasn't enough.

Sam kept firing, making his way toward the car. She eyeballed the distance between him and the car. He wasn't going to make it.

Emily revved the Porsche and tried to move closer. There wasn't much room to maneuver and moving closer to Sam meant moving closer to the zombie horde. Sam had walked nearer to them while shooting and stepped backward as they advanced.

Something thudded against the back of the car.

A quick look back told her there were even more of the creatures coming up behind them. They were cutting her off from Sam!

She could hear him yelling into his phone. He was ordering the air strike.

"Send the missile now!" he screamed. "Do it now. There are too many of them."

Twenty of the creatures got between her and Sam, cutting off her view. She tried to ram them with the car, but they felt no pain. They didn't move out of her way and she couldn't get up enough speed in the small space to push them or throw them. One broke the passenger side window and a flash of bloodstained claws swiped at her face. More were coming around to the driver's side. If they surrounded her, she was dead.

"Emily!"

She could hear Sam screaming her name above the inhuman moaning of the creatures and the purring of the high performance engine.

"The bombs are on their way," he shouted. "Get out of here! Go now!"

"Sam," she whispered, tears running down her face as she saw him fighting hand to hand with one of the creatures. He was totally surrounded now and bleeding.

Oh, God! He was bleeding. He'd been scratched or bitten. It didn't really matter which. Either way, according to what he'd told her, he was dead already.

"Sam." She felt tears streaming down her face as she put the car in gear, cutting sharply to the left, away from Sam and the majority of the monsters. "God, Sam, please forgive me." She gunned the engine and drove away from the horror scene as fast as she could.

In her rearview mirror, she saw the giant, all consuming fireball a few moments later. The thunder of it roared in her ears and the pressure wave beat against her chest like a bass drum. The ranch house had sustained a direct hit.

No way anything survived that. Or anyone.

Emily stopped the car and cried in great, heaving sobs for the man she loved.

It could have been minutes or it could have been hours before she was startled out of her sorrow by a tapping noise.

Someone was tapping on the hood of the car. She looked up, fearing the worst, half-expecting to see one of the creatures who'd escaped the blaze.

But it was a man in black combat gear, heavily armed, concern on his face.

"Ms. Parkington?"

He knew her name. That meant he was most likely part of Sam's team.

Oh, God. Sam.

"Sam was back there..." she hiccupped and pointed behind her.

"It's okay, Ms. Parkington. We'll find him. Stay here." A group of similarly outfitted people started jogging through the drifting smoke toward the flames.

She'd be damned if she was going to stay here. She had the car. If those creatures were still out there, she could drive away again before any of them got to her. She was pretty sure they were all gone. Blown to kingdom come and then fried to ash in the inferno that followed the explosion of the most destructive missile she'd ever seen.

Of course, she'd never seen ordinance explode at this close range before, but she'd heard about it from her brother. Knowing he'd been the one to fire the weapon made it somehow more surreal than it already was. And she'd been on the ground. She hadn't heard anything overhead. He must've fired that sucker from miles away.

All that ran through her mind as she shoved the car in reverse. The car almost spun out when she turned it around too fast. Then she was on her way, back the way she'd come. She passed some of the black-outfitted team members on her way. She caught an expression of surprise on one of their faces. A woman. She would have been surprised herself if she'd given any thought to the fact that they had a woman on their team at that moment. As it was, she sped past the surprised woman and her partner—a man who shouted at her to stop.

Yeah, right. Nothing was stopping her until she knew for

certain what happened to Sam. If he was dead… Oh, God. If he was dead…she had to see it for herself. If not, she had the fast car. She'd get him to a hospital if these mysterious soldiers didn't have the means to treat him on the spot.

The majority of the soldiers were clustered around the far wall of the barn. It was the only part of the structure still standing. Emily maneuvered the bright red car around to shine her headlights on the scene from the other side of the bonfire that still raged from the direction of the house.

She heard gunshots as she approached and realized not all the creatures had been destroyed by the bombardment. Then she saw them in her headlight beams. The soldiers had formed a line and were gunning down the remaining creatures. There were only a few and the team made short work of them.

Then she saw the figure on the ground. The zombies had been clustered around him.

Sam.

She slammed on the brakes and threw the car in park even as she opened the door.

"Get back in the car, Ms. Parkington," a man ordered her but she wasn't listening. Nothing would keep her from Sam.

"There could be more of them. This area's contaminated." Another man tried to prevent her from getting to Sam, stepping in front of her.

"I don't give a damn," she cursed him, trying to push him aside. "I need to see Sam."

"It's best if you don't," another man walked up from where Sam lay a few yards distant. He had a kind face, but his expression was hard.

"I need to see him." She stood her ground, facing the two men down. She wasn't giving an inch. "Please."

One of them shifted on his feet. He was weakening. Finally, he turned to his side, allowing her to pass.

"Don't touch anything," the other one called out, following her as if he were an honor guard.

There was a woman at Sam's side, dressed like the others,

all in black. But this woman had gloves on her hands and she seemed to be treating Sam's wounds.

"Is he alive?" Emily's voice shook as she approached.

The woman kneeling at Sam's side looked up in surprise. She looked from Emily to the silent soldier at her back. Seeming to get permission to speak, the woman answered her.

"He's alive."

"How is that possible?" Emily had seen the blast. She'd been sure nothing could have survived the maelstrom.

"This part of the barn shielded him, as did a few of the creatures who landed on him. A couple of them made it too. We had to put them out of their misery," the man answered.

Emily edged closer. "Can I see him?"

The woman silently leaned back so Emily could see Sam's face. He was unconscious and every spot of flesh she could see from his face to his arms through his ripped up shirt was covered in blood, scratches, deep gouges, and burns. He'd most likely be horribly scarred if he made it through this alive. Her heart broke. She loved him. At that moment she knew she'd stand by him no matter how it turned out. She'd stay by his bedside and nurse him if he let her. It would be her honor.

She moved closer. "Sam?" She knew he was unconscious, but she hoped somehow he heard her. "I'm here, Sam. I'm not going anywhere, so don't you leave me." Her words choked out on a pained whisper. She didn't care who heard. The only person who mattered lay bleeding and burned on the ground at her feet.

"Sam'll be okay. You'd be surprised what a man can take and still come out of it okay." The man was at her side awkwardly trying to comfort her.

"It looks a lot worse than it is," the woman offered. She had a kind face and she was trying to be nice but Emily wasn't a fool. Sam would never be the same carefree man she'd fallen in love with but it didn't matter. She loved him. He loved her. He'd said so and she'd hold him to it, if he made it out of this alive.

"Do you have a helicopter or something to get him to a hospital? If not, that Porsche can move fast. He needs medical care."

"I'm a doctor," the woman said. "Don't worry. I'll look after him. I've done it before." A small smile touched her mouth.

"What about the contagion?" It suddenly dawned on her that he was scratched up and even bitten in a few places that she could see, but he was still breathing. He wasn't dead. From what she'd witnessed earlier, the contagion should have ended his life long before now.

"He's immune," the woman said offhandedly. The soldier at Emily's side shifted uncomfortably.

"That's need to know, doc," he reminded her.

"For goodness sake, she's seen these things up close and personal. I think she'd have figured it out when things calmed down anyway." The woman went back to treating Sam. She had some kind of swabs she was using to clean out the worst of the dirt and dress the deepest wounds.

The relief that hit Emily when she learned that there was such a thing as immunity to the zombie bug calmed her nerves somewhat. Sam was immune. Such a simple statement that meant so much. No wonder he'd claimed the creatures couldn't hurt him. They couldn't turn him into one of their number. He'd never succumb to the contagion. That's why they sent him after the zombies in the first place. His immunity had no doubt been his ticket onto this eclectic team that seemed to be made up of both men and women, soldiers, doctors, and who knew what else.

"Is there anything I can do to help?" Emily asked the woman.

"Not really. I'm just doing a quick field dressing so we can move him without his losing more blood. We'll give him a thorough decon once we get him someplace cleaner. Where are we going, by the way?" she asked the soldier.

"The air base." The man touched his ear and turned

slightly away, indicating he was communicating with someone over his tiny headset. He turned back and his gaze pinned Emily in place. "You're welcome to come with us, Ms. Parkington. We'll send someone to the B&B to get your stuff."

"And release Mrs. McGillicuddy. Scott tied her to a chair in the front parlor," she said absently. Everything was taking on a surreal quality again. Relief that Sam was alive battled with worry that he was so badly injured, and left her numb. The adrenaline rush that had kept her going was leaving her now. She was crashing hard, her limbs shaking.

She knew one thing for certain though. She was going with them. She'd go wherever Sam went. She'd stay by his side and see him through this. However long it took.

"Chopper's coming in," the soldier said only a moment before Emily heard the blades.

A black helicopter landed in the small pasture behind where the barn had once stood. Men piled out with a stretcher and ran over to them. They made short work of loading Sam on it and running back toward the waiting chopper. Emily followed behind the doctor and jumped on board, claiming a seat and strapping in automatically. Before she knew it, they were airborne.

She didn't know how long they were in the air or even what direction they were going in. Normally, such knowledge would be second nature to her but right now, she just didn't care. She didn't care about anything except Sam's condition. The doctor, true to her word, kept careful watch on him, doing what she could even during the flight to make him more comfortable.

By the time they landed on a rooftop of what she assumed was a hospital, she'd started an I.V. and had stopped the bleeding from the worst of his wounds. The two men who'd loaded Sam on the chopper jumped out first and took charge of getting him out of the helicopter once they landed. Only then did she realize the two men were in hazmat suits with breathing apparatus and thick gloves. She assumed the helicopter and everything they touched would be decontaminated once they'd disembarked. From what she'd seen that night, it was good they were taking such extreme precautions.

She never wanted to see another zombie in her life. They were worse than the few horror movies her brother had dragged her to in their teens. Movie makeup guys had nothing on the true horror of what she'd seen. Nothing could match it and she only prayed she could forget, but feared she'd be having nightmares about it for the rest of her life.

Emily followed behind the little parade led by Sam, now on a rolling gurney, with the two hazmat suited men. The doctor was right behind them and Emily followed her. It was a short walk into the hospital and into a fully equipped private room. There were no windows and the doors had a special entryway that felt like it had negative air pressure. Being a pilot, Emily's ears were sensitive to such things.

"We're getting a sealed suite. It's where they quarantine possibly contagious cases of various kinds," the doctor said, falling back to walk at Emily's side.

The hazmat men rolled Sam into the center of the room and lowered the sides, making him more comfortable. The doctor talked with them for a few moments, then let them go. They left the room without another word and disappeared.

"Well, we're on our own for now," the woman said, moving to Sam's side. "I'm Eileen, by the way. I'd shake your hand, but you're not immune, so you need to be very careful about what you touch in here."

"So you are? Immune, I mean."

"Yep," Eileen answered with a small grin. "I guess Sam didn't tell you about that part. Don't get mad at him though. He was under orders. The contagion alone is bad enough but if Sugden knew there were more cases of spontaneous immunity—or in Sam's case, manufactured immunity—he would have hunted us down to get his hands on it."

"Manufactured immunity?"

"Something I developed. A serum that works in only a

small fraction of the population right now, unfortunately. Luckily, it worked for Sam when he played hero and jumped out of a chopper to help one of the other men. He got infected and would have died but the serum worked on him, thank goodness."

Emily could picture it. After seeing him in action that night, she knew firsthand how brave he was under fire.

"That sounds like Sam. I'm glad you were there to save him."

"He's special, isn't he?" Eileen agreed as she cut away his shirt. "A terrible patient, but a good man."

"I heard that."

Sam's voice. Whispery and weak, but Sam was definitely awake. Emily rushed to his side.

"Don't touch," the doctor reminded her when Emily reached out. "Not 'til we get him cleaned up and decontaminated." Emily pulled back reluctantly. It hurt not to be able to touch him.

"How do you feel?"

"Like I just got blown to hell and back with a few dozen zombies. How do I look?" His mouth tilted upward at one corner in a roguish smile. Even battered, bloody, and burnt, he still managed to be charming.

"About the same," Eileen answered.

"Em?" His head turned toward her. He moved slowly, as if in pain.

"I'm here." How she wished she could at least hold his hand, but even that simple touch was denied her.

"Tell your brother I owe him."

A startled laugh escaped her. That wasn't what she expected him to say by a long shot, but it was typical, irreverent, vintage Sam.

"I'll tell him." Tears gathered in her eyes but she didn't let them fall.

"Don't worry, Em. I'll be okay. You'll see."

"You're reassuring me?" She gave him a tearful laugh. "I think you've got it backwards, Sam."

"No I don't. Doc, tell her. She doesn't know." Sam's head rolled so he could look at the doctor.

Eileen's eyes widened. "Oh my gosh, I'm sorry." She looked truly contrite. "He really will be all right. Tomorrow at this time, you probably won't even know he was hurt."

Emily frowned. "What?"

"You might as well know it all," Eileen replied, going back to work bathing Sam's wounds. "The original goal of the research was to develop something that would make soldiers heal faster. In the few people that are immune, that goal has been achieved. Unfortunately, only a micro-percentage of the normal population is spontaneously immune, according to my calculations. And my serum only works on another small segment. The risk of the contagion is too great to use, even with the few successes we've had. Like Sam."

Emily almost didn't believe the doctor's words. They didn't make sense. Not when confronted by Sam's injuries.

"Here," Eileen pointed to an area on Sam's chest. "Watch."

The patch of skin had been exposed to the flames, torn by claws, and then burnt. It was covered with a bloody, crusty brownish scab of material that made Emily wince. Eileen irrigated the area with a small amount of saline solution, then wiped it away.

The skin beneath the crusty mess was pink and healthy. Newly healed and unscarred.

"Dear Lord," Emily breathed. "He'll heal? He really will heal?"

"Yes, Emily. He'll be good as new by tomorrow, if I'm any judge. Right, Sam?"

"Good as new, doc. But right now I really need some shut eye. Sorry, Em. Can't stay awake."

"It's a side effect of major healing," Eileen explained. "Don't worry. It's normal."

"Love you, Em," Sam whispered as he drifted off to sleep on the gurney, while the doctor continued her work.

Emily let the tears fall. Tears of relief and joy. She was in a daze. He would be all right! Praise God, he would be all right.

Eileen watched her, peering upward every few moments as if checking on her. Finally, she spoke.

"Why don't you use the restroom there to clean up a bit." She gestured toward a door at the end of the room with her chin. "We can't take any chances with decon, so you'll have to strip off and put your clothes and anything else you're wearing in a plastic bag. It'll be returned to you once it's been through decontamination. There should be scrubs in the bathroom. You should take a shower while you're at it and scrub your hair and under your fingernails thoroughly."

Given a task, Emily was grateful to have something to do. Relief rushed through her veins, renewing a little bit of the adrenaline that had kept her going thus far. Emily did as she was told, using a plastic garbage bag she found in the bathroom to wrap up her clothing and shoes before stepping into the shower. The hot water felt good and if she cried happy tears, they meshed with the gentle pelting of rain from the showerhead to disappear down the drain.

When she emerged from the shower, she felt renewed. Sam would heal. Their lives would go on—hopefully together. He'd said he loved her a few times now. He couldn't take it back. She wouldn't let him. She wanted to be with him, no matter what that meant. She'd even give up the airline if it meant being with Sam, but that was putting the cart before the horse. First they had to answer to his superiors and Sam needed time to heal.

Everything else could come later…now that she knew there would be time for them to be together. She wasn't letting him go. Not now, not ever.

Sam was sound asleep when she emerged from the bathroom, dressed in loose scrubs with little booties on her feet. Eileen looked up at her and smiled.

"There's someone who wants to see you outside. Don't worry. I'm staying with Sam. He'll be fine."

Emily took a good look at Sam. Yes, indeed, he did look a whole lot better than just a few minutes ago. Eileen had cleansed his wounds and many of them were already healed. The angry scratches were mostly gone. Only the deep wounds still required bandages to hold them closed. He had a few of those on his face, along with some burns, but his face was looking much better than it had. The burns were healing. If she hadn't seen him when it first happened, she wouldn't have known how bad he'd been hurt. It was truly amazing.

"Get some rest if you can," Eileen said, breaking her intense reverie. Everything was still a little fantastical to her. "Go. I'll take good care of him. I promise."

"Thank you, Eileen." Emily had to drag herself away from Sam's side but knew there were people she probably had to talk to after what they'd been through. No doubt there would be reports to file and information to impart. She headed toward the door reluctantly, but made herself go through it, confident that Sam was in good hands.

She hit the button to open the inner door then passed into the air lock area before the doors at the far end opened for her. What she found waiting for her was something totally unexpected.

It was a huge hug from her twin. His arms enveloped her even before she realized what was going on. He tugged her into his arms and lifted her clear off her feet, holding her tight.

"God, punkin, don't ever worry me like that again." He kissed her cheek before lowering her to the ground again, his worry clear in the slight tremble in his arms.

"Henry," she could barely speak, so glad to have him nearby.

"I'm here." He stroked her hair, soothing her. The shakes hit her bad as she finally released all the worry, tension, and emotion that had stormed through her since being kidnapped from the B&B earlier that night.

A throat cleared behind them and Henry reluctantly let go of her. He turned them both to face the man who stood watching them.

"Emily, I'd like you to meet Commander Sykes."

The slightly older man held out his hand and Emily shook it. He had striking denim-blue eyes and a friendly smile that he used, no doubt, to try to put her at ease.

"I'd like to talk to you about what happened tonight if you're up to it, ma'am."

Emily went with him into a small room that looked like it had been commandeered in a hurry. A mismatched table and chairs had been crammed into what had probably been a break room. Her brother came with her for moral support and doled out coffee for them all from the coffeemaker on the counter behind the chair she'd taken.

"Can you tell me how you ended up at the ranch?" Sykes began, his voice gentle.

"Scott Southerland kidnapped me from the bed-and-breakfast. He tied up the old lady who owned the place. I saw her on the way out the door. He forced me to get into his car at gunpoint and drove me up there."

"Did he say anything?" Sykes prompted.

"He was ranting about how I shouldn't have stuck my nose into his business. How I'd almost ruined everything for him. Then he started gloating, saying that I wasn't as smart as I thought I was. How he was smarter and that he always had been despite the fact that he'd never been able to get his pilot's license. That was always a bone of contention between us, even as kids. His father always wanted him to earn his wings but Scott never seemed to give a damn one way or the other. When it really counted, he never passed the exams. He nearly had a cow when Shotgun went to the academy." She looked at her brother and smiled. He nodded, allowing his mouth to lift in a small grin in response.

"What happened to his weapon?" Sykes asked, taking notes.

"It's in the plastic bag with my clothes. I left the other weapon in there too. Scott's gun only had three conventional rounds left in the clip. The gun that Sam gave me was empty. I used all the rounds before I took off in the car. But I'm getting ahead of myself." She took a breath, trying to focus.

"When Scott pulled up in front of the house, he held a short conversation with the three men on the balcony. They seemed to be stalling him and it became apparent why when the first zombie showed up. Scott shot wildly and used most of his ammunition. I retrieved the gun from the dirt when Scott went down but I didn't end up firing any shots from it."

"That's when Sam broke cover, right?" Sykes prompted.

"I didn't see where he came from, but suddenly he was there."

"I heard the rest. He had his phone on speaker." Sykes jotted a few notes before returning his gaze to her. "Can you account for what happened to the three on the balcony?"

"Scott shot one, I think. The Asian man. Sam got the other two when we ran for the car. There was a lot of shooting. One guy was shooting darts. The other had a pistol with conventional ammunition and they were both shooting toward us. Sam got them before they could get us. It was self defense."

"I'm not a cop or a lawyer, ma'am." Sykes gave her that charming smile of his, though it was edged with steel this time. There was a glint in his eye she recognized. She'd seen it in Sam's eyes many times over the past few days. "Archer won't face any repercussions for his actions. Our team was sanctioned directly by the President. Hell, he'll probably get a medal."

CHAPTER 17

There was a brief knock at the door before Eileen entered. She'd changed her clothes since Emily had last seen her. The doctor sent a smile at Commander Sykes that made Emily think there was something between them. That made Sykes seem somehow more human to her.

"Sam's being moved to a normal room. It'll be private and secure. He's been through decon and woke up for a bit, though he's still pretty groggy. I expect he'll sleep until morning but he was asking for Emily. If you're done with her, I thought I'd take her to him."

"We're finished here," Sykes said, putting his papers into a folder. "Ms. Parkington, I'd like to thank you for your part in tonight's events and the investigation leading up to it." Sykes held out his hand and she took it. She liked this gentle giant of a man and could see why he inspired such confidence and loyalty in his troops.

Emily left, but the commander asked her brother to stay behind. He promised to catch up with her later. Emily followed Eileen, sad to leave Henry behind but eager to see Sam again.

Eileen led her to a much cozier room that had a window and two beds. Only one was occupied. Emily was amazed by how good Sam looked as he sat propped up in the hospital bed. He smiled when he saw her and there was only one healing wound left on his face that she could see. She rushed to his side, reaching for him, even as he opened his arms to her.

"Are you a sight for sore eyes," Sam said as she kissed his cheek and stroked his hair lightly. She was afraid to touch him too hard in case she hit a sore spot.

"How are you feeling?"

"A lot better. So…are you okay with this? The super fast healing thing? I know it's a little weird." He seemed so nervous about her answer, she rushed to put him at ease.

"How could I not be grateful for something that keeps you safe and healthy? Thank God for this miracle, Sam. You were so badly injured. I doubted you'd ever be the same and now here you are, almost back to normal only a few hours later. It truly *is* a miracle."

He looked so relieved by her answer she had to kiss him. Just a quick brush of her lips on his that turned into something longer and more lingering. But he was still hurt, no matter what he said, so she kept it light and backed off before anything truly interesting could get started.

"God, Em," he whispered when she snuggled lightly into him. It was an awkward position but she didn't care. She wanted to be near him. To smell his clean, masculine scent. To touch his strong, muscular body. "I love you so much."

She drew back to look into his eyes. "And I love you, Sam."

He reached up to stroke her cheek with one calloused hand. "Can you live with this—with me—now that you know what I am?"

"Are you asking me to?"

He swallowed, clearly nervous, which endeared him all the more to her.

"I'm asking. Will you marry me, Em? I never thought I could love somebody as much as I love you. I tried to keep it light and easy but it was impossible from the first. I love you,

Emily, and I want to spend the rest of my life with you, however long that may be."

She smiled. "I'm glad. Because I feel the same about you, Sam."

"Is that a yes?" Hope lit his gaze.

"Definitely a yes," she whispered before meeting his lips with hers one more time. This kiss was deeper and even more joyous.

His hands cradled her head and guided her, demanding more pressure and deeper access. She gave him everything he asked for and got all she could ever want in return. He'd just given her his love and his commitment to a future together. She never knew she could be this happy or this blessed.

When she drew back this time, his gaze sought hers.

"You make my life complete, Em."

Her heart overflowed with happiness at the look in his eyes.

"You do the same for me, Sam."

"I hate to interrupt," Henry cut in from the doorway, "but I'm heading for the barracks for the night and wanted to say goodnight."

Emily turned toward the door, but Sam caught her hand and held it tight. Henry moved into the room, clearly bristling.

"You can be the first to congratulate us," Emily broke the news to her twin. "Sam and I are engaged."

Henry's brows drew together as he studied the scene. His gaze went from her to Sam to their joined hands and back again.

"Is he what you really want, Em?" he asked finally.

"More than anything or anyone. I love him." She shrugged her shoulders at the simplicity of those words. It felt so good to be able to say it out loud and proclaim it to any who would listen. She felt like shouting it from the rooftops, but this would have to do for now.

"How about you, lieutenant? Will you take care of her better than you did tonight?"

"Henry, that's not fair." She jumped to Sam's defense.

Sam squeezed her hand, stilling her words. "Hold on there, Em. He's right. I should never have left you vulnerable to Southerland. I messed up and you almost paid the ultimate price."

She turned to face him. "I don't believe that, and I refuse to see it that way."

"But I do. And so does your brother." Sam's gaze went to Henry's and he nodded just once. "I'd die for her," he said simply, making her heart flutter at the surety in his tone.

"You love her? You won't hurt her?" Henry pressed.

"I'll never deliberately hurt her. And I do love her. It'll be my honor to take care of her for the rest of our lives." Sam squeezed her hand again and caught her gaze. His heart was there in his eyes for all to read.

Henry nodded. "See that you do. Or you'll answer to me."

He walked up to Emily and bent to kiss her forehead in something like a benediction. The moment was tender and moving. Then he moved back toward the door.

"I'll see you tomorrow, sis. And congratulations to you both."

Henry left them and Emily pulled up a chair to the side of Sam's bed. They spent almost half an hour talking and just being with each other in safety for the first time in what seemed like ages. Sleep overtook Sam again and Emily just watched him sleep for a while, glad he was getting better almost before her eyes. The gash on his head looked like it was healing really fast and she watched it scab over and shrink in wonder.

Eileen came in about an hour later to check on him. He was still asleep and slept through the examination of his cuts and bruises.

"Why don't you get some sleep," Eileen whispered to Emily. "You can use this bed." She pointed to the other bed that was neatly made up. It looked really inviting and Emily sought it out gratefully.

When she woke, sun was streaming in the window. It was

well into the next morning and Sam was gone. She sat up in the bed and looked around. Sam's bed was empty. For just a moment, she panicked.

Then she heard the toilet flush. The door to the small bathroom was closed. Maybe he was in there. She held her breath until the door opened. Out stepped Sam, fully dressed in fatigues, looking as if he'd never been burned or scratched nearly to death last night.

"Amazing," she breathed.

He grinned, walking over to her. He leaned forward, pinning her to the bed.

"You look pretty amazing yourself." His mouth dipped to capture hers for a brief good morning kiss. He nuzzled her neck before straightening away much too soon. "I'd love to take this further but we've both got places to go and people to see this morning. Your clothes are over there. Get dressed, captain. The clock's ticking."

His playfulness made her want to cry. He'd been so badly injured. She'd thought he was dead. Then, when she knew he'd lived through the bombing, she had mentally prepared herself to nurse him for as long as it took and accept whatever limitations he'd have from then on. Instead, here he was, laughing and joking with her, whole and healthy, as if nothing had ever happened to him. It truly was a miracle.

He must've seen the way she was looking at him. His expression grew more solemn and he sat on the edge of the bed, next to her.

"I know it's a lot to take in," he said in a gentle voice.

"I'm just so glad..." Her voice broke and he turned to gather her in his arms as she hugged him tight. It was so good to feel his strength against her. So good to know he was real and strong and hers.

"I am too, sweetheart." He held her, rubbing calming circles on her back for a long moment before finally pulling away. "I wasn't kidding. There are people waiting for us. Are you up to it?"

"Yeah." She stood wearily and pushed back her messy

hair. "Give me a minute to freshen up and change."

He patted her ass as she passed him on the way to where her luggage sat and she jumped. His grin made her want to giggle when she looked back over her shoulder at him. That set the tone. The danger was past for now, and it was time to be happy they were both still alive and together.

"Your comrades got our luggage from the bed-and-breakfast?" She noted that her pilot's case was fully packed and all her toiletries had been gathered from the B&B's bathroom.

"The team can be quite efficient when put in motion. They checked us out and returned the rental car too."

She was impressed. "I'll just be a minute," she told him, disappearing into the bathroom with a few things. She emerged a couple of minutes later, coiffed, perfumed, and dressed in fresh clothing. She would've liked a shower but there wasn't time and she was clean enough, she supposed. She'd showered last night after the battle.

Sam was waiting for her by the door, talking to someone she couldn't see outside the room. She went over and waited for him to finish but he turned, including her in the conversation. He was talking to her brother about his ride.

Emily loved hearing the details Shotgun hadn't been able to share with her before. He was one of the select few top pilots who'd been chosen to test the newest generation of strike fighters. Before, she'd just been a civilian who wasn't cleared to hear the nitty gritty of his ride. Now, apparently, things had changed. He was telling Sam about range and ammunition specs that he never would have disclosed before.

No doubt Henry had been given the go ahead by whoever commanded them all now. She supposed there couldn't be much more top secret than what she already knew about the zombie contagion. Letting her in on some information that a lot of people in the Air Force already knew probably wasn't such a big deal after that.

Henry greeted her with a grin and went right on talking about his favorite subject—his jet. She didn't mind. She loved talking airplanes too. They'd both grown up in the airline industry and had jet fuel running through their veins. They talked all the way down the corridor and down the elevator, and right out the door. She was able to ask questions about things he'd only hinted at before and listened avidly, as did Sam. It was so great to share her passion about aircraft with him.

They walked out into the sunshine, Henry leading them to a little corner of what had to be his home base. She saw uniformed Air Force personnel everywhere. Several saluted Henry and Sam in passing. Now that was cool. Nobody ever saluted her, even though she owned a good percentage of Praxis Air.

The men took it in stride. Emily felt a little out of place being the only civilian in sight. Of course, her only clean clothes had been her pilot's uniform, so she was in dark pants with a white shirt. Praxis Air's uniform was casual but neat. Still, she definitely didn't look military and that was easy to spot. She got a few questioning glances as they walked through the heart of the highly restricted base but nobody dared question her with her two high-ranking bodyguards.

They entered a small building on the edges of the airfield that looked like it had seen better days. Looks were deceiving, she realized, as she went farther inside. The outer rooms were as shabby as the façade but inside a state of the art conference area hummed with electronic gizmos, computers, and audio/ video equipment. Many of the people she saw looked somewhat familiar to her from the night before.

There was a giant conference table at the center of the room and lots of people milling around, some going over papers, some just chatting. They arrived only moments before Commander Sykes. When he walked in, the room drew to order, everyone taking their seats and quieting down. The meeting had begun.

Emily sat between Sam and Henry. Her brother had procured coffee for them all and sat back down before the meeting got going. Sam's leg brushed deliberately against hers under the table. Cozy.

"First off, I want to thank Ms. Emily Parkington of Praxis Air for her cooperation and assistance. Last night's action—while not ideal—accomplished a major goal. Forensic investigation this morning confirmed that Dr. Sugden and his buyers Bin Zhao and Aleksander Krychek are all dead. No further creatures have been found in the area and we've locked down the entire mountaintop with military personnel until further notice. We've put out a story about an illegal weapons factory operating at that ranch with national security implications and the possibility that they were working with bio-weapons, which allowed us to evacuate the surrounding homes and communities on both sides of the mountain."

Commander Sykes had been busy while Emily and Sam had been sleeping. Of course, he had the full might of the American military and the backing of the President himself to get this handled. She'd be surprised if he was anything less than efficient in the carrying out of his duties.

"We're going to stay on station at the ranch and the surrounding woods until we're certain none of the creatures escaped," he continued. "The combat team will be patrolling the woods every night for the next week at least, in alternating shifts, flowing in by helicopter. We'll use the burnt out ranch as our base of operations while the decon teams go through the area with a fine toothed comb. I don't want any trace of this contagion left behind."

Nods of agreement met that statement and a few of the folks around the giant table made notes. Sykes tapped a key on the keyboard in front of him and the lights went to fifty percent. A projector came on, displaying a flow chart with names.

"This chart lists all the members of the original science team. The ones marked in red are dead. The yellows are being watched to confirm that they have given up the line of research completely. They've already undergone rigorous investigation and have been cleared but they'll be watched—probably for the rest of their lives, in one way or another.

The lady in green is our own Dr. McCormick." Sykes shot a smile at Eileen and it was clear to Emily there was something going on there. "As you can see, we've accounted for everyone from the science team." He tapped another key and a new chart came up on the screen at the far side of the room. "This lists all those we know have been involved in one way or another. Same color coding applies."

Emily noted Scott's name up there in red and her own, listed in green. Just that easily, one life ended and another life went on. A chill went down her spine, remembering how Scott had died. Sam's hand reached for hers under the table, squeezing her fingers in silent reassurance. There were precious few names in green on that chart. Most were red. Red for dead.

It was driven home to her how many people had died because of this science experiment. And she didn't even want to think about all the people who'd been savaged by the zombies or killed by the scientists and sent out to make more like themselves. So many people had died.

And yet, if not for this awful chapter in the secret history of military science, she never would have met Sam. Life had a funny way of working out sometimes. Good had come of the evil. As she looked around the room, she saw more than a few couples sitting side by side as if they belonged together.

"As of today, we're in wrap up mode," Sykes went on. "Before you ask, the team will stay together. For the next few weeks we're going to be working up on the mountain, making absolutely certain that nothing remains of the zombie research. After that, the Chairman of the Joint Chiefs, the Special Operations Command, and the President have agreed that the majority of our little combat group has too many attributes that might set us apart if we were to return to our original assignments. I've made the argument and it's been accepted that the combat team in particular, would be better utilized as a separate Special Ops group. The affected team members will be notified over the next week or so and offered a chance to remain part of the new formulation of our team. This is a turning point for us all. The reason we joined together in this special team has been eradicated. We've done our job and achieved our goals with the grateful thanks of the leaders of our services and our nation. We have our pick of assignments. As a result, I'll be scheduling individual meetings with all of you over the next few weeks. I want you to think about where you want to go from here. I'll want honesty from you when we meet. You've earned your right to choose your destiny—something few warriors are granted. So I want you to think about it. In the meantime, are there any questions?"

Sykes waited a moment but nobody seemed eager to speak.

"Then I guess it's back to the mountain for most of you. Then we have a few weddings to attend—including my own. I'd like to officially invite all of you to the party. Eileen and I are getting married the second weekend in November. Hold the date. Details will follow as to location and time."

Everyone broke protocol then and cheered for the couple. Sykes grinned, accepting congratulations from everyone as Eileen beamed at his side. The meeting broke up soon thereafter, most people stopping to congratulate the commander and Eileen. They looked happy. As happy as Emily felt when Sam took her hand in his and reminded her of the question he'd asked the night before.

"Do you still mean it?" she breathed, while the rest of the room focused on Matt and Eileen. "Or was it just the fatigue and stress talking?"

"Are you kidding me?" Sam looked almost insulted. "You said yes. I'm not letting you back out now." His hands went around her waist and he dragged her closer. Close enough to kiss, though he didn't. He made her think about it though, and she wanted it…bad.

"I was just making sure," she told him, wanting that kiss more and more.

"None of that, you two," Henry chided them as he stepped right next to them. "You're in uniform." He sent her a mock stern look that made her laugh.

Sam let her go by slow degrees, letting out a heavy sigh. "He's right. No hanky-panky while in uniform. But wait 'til I get you alone, Em." He leered at her in a teasing way that made her laugh. Especially when Henry held up one hand and made a face.

"I do *not* want to hear this." Henry made a show of turning away but she knew it was all in fun.

Henry and Sam had hit it off and she thought they'd become good friends given time. They both loved aircraft and they both loved her. She marveled at that for a moment. They both loved her. In different ways, of course, but Emily counted herself lucky and blessed to have two such wonderful men in her life.

"Sam," Sykes came up to them as he was on his way out of the room. "I want you to take a couple of days off. You've earned it." He clapped Sam on the back and Emily could see why people responded to the commander's easy charm and confident leadership. "Thank you again, Ms. Parkington." He held out his hand for her to shake.

"Please, call me Emily."

"Emily." He gave her that full-wattage smile. "After things settle down a bit, I'd like to talk to you more about Praxis Air. There is a possibility that we could take some of those cargo-outfitted jets off your hands, or, if you're willing, we could hire Praxis for some of our travel. Groups like ours like to fly under the radar from time to time."

Emily was intrigued and more than willing to discuss business with the military. She would have a huge mess to clean up when she got back to Wichita. Scott's death was going to throw the company into disarray and she had a feeling she was going to end up taking on a lot of the day-to-day responsibility he'd once had.

"By all means. I'd be happy to work with you again, sir."

"I have to thank you also for bringing Henry to my attention." He nodded toward her twin. "Because of him and the good work we've done on this mission, I've been given the go ahead to form a new kind of combat team. Last night's action will have long reaching aftershocks. I think a lot of good things will come out of our success here, and that's due, in large part, to you, Emily."

She felt the heat in her cheeks. She wasn't used to such high praise especially from a man she read as hard to impress.

"Thanks, commander. That means a lot. And congratulations on your engagement. Eileen really helped me cope last night. She's a great person and a fine doctor."

"You can say that again." His smile widened as Eileen stopped next to him. The room was mostly empty now except for the five of them.

"So what about you two?" Eileen asked point blank.

Sam surprised her by putting his arm around her waist and drawing her to his side. She hadn't been sure he wanted to go public so soon, but it appeared she'd been wrong.

"We're engaged," Sam announced with simple candor.

"Damn," Matt shook his head but he had a grin on his face.

Eileen and the commander congratulated them. Emily felt the enormity of the moment. Sam was her future as she was his. They had a lot of logistics to work out and she had an airline to save, but they'd figure it out. Together. Forever.

Sam and Emily took the time off that Sykes had given Sam together. They flew back to Wichita where the news that Scott Southerland had died in a freak accident had already been delivered. The cover story had been supplied by the military and the very organized commander. The lawyers were working through the particulars of who exactly owned the majority position in Praxis Air now, but Emily didn't really care. She'd fix the broken airline with whoever ended up in charge.

She had better things to do over those first few days. Like making love to her new fiancé. They closeted themselves in her bedroom and only came up for air when they got hungry. In fact, with the leisure time, Sam introduced her to some new and exciting things that she knew they'd have a lifetime to explore.

He'd found some silk scarves she'd bought in her travels in Asia and they immediately became instruments of pleasure. He held her captive, teasing her skin with the soft slide of silk, then he added a new twist, tying her hands to the bedpost. She wasn't sure she would enjoy it at first, having never dared anything like this with the men in her past. When it came down to it, she hadn't trusted those other men enough to let them tie her up. Sam was a different story. She'd already trusted him with her life. It wasn't much of a leap to trust him with her pleasure.

Facing death together had brought them an intimacy and a level of trust she'd never experienced in a relationship before. This time, she knew their love was built to last. Few couples went through what they'd faced together. They'd been tested in the crucible and made stronger for it.

"What are you thinking about?" Sam asked as he teased her skin with the soft fringe of one of her silk scarves.

"You." She squirmed under his skilled touch.

"You'll have to do better than that."

"I'm thinking about you, sir, and what you do to me."

He grinned as he guided the scarf fringe down over her breasts, pausing at the peaks that made her shiver. He watched her with a hungry, patient gaze as the scarf drifted downward over her abdomen, making a ticklish area suddenly become an erogenous zone.

"And what is it, exactly, that I do to you, Captain Parkington?" Using her title was just another part of the wicked game he'd introduced to her. It was a game of gentle dominance and sweet submission and he played it really, really well.

"You drive me crazy, lieutenant. Crazy in the best possible way."

He lowered his head to spread licking kisses over her abdomen, letting his tongue circle her belly button.

"I like the sound of that, captain. You've earned a

reward."

She nearly shrieked when his head trailed downward even farther, pausing between her spread legs to torture the most sensitive place on her body. She skyrocketed upward with his first touch and he held her there, just touching the tips of the stars for an excruciating, incredible time out of time. He knew just how to play her body now. He was the master of her pleasure in every way.

When he moved back, letting her come down just a bit from the plateau of pleasure, she sagged back against the bed. Her arms and legs were tied. He'd secured her hands together above her head. Her legs each had a scarf around the ankle and were spread apart. He'd left enough room for her to squirm but she wasn't getting free until he untied her.

After the pleasure he'd given her over the past hour, she didn't really care if he never untied her. But that wasn't really fair to him.

"Don't you think it's time for your reward, lieutenant?" Her gaze drifted upward lazily, over his impressive abs and awesome chest to meet those blue, blue eyes she loved so much.

His smile was another thing she loved and he gave her one now. "I think you're right, captain."

He slid over her, taking his place between her thighs, pushing deep. There was no hesitation, no insecurity. He simply glided inside, into the place he belonged. He owned her. As she owned him.

After the long session of foreplay, it didn't take much to send her into orbit again. He kept her there with a slow, steady rocking rhythm. She couldn't believe his willpower but he had proved to her time and time again over the past few days that he was in complete control of himself…and her. It had become a personal challenge to make him lose control.

She'd succeeded a time or two, but only at the very last moments before climax. That's when he'd decided to tie her up, so she couldn't ply her tricks on him, or so he'd said. She knew darn well he'd enjoyed her taking control for those moments, but it was all part of the game and she was a willing player. She'd play with him for the rest of their lives.

And every now and again, she'd come out on top.

#

ABOUT THE AUTHOR

Bianca D'Arc has run a laboratory, climbed the corporate ladder in the shark-infested streets of lower Manhattan, studied and taught martial arts, and earned the right to put a whole bunch of letters after her name, but she's always enjoyed writing more than any of her other pursuits. She grew up and still lives on Long Island, where she keeps busy with an extensive garden, several aquariums full of very demanding fish, and writing her favorite genres of paranormal, fantasy and sci-fi romance.

Bianca loves to hear from readers and can be reached through Twitter (@BiancaDArc), Facebook (BiancaDArcAuthor) or through the various links on her website.

WELCOME TO THE D'ARC SIDE…
WWW.BIANCADARC.COM

OTHER BOOKS BY BIANCA D'ARC

Brotherhood of Blood
One & Only
Rare Vintage
Phantom Desires
Sweeter Than Wine
Forever Valentine
Wolf Hills*
Wolf Quest

Tales of the Were
Lords of the Were
Inferno

*Tales of the Were ~
The Others*
Rocky
Slade

*Tales of the Were ~
String of Fate*
Cat's Cradle
King's Throne
Jacob's Ladder
Her Warriors

*Tales of the Were ~
Redstone Clan*
The Purrfect Stranger
Grif
Red
Magnus
Bobcat
Matt

*Tales of the Were ~
Grizzly Cove*
All About the Bear
Mating Dance
Night Shift
Alpha Bear
Saving Grace
Bearliest Catch
The Bear's Healing Touch
The Luck of the Shifters
Badass Bear

*Tales of the Were ~
Were-Fey Love Story*
Lone Wolf
Snow Magic
Midnight Kiss

*Tales of the Were ~
Jaguar Island (Howls)*
The Jaguar Tycoon
The Jaguar Bodyguard

Gemini Project
Tag Team
Doubling Down

Resonance Mates
Hara's Legacy**
Davin's Quest
Jaci's Experiment
Grady's Awakening
Harry's Sacrifice

Dragon Knights

Daughters of the Dragon
Maiden Flight*
Border Lair
The Ice Dragon**
Prince of Spies***

Dragon Knights ~ Novellas
The Dragon Healer
Master at Arms
Wings of Change

Sons of Draconia
FireDrake
Dragon Storm
Keeper of the Flame
Hidden Dragons

The Sea Captain's Daughter
Book 1: Sea Dragon
Book 2: Dragon Fire
Book 3: Dragon Mates

Guardians of the Dark
Half Past Dead
Once Bitten, Twice Dead
A Darker Shade of Dead
The Beast Within
Dead Alert

StarLords
Hidden Talent
Talent For Trouble
Shy Talent

Jit'Suku Chronicles ~ *Arcana*
King of Swords
King of Cups
King of Clubs
King of Stars
End of the Line
Diva

Jit'Suku Chronicles ~ *Sons of Amber*
Angel in the Badlands
Master of Her Heart

StarLords
Hidden Talent
Talent For Trouble
Shy Talent

Gifts of the Ancients
Warrior's Heart

* RT Book Reviews Awards Nominee
** EPPIE Award Winner
*** CAPA Award Winner

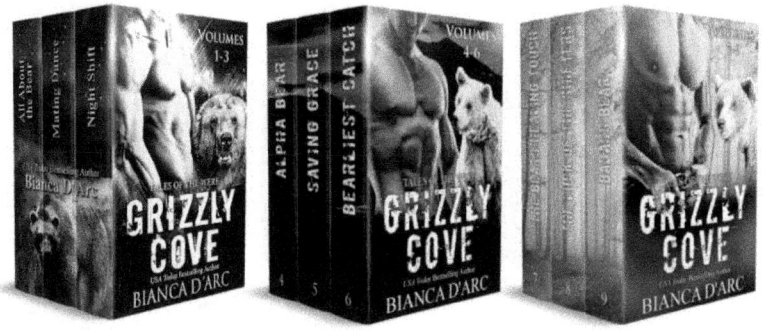

Welcome to Grizzly Cove, where bear shifters can be who they are - if the creatures of the deep will just leave them be. Wild magic, unexpected allies, a conflagration of sorcery and shifter magic the likes of which has not been seen in centuries... That's what awaits the peaceful town of Grizzly Cove. That, and love. Lots and lots of love.

This series begins with…

All About the Bear
Welcome to Grizzly Cove, where the sheriff has more than the peace to protect. The proprietor of the new bakery in town is clueless about the dual nature of her nearest neighbors, but not for long. It'll be up to Sheriff Brody to clue her in and convince her to stay calm—and in his bed—for the next fifty years or so.

Mating Dance
Tom, Grizzly Cove's only lawyer, is also a badass grizzly bear, but he's met his match in Ashley, the woman he just can't get out of his mind. She's got a dark secret, that only he knows. When ugliness from her past tracks her to her new home, can Tom protect the woman he is fast coming to believe is his mate?

Night Shift
Sheriff's Deputy Zak is one of the few black bear shifters in a colony of grizzlies. When his job takes him into closer proximity to the lovely Tina, though, he finds he can't resist her. Could it be he's finally found his mate? And when adversity strikes, will she turn to him, or run into the night? Zak will do all he can to make sure she chooses him.

Phoenix Rising

Lance is inexplicably drawn to the sun and doesn't understand why. Tina is a witch who remembers him from their high school days. She'd had a crush on the quiet boy who had an air of magic about him. Reunited by Fate, she wonders if she could be the one to ground him and make him want to stay even after the fire within him claims his soul…if only their love can be strong enough.

Phoenix and the Wolf

Diana is drawn to the sun and dreams of flying, but her elderly grandmother needs her feet firmly on the ground. When Diana's old clunker breaks down in front of a high-end car lot, she seeks help and finds herself ensnared by the sexy werewolf mechanic who runs the repair shop. Stone makes her want to forget all her responsibilities and take a walk on the wild side…with him.

Phoenix and the Dragon

He's a dragon shapeshifter in search of others like himself. She's a newly transformed phoenix shifter with a lot to learn and bad guys on her trail. Together, they will go on a dazzling adventure into the unknown, and fight against evil folk intent on subduing her immense power and using it for their own ends. They will face untold danger and find love that will last a lifetime.

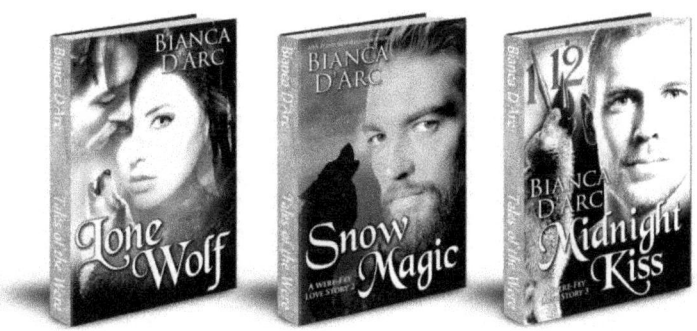

Lone Wolf

Josh is a werewolf who suddenly has extra, unexpected and totally untrained powers. He's not happy about it - or about the evil jackasses who keep attacking him, trying to steal his magic. Forced to seek help, Josh is sent to an unexpected ally for training.

Deena is a priestess with more than her share of magical power and a unique ability that has made her a target. She welcomes Josh, seeing a kindred soul in the lone werewolf. She knows she can help him... if they can survive their enemies long enough.

Snow Magic

Evie has been a lone wolf since the disappearance of her mate, Sir Rayburne, a fey knight from another realm. Left all alone with a young son to raise, Evie has become stronger than she ever was. But now her son is grown and suddenly Ray is back.

Ray never meant to leave Evie all those years ago but he's been caught in a magical trap, slowly being drained of magic all this time. Freed at last, he whisks Evie to the only place he knows in the mortal realm where they were happy and safe—the rustic cabin in the midst of a North Dakota winter where they had been newlyweds. He's used the last of his magic to get there and until he recovers a bit, they're stuck in the middle of nowhere with a blizzard coming and bad guys on their trail.

Can they pick up where they left off and rekindle the magic between them, or has it been extinguished forever?

Midnight Kiss

Margo is a werewolf on a mission...with a disruptively handsome mage named Gabe. She can't figure out where Gabe fits in the pecking order, but it doesn't seem to matter to the attraction driving her wild. Gabe knows he's going to have to prove himself in order to win Margo's heart. He wants her for his mate, but can she give her heart to a mage? And will their dangerous quest get in the way?

The Jaguar Tycoon

Mark may be the larger-than-life billionaire Alpha of the secretive Jaguar Clan, but he's a pussycat when it comes to the one women destined to be his mate. Shelly is an up-and-coming architect trying to drum up business at an elite dinner party at which Mark is the guest of honor. When shots ring out, the hunt for the gunman brings Mark into Shelly's path and their lives will never be the same.

The Jaguar Bodyguard

Sworn to protect his Clan, Nick heads to Hollywood to keep an eye on a rising star who has seen a little too much for her own good. Unexpectedly fame has made a circus of Sal's life, but when decapitated squirrels show up on her doorstep, she knows she needs professional help. Nick embeds himself in her security squad to keep an eye on her as sparks fly and passions rise between them. Can he keep her safe and prevent her from revealing what she knows?

The Jaguar's Secret Baby

Hank has never forgotten the wild woman with whom he spent one memorable night. He's dreamed of her for years now, but has never been back to the small airport in Texas owned and run by her werewolf Pack. Tracy was left with a delicious memory of her night in Hank's arms, and a beautiful baby girl who is the light of her life. She chose not to tell Hank about his daughter, but when he finally returns and he discovers the daughter he's never known, he'll do all he can to set things right.

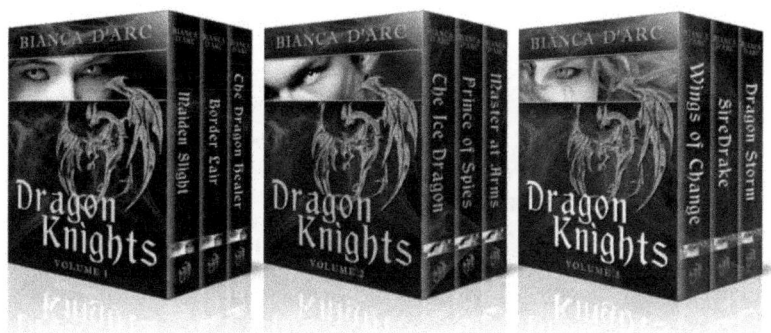

Dragon Knights

Two dragons, two knights, and one woman to complete their circle. That's the recipe for happiness in the land of fighting dragons. But there are a few special dragons that are more. They are the ruling family and they are half-dragon and half-human, able to change at will from one form to another.

Books in this series have won the EPPIE Award for Best Erotic Romance in the Fantasy/Paranormal category, and have been nominated for RT Reviewers Choice Awards among other honors.

The first three novellas in the critically acclaimed vampire romance series…

One & Only
Atticus is about to give up and greet the sun when he finds the love of his eternal life…by accident.

Rare Vintage
Marc, Master vampire of the Napa Valley, can't keep away from Kelly, no matter how many sparks fly between them. When an enemy challenges his authority, will she sacrifice her life for his?

Phantom Desires
Master Dmitri's lair is located under a farmhouse in rural Wyoming. Spying on the new owner while she sleeps could be more dangerous than even he suspects.

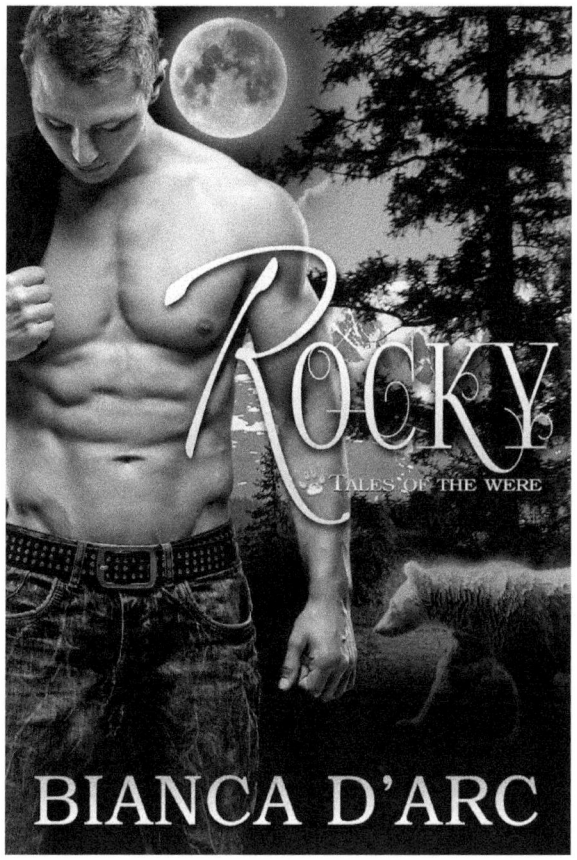

Rocky

Maggie is on the run from a killer, directly into the arms of Rocky, a man from her past. He's much more than a man, though. He's a shapeshifter. A grizzly bear who can protect her and her babies from the demon who murdered their father - Rocky's childhood friend. Magic, fists, claws and blood will determine the winner when the demon tracks Maggie to his door... but will their love prevail?

Also available as an audiobook.

WWW.BIANCADARC.COM

Lightning Source UK Ltd.
Milton Keynes UK
UKHW011846041119
352881UK00019B/433/P